The Name is Thompson

A Novel of Old Belfast

by

ELIZABETH MAY

Copyright © 2021 Elizabeth May

All rights reserved.

ISBN: 9781708474867

I should like to express my sincere thanks to the many people who helped me in obtaining detail and information for this book, especially the staff of the Belfast Public Libraries.
E.M.

CONTENTS

	Foreword	vi
1	Chapter One	1
2	Chapter Two	Pg 32
3	Chapter Three	Pg 45
4	Chapter Four	Pg 62
5	Chapter Five	Pg 85
6	Chapter Six	Pg 107
7	Chapter Seven	Pg 128
8	Part II	
	Chapter Eight	Pg 154
9	Chapter Nine	Pg 183
10	Chapter Ten	Pg 210
11	Chapter Eleven	Pg 248
12	19th Century Map of Belfast	Pg 270
13	Resources	Pg 272
14	About the Author	Pg 274

FOREWORD
By Sam Hanna Bell

In a recent television interview a prominent Irish historian expressed mild surprise that so few Irish writers today turn their attention to the historical or period novel. It was not always so. It is possible to trace about thirty titles of romances that dealt with the '1798 Rising' and almost as many with the Williamite Wars. That almost all these works have disappeared from the library shelves is probably no more than their literary due. Not that the Professor was suggesting that such momentous occasions should be left to the writers of fiction. Certainly Elizabeth May has not fallen into that snare. She writes of humble anonymous people. And it might be said here that, as far as the city of Belfast is concerned, there are no lives more difficult to trace. This is a tribute to her painstaking research into the period, for the historians were preoccupied in following the political or mercantile fortunes of the originals of the statues round the City Hall. Miss May's novel opens with the unveiling of a statue erected to a notability (removed, ironically, some twenty years later, to make room for the likeness of a disputatious cleric). But in that dismal November evening in 1855 we see the newly erected statue through the eyes of a little pinafored girl gazing up in fear. For Alice Storey was "nearly sure that it was a real man up there; some of the other children said it was only a statue and couldn't touch you, but Alice believed it was a live man and she was terrified that if she walked past him, however softly, he might come down off his pedestal and chase her and maybe catch her".

Other and more significant historical events take place during the course of *The Name is Thompson*. Belfast is riven by street rioting, and from afar come the muffled cannonades of the American Civil War. Miss May, like a good storyteller, describes these events as they affect the lives of her characters. But the lasting impression left with the reader as he follows Robert Thompson from childhood to manhood is that of a warm and sympathetic understanding of neighbours living together in narrow gaslit streets. There are, of course, excursions to the countryside, for the Thompsons, the Storeys, and many of their fellow citizens still claim kin who farm in the green townlands looking down on the growing city.

Robert Thompson, as you will learn, is faced by a dilemma as he stands on the threshold of manhood, his decision likely to have far-reaching consequences on his future life. Who will say that he was not led to a wise decision by the example of that sober, honest man, his father, his warm-hearted mother, their Catholic neighbour, Mrs McKenna, the gentle Alice, whom he marries, even the garrulous, bigoted Mrs Storey? Readers, I feel sure, will enjoy meeting the people of Killen Street and College Place who enliven the pages of Elizabeth May's novel.

Sam Hanna Bell

CHAPTER ONE

Dusk was falling over the town of Belfast, and a slight mist creeping down from the mountains was turning into a dismal drizzle. College Square looked deserted and desolate; it was too early yet for the lamplighters to come round and light up the gas lamps in the streets, but and many of the big houses in the Square had welcome gleams of gaslight beckoning from halls and drawing rooms. It was very quiet in the Square, with only an occasional carriage driving past, and a few country carts plodding along in single file, homeward bound with goods and merchandise for the town of Lisburn. Even the College, beyond the green lawns that separated it from the Square, was silent; the scholars and the young gentlemen studying to be doctors and ministers had gone home.

Near to the centre of the Square, almost opposite the front gate of the College, was the statue, which was to be unveiled the next day, 1st November 1855. The workmen had been busy all day lifting it up onto its pedestal, but there hadn't been time, before darkness descended, to engrave the inscription on the statue, and this job was left to be done after the unveiling had taken place. A crowd of the children from the nearby streets had stood watching the men as they put an ornamental arch around the statue, gay with the colours of the

Donegal clan, to which illustrious family the young nobleman depicted in the statue had belonged.

Alice Storey had stood with her brother Alfie and the other children, crowding around, jumping in the way of the workmen, until they had tired and wandered off. Alfie went with some boys to see the soldiers returning to their barracks, and Robert Thompson, who lived near the Storeys and went to school with Alfie, wandered off too, and Alice found herself alone. She wandered up as far as Fisherwick Place, then had daringly crossed the road, although she knew very well she wasn't allowed to cross by herself, on account of the traffic of horses and carriages passing this busy spot. She stood looking at the houses and gardens in Murray's Terrace, but now it was getting dark, and Alice wanted to go home to Killen Street which was away on the other side of the Square, and she'd have to pass by the statue-man to get there.

Alice was nearly sure that it was a real man up there; some of the other children said it was only a statue and couldn't touch you, but Alice believed it was a live man, a black one, and she was terrified that if she walked past him, however softly, he might come down off his pedestal to chase her and catch her.

She crossed the road again, which was fortunately free of horses, and ran to the railings of the houses at the corner of Wellington Place. She stood there shivering, trying not to cry.

A slight breeze whipped the sheet in front of the statue, and Alice screamed as she saw the outline of the man, black and fearsome looking. She sobbed hard, in a wild panic, afraid to move, for there was another terrible hazard to be met, just around the corner, at the side of the College, where the young gentlemen studying to be doctors went in and out by a little side door. It was whispered among the children of Killen Street and College Place that these young doctors came out after dark and snatched up little girls and boys and cut them up for experiments. Even in the daytime the children took hands and ran quickly past this door. To go past it in darkness was something too awful for Alice to think of. She had never been out so late before, not since she had come to live in Killen Street, a few weeks previously, with Pa and Ma and her brothers Alfie and Arthur. They had lived in Duffy's Place before and there was nothing there to frighten a little girl. Her crying was now a steady sobbing, and she twisted her white pinny in her hands and clutched it to her.

In the house behind her, Mary Murtagh heard the crying, and came out down the steps to see what was the matter. Mary was the parlour-maid in the house of Mr Marshall, the wine merchant. She wasn't very long in service in the house, and found it very quiet in the Square, after the bustle of her previous place in a doctor's residence in the Parade.

"What's wrong, love?" she asked Alice, leaning over the iron gate.

"I'm afeard, so I am. I want to go home to my ma."

"Where do you live?" Mary knew it wasn't one of the children from the Square, as they didn't play out in the streets, and would not, in any case, be dressed in pinnies, or have dirty faces.

"In Killen Street," Alice sniffed.

"I'd take you there myself, pet, but I've my work to do. The mistress'll be back any minute on top of me. It's not far, though, round that corner, and there you are, safe and sound."

"I'm afeard of – of – him!" Alice whispered, pointing a chubby fist towards the statue.

"As true as God, I don't blame you!" Mary blessed herself quickly. "Put the heart across me, it did, looking out of the window a short while ago and seeing a black man up there, even though Cook says it's only a bronze statue. And it's me that will have to look at it every day now, and me thinking it so lovely here, with the green lawns of the College to look at. What did they want to put their oul' statue here for?" She paused, then firmly pushed Alice towards the end of the Square. "But there, it's only a statue, love, it's not real. Go on home now."

But Alice had no intention of facing the darkness now that she had someone to comfort her, so she resisted the push and stood firmly, whimpering.

Just then Robert Thompson came running round the corner from Wellington Place, hurrying home, for he had strict orders from his father to be in the house before the street lamps were lit.

"Here boy!" Mary shouted at him. "Are you going near Killen Street? Will you take this wee girl home to her ma?"

Robert halted, and pulled the crumpled pinny from Alice's face.

"It's Alice, wee Alice Storey, she lives round the corner from me."

"Well, take her home, that's the good boy!" Mary said firmly. "It's no time of night for children to be out roaming the streets." To herself, more than to the children, she added, "There's to be the great excitement here in the morning, with the Viceroy himself coming all the length from Dublin, and we'll have more than enough to do with all the visitors the mistress has coming to watch from the windows. We'll have the grand view of it all." But for all her assumed bravery she hurried up the steps and quickly shut the door, shutting out the view of the silent black man standing shrouded on his pedestal.

"Come on, Alice," Robert shouted impatiently, "stop your crying and come on home. I'll leave you to your door." He pulled her sharply by the hand. Girls were a great nuisance, always whining and gurning, at least Alfie said they were. Robert was an only child, but he knew that girls were always frightened, even a big girl of seven like Alice. "Come on," he snapped, as she held back.

"Robbie, I'm afeard," she whimpered. "I'm afeard of him, that man up there. And I'm afeard of the doctors. Did you know they catch wee girls and boys and cut them up?"

"They do not! My da says it's all nonsense," Robert told her and pulled her after him, right across the Square. Then, of a sudden, it struck him ... it was getting very dark ... that statue did look like a man when the sheet moved ... maybe it *was* true that the young doctors came out from the College and caught little boys and girls and cut them up. A wild panic came over him.

"Run, Alice, run!" he shouted, and pulled her along in a mad race until they came to the corner of College Place, to the safety of his own corner, where they could stop and get back breath.

"Did he run after us, that statue man?" Alice gasped.

"Not at all!" Robert said stoutly. "I ran to get you home quick, and keep us warm. Come on, I'll bring you to your ma," and he ran with her along the Place, up the two steps and into Killen Street.

Alice held his hand tightly. "Come in with me, Robbie," she pleaded, "our hall is dark, and I'm still afeard."

Robert followed her through the half-opened hall door and into the gloom of the house. Alice opened the kitchen door, and pulled him with her. The gas light was dazzling to Robert's eyes after the gloom outside, and it was a second or two before he could look around. It looked a cosy room, the Storeys kitchen, with a glowing fire in the hob grate. He had never been in the house before and felt a bit shy now, walking in with Alice.

Alice ran over to her father who was sitting in a rocking chair in front of the fire.

"Pa, Pa" she cried, and started to sob, "I was afeard, Pa, and Robbie brought me home. Our Alfie left me and I was afeard of the statue and the doctors." She clung to him, then climbed on his knee and put her arms around him. Mr Storey patted her and murmured soothingly. He was a small man, with very blue eyes, and a pasty white face, and he coughed and wheezed all the time. His voice was low, as if he was slightly deaf.

"Wait and I'll give that Alfie something," he said crossly. "I'll warm his backside for him, leaving a wee child in the dark. There now, love, you're all right now," he soothed her.

Mrs Storey came bustling in from the scullery. She had a torn frilly apron and a mob cap from under which wisps of fair hair streeled. She was good-natured looking, Robert decided.

"Did you bring Alice home, Robert?" She smiled at him. "You're a good boy. You see, William," she addressed her husband, "Alice wasn't on her own, this wee boy brought her home. Alfie likely asked him to."

"He didn't! He left me," Alice howled.

"He left her all right, and after all I've warned him, and us in a strange part of Belfast and all them horses dashing about," Mr Storey said emphatically.

"Maybe it wasn't Alfie's fault, Alice could have left him. She does that, you know, William, she wanders away from him."

Mr Storey grunted. "Maybe! Maybe not, more like! Where's my boots, Sarah?"

"I was just going to clean them," his wife replied affably, "and I don't know where I put them." Behind her husband's back she winked at Robert, while looking intently around.

Robert thought the Storeys' kitchen very different from his own house where everything had to be neat and tidy. Here there seemed to be a clutter of chairs with faded cushions, and there was a huge dresser taking up most of the room, with bowls and plates and brassware sitting untidily on it. Newspapers were thrown on the floor and a cat had a litter of kittens on an old cushion under the table.

"Is your ma going to see the statue unveiled?" Mrs Storey suddenly addressed him. "Oh, I believe it's going to be great, with lords and ladies there, and soldiers on their horses and all the gentry."

Robert replied that he didn't know, his ma hadn't told him.

"I expect she will," Mrs Storey went on, "for it's going to be a great day round these doors, and there'll surely be room for us that lives practically in the Square. I tell Mr Storey that we're very lucky to move into such a nice neighbourhood, so near the College and all. It's nice to be near the gentry again," she added in a polite voice, rubbing her nose on the corner of her apron.

Robert wondered, although he was too shy to ask, if the Storeys had lived among gentry in Duffy's Place, and as if she read his thoughts Mrs Storey went on:

"I'm from Antrim town myself, you know, and not a day went by but his Lordship passed our window, and once her Ladyship from the castle come into Pa's emporium." She paused to let this sink in. "He's a linen draper, you know, my pa, and a cousin of mine on my mother's side has a niece that has a good place in the castle, under the housekeeper herself she is with very good chances of improving herself."

"Did you find my boots, Sarah?" Mr Storey wheezed impatiently.

"Now where did I put them," Mrs Storey said loudly, winking again at Robert. "Maybe they're in the room. Come and hold the candle for me, Alice pet, and I'll look."

Alice whined, "No, I don't want to," so Robert politely offered.

"I'll hold it for you, if you like," he said, and was handed an old tin holder with the butt end of a tallow candle stuck in it. He followed Mrs Storey into the front parlour which the candlelight revealed to be just as untidy as the kitchen. Coats and shawls and dresses were thrown on the chairs and a hamper stood under the window.

"Look at the cut of this place!" Mrs Storey exclaimed. "We're still unpacking from the flitting. I must call and see your ma, Robert. She'll think it odd of me, here three weeks and never introducing myself. Her and Mrs McKenna next door to me is very friendly, I see. The McKennas is Catholics, I hear. I never like to bother much with the likes of them, but I suppose you can't avoid it. I hear that your da's a precentor in the Presbyterian Church. Is that right? We're church goers ourselves."

"No, my da isn't. His da was, though. A precentor, I mean."

"Well, it's little odds which, it's nice to have the like of that in a family. Very respectable."

"Mrs Storey, the candle is going out," Robert remarked, trying to shield the guttering flame from the draught coming through the door.

"So it is! Well, there's no boots here!" she said in a loud voice, then whispered to Robert, "I don't want him to find them, for he'll only go to the public house and take drink, and miss his work. He's a baker, you know, and so is our Arthur and they have to work at night-time. God oh! What's the time? That Arthur fellow's still in his bed. I'll have to rouse him out."

The front door burst open and Alfie dashed in, his cheeks red with exertion and holding a large turnip clutched to his navy jersey.

"Ma, look, I've got a turnip, and I'm going to make a lantern out of it and put a candle in it and light it for Hallowe'en!"

From the kitchen Mr Storey's voice rasped, "Is that you, Alfie? Come you here to me! Did you leave your wee sister?"

Alfie looked alarmed, and his mother caught hold of him. "Your da's raging at you, and you're going to get a good beating." She whacked a cushion on a chair and winked at the two boys. "There, that'll learn you to leave your wee sister," she shouted, then whispered fiercely to Alfie to cry. He raised a loud shining to accompany the beating of the cushion.

"You're not touching him!" Mr Storey shouted out. "Come in here and I'll give you something to cry about.Mrs Storey dashed into the kitchen and lifted Alice off her father's knee. "Now, William, I gave him what for. Look at the time and that Arthur fellow still in bed. Will you get him up and I'll see to the supper. I've a lovely dumpling in the pot for Hallowe'en. Here you, Alfie, take that oul' turnip into the scullery. Robert you'd better go home, your ma will wonder where you are."

Deftly she pushed Alfie out of his father's way, into the scullery, and closed the door on him. She sighed. William was hard on the boys, particularly Alfie, who was her darling, whom she saved from many a beating. Alice was her da's pet, and he gave her everything she wanted.

She went into the dark hall and yelled up the stairs, "Arthur, get up out of that, you'll be late for your work," and almost ran into him coming down the stairs, stretching himself, his hair tousled, in bare feet and his braces dangling from his trousers.

"All right, all right, I'm up! You couldn't sleep in this house with all the shouting. Is the supper not ready?"

"Away you go into the scullery and wash yourself and don't be fighting with Alfie, for your da's as cross as two sticks as it is and I want to get the two of you to your work in time for once."

"I was thinking I'd stay off and give myself a holiday in the morning. There's a statue getting unveiled, and I'd like to see it."

"You'll get paid off, that's what'll happen to you, and where will you get such a good job? Lamont's is a good job. Where else would you be let come in late just because your da and Lamont was friends as boys?"

Arthur yawned. "Didn't Da help him build up his baking business? Hasn't he the right to treat him, and me too, different? Sure you have only to look at him, old before his time, and bad with his chest from all that hellish heat in the bakehouse and then going out in all weathers to sell his rotten loaves. Don't talk to me about Lamont! He's an oul' skinflint and a slave driver, him and his big house and his carriage and horses, and my da still a poor baker and an old man near worked out."

"That's no sort of talk," Mr Storey said mildly. "I've a good job with Joe Lamont and nothing to complain of. Two pounds ten I'll have when I'm a master baker, and I only hope you'll earn half as much a week when you're my age."

"I've other ideas," Arthur retorted. He was a tall, dark-haired young man, but already his complexion was getting the white, pasty look of the bakers who worked in too much heat.

"Oh, maybe they'll put up a statue to you some day," his Father retorted.

Mrs Storey pushed Arthur into the scullery.

"What are you doing?" she whispered fiercely to Alfie, when she discovered he was trying to scoop out the heart of the turnip with a knife. "Take that oul' turnip out of my scullery before you cut the hand off yourself. Here, ask your da to do it for you."

Alfie brought the turnip and the knife over to the rocking chair where Alice still stood beside her da's knee. The two children watched as Mr Storey completed the job of making a turnip into a Hallowe'en lantern.

Mrs Storey sighed, thankful for a bit of peace to let her get on with making the supper.

She hadn't got really settled yet from moving house at Duffy's Place, at Boundary Street. It had been a good enough place to live, but she had always wanted a house with a parlour, and now she had got one, and had the gas too, and running water which was wonderful. No more lamps— except of course for going up to bed at night, for the gas was only downstairs. Killen Street was a good open neighbourhood, too, with open ground in front and a clear view of the mountains. She hoped it might help William's health; his cough wasn't getting any better, and coming on another winter it had her worried. It was the heat of the bakehouse, of course, and then having to go out into the cold and damp with the basket and sell the bread. It was no wonder that William liked a wee drop of spirits to cut the phlegm and help his breathing, but she knew that if he went round to the public house—and that was one thing about Killen Street, there were far too many pubs about, with one at every corner of nearby Smithfield Market—he wouldn't go to his work, and then he would miss his pay. Arthur, too, was getting a bit rebellious. He didn't seem to like the baking very much. It was hard to know what to put a boy to, and what her Alfie would be when he left school she just didn't know. She had great hopes that he might be a minister, or an apothecary. Nothing would be too grand for her Alfie, and as she peeled the boiled potatoes and mashed them with sweet milk into a big bowl, in her mind's eye she saw a statue being put up, and the figure on it was her Alfie—Alfred Storey—but what he had done to deserve the statue she just could not decide.

Anyhow, tomorrow would be a great day in the Square. There would be a lot to see, all the ladies of fashion, and great crowds and carriages. Maybe that Mrs Thompson—Robert's mother—would go with her. She didn't seem too friendly, but of course they hadn't really had the chance to know each other yet. And maybe some of her own people might get up from Antrim. Her sister, Aggie, was to come the first time McQuillan's country cart was coming; it would be great if Aggie could see the nice place they lived in, almost in College Square you might say, among the merchants and gentlemen, and she would love to see the style at the unveiling of the statue. It would be something to tell about in Antrim, to boast of to the neighbours. She'd wear her good shawl and her cashmere dress and the new bonnet she had for churchgoing on Sunday, though of late the Storeys hadn't gone very regularly to church.

Robert Thompson went home disappointed. He had wanted to see what a turnip lantern looked like, but he wouldn't now, for once he got home he would not be allowed out again. It suddenly occurred to him that it was late; the lamps had been lit a long time ago, and his mother would be looking for him. He hoped his father wasn't home yet from work, or he would be in real trouble for staying out past the allowed time. Running along Killen Street and down the steps into College Place took only a minute, but there was his mother, standing at the door, peering out. She caught hold of his arm and pulled him into the house.

"Where were you?" she demanded. "You know well you have to

be in before the lamps get lit. And your jacket is damp. Were you out in that rain?"

"I brought wee Alice Storey home," Robert whined. "She was frightened of that statue in the Square. And then Mrs Storey asked me to hold the candle for her to look for Mr Storey's boots, but she didn't really want to find them for he'd only go out for drink and she didn't want him to."

"What nonsense have you got hold of! You'd better get your slate out and your book, too, and do your lessons before your father comes home. But first of all, run round to Mrs McKenna's with this bit of pork. Poor woman, tell her I got it only this evening from Moneyrea."

"Ach, did I miss Uncle George? Was he in from Moneyrea?"

"Don't let that bowl fall now, and don't be delaying. And yes, your uncle wanted to know where you were. That'll learn you not to be late.' Bring that bowl back. And ask Mrs McKenna if there any news yet of her husband's ship."

"I think maybe Mr McKenna has got shipwrecked and he's on a desert island. Sure he'd get coconuts to eat."

"Don't talk silly!"

Robert walked cautiously along, holding the bowl carefully. He knocked at Mrs McKenna's door, next to the Storeys'. Mrs McKenna's husband was a sailor and his ship was months overdue on a voyage from Australia. By now, hope of his safety was fading.

Robert tapped once again at the door and Mrs McKenna opened it. She was a small woman, with red, straight hair scraped back from her face in a bun. Her eyes, too, were red as if she had been crying.

"Is that you, Robert?" she said. "Come in, boy."

"I can't, Mrs McKenna. Ma said I was to hurry back, but she sent this bit of pork. My uncle George was down from Moneyrea today and he brought some of the killing of their pig. I missed him, though, I was in Storeys'."

"God bless your mother, she's one of the kindest creatures in the whole of Belfast. She never forgets me if she has anything. This'll be a nice bit of kitchen for my Jim's supper, and maybe I can get Mary to take a pick of it. She had to come home sick from her work today again. It's that oul' brewery at the corner of their street, the smell of it makes her sick."

Mrs McKenna had two children, Mary and Jim. Mary was only fourteen and was at the hemstitching in a linen wareroom, earning a few shillings a week to help out when there was no money from Mr McKenna. Young Jim wanted to be a sailor, too, like his father, and was planning to go away to sea again with him on the next voyage, but the weeks went by and there was no news of the *Oranda* coming to port.

"Can you get me a message, Robert?" Mrs McKenna asked.

"Ma said I was to hurry back, but maybe if I ask her..."

"I'll go down with you and ask her myself."

Mrs McKenna threw a shawl round her shoulders to keep out the chill air of the evening. The rain had ceased but there was dampness about that was unpleasant. She walked the short distance with Robert to his house.

"Is that yourself, Mrs McKenna?" Mrs Thompson greeted her. "Come on in. Any news?"

"Jim was down at Lancaster Street this morning, at his grannie's, to hear if there was any news from any of the seamen. A man just in off a sailing ship at Derry from the America run said he heard in Liverpool that the *Oranda* had foundered."

"Pray God he was wrong," Mrs Thompson said softly.

"Pray that he is, but if it's the truth I'll not be the first nor the last woman in the port of Belfast to lose her man to the sea. Look at poor old Grannie down there in Lancaster Street; her man was lost, and her two sons with him. She's been left with a daughter to help her keep a lodging house for seamen. My man is her only son left to her, and I can't think that God would take him from us all. I still have hope, and

I'm praying hard. I went to the nuns in Bankmore Street and they're praying too."

"We'll not forget, in our prayers," said Mrs Thompson. "You may be sure my John has made many a prayer for the same purpose, and sure Mrs McKenna, dear, it's the same God that hears us all."

"That's the truth, it is indeed. I wonder, Mrs Thompson, could you let Robert do a wee message for me? I need a few things but I don't want to go down to oul' Wilson myself. I have a bit owing there, and if he saw these few shillings I have he'd take it off and give me nothing more. I know him of old! He's had many the sovereign off me in his time, but the fuss he makes about letting a small bill stand over, you wouldn't believe."

Mrs Thompson was quite agreeable for Robert to go the message.

"I'll have a few shillings more from my sewing, and young Jim got work at the docks today, so we'll be able to manage maybe, doing with less. It's a time like this a body knows their friends, Mrs Thompson, and you're one of mine."

Robert was given the basket and memorised the items he was to get at the shop. On his way to Durham Street, he took care to pass the Storeys' door again, in the hope of seeing Alfie and his turnip lantern. Robert had set his heart on getting one for himself, if he could get hold of a turnip and a bit of a tallow candle.

At the shop in Durham Street he had to wait his turn to be served, for old Mr Wilson, the grocer, was in no hurry; and moved around the dimly lit, cluttered shop at a snail's pace. An elderly woman with a shawl wrapped round her head and shoulders was getting snuff, and couldn't wait until she got outside to take a pinch. Then lamp oil had to be measured for another woman, and after what seemed an age, it was Robert's turn.

"Half a pound of butter, a big loaf of bread, half a pound of candles," he recited off.

"You're in a quare hurry," old Wilson muttered gruffly. "Have you the money to pay for all this?" Robert said he had, so the old man grunted.

"Tell your ma that butter's up the day; it's fivepence a pound and the loaf's fivepence too. With the candles that's ninepence."

Robert handed over three fourpenny pieces and got his change, which he carefully wrapped in a screw of paper from the floor.

"How much is a turnip?" he asked the old grocer. Mrs McKenna sometimes gave him a farthing for going her messages, and he might be able to get a turnip if she gave him one now.

"I have none!" snapped old Wilson.

Robert sauntered back home in the darkness, wondering where he would get a turnip, and at the same time, putting in as much delay as he could to going home, where he would have to settle down with his slate and sums. Going the message for Mrs McKenna was a Heaven-sent excuse; even his da couldn't fault him for it and say he was an idle, useless boy if he hadn't a slateful of sums done by suppertime. Mrs McKenna gave him a farthing when he got back. She went to her own house then and Robert was sternly put to his lessons by his mother. The Thompson house was neat and spotlessly clean.

The hob in the kitchen was blackleaded, and the flames of the fire reflected in the highly polished brass fender on the hearth and in the two huge candlesticks on the mantle-board. The yellow flags of the floor had been freshly scrubbed and there was a pleasant smell of soapy water mingling with the appetising scent of the boiling pork simmering in a big black pot at the back of the hob. Some pieces of crockery sat tidily on the big mahogany dresser, all in keeping with the general air of neatness.

Mrs Thompson bustled around, finishing off her preparation for the evening meal. She was a tall, stately woman, with black hair and pale complexion, a kindly - but stern - face, and smiling eyes. Robert resembled her in his black hair and his brown eyes, but for the rest, he strongly resembled his father.

He sat dreamily on a stool in front of the fire, his slate blank on his knees.

"Ma, have you a turmit?"

"A turnip, you mean. Turmit is a country way of talking. What do you want a turnip for?"

"Alfie Storey is making a Hallowe'en lantern out of one." His voice was eager. "You just scoop out the middle with a knife, put in a bit of a tallow candle, and make a hole in the front, and you have the great lantern for Hallowe'en. Oh, Ma, I'd love one! Gould I get one? I have a farthing Mrs McKenna gave me and I could get a turmit - I mean a turnip - in Smithfield. It would be great, running a turnip lantern up and down the street. Can I get one, Ma? Please?"

Mrs Thompson shook her head. "I doubt your father would think little of nonsense like that. What the Storeys do is their own business, and I'm tired telling you that. What call have you to heed the likes of them that's only got their foot in the neighbourhood. You do your lessons, boy, or your da'll take the taws to you."

Robert was silent for a moment or two, and with his slate pencil idly put a few figures to start off a sum. The firelight gleamed and made a cosy brightness; his mother sat on another stool beside him and looked over his shoulder.

"How much have you done? You're sitting there dreaming!"

Robert looked up at her, his face flushed from the fire. "Ma, haven't I a brother? Alfie Storey says I haven't, that it doesn't count if they're dead. But it does, doesn't it? Haven't I a brother that's dead?"

"There you go again," his mother retorted sharply. "Alfie Storey says this, Alfie Storey says that! Sure, what does he know!" A wistful far-away look came into her eyes as she sat for a few seconds looking into the flames.

"Aye," she sighed, in a low tone. "You have, son, you have a wee brother, you've two of them, and they're both in Heaven, and a wee sister too. Your wee sister would be the age of that Storey girl, Alice, just the same age, and going to school with you taking her hand - if she'd lived."

"Alice is an oul' cry-ba," ventured Robert. "All girls is cry-bas. Alfie says so -"

"Don't mention that Alfie to me again. I'm sick of hearing what he says."

"Mrs Storey is nice. She says are you going to see the statue getting unveiled to-morrow. She says she must come and see you, that she's three weeks here and you'll wonder at her not coming."

"Indeed and it's not worrying me! From what Mrs McKenna tells me I'm in no hurry getting friendly with Mrs Storey. Neighbours and friends is two different things."

"Was Uncle George by himself, or was wee Danny with him?" asked Robert, switching the conversation.

"He was just his lone, and you might have got to the end of the Square in the cart if you'd done as you're bid and come home in time. He brought me the right load of potatoes from the farm. They had a good harvest, he says. 'Deed I must try and get for a walk: out to Moneyrea in the spring. It's the quare while since I saw it."

Mrs Thompson sat on by the fire, her work done, the supper ready and waiting for her husband John. She thought of her old home in Moneyrea, up in the Hills. She'd love to see it again, but of course, it was all changed now with her ma and da gone and brother George with his own houseful of children. She'd like to see Aunt Aggie, her father's sister, who had a wee place further up the Kills, the cottage and bit of land and the few animals. It must be lonely now for poor old Aunt Agnes, and her by herself. It was a pity about George's wife, her and her wicked tongue. They had words every time they met and it spoiled her visit to the old homestead, but by what George had told her to-day, his wife got on with nobody. She had fallen out now with old Aunt Agnes and none of them had seen her for a month. Mrs Thompson knew that George wasn't too happy about it, though he said little; apart from being fond of the old lady he would have his eye to the bit of money she was supposed to have that came to her from the son in America that died out there. Nobody likes to fight with relations that have the gold. Poor George! He hadn't drawn it lucky, with a wife with a shrewish tongue and an untidy, dirty clart of a woman if all that was said was true. And no doubt the old home wasn't the same; you wouldn't know the place for muck and clabber. What possessed George to marry that one was more than she could understand, but of course, sisters didn't always approve their brothers' choices. George's wife likely had a bit of money with her. That was what she surmised.

Martha Thompson yearned now and then for the old days at home, before she got married. The farm was well-run and the place neat and clean, and there was none of this bickering going on, so that you wouldn't know who was speaking to who. Martha had been lucky enough to get a place in service at the manse in the Hills, with the Reverend Jackson's wife, just a few miles from home. Mrs Jackson was a great housekeeper and a wonderful cook; Martha had learned a great deal from her in the three years she had been in the house. It was there that she first met John when he came to visit the minister and attend a Sabbath service. His stern look and solemn manner caught her and she found herself hoping he would come again. He seemed a very serious, studious young man, and it was known about him that he was in the linen business and came originally from Lisburn. He had a lovely singing voice and had come up to the Hills from his lodging in Belfast to help the precentor to raise the tune. Martha watched out for him. Then one Sunday he walked her back to the manse, and after that it was a regular thing for him to accompany her home from the service. Not that he talked much or gave any indication of his intentions; indeed Martha had the surprise of her life when her father told her that John Thompson had come to him and offered for her and that it would be a good match for her and she was to take him. She was greatly flattered; a young man in the linen trade -- the son of a precentor, too, it seemed - to offer for her, a girl in service. True, her father had one of the snuggest farms in the Hills and was a well-doing man, but still, it was a great thing for Martha and she was thought to be a very fortunate girl the day she married John Thompson.

She liked him, and respected him, but even now, twelve years after, she did not know what went on in his mind. He was quiet and reserved, liked his home orderly and quiet so that he might read, and think. He was deeply religious and observed the strict order of the Sabbath, when no cooking or work of any kind was permitted. Martha Thompson would have declared - if anyone had asked her - that she was happy, and that hers was a happy marriage, but deep in her heart she had a longing for a companionship that she did not get from her husband. With the sorrow of three children dying soon after birth, she was becoming almost as quiet and reserved as her husband, and at times was as sharp with Robert as he was. Only with Mrs McKenna was she neighbourly and friendly; to all others she was withdrawn and reserved, but there was something about the small red-haired Mrs McKenna that drew her, some unaffected, forthright quality that matched her own direct character. Her house was her pride, and to have it clean and shining her constant aim. Robert had known from babyhood that things must be kept tidy, and now he took it as a matter of course.

"Ma," Robert suddenly said, looking up from his slate, "will Uncle George be back soon again? Could I go and stay sometimes in Moneyrea? You said once that I could."

"It's manners to wait till you're asked! But hush now, here's your father coming in the door. Run and take his coat from him."

The tall, broad-shouldered, sandy-haired man came slowly and calmly into the kitchen, the master home to his own house, after his day's work. He sat by the fire in his chair, and picked up Robert's slate from the stool.

"What's this, boy?" he asked. "You didn't do your sums." Robert hung his head, and replied in a whisper that he hadn't got them done yet.

"Where were you? Were you out wasting time?"

"I went with Alfie Storey to see the soldiers on their horses, and we saw the men putting up the statue on its stand in the Square, and then I was coming home to be in before the lamps was lit and wee Alice Storey was standing crying and one of the maids from a big house asked me to take her home, and I did, and then Mrs McKenna wanted a message and Ma said it was all right."

"To-morrow you must do better, but it's right of you to be useful to Mrs McKenna. Is there any news to-day of her husband's ship, Martha?"

"No, poor woman, the strain is hard on her, and Mary had to come home to-day again from her work, sick from the smell of the brewery. Young Jim got work at the docks, and that'll help her, poor soul. Supper's ready now, there's a lovely bit of kitchen for us. George came down from home and brought a bit of the killing of the pig."

The steaming pork and potatoes was set on the table and John Thompson bent his head to make a prayer before eating.

"Pa, Alfie Storey got a turnip, and he's making a lantern for Hallowe'en," Robert ventured, then added eagerly, "You scoop out the middle and put in a candle and you have a lit lamp. It's for Hallowe'en. To-night's Hallowe'en." He was hopeful that his father might show enthusiasm for a lantern.

"Indeed I'm well aware that it is Hallowe'en, son," his father said calmly, "and we have here a feast of pork that not many in this town will put on their table. I hope you pointed out to this Storey boy that to cut up a turnip and throw part of it away is a sinful waste."

"No..." Robert mumbled.

"Such waste! I wonder his mother countenances it! We should

none of us forget that a turnip would have kept some poor person alive not many years ago. People died here in Ireland, boy, and not so long ago, because they had nothing to eat. We should never forget that. If the good Lord gives us plenty we should not waste it."

Robert was dashed, his hopes of a turnip lamp gone. He thought wistfully of the Storeys' house, where no shadow of the famine years of nine years ago crept into a boy's dreams, where turnips could be cut up without having to think of starving families. He knew now there was no hope at all that he would be allowed to have his lantern. He knew too that to rebel would bring retribution from his father's open hand.

Supper was finished, and his mother cleared the table and washed the dishes and the pots, then Robert went to the parlour and in the dark lifted from its familiar place on the table by the window the huge family Bible. Carefully he placed it on his father's knees, for the ritual of Scripture reading. John Thompson opened the book leisurely and picked his passage, and in a droning voice read from the New Testament.

Robert sat quietly, his mind occupied more with soldiers and with the Storey family than with the Scriptures. Mrs Thompson sat with her eyes closed, rocking herself to and fro, the better to concentrate on the passage, and to enjoy her husband's rich, easy reading. Then the Bible was put back on its table and the three of them sat around the fire, Mrs Thompson to knit the black stockings that Robert wore out so easily, and Mr Thompson to read over his weekly newspaper. Robert was supposed to read his book, but to-night he had his slate on his lap to do the sums he had neglected earlier on.

"The war is drawing to a close in the Crimea," Mr Thompson read out. Robert remembered the soldiers he saw dashing back to their barracks. Maybe he wouldn't be a soldier now after all, if there was no war to fight. He yawned.

"Time for bed," his mother said quickly.

"Just a minute," Mr Thompson interrupted, "I want to read out something that should interest Robert - and you, too, Martha. As you well know, a statue is to be unveiled in the Square to-morrow, and it tells here in my newspaper the history of the young nobleman who is being honoured."

Robert hadn't thought at all about who the statue was of, but now, with sleepy eyes, listened while Pa read from the paper about the young boy who had become Earl of Belfast when only seventeen years old, who had been a musician of much taste and refinement, as well as displaying marked literary talent and possessing a highly cultured mind. His death at an early age in Italy had aroused the deepest feelings of regret and sorrow among all classes - the paper said - and a movement had been set afoot to erect a statue in his memory.

"This is to be unveiled on 1st November, and it is expected that a large and distinguished gathering will be present," concluded Mr Thompson.

"Mrs Storey is going," Robert added, "She said would you like to go with her, Ma?"

"I've no time for the likes," retorted Mrs Thompson, "and if I had, it wouldn't be the likes of her I'd go with."

"This is a surprise for you, Martha." Her husband smiled at her. "Mr Aspinall was kind enough to give me the day off my work for the express purpose of witnessing this event, so you and I will be there together."

"A day off!" his wife echoed with wonder.

"Yes, and he also gave me two tickets for the concert to be held in the evening; we can look forward to a great deal of enjoyment from the music."

"It's manys the long day since you had a day off, John! It must be six years if it's a day."

"I believe you're right, it's six years, the day Queen Victoria came to Belfast. That was a day of excitement!"

"Aye, I mind it well. It was just the next day our wee girl took sick. I was just looking at the Storeys' child, and there was something about her that minded me of our wee one." Mrs Thompson looked sad.

"Time you were in bed, boy," Robert was told brusquely by his father.

"Take your candle, son," his mother instructed, giving him a shining tin holder with a new tallow candle.

"A candle! I had no candle when I was your age. You spoil that boy, Martha. When I was your age, Robert, I was out working."

"Now I had no candle when I was young, either, John, how times has changed, and if I had my way of it no child would go to work until it got a good schooling. I think I'll go up myself, for if I'm going to be out of my house in the morning I'll need to be stirring early and get well red up."

She went off upstairs, leaving John to sit in front of the dying embers of the hob fire. It had been a hard day for him at his work, in the firm of Aspinalls at Mountpottinger. John was in the warehousing department. The manager, old Fred McClure, had been ill with gout for weeks, and it was known that he would probably never work again. John was confident that the job would be his, and hoped each day that he would be told it was so, but week followed week and Mr Aspinall did nothing about it. It would have been different in the old man's time, John reflected; old Mr Aspinall would have settled the matter promptly, as he settled most things. It was this way that had built the business. His son, young Mr Aspinall, was a different type; he had been educated in England and in Switzerland, and at times seemed to have very little interest in either living in Belfast or in maintaining the prosperous business he had inherited. The family had wealth from other interests than the linen business; ship-building interests in England, and there was a business in Switzerland too.

Aspinalls was a fairly small, self-contained factory and warehouse, workers would weave from bought yarns, the cloth they then made into sheets, pillowcases, handkerchiefs, and dress linens, which they sold all over the British Isles and a fast-developing trade in North America. It was an order for America that the warehouse had been working on that very day, and the absence of a manager of the department to co-ordinate the work and speed the order, had been sorely felt. The girls had finished the folding and ornamenting of the order, then had to stand idle because no further instructions had come from Mr Aspinall, who had assumed the management of the department in Mr McClure's absence. The packing case was not ready, was not, in fact, even ordered; the office hadn't the invoices ready, and to crown it all -when all these obstacles had been overcome by John Thompson's efforts - the carter was late in coming for the shipping and there was the chance that the particular order for America would be late getting to Liverpool and so miss the shipping connection. It was a day of frustration for John; he had spent most of it chasing after Mr Aspinall for instructions, in whatever part of the building he could find him. He could have managed the business of the department quite easily; Mr Aspinall would not have countenanced this. He was the governor, it was his firm, although he had not the fraction of knowledge of the linen trade that John Thompson had, and it was unlikely that he ever would know as much about it as any of the senior men in the warehouse. He would never be the man his father was; he had inherited none of the old man's stern resolve and directness of purpose, but where the old man was hard, though just, the son was easy-going in an erratic way. To John Thompson and the other men of the firm, his greatest fault was that as a younger man he had, by the accident of birth, inherited a business which he knew very little about, and through either stubbornness or stupidity was unwilling to accept advice from any of them.

That afternoon, John had eventually found him in the weaving sheds. John wanted details of the next order in the book for the warehouse. It wanted only fifteen minutes to the closing time of six o'clock, and the weavers were finishing off and examining their work for flaws. It was a long day for them, from half-past six in the morning, and many of them, John knew, had long distances to walk. Mr Aspinall was now talking to Paddy McFall, the foreman, and was telling him that some of the weavers would have to be laid off work, that business was not too good and the firm was over-stocked. This was not true, John knew; in the handkerchief department alone orders were being delayed for want of cloth; other departments were similarly affected, and yet here was Mr Aspinall laying off good workers.

John sighed to himself. He really feared for the future. Was he going to get the position of manager? Was he wise in staying on with the firm? He was young enough yet to look around and find a good position elsewhere, and with his experience and knowledge of the trade should hardly have much trouble in doing so. And there was Robert's future, too, to consider.

He had decided to put the boy into the linen trade, and had been promised he would be taken into Aspinalls when he was about thirteen, as an apprentice, but now he wondered if the firm would still be in existence in a few years' time, if things continued the same way.

He had stood in the weaving-shed, respectfully at a short distance, and waited until Mr Aspinall's eye took him in.

"Ah, Thompson," he boomed, "just the man I want to see."

"Yes, Mr Aspinall, sir, if we might have the next order…"

"It's not work I wish to see you about - for a change. It's a surprise for you, Thompson! You're a musical man, I hear."

"Well, sir, I'm fond of music, and do a bit of singing in the church."

Mr Aspinall fumbled in his inner pocket, and drew out first a cigar case, then a bundle of papers which he leafed through and from which he extracted two tickets. These he handed to John.

"Here you are! This is something to interest you, then. A grand concert to be held in the Victoria Hall to-morrow night, the Belfast Harmonists' Society inaugural concert, sees it says so here, on the ticket. There's to be quite a gathering I hear, including the Lord Lieutenant, and my Lord Dufferin. I was asked to take a pair of tickets, but what would I do at such a display of talent. Haven't a note of music in me!" And he laughed heartily.

"It's very kind of you, Mr Aspinall," John said dubiously. "No doubt it is to finish off the festivities of the day. I believe a statue is to be unveiled to the late Earl of Belfast."

"Yes, yes, that's it! I knew it was something formal and official. Can't stand these things myself. Tell you what, Thompson, why don't you see the statue unveiled! Make a day of it. Take the good wife along to see the gentry and the style. And your boy, too, Thompson. Must be quite some while since you had a day off."

John replied quietly that the last occasion had been the visit of Queen Victoria, six years previously.

"Take the day off, then, you've earned it! You Belfast fellows annoy me, you know, so dashed earnest about work, never do anything about enjoying life. My poor old pater always held you fellows up to me, said if I'd as much application as you had, I'd do all right." Mr Aspinall chuckled to himself. "Dull existence, I call it."

"The department, sir," John queried, dazed, "what about the orders for to-morrow?"

"Now you leave that to me to look after! You go and enjoy yourself, and McCrum and I can see to things. That's the trouble with you fellows. You think nothing can be done if you're not around, but you know everyone can be done without. My father thought that; the world would have ended if he hadn't been early to his blessed warehouse, and look at it now, still going strong, when he's dead and gone. You go and have a bit of gaiety, my dear Thompson, and leave the department to McCrum and myself. We'll see to everything."

Although loath to appear ungracious, John found it hard to express thanks to Mr Aspinall, and had to struggle to hide the feelings of amazement and apprehension at this extraordinary outburst. What, he wondered, was behind all this sudden burst of feelings? It had never happened before that a man in his position was given a day off, in the working week, without being ill. And what did he mean by saying "everyone can be done without"? Was McCrum going to get the position of manager of the department? Was he, John Thompson, to be ousted from it, and even worse, was he going to be got rid of from the firm completely?

John had walked home slowly, in a daze, pondering in his mind the possible motives behind this seemingly generous gesture. He wished he knew where he stood with young Mr Aspinall, and where his best prospects lay. Aspinalls wasn't the only linen firm in Belfast, of course. Still, it didn't do to change too much, especially if it meant leaving what could eventually be a promotion. Young Mr Aspinall might tire of playing at being head of the firm, and there would be a good position for someone who could accept the responsibility of general managership.

John Thompson knew his work inside out, having been all his working life in the linen trade, and most of it in Aspinalls. He was a Lisburn born man, and his own father had been in a small way in the linen business, with a weaving shed of his own, employing a few men. There had been the farm, too, but John had no interest in it, and his brother Thomas came into it. Many an hour John had spent, roaming around the district, watching the weavers at work, in their cottages and sheds. The long lines of linen on the bleach greens were familiar sights to him, and he remembered listening to his elders talking, when he was but a lad in his teens, of the competition of the wet yarn which was introduced to Ulster from England, with which the local hand-spun yarns could not compete. And then the biggest cotton mill in

Belfast had burned to the ground, and the owners had decided, because of competition from English and Scottish firms, not to rebuild a cotton mill. Instead they erected a new flax wet-spinning mill with steam-driven machinery. Within two years this mill had about one thousand spindles, and subsequently, over eight thousand were erected.

Mechanical power spinning of flax produced a yarn that was better and cheaper than the finger-spun product. This gave a new lease of life to linen manufacturing and the yarns spun in Belfast became popular throughout the trade. Power looms were slow in coming to Belfast. Labour was plentiful - and cheap - and mill owners saw no reason for introducing power for their looms when they could get human beings to do the job. But with the Irish Famine of 1846 came a great change in the labour situation. Belfast had a lot of distress; soup kitchens were established and societies set up to give relief in the years of hunger to the poor who suffered. The widespread emigration that followed meant that labour was not so plentiful, and there was a wonderful revolution and improvement in the conditions of the working classes. The people who worked in the linen and still active cotton industries benefitted.

All this John Thompson had lived through in his working life. His father had got to meet old Mr Aspinall and John had been taken on to work as an apprentice. There wasn't much he didn't know about the manufacture of linen, and he was sure and certain now, in this year of 1855, that it was going to increase in importance. It was a far cry, this huge industry, from the early start, away back in the 1700's, when the French Huguenot refugees had brought their craft with them to the Lisburn district, when flax was spun by hand and woven by hand, and the wives of the small farmers paid the rent with the yarn they spun and themselves sold at the nearest market. Businesses had sprung up - bleaching, dyeing, printing and finishing of cotton piece goods - all bringing prosperity to the merchants of the growing town of Belfast.

John had quickened his step when he reached the Queen's Bridge on his way home. It had turned into a raw, cold night, and there was a chill air from the river. The port was full of ships - the steamers that crossed to England and Scotland; the sailing ships that plied to America and Australia with emigrants and cargoes. It was in these ships that the smooth white linen went, the snowy fabric whose manufacture fed so many mouths in Belfast. Just now, John reflected, the mills and warehouses of the town would all be finishing off work for the night. To their homes would go the spinners, the doffers, weavers, stitchers, the flax dressers, and all the people who tended in some way to the raw flax to turn it into the snowy white linen. To-night the doffing mistress would have blown her whistle, and the tired little girl doffers, some of them half-timers at the mill, would wind their frames for the last time in the day's work; the hacklers, the lappers, the reelers, the finishers, all would leave work with relief, to be away for a time from the heat, the clamminess, choking dust, and the back-breaking weariness of the day. Into this cold, chill night they would emerge, the women with shawls thrown round them, to keep out the damp after the steaming heat they had worked in.

College Square had been quiet as John passed through it, noticing on his way the shrouded figure of the statue, awaiting the morning's ceremony. He would be there to see it, reluctantly, worrying and wondering what events were afoot, and how his future would be affected by them. He would pray for guidance, that he might do the right thing for himself and his family.

When Martha went off to bed, John sat thinking by the dying embers. He gave no hint of his worry to Martha; it was not for a woman to worry about these matters of a man's world. But he knew he could not sleep yet awhile, with this worry on his mind, though common sense told him that thinking more about it would do little to solve the problem. The next few weeks, even perhaps the next day or so, might show how it would turn out. When he got back to work, after his unwanted day off, John would know if McCrum had been made manager. If he had, then John's way would be clear; he would look around for a position with another firm. Then he would have to think of Robert's future. Old Mr Aspinall had promised that Robert would be an apprentice in the firm. He would mention it, perhaps, to the young Mr Aspinall, but possibly it would be better to wait and see what happened. He wanted Robert to be in the linen trade. Linen, or railways, either was gilt-edged for a boy. It was the age of opportunity, of course, and with the coming of railways, steam ships and the vast expansion in shipbuilding. Robert could be well-placed in the shipyard, for John was acquainted with some of the men who worked at Hickson's yard, and he knew the manager of a ropewalk who would take the boy. Martha wanted Robert to be a minister, but Robert showed absolutely no leanings towards deep learning or piety, and his father never even considered the possibility. No, Robert would do well in the linen trade. It was a fine opening for a boy. First he would serve his apprenticeship then, as a journeyman, would have a good position and could become a traveller for his firm, maybe become a manager in time. For many little boys and girls of Robert's age it was a different story. They worked as half-timers, half work and half school, progressing little, either as scholars or as working little drudges. It was grinding work for the poorer classes. John Thompson knew many linen workers. Some had done well for themselves, many others were poor spinners or weavers, with the years coming on them, and finding them in poverty from the grinding long hours and poor wages, ending in ill-health from the dampness and heat of the mills and warehouses, and the squalor of the small houses, clustered in narrow cobbled streets in the shadows of the mills.

 John poked the cinders in the hob grate, and turned off the gas jet, and went slowly up to bed. Out in the street voices echoed, and far-off footsteps and the sound of horses' hooves on the cobbles were a reminder that not all citizens of the town of Belfast were as early to bed as he was. He brought with him a worry that would give him little sleep; he looked forward, not to the unveiling of the statue, but to getting back to his work the day after that, to see if he still had his position in the firm, or if George McCrum had been made manager over his head. With such a worry, the unveiling of a statue to a young Earl seemed not important.

CHAPTER TWO

There had been heavy rain during the night, and the streets were clean and drying by the morning. It was a brave day, with the weak sun trying to shine in opposition to the gray skies. From an early hour the streets of the town were busy with traffic with an unusual activity for a midweek morning, but then it was not every day that Belfast had a visit from the Viceroy of Ireland and from a host of lords and ladies, as well as the military escort to the Viceroy. The more important citizens were early astir to grace the proceedings of the day with their presence. Those of the less important class were mostly busy at work in factory and shop, and had to take on trust this sudden grandeur in their midst, but even so it was surprising how many of the people managed to present themselves in College Square, or as near as they could reach it, to witness the unveiling of the statue.

From the very crack of dawn the maids in the houses of the Square had been hard at work, washing steps, lighting fires in drawing rooms and preparing refreshments. Masters and mistresses had invited a throng of visitors to the houses to view the proceedings from the comfort and height of the upstairs windows.

Mary Murtagh, the parlour-maid at the wine merchant's house, hadn't a minute all morning to wonder if she was still afraid of the Blackman's statue. In the light of day these fears seemed foolish.

"Sure, what harm could a bronze statue do to a body?" she asked the cook, and hoped that she and the other maids might get up to the attic room for a peep from the skylight at the gentry below.

Donegall Place, Wellington Place, Chichester Street and King Street were choked with carriages, and with people on foot, all going in the direction of College Square. The dealers in Smithfield Square found few customers at their stalls, though the public houses in the entire district had a grand turn of trade. At the Royal Hotel the stage coaches drew up to disgorge more than the usual number of passengers from the country towns of Lame, Armagh and as far away as Enniskillen, while up at the new railway station a big throng of people had travelled up from Lisburn and Lurgan. Soldiers on horseback lashed by, their gleaming horses the object of admiring eyes. Foot soldiers in brilliant scarlet made way for the gentry to alight from carriages and to escort them to the newly erected stand near the statue.

The sun won its battle with the skies and in a wintery brilliance that added gaiety to the crowds the face of Belfast seemed to put on its best look for its visitors. The Cave Hill stood out black and dignified, like a guardian over its town, and the mountains were clear cut and adjacent., giving a clean, blue background to the Square, like a backdrop in the theatre. An excitement mounted in the crowd as the procession of the Viceroy and his attendant lords, the Mayor of the town, and the important ones connected with the statue approached.

For the residents of Killen Street and the other small streets nearby, there was no special accommodation—as Mrs Storey had hoped—and they had to make their own ways and use their elbows to gain positions of advantage. Mrs Storey took Alice and Alfie with her, and set off in good time, herself in her best bonnet and shawl. Arthur had said he would get up out of bed later and have a look, but his ma had her doubts. William Storey was only too glad to get some sleep and rest. His cough had bothered him in the wet morning as he made deliveries of bread before coming home. Mrs Storey left dishes unwashed and front unscrubbed, without a thought, and gaily pushed her way in as near the centre of excitement as she could get. The Thompsons got a position behind the ceremonial arch. They had a fairly good view, though when the speeches began the voices were practically inaudible. There was the reading of the inscription by the Secretary of the Committee, then there was an oration, and a speech from Lord Dufferin. Speech followed speech, with rounds of applause and cheers from the crowd as the statue was eventually unveiled.

Mr Thompson enjoyed it all. To his mind the young Earl of Belfast deserved to have a statue put up to his memory. He had been an accomplished musician, this young Earl, and had given away a hundred pounds that he had got for his musical compositions to the fund for the relief of famine victims. John considered this was a wonderful gesture and a lot more than some lordships did in those terrible years to help the starving people.

Robert stood beside his parents in acute unhappiness; he could neither see nor hear, and he had particularly wanted to see the soldiers on horseback. Instead he was stuck with his nose pressed against the black greatcoat of a worthy citizen in front and might as well have been at school for all the thrill or enjoyment he got.

Mrs Thompson enjoyed the excitement of the event; she had been up unusually early to put her house to rights, and to leave all the work done before setting off. She thought her husband was enjoying his day off; he was, to an extent, having put to the back of his mind the worry of what lay ahead of him at Aspinalls when he got home. He had been given a day off; he would enjoy it; that was how he reasoned to himself.

Mrs Storey was elated. She had never before in her life seen such a crowd, and was mentally taking notes to relay to Antrim. She noted the fashions carefully. Flounces and bell-shaped sleeves were in full style, as were numerous starched petticoats under the gown, though they made walking something of an ordeal. Eagerly she scanned each grand lady who came within sight. It was a great pity that her sister Aggie hadn't managed the trip from Antrim for a stay with her. What a sight it would have been for her country eyes; the grandeur of so many lords and ladies in the one square, the brilliant colours of the soldiers' uniforms, the carriages coming as thick as blackberries, the grand speeches, and the eloquence of the speakers, the pomp of the Viceroy that had come up all the way from Dublin. Ah well, she'd be able to tell all about it when Aggie came the first time McQuillan's cart was coming the length of Belfast. On her return at the end of the visit Aggie would certainly have something to crow about over their cousin Mary Ellen who was so superior because she worked with the gentry. If there was a chance of getting down to Antrim herself, Sarah Storey would have jumped at it, but there was no hope just at present. William was none too well, and she feared he was in for a bad winter of it with his cough.

The day ended in a blaze of glory with the grand concert in Victoria Hall, for which the Thompsons had been given the tickets. It was an anti-climax for them; the place was full of gentry, to be sure, with great elegance of dress from the ladies; their seats were at the back of the hall but gave a clear view of the platform, and they could hear the singing very clearly. Still, they felt out of their element amongst so many gentry, and Mrs Thompson was tired after the early excitement of the day, and worried, too, about Robert, who was sitting between his mother and father, fast asleep; it was time the boy was in bed. John Thompson tried resolutely to enjoy the music. There was an ode, specially written and recited by Denis Florence McCarthy for the event, and some of the late young Earl's compositions were sung. In the back of his mind the worry of his work would not stay quiet, but like a mouse in a cage kept going round and round, wondering, wondering. Why did Mr Aspinall give him the day off? Was George McCrum going to be made manager of the department? Would he be able to get young Robert in as an apprentice? It spoiled the music for him. Mrs Thompson said she enjoyed it all, but privately thought it would have been more to her taste to have a bit of fiddle music, and maybe a step dance and an Irish ballad or two. They were glad to get home and get to bed, and in the black darkness walked tiredly across the square, past the black statue of the young Earl, now standing in full unshrouded glory surveying the scene, the crowds gone, the oratory all but forgotten, the statue to be soon a part of the landscape of the town, a landmark for those seeking direction near to

College Square.

John Thompson was full of apprehension the next day as he set off for work. Would he find himself by-passed and McCrum manager? To-day would likely tell, he told himself stoically. He went about his duties in the department as though he had not been off for a day; the girls were busy and he was kept occupied all morning, without seeing Mr Aspinall, or McCrum, and after the meal hour the evening passed without any indication of any change, or without any visit from the Governor. Home coming time arrived and John was walking out of the warehouse when he heard footsteps behind him, hurrying. Turning round he saw it was George McCrum, trying to overtake him.

"I'll walk with you, if I may, Thompson," McCrum gasped, out of breath. He was a small man, inclined to be portly and obviously unused to the exertion of walking fast.

"Fine night, that, for November," John remarked casually.

"'Tis, 'tis, indeed," McCrum replied. They walked a short way in silence, then McCrum asked cautiously,

"What do you make of the young Governor, Mr Aspinall?"

"Well," John was equally cautious, "he's not the man his father was."

"No, indeed." McCrum breathed deeply, then burst out, "To tell you the truth, Thompson, I don't know what to make of him. He came to me to-day and told me to take the day off work to-morrow, and gave me a gold sovereign, to boot! A sovereign, and then—wait till you hear this—he says to me, 'Take your good lady for a day on the town, McCrum, bring her to the Theatre Royal, and treat her regally,' he says, and handed me the gold piece. I don't know what to make of him! Do you think he's right in the head?"

John Thompson had to smile. He nodded his head in wonderment. Mr Aspinall obviously did not know McCrum's taste, nor could he have been aware that Mrs McCrum was a strict

Methodist, to whom the very name of a theatre was repugnant.

"He gave me the day off, too, you know, and two tickets for a grand concert. My impression was that he intended making certain, eh, changes, and wanted to be rid of me for the day while he did so."

"You mean you thought he was going to make me manager of the department?" McCrum asked directly.

"Yes, I did, I must admit that was my mind."

"Sure and here's me thinking I was being got out of the way so that you could take over the whole place. We're both wrong, and I tell you what I think, Thompson, and that is that young Mr Aspinall has no intention of making anybody manager of the department, and moreover, he has very little idea what he's doing. I tell you, I think he's not right in the head. He was reared in England and went to one of them fancy schools somewhere abroad, and they get funny notions in them places. They're near all Papists, you know, and foreby he was a Christian born, I don't think he's one now. He mustn't be, for he knows right well what I am, and yet he turns round and tells me to take my missus to the Theatre Royal! He's far off his mark!"

John sighed. "I just don't know what to think, McCrum. Anyway, he's not running the firm the way his father did, and I'd say it behove us to watch out." John was cautious enough not to tell his mind to McCrum, knowing that the other was not to be relied upon to keep a still tongue in his head, but was likely to blab out any secret he might be told. "Wait and see," was all John said, and he intended doing that, in his own interests in particular.

To this end he asked permission to speak to Mr Aspinall about a week later, and in the private office, stood with the large mahogany desk between the Governor and himself.

"Well, Thompson, just the man I want to see," Mr Aspinall said, swinging his legs down from where he had stretched them on the table.

"Yes, sir," John replied gravely. He would hear what Mr Aspinall had to say first.

"I'm going away for a short time, Thompson," the Governor told him, "maybe until before Christmas. And I want you and McCrum to keep things going for me. I know that either of you can be relied upon, or together you can see that things run smoothly in my absence. Wilson in the counting house will attend to that end, and I'm sure everything will go along in fine style. I'll have you and McCrum in with me before I go, in a few days, and you'll know what to do."

"Yes, sir, Mr Aspinall." John was too surprised to say much more for a while, and stood silent.

"You want something, oh, yes, you wanted to see me."

"It's about my son, Mr Aspinall. It was an understood thing with your late lamented father that my son would be taken as apprentice when he was old enough."

"And he's old enough now, is that it?" Mr Aspinall smiled, and smoothed down his brocaded waistcoat with his fingertips.

"In another year he'll be old enough, and I hoped it would be acceptable to you, Mr Aspinall, to have him."

"Well now," Mr Aspinall replied lightly, "a year is a long time and I would not care to say if we would be in a position to take on an apprentice then. We have a few running round the place now, I understand."

"Yes, sir, the last to be taken on was Baxter, just before your father died, and there are four other boys serving their time, Moreland, Best—"

"Just so: I think we may leave it at that, Thompson. When the boy is older—"

"Thank you, Mr Aspinall," John replied solemnly, and turned to go. This was an unexpected turn and he was quite confused by it.

As he got to the door, the Governor, who had been standing by the desk, apparently deep in thought, said softly, "Just a minute, Thompson."

John came back and stood, silent, waiting. He felt angry now, and tried to control it. A bargain was a bargain, and this young man should at least honour his father's memory by honouring his bargains. It should have been an understood thing that an apprentice bespoke by the old man would in due time come into the firm. If not Robert for an apprentice, then who? Or was he not going to take on any apprentices at all? For a second John felt that McCrum's estimate of young Mr Aspinall was most apt, that he was not right in the head.

The young man looked straight at John, his face very serious.

"I think I had better tell you, Thompson, I'm quite certain you wonder how things are going. You would be at liberty to wonder, indeed, for I know that in my father's day it was different."

John inclined his head, not trusting himself to speak. He did not often become angry, and on this rare occasion struggled to master his feelings.

"I'm thinking of becoming married, Thompson."

Mr Aspinall had turned now and was looking out of the grimy window at the cheerless yard. "It's possible that I may not live in Belfast if I do," he went on. "The lady in question is of another country, and does not care for this climate. So you will understand that I cannot plan too far in advance. I may have to consider the position of the firm here."

"I understand, Mr Aspinall," John replied woodenly.

"My idea in giving McCrum and yourself a day off was to recompense you both for the extra work which will devolve upon you in my absence."

"You can rely on us, sir."

"And I can rely on you to keep this matter I was talking to you of, to keep it to yourself?"

"Of course, sir. And may I wish you joy, sir?"

"Thank you, Thompson. You may go now."

John went back to the department, his head in a whirl. So that was it! He was going to get married. There had been talk going round, though John never had paid much attention to it, that the young Governor was infatuated with an Italian opera singer. He was a gay young man who was well known, and spent more time in London than in Belfast, in his father's time, with frequent trips to the Continent. So he was going to marry his opera singer, and she wouldn't live in Belfast: the climate didn't suit! No doubt it would be Switzerland for them, or Italy. He had enough means to live wherever he had a fancy, and was not depending upon the linen firm for a livelihood. But so many others were, John thought angrily, so many workers who had given loyal service to the firm. What would happen to them all when his young lordship decided to finish with them, as assuredly he would, John knew. Likely he would sell his interests to another firm. There would be little hope of a managership then, in fact he might have to take a lower position under an amalgamation.

Furiously his thoughts ran. He would get Robert apprenticed elsewhere, he had many friends in the trade. For himself he would stay on awhile, but be on the lookout for a change of position; opportunities frequently arose that he had previously ignored, feeling he was secure where he was. Now he knew there was no security in Aspinalls. Let him stay until after Christmas anyhow, to collect the bonus that was part of his yearly salary of eighty pounds a year. That was his due, and Mr Aspinall was not going to deprive him of it. Keep his counsel he would: he had been asked to keep Mr Aspinall's news to himself, and it was not in any case in his nature to share his thoughts or business with any person, not even his own wife. He would keep all this to himself, but quietly his own plans would be laid.

During the weeks that followed, if Martha wondered at her husband being more than usually quiet, she had to keep on wondering, for he told her nothing of his troubles. She had trouble of her own now, and had confided to Mrs McKenna that she was expecting to be confined again, and was having a lot of sickness. It was nearly seven years since her last child, and she was most apprehensive of this child's coming.

"I never felt this way before, Mrs McKenna. I have terrible sickness every day, and I could retch my insides out as easy as wink."

Mrs McKenna waved her hand in a careless gesture. "You'll be as right as a trivet, woman dear. Sure that's nothing at all. When will your time come?"

"July, I think. I'm glad, of course, but I never felt this way before."

"Of course you're glad, and when you have another wee fella in your arms you'll forget all this. I'm sure Mr Thompson is glad too. He'll be looking another son."

"Well he doesn't say much. You know how men is. They don't like to talk of these matters. And he's worried enough, anyhow. I think he has business worries, and sure my bit of trouble would seem trivial."

"Soul, it wouldn't be trivial if he had it! They get off light." Mrs McKenna laughed.

It was a clear January day, with the evenings on the turn, and the promise of spring in the air. Christmas had passed quietly for both families, and if Mrs McKenna had a sad heart for her husband missing at sea, she did not show it in her demeanour, but went quietly and cheerfully about.

She came round to Mrs Thompson of an afternoon and the two of them sat at their stitching, having a good gossip at the same time.

"How is Mrs Storey getting on?" Mrs Thompson asked. "Oh, her! She's never done knocking the entry door, asking for the loan of a pick of this and a crumb of that. I hate a neighbour always borrowing! If I hadn't a thing I would do without it!"

Mrs Thompson had to smile at her forthright friend.

"They say she's not a bad sort, if you can stick all the bumming and blowing she does about her da and her Antrim relations. But if you ask me, I think she's a bit of a dart. Did you ever see the cut of that child's pinny? And the wee fella, Alfie, that plays with our Robert, his heel's out of his stocking more often than it's in."

"She's them childer ruined, particularly the wee fella. I tell you," Mrs McKenna wagged her head, "if he was mine he'd get a good beating."

"I think the da's hard on him. I hear Robert telling that Alfie made noise with dropping marbles the other morn, when the da was sleeping, and wakened him and he got up and gave the wee fella a good leathering. Robert says he come till school crying and saying he was going to run away to his grannie in Antrim."

"The oul' fella takes a drop, I hear," Mrs McKenna said, pursing her lips. "Sure you wouldn't blame the creatur, and him fighting for breath and working in thon oul' bakery. The big son, Arthur, he's a brave fella now. He come round one night to ask if Mary would sew a shirt for him. I think he's sweet on our Mary."

"Your Mary? Sure she's only a child!"

"Child! She's near sixteen, and young Jimmy's fourteen. I'm more worried about him, Mrs Thompson."

She paused at her sewing, and put the white linen on the table beside her while she rubbed her eyes, and pushed the strands of red hair back on her forehead. Mrs Thompson's kitchen was cosy, with a fire red in the hob. The two women sat in companionable silence for a few minutes. Martha Thompson would not force a confidence; if Mrs McKenna wanted to tell her troubles, she would, in her own time.

"He's talking about the sea," Mrs McKenna said at last to break the silence.

"Sure he's too young!"

"Not a bit of him, they would take a boy of twelve on the ships. It was always the sea for my Jimmy, ever since he was a wee lad. I've fought it, Mrs Thompson, I've fought the sea, ever since I was married, but I've wasted my time. He tells me that he'll run away to sea if I don't let him go, and sure how can I stop him, when the salt water's in his veins."

"'Deed aye, and his father a sailor, too."

"And his father before him. Do you know what I'm going to tell you, Mrs Thompson? My own mother warned me how it would be. 'Never marry a sailor,' she used to say, для your heart'll be broke, waiting and watching and wondering', and when I told her I was going to marry McKenna she said she'd rather see me married till a man pushing a handcart for a living. But marry him I did. Sure from the start, from the time we met, he was the one for me, and I was for him. I never regretted it, but I tried to fight the sea. I moved up here to Killen Street, from way down in the Docks, thinking maybe if McKenna was out of the sight and the sound of the ships in the Lough he'd stay on dry land for a bit. And many a time I thought I'd won, when he'd come in home from a voyage and throw down his handful of money on the table. 'There's hard-earned silver,' he would say, 'and as true as my name's James McKenna, I'll never put foot on a sailing ship again.' But then ... after the week or two went by, there'd be restlessness about him. He wouldn't say nothing, but I'd know, and I'd make him go round to the Chapel and see to his duties, and when he went off I put him in God's hands, knowing I could do nothing to hold him on land."

Mrs Thompson nodded her head and tut-tutted as sympathetically as she could, her eyes full of tears.

"And now my son is going. I'm to lose him too!" Tears trickled down Mrs McKenna's face, and she wrung her hands. "Am I to lose him too, Mrs Thompson? For I'll tell you this day what I never admitted to myself before: I'll never see James McKenna again. I know now in my heart of hearts that I'll never see him again."

She laid her head on the table and sobbed quietly, heartbroken.

Mrs Thompson said nothing, but patted the arm near her. It was her guess that this was Mrs McKenna's mourning that she could not allow herself to do in front of the children.

"There, now," she murmured, after a few minutes. "Don't distress yourself more, woman dear. The Lord above knows your trouble and He'll give you strength."

Mrs McKenna wiped her eyes with the end of her white apron, and pushed back a few wisps of the red hair that had fallen over her eyes.

"You'll pardon me opening my heart to you," she said sadly, "but there's no other body I can talk to. But I'm finished now. I'm done. That's my mourning done; the rest will be in my own heart. I'll never forget him."

After Mrs McKenna had gone home, Mrs Thompson sat thinking about her. Left a widow, her own way to make, and her son leaving her for the sea. But for all that her own position compared so favourably, she knew full well that Mrs McKenna had enjoyed a happiness and excitement with James McKenna that she, Martha Thompson, would never, never know with her husband John.

CHAPTER THREE

From Killen Street there was a fine view of the mountains on the west side of the town, and on a clear day they looked, to Robert, near enough to touch. He used to gaze at them and wish he could wander off and see what they were like on the top, but he never did, for he was not allowed to be far away from his own street for long. His da didn't like the idea of boys roaming the streets of the town, but Alfie Storey had no such restriction. He wandered far and wide, and often got lost. Once he walked as far as the Lagan River and stayed with the lightermen on their barges until it was dark. He went on the train once by himself as far as Lisburn. This, to Robert, was a wonderful exploit and he admired Alfie for it. Robert had never been on a train. Neither had Alfie, but that didn't stop him going on one, where he got a lift from a carrier in his cart. The most amazing thing to Robert was that never once did Alfie get a beating from his mother for these wanderings. Mrs Storey would run round the streets, asking everybody if they saw a wee boy called Alfie Storey, and when Alfie did get back, late in the dark, he was greeted by his tearful mother who hugged him and put him to bed with a big supper.

Robert had been told that he was not to try any such wanderings, either by himself, or with Alfie, but he was sorely tempted when Alfie asked him, one day coming home from school.

"Do you see them hills up there, Robbie? Were you ever up one?"

"No, I wasn't," Robert replied solemnly.

"I'm going up there the day. Will you come with me?"

"I'll have to ask my ma!" Robert said.

"Ach, never bother," Alfie said contemptuously. "I never ask my ma nothing. I just go. Come on."

But Robert hurried to his house and burst into the kitchen where

Mrs McKenna sat talking to his mother.

"Ma! Ma! Can I go with Alfie? Can I go up the mountain with Alfie?"

"Shut your noise, will you," Mrs Thompson snapped at him, giving him a swift box on the ear at the same time. "You and that Alfie. You cannot! But you can make yourself useful for once and do a wee message for Mrs McKenna."

Robert stopped snivelling and took his hand from his injured ear. His ma was awful cross these days. She was always boxing his ear for him.

Mrs McKenna had a big bundle on the table beside her. She smiled at Robert, and took hold of his arm.

"Do a wee message for me, Robert, will you? I have to send this work over to the wareroom in Hamilton Street. Do you know it?"

Robert nodded.

"Well, you take this for me, and I'll have something for you when you come back." Mrs McKenna turned to Mrs Thompson. "I wouldn't ask him, only our Mary couldn't carry it herself, it's that heavy, and her not feeling well. She had to leave the wareroom, you know. She was taking sick and fainting every day."

Mrs Thompson nodded agreement. "I just thought so! I seen her coming down the Court early. What is it that makes her faint? She's not a strong girl, maybe."

"It's the brewery at the corner, that's what it is. The smell of it makes her sick, and then you know what it's like, the closets in the wareroom is none too clean. Only once a week the buckets is emptied, and her being sick into them, you know, it makes her worse, and she faints. So her and me is doing out-work, hand-stitching, and here's a full week's work in this bundle that I'll get the most of five shilling for. Can you carry it, Robert?"

Robert nodded, not too eagerly, for it was a very big bundle.

"Do you know the way?" his mother asked sharply.

"I think so..." he said doubtfully. He was none too sure but to say so would invite another box on the ears. "It's over beyond McClean's Fields, I think...."

"That's right," said Mrs McKenna, "beyond St Malachy's Chapel. But maybe you'd lose yourself. I'll tell you what, I'll get Mary to go with you, and then you'll have company and you'll get there for sure, and maybe"—she turned to Mrs Thompson— "maybe the oul' fella might think of giving her the money for the work, and save me the journey in the morning."

"Would he not want to check it?" Mrs Thompson asked shrewdly.

"Soul, aye, he would, you're right. That oul' lad wouldn't trust God Almighty with half a farthing piece."

Mrs McKenna went to get Mary, and Robert followed her with the bundle of linen in his arms. Alfie came sidling up to him as she walked down the street.

"Where are you for?" he asked.

"Going a message with Mary McKenna."

"I'll come too," Alfie announced, then his sister Alice appeared from a doorway where she had been standing singing to herself.

"Let me come, I'm coming too!"

"You can't," Robert snapped. "We don't want no wee girls. You're an oul' nuisance, so you are," and Alfie added his, "You're an oul' cryba," and gave her a push.

Alice started crying, and ran homeward, sobbing, "I'll tell so I will!"

"Ah come on quick, before she brings my ma out," Alfie urged.

"I can't go without Mary," Robert said crossly. Mary McKenna came round the corner at that moment from her house, and Robert went forward to meet her. He liked Mary, very much, and he didn't want the Storeys coming with him now, for he wanted Mary all to himself.

She pulled her fine lavender shawl round her shoulders and shook back her fair hair.

"Amn't I the lucky girl, having a young man to walk with," she teased. "Don't drop that bundle, whatever you do, Robert," she added. "If you knew the work my ma and me had to do, you'd be very careful of it."

Robert's arms were aching slightly already, but manfully he tightened his grip. "I'll mind it, Mary, never fear," he assured her. He would do a lot more for Mary, if he had the chance, for he had lately decided that when he grew up she was the girl he was going to marry, and nothing he could do for her or buy for her would be half good enough for her.

"I'm coming, too." Alfie danced forward. "But we'd better hurry up for our Alice wants to come. Ach, here she is." He sighed as Alice came running.

"Let her come, poor wee Alice," Mary said kindly. "Sure she's a good wee thing and she'll like the walk in the fields, she can get wild flowers."

The party was walking off, down Killen Street, when the Storeys' door opened and Arthur came quickly out, pulling on his jacket and cramming a cap on his head.

"Where are you for, Mary?" he asked pleasantly. "Alice says you're going a walk, and if you knew how long it is since I had a breath of fresh air in the daytime, you'd be sorry for me and ask me to go with you."

"Oh, I'd break my heart, I'm sure," Mary retorted lightly. "It's the quare pity of you! Do you think you'd last as far as Hamilton Street?"

Arthur took Mary's arm and they walked on, leaving Robert still carrying the bundle. He resented Arthur coming. What right had he, pushing in where he wasn't wanted? And anyhow, nobody had asked him. Alfie pranced on ahead, and Robert was left with Alice. Their progress was slow, and as they passed the statue in College Square, the others were far ahead, and after crossing the road carefully at Murray's Terrace, by the time they got to the fields Mary and Arthur were sitting on a tree stump laughing, and Alfie was nowhere to be seen.

"Come on Alice," Robert urged crossly.

"I'm tired, you're walking too quick," Alice whined.

Robert was annoyed; it was all very well for the Storeys to come unasked, and leave him to carry this huge bundle that got heavier at every step, but it was a bit much to leave him to mind Alice too, and he was fed up with her hanging onto his coat and gurning at him. He noticed that Arthur was helping Mary over the ditches, and laughing and talking in low tones, and taking her hand and putting his arm round her whenever he could. Why didn't Mary give him a box on the ears and send him about his business! Mary shouldn't be anybody's girl, not yet at least, until he, Robert Thompson, was old enough to make his fortune and offer his hand.

The party straggled on and reached McClean's Fields. Robert had been once before with his father on an evening walk, as far as St Malachy's Chapel, which stood in the midst of the fields, with cows grazing peacefully in the shadow of the towers.

"Where's Alfie?" Mary turned to ask, and noticed Robert still carrying the bundle. "Ach, Robert son, have you carried that all by yourself the whole road? Aye, it's right gentlemen I have with me, I must say," she said mockingly to Arthur.

"Here, give it to me," Arthur said sharply, snatching the linen from Robert's aching arms. "Wait and I'll give that Alfie a clout on the lug. Where is he? Alfie! Alfie!" he yelled, and his young brother came running.

"Take you that," Arthur said, pushing it into his arms, "and you take care of it, mind, and don't drop it. You're getting it soft, boy," he added, "we're near Hamilton Street."

"I'm going into the Chapel to say a prayer," Mary announced. "Coming in with me, Arthur?" she asked, with a trace of ridicule in her voice.

"No, I'm not," Arthur answered curtly.

"I'll go, let me come," Alfie offered, and Alice chimed in, "Me too, take me!"'

Arthur's face got red. "You're not to go in there," and then he turned to Mary. "No harm to you, Mary, but I've never put a foot in a Papish chapel in my life, nor no one belonging to me, so if you don't mind, we'll stay out here."

"Just as you like," Mary laughed. "What about you, Robert?" she asked, and all eyes turned to him.

"I'll go, Mary," he said eagerly. He would have faced fire for her, and now was his chance to show Arthur Storey up.

"Come on then." Mary was walking up the stone steps, covering her head with her lavender shawl, and Robert trailed uncertainly behind her, hearing Alfie jibe, in a low voice, "I'll tell your ma on you, going into a Roman Catholic chapel."

Robert paused to put out his tongue, but his heart was beating and he felt he was doing a momentous deed. He never before had the opportunity to go into a chapel, and he didn't know what his ma and pa would say, but it didn't matter now, he was doing a brave thing, and the consequences could follow.

Mary paused in the porch and dipped her hand into an aperture and made the sign of the cross on herself. She opened the glass and wooden door and went into the church, and Robert followed, glancing fearfully around him, at the long rows of seats, at the gallery upstairs with its box-like pews. He stared at the stained-glass windows, and the banks of burning candles, dancing with brilliance in the half darkness of the church interior. His eye was caught by a red lamp, hanging in front of the brown wooden altar, and when Mary knelt in one of the seats and bowed her head, Robert sat beside her, noticing, now that his eyes had grown accustomed to the dim light, that other people were in seats, praying. Mary got up to leave, bent suddenly on one knee, so quickly that Robert bumped into her, then he stumbled after her, his boots clattering on the wooden floor. As they got to the huge, studded, timber door of the church, a bell rang, high up in the church spire, and as they got outside it was loud and clear; he looked up, but could not see it, and as the booming went on, it gave him a strange feeling of happiness and contentment.

"What's that, Mary?" he asked.

"That's the Angelus bell ringing," Mary said, and stood for a moment, her head bowed in prayer. She then caught his arm. "The Angelus rings at six o'clock. We must hurry for the wareroom closes at half-past."

"It was a lovely chapel, Mary," Robert murmured.

Mary smiled. "Will you get into trouble for coming in with me?" she asked kindly. "I wouldn't like you to."

"It doesn't matter, Mary." Robert wished he could say something to express his feelings, to tell her that he would brave his father's displeasure for her sake.

Arthur and Alice were strolling in the fields, and Mary shouted, "Yo-ho," and waved, and as they came towards the chapel, Robert saw that Arthur was not carrying the bundle.

Mary saw the same, for she asked immediately, "Where's the linen? Who has it?"

Arthur jerked a thumb towards Bankmore Street. "I got young Alfie to take a turn. He's over there," and he shouted Alfie's name several times.

"He's over the fields. I can see him," Alice remarked dreamily, and pointed a chubby finger to a figure beyond the trees.

Arthur shouted again, and slowly Alfie approached. As he came nearer it was obvious that he hadn't the bundle with him.

"The bundle, where is it?" Mary shouted.

Arthur commenced to run towards the figure in the navy-blue jersey which was trudging slowly towards them, then they all ran as it was seen that Alfie was soaking wet. His fair hair was flattened into his head, his pale face was streaked with mud, and water oozed from his jersey and trousers, and squelched in his boots with every step he took.

"I fell in!" he whined, half crying. "I fell into the river, so I did, and I was near drowned. I'm all wet!"

"Look at you!" Arthur yelled in a furious voice. "You're wringing. What took you near the river anyway? Ah, God oh! Can I not take a walk for once without you causing trouble? Here, dry yourself with this," and he took a large red handkerchief, none too clean, from his pocket, and roughly dried at Alfie's hair.

"A man pulled me out, so he did," Alfie sobbed. "I was near drowned, so I was."

"Ah, shut up, you're all right now! You wouldn't drown that easy," his brother snapped.

Mary went over and took his arm. "Are you all right, Alfie?" she asked, and as he nodded tearfully, she continued, "Where did you put the bundle you were carrying?"

Through teeth now chattering from the vigour of Arthur's rubbing and the cold, Alfie pointed a finger, and mumbled about "over thonder by the trees".

"You didn't drop it in the river?" Arthur demanded.

"The man that pulled me out has it," Alfie whined. "He's bringing it."

Just then a working man came up to the little group, the bundle in his arms. It had become untied, and the items of sewing were trailing out, all freely spotted with green slime and cow clabber.

The man spoke to Arthur. "This wee fella fell in, and here's the things he had. I'm afraid the cows has stood in it, and it's got a wee bit dirtied, like, but it'll wash. Are you all right, wee fella?" he asked Alfie.

Nobody answered him. Robert stood with his mouth open, looking at the bundle, Alfie still whined and shivered, and Mary turned deathly pale. She clutched Arthur's arm for a second, murmured, "I'm dizzy," then fell to the ground in a dead faint.

All was commotion. Arthur held her in his arms, whispering, "Mary, Mary, love," then he tried to revive her by patting her cheeks and rubbing her wrists. In no time at all a crowd gathered, of men going home from their work, and women from the nearby warehouses. Much advice was given freely, every person having an opinion as to how Mary should be brought out of her faint. She looked like death, Robert thought; he was afraid that maybe she *was* dead. If so, he would be blamed, of that he was quite sure.

Mary came round inside a few minutes, still looking pale, but able to stand up. Arthur gave directions to the party.

"Alfie, you run on home as quick as your legs will take you. Robert, you carry the bundle and take wee Alice by the hand, and mind now and don't lose any of them things. It's bad enough without that," he added crossly, looking as if it was all Robert's fault. Then to Mary he said, "Come on, Mary, love, we'll get you home. Just take my arm and lean on me, and we'll walk slow. Do you feel a wee bit better?"

Mary nodded her head, but didn't in fact look anything but very sick. She took Arthur's arm as if she was glad of it, and they walked slowly off. Alfie trotted alongside them, still shivering and snivelling.

"Come on, Alice," Robert sighed, "we have to take these oul' wet things," and he gathered up the sewing as best he could in his arms, trying not to hold the dirty parts near himself. It took him all his time carrying the dirty linen without being able to take Alice's hand, so he instructed her to hold firmly on to his jacket, and not to leave his side until they got back to Killen Street. Alice was tired and whimpered a bit, but Robert firmly urged her on, and together they tried to keep up with the others, as they walked back over the fields and back on to the road. Their progress was a snail*s pace, and they were soon left behind. As they trudged along, people in the street stopped to laugh at them, and Robert knew that he was a sorry sight, with a wet bundle clutched to him. He was apprehensive of his reception, and now and then would drop one of the sodden pieces of linen, making it even dirtier, so that when Killen Street was reached, there was no resemblance between the white bundle that had left a short time ago, and the ill-smelling, grimy collection that had Robert's arms feeling as if they would fall out.

Mrs Storey stood at her door, and when she spied the pair, she came running towards them.

"So here you are," she shouted. "What do you mean, Robert Thompson, making my Alfie fall into the river? Near got his death he has, and look at poor wee Alice. Come on in home, love!" She took Alice by the hand, and into the house, pausing only to shout at Robert, "You're a right one to go a message for anybody."

Robert leaned limply against Mrs McKenna's door, then, taking courage, pushed it open just as Mrs McKenna was about to. In the back of the hall Robert saw his mother looking sternly at him. He let the trailing armful fall from him on the hall floor. Mrs McKenna, without a word, reached down and gathered it all into her arms, and at the same time his mother reached forward and pulled him into the hall, and commenced slapping his ears, his hands and his legs.

"Take that, you brat," she shouted, slapping hard. "Next time you go a message for Mrs McKenna, do it right!"

"Now don't be beating the child anymore," Mrs McKenna intervened. "Sure we don't know what happened. Maybe it wasn't his fault."

"I'll find out what happened," Mrs Thompson snapped, her usually pale face flushed, and her eyes flashing with temper. She gave Robert's hair a hard pull.

"Come on home, you, and I'll give you the best lick of the taws you ever had."

"Don't, Mrs Thompson, don't!" Mrs McKenna shook her red

head sadly. "Don't beat wee Robert no more, there's a good woman. I'm sure it wasn't his fault, was it son?"

Robert sobbed, "No, no!"

"I thought not. My Mary doesn't faint for nothing and I'll lay that Alfie Storey had a hand in it, hadn't he?"

"Yes," Robert nodded. "I'm sorry, Mrs McKenna," he stammered out. "Arthur Storey came with us too, and wee Alice, and Arthur said we had to take turns to carry, and Alfie was doing it, and we went into St Malachy's Chapel, and when we come out Alfie fell in the river."

Mrs McKenna patted his head. "Go on home now with your ma. You're a good wee boy, and I'm sure you wouldn't do the like of this on purpose. Mrs Thompson, promise me you won't beat him."

Mrs Thompson nodded her head, as if she couldn't trust herself to speak. She caught hold of Robert's arm, and together they went round the corner, Mrs Thompson pausing only to call back to Mrs McKenna, "I'll call round and see how Mary is after I get this fellow cleaned."

Robert's feelings were hurt as well as his ears, and he sensed that his mother blamed him for letting her down. In their own house he caught her hand.

"Ma, I'm sorry, it wasn't my fault. It wasn't!"

"All right. Maybe it wasn't, but you got the blame. First of all, that Alfie one come screeching up the street as if he was being murdered, and his ma runs out to see what's wrong with her wee pet and him all wringing wet. Then Arthur comes, half carrying Mary, and her hardly out of a faint, and both Alfie and Arthur shouting at their ma that Robert Thompson had the bundle, and poor Mrs McKenna herself half fainting with worry. Then you come, and the decent woman's stitching is all cow clap and soaking with dirty mud. I tell you, Robert Thompson, she'll not send you on a message again.'

Robert hung his head, ashamed.

"But Ma," he ventured, "I carried the bundle all the way to St Malachy's and my arms was near broke, and that big Arthur Storey one never helped me at all, and then he bid Alfie take it when we went ..." his voice trailed off.

"When you went where?" his mother took him up sharply.

"Well, Mary wanted to go into the chapel, and Arthur wouldn't go and wouldn't let Alfie and Alice..."

"Did you go into the chapel?"

Robert nodded his head, and sniffed. "The Storeys wouldn't put foot in it, and that Arthur is always telling people what to do. He was calling Mary 'love' when she fainted. Ma, what's an Angelus for? The Angelus bell rang in the chapel."

"Ah, hold your tongue," Mrs Thompson snapped. "Ask your Pa, but I don't think he'll be any too pleased at you running in and out of Roman Catholic places of worship."

Robert thought this was unfair: he had never been in a chapel in his life before, but he knew better than to argue with his mother when she was so cross.

"Away and wash yourself," she directed him, "and mind and do it well or I'll come and do it for you. We'll see when your father comes home if you'll get any supper or not."

Mr Thompson heard of the day's adventures, and decided that Robert could come down for his supper in his good suit: his everyday clothes were muddy and soiled and would have to be dried and well brushed.

"It was a most unfortunate affair," was Mr Thompson's verdict when he had listened to Robert's telling the tale, "but I feel that Robert has been punished enough by Mrs McKenna's distress. Isn't that so?"

Robert nodded, not mentioning his mother's hard slaps and hair-pulling.

His father seemed in a reflective mood. "St Malachy's is a very beautiful house of God," he told them, "even though it is a Papist one. I well remember the great celebration dinner there was in Devlin's guest rooms the day the foundation stone was laid. I was a young fellow at the time, but I remember reading about it in the newspaper. In 1841, I think it was. Anyway, Papist and Presbyterian both attended the celebration, and the toast was made to Mr Adam McLean, a good Presbyterian man. He gave the land for St Malachy's Chapel—gave it free of rent forever."

Robert was delighted that the conversation was changed. He kept thinking, as his father spoke, of the sound of the bell ringing out over the peaceful fields. He must ask Mary some time what an Angelus was.

After supper, and when the dishes were tidied away, Mrs Thompson threw a light shawl over her head, and walked round from College Place to Killen Street, to ask how Mary McKenna was.

"Come on in, Mrs Thompson dear," Mrs McKenna greeted her. "I have Mary in her bed and she took a wee sup of tea. She told me all about the affair, and it wasn't your wee fellow's fault at all. And it was as much the smell of that brewery or for sure the chapel that made her faint as well as the upset she had over wee Alfie falling in the water."

"What about your sewing? Is it not ruined?"

"I'll have to wash every bit of it, for any that didn't get the clabber has big dirty streaks of mud and slime. I wonder, missus dear, would you have a wee taste of starch? I slipped down to the starch factory at the corner for a penn'orth, but they'd stopped for the night."

"Certainly I've somet. I'll just run down for it," and Mrs Thompson turned to the door immediately.

"Now take it easy, missus dear," her friend urged. "Remember your condition, woman. 'Deed I was sorry to see you in such a state this day, and your wee Robert getting chastised. He's a good child."

Mrs Thompson was barely out of the house when there was a light tapping at the back door and Arthur Storey peeped his head in.

"Can I come in, Mrs McKenna? How's Mary?"

"Come on, sure aren't you in already. Mary's in her bed, and no thanks to you or your wee brother she isn't worse."

"Now don't be too hard on me," Arthur pleaded. He was paler than usual and sank his large frame wearily into a chair. "Don't be too hard on me," he repeated, rubbing his hand across his brow. "I've lost my work over this day's events."

"Ah, God oh, you never did!"

"Aye, I was late going, and the boss himself, oul' Lamont, was standing waiting for me. Looking the chance if you ask me, for there's no love lost between us. To tell you the truth, if it hadn't been for my da, I'd have lost my work long before this."

Immediately Mrs McKenna was sympathetic, all her resentment forgotten.

"Ach, Arthur, I'm sorry, I really am. Sure my few bits of dirty sewing can be washed and starched up and no harm done, but you've lost your employment. It's too bad."

Arthur stretched his long legs over to the fender in front of the hob grate. He sighed.

"Aye, and what my ma will have to say is another thing. She'll screech the street down when she hears."

"Does she not know yet?"

"No. Nobody but you knows. I thought I'd call in first and ask about Mary and tell her about it."

Mrs McKenna grunted, gave Arthur a sidelong sceptical look as she lifted her iron pot of linen on to the grate to boil.

"I'm sure Mary's worrying about you," she remarked drily. "You all of you gave her the right time of it the day."

Arthur looked taken aback.

"I'm sorry, Mrs McKenna. Honest I am and if I could do

anything, I would. Do you need help with the washing of them things? Will I scrub them for you?"

"No, I'll manage. I'm giving the worst pieces a bit of a boiling to get the clabber off, and Mrs Thompson is away for a bit of starch for me, and I'll do them all up as good as new."

Arthur still sat on, apparently in no hurry to leave. Mrs McKenna kept bustling between the hob, to give the boiling clothes a push down in the pot, and the sink in the scullery where the rest of the linens were steeped.

The long silence was suddenly broken as Arthur exclaimed, "Mrs McKenna!"

"What?"

"I've been thinking hard, so I have." Arthur's pale face had a serious look on it.

"Well, I knew you were doing something, sitting there."

"It's something I've had in the back of my mind for a long time, and suddenly it's now clear. I think that leaving my work has maybe made it all plain. Do you know what I'm going to do, Mrs McKenna? I'm going to start up in business for myself!"

She laughed at him. "Are ye indeed! And what are you going to be? Lord Mayor of London?"

"You can laugh," Arthur said solemnly, "but I've got it all worked out. I'm going to start at the baking on my own. All I need is the bit of money to begin with."

"We could all do with a bit of money! Indeed if I had it, I'd start in business too." Mrs McKenna sat down on her wooden settle, and laughed heartily. "Talk sense, man dear. What you should do is to go up and see Mr Lamont and make an apology to him and ask to get back."

"Damn the fear! I'd see him in Hell first!" Arthur sat bolt upright in the chair. "You don't take me seriously, Mrs McKenna, but I'm telling you that I'm going to start in business for myself, and I'll tell you something else while I'm at it. I'm going to marry your Mary!"

The merriment went out of Mrs McKenna's face. She stood up suddenly and came over to Arthur's chair. She spoke firmly.

"Now listen to me, Arthur Storey, a joke's a joke, but don't you carry it too far. My Mary is not for the likes of you. You go and marry one of your own sort and you'll be happy. Foreby, my Mary's only sixteen; she's no notion of marrying anybody. I hope you haven't been talking to her."

"I told her she was the girl for me, but she just laughed."

"Aye and she was right to laugh. She's not for you, Arthur Storey. You needn't think I'd let my only daughter marry a Methodist that's an out-of-work baker."

Arthur sat for a second, then slowly walked to the door, controlled but flushed with anger.

"I've made up my mind, and you nor nobody else is going to get in my way. I'm going to have a big bakery, and I'm going to marry Mary. The religion is nothing to do with it. She can be as good a Methodist as I am, if she likes, or she can stay a Papish. It's all one to me."

Mrs McKenna gave him a sudden push. "Here, get out of my house! Have I not enough to put up with this day without you bringing me more! Away with you, go home, Arthur Storey, and don't let me hear any more of your nonsense!"

Arthur stopped and put his hand on her shoulder, angry. "Don't push me!" he shouted. "I'm going, but I'll do it in spite of you. You wait and see!"

Mrs Thompson arrived just in time to see Mrs McKenna shove him out of her front door.

"What is it at all?"

"Ach, Mrs Thompson, dear, wait and I'll tell you! Sure that Arthur Storey must be out of his mind." She related all that had happened.

Mrs Thompson pursed her lips. "It's what I'm always telling my Robert. Them Storeys has too much to say. Never heed him, missus dear, sure your Mary wouldn't look at him if he was decked in jewels."

Later, when the linen pieces were boiled, starched and hung on the fireboard to dry sufficiently for ironing, Mrs Thompson went home. Her husband was still reading at his newspaper, and Robert was long since in bed.

"You were a long time gone - is all well with Mrs McKenna?" her husband asked.

"Wait and I'll tell you the latest!" she announced. "Arthur Storey is talking about starting business for himself. He's lost his work at the bakery over being late to-night, and he says he's going to marry Mary McKenna someday when he's made a success!"

"Start business for himself! If he's nineteen years old it's the height of it!" John Thompson exclaimed. "Surely some wild notion has got into his head. I'm surprised at you, Martha," he said sternly, "idle gossip isn't like you at all." He took up his paper again to read, while his wife, rebuffed by his tone, went about her work in the scullery.

For all his outward show of indifference to the news, John Thompson's mind was racing, suddenly spurred by the idea that had sprung into it. Start business for himself, would young Storey? Well, why not himself, John Thompson start up for himself? Opportunities were there to do good business if he had some way of starting. He could start small, get a floor of a building and put in machines for a small warehouse to produce household linens, sheets, pillowcases and the like. His mind raced on, as though the idea had been lying dormant awaiting the impetus to start planning, but to be in business for himself - the idea fascinated him.

Then slowly but surely the cold logic of his common sense had to reject the whole image regretfully. Where would he get the money to start business? He had a little savings, but nothing near enough to start up for himself, no matter how small a way it was. Ah well, he would dismiss the dream, for it was only a dream, as no doubt young Storey's ideas were too. He took up his newspaper and started reading again.... His brother in Lisburn might have some money to lend him ... it would be worth a try surely. Before dismissing the idea finally, he might take a trip out to the farm someday soon and prospect the idea. The time was coming when some change would have to be made. Aspinalls could close down any day. He would have to get Robert settled as apprentice very quickly. He should be looking out for another position himself ... but let him play with the notion of having his own small warehouse, remote though the prospect might be. His serious, calm expression gave no hint to his wife, sitting at her knitting, that he was not reading the news, but was dreaming.... He, the serious man who rebuked her for idle talk was away in the realms of fantasy himself, fearing in his realistic mind that it was indeed only fantasy.

CHAPTER FOUR

Sunday in Belfast was a day that varied according to the religion a person professed. For strict Presbyterians it meant sitting with lowered blinds, and eating meals prepared the day before. It meant attending at church morning and evening, and Sabbath school for the children before morning service and again in the afternoon. Robert Thompson did not like the Sabbath; the usual Saturday preparations of cleaning boots and his mother cooking the next day's dinner filled him with a dread dullness. He was more conscious of this feeling ever since the Storeys came to the district, because he could see that their Sabbath was nothing remotely like his own. Alfie and Alice went to Sabbath school if their ma happened to get up out of her bed in time to have them dressed. If not, an evening visit to the church sufficed, and so far as Robert could gather—for he was not allowed to visit the

Storeys on Sundays, or even look out of the windows to see what was going on from talking to Alfie and Alice, he knew there were exciting walks after church and special Sunday suppers.

One Sunday morning early in August, Robert was wakened by his father shaking him. "Wake up, boy," he whispered. "Wake up!" And when he got the sleep out of his eyes his father told him to get dressed quickly and run round to Killen Street for Mrs McKenna.

"Your ma isn't well. Hurry, Robert son, hurry!" Robert struggled into his Sunday black suit laid on the chair, but didn't take time to fasten on his stiff collar or pull on his black stockings. Barefoot he ran down the stairs and undid the front door. It was a beautiful morning, with a slight mist on the bulk of Divis and Black mountains which dominated the landscape from the steps of College Court. It was quiet, except for a bell ringing in the distance which Robert fancied might be St Malachy's. He hurried along to Killen Street. It was exciting, getting up so early in the morning and going for Mrs McKenna. It did not feel like a dull Sabbath morning, but had a holiday freedom about it. Mrs McKenna was just returning from early Mass in St Mary's Chapel.

"What is it, Robert?" she asked anxiously. "Is it your ma?"

"Pa said would you come. Ma's not well."

"Wait and I'll throw on my shawl, and I'll be with you. No, Mary is behind me, coming from Mass, she'll wonder where I am. You stay here, love, and tell her I'm away round to your house."

She rushed off and Robert sat in front of the warm fire in the hob, warming his toes. He looked curiously at the ornaments on the mantle and the sideboard, and wondered what part of the world they had come from. Mr McKenna had likely brought them home from his sea-going trips. Maybe those big shells were from a desert island, and that carved box, would it be from China? Robert's fingers itched to handle these treasures, but he just sat and gazed at them until Mary came in and he explained his presence to her.

"Your poor ma, is she near her time?" Mary asked him, but he looked blankly at her, and said that his ma just wasn't well.

"I'll better go home now, Mary," he said, taking a backward glance at the sea shells.

There was a bustle in the house unusual to the Sabbath. His father was still in his night-shirt with his trousers pulled over, and was standing at the hob grate waiting for the big black kettle to boil. Mrs McKenna came down the stairs and got a basin of the water. Robert was sat down at the table to a sketchy breakfast of bread and a cup of cold milk. Then he was sent into the back to wash his hands and face in the sink. His father took him by the arm when this was done.

"Go up the stairs very quietly now, and don't go near your ma. Get yourself dressed and ready for church. I'll likely not be able to go this morning, so you go straight on by yourself. Be a good boy now."

"Is Ma very sick?" Robert asked, suddenly alarmed.

"She'll be all right, son. Be sure to pray for her when you go to church. Ask Almighty God's blessing for her."

Robert walked down College Court and into College Square with a queer, light-hearted feeling of freedom, the same as he felt earlier when going for Mrs McKenna. He clutched his Bible in his hand, set his good cap firmly on his head, and sauntered slowly along towards Berry Street and the Presbyterian church. He was quite early and in no need to hurry.

At the corner of the Square, near the statue, he met Alfie and Alice, both dressed in their Sunday best, Alfie in a brown suit and a round hat, and Alice in a blue gown and white bonnet.

"Where are you going?" Robert asked them, feeling very grown-up being on his own and on his way to church, even though he was taking the long way round to get there.

Alfie said pompously, "We're going to church, and you needn't think you're the only one to go. You think you're great because your oul' granda was a precentor. My granda in Antrim is a Methodist precentor, which is far better nor a Presbyterian one."

"Methodists don't have precentors," Robert said curtly.

"How do you know?" retorted Alfie. "Of course they do. All churches have precentors. The Roman Catholics have them, Mary McKenna told me, they have hundreds of them."

Robert didn't believe him, but he had no arguments or facts to disprove him, so he walked on ahead with a stern look on his face.

"Ach, wait a minute, Robbie, sure you're far too early, and so is Alice and me. We're going round by Castle Place to see the stage coaches. Come on with us. It's too soon for Sabbath School."

Robert wavered between keeping his dignity and gratifying his curiosity. Never before had he the chance to see the passing parade on a Sunday morning, and he loved to watch the stagecoaches coming in from their journeys, on any occasion that he could. There was something terribly exciting about seeing the dusty coaches and panting horses arriving from the far-off places like Dublin and Larne. He stood, undecided. Then Alice held out her hand to him.

"Come on Robbie," she said shyly, "come a walk with us."

Off they went, the threesome, hand in hand to cross the road carefully and avoid the traffic of carriages drawing ladies and gentlemen to church. On they walked, slowly, down High Street, and as if attracted by a magnet, towards the tall masts of the ships in the river. Sabbath school and church were forgotten.

However wrong Alfie was on precentors, he had his facts right about the ships. He knew the name of every one tied up in the port, where it had come from and how long it had taken. This was by no means Alfie's first visit to the ships, that was clear.

"Here's the iron steam ship." Alfie pointed to the *Blenheim*. "She goes to Liverpool four times a week. And the *Waterloo* goes, too. You can get to Liverpool for three shillings on deck or steerage. That there"—he pointed to a tall masted sailing ship, huge and impressive in its shrouded silence—"that's a packet ship. That goes to Australia."

Robert nodded, fascinated. He felt a new, deep respect for Alfie. He gazed at the packet ship, wondering was it such a one that Mr McKenna sailed in, and would James McKenna sail off too in a wonderful ship like it.

The children sauntered along the quayside, picking their way through the bundles of cargo that littered the cobbles, walking carefully over piles of ropes and kegs and barrels. Few people were around on the quiet Sunday morning; some seamen came and went from their ships, and to one of them Alfie said "Hello" and got a friendly nod in reply.

"Do you know him?" Robert asked excitedly.

"Surely," Alfie swaggered. "James McKenna brought me down one day and I got on a packet sailing ship that goes all the way to America. And the men talked to me."

"James McKenna is going away to sea," Alice said dreamily.

"Of course!" Alfie was brusque. "He's just waiting his call on a ship." He paused, looked at Robert for a brief second, then dropped his voice.

"Could you keep a secret?"

"Yes. I think so."

"Swear you'll never tell." Alfie's voice was an urgent whisper. "Swear to God you'll never tell the secret, if I tell it."

"Yes ... yes, I'll swear," Robert promised hastily.

"Well..." Alfie looked mysterious. "Nobody knows but me and James McKenna."

"I know! Me too!" Alice chirped.

"Well, you too, but girls don't count."

"What is the secret?" Robert demanded. "Sure I know rightly that James McKenna is going to sea. The whole street knows that."

"It's very important," Alfie said. "He's going to take me with him!"

Robert gasped. Suddenly a new world had been opened, the sea and ships, a wonderful, dreaming, shining world, and Alfie was going to be in it.

Alfie went on, his eyes shining,

"As soon as James gets a ship he'll write me a letter, and I'll go and meet him. I might have to go to Liverpool, or to Derry, because he mightn't get a ship that sails out of Belfast!"

"Liverpool!" Robert gasped. "How would you get there?"

Alfie's voice dropped to the merest whisper. "I have money saved, and even if I hadn't enough money to go on the iron steamship, I'd hide myself on it. I have a fourpenny piece and Alice is going to lend me her silver sixpence."

"Ah, Alfie, take me with you," Robert begged. "It would be wonderful, going away in a big ship…"

"Well… I might."

"I'll save my money too. I'll put by every farthing I get for going Mrs McKenna's messages."

"Well, all right, but don't you go and tell anybody." Alfie walked on, his stride longer, with the nearest he could manage to a seaman's gait. Robert followed humbly. Alice trailed behind them.

"We're late for church, so we are," she whined. "I'm tired walking."

"Church!" Robert echoed, panic stricken. "Oh, come on Alfie, come on quick, we'll be late. What time is it?"

"Maybe we're too late to go now," Alfie said hopefully.

"But I must go! I have to go to church!" Robert turned on his heel to walk back the way they had come.

"Wait a minute, I know a short-cut," Alfie shouted. "It'll save us time if we take it. Come on," and he led them up a little lane, off the quayside. "This brings us out near the town," he said cockily. "I know the way, follow me."

The little lane led them into a narrow street, and off that was an even narrower street, with houses in very bad repair, and seeming ready to tumble down at a breath of wind. Windows were bare of curtains, and few had even glass in them. Doors lay open, with blackness beyond, and refuse and dirt and filthy heaps of horse manure and dirty straw. The smell was overpowering. At a corner a group of ragged children stood aimlessly, bare-footed, their hair unkempt, their faces thin and pale beneath the crusts of dirt. At the sight of the three well-dressed children approaching they stared hard, then slowly walked towards them: it was obvious from their unfriendly looks that they planned some harm, perhaps even to take some of the children's clothes.

"Is this the way?" Robert whispered.

Alfie looked scared, and Alice whimpered.

A tall boy from the ragged group suddenly darted over and snatched Alfie's hat from his head.

"What are yous ones doing here?" he demanded cheekily.

"Run, come on Robert, run," Alfie shouted, and he grabbed Alice's arm and dragged her along, away from the corner, dashing along the street and round another corner into a different street. Headlong they went, from one narrow street to the other, their one thought to escape from the maze of the slums.

At length, out of breath they stopped, unable to go any further, and were glad to see that nobody had followed them. Robert looked round anxiously, and at the end of the street glimpsed the top masts of a ship: they must be near to the quayside, and in fact, a few steps took them on the quay, to the spot they had left a short while before.

"We'll go home the way we came, up High Street," Robert said crossly, "and if we hurry we mightn't be too late for church."

"Sure the people's coming out of church," Alfie snapped, pointing to the groups of worshippers strolling out from the various congregations, homeward bound in leisurely fashion.

Robert felt stricken: never before had he missed Sabbath school or morning service. What would his father say? Desperately he urged Alfie and Alice to hurry along, to get home as quickly as possible and he was on the point of blurting out his terrible crime when a grey-haired man in a top hat hurried down College Place, and went into the house. Robert was pushed firmly out and the door closed, and he went slowly up the steps to Killen Street, his heart heavy. Doctors cost a lot of money to bring to the house and his ma must be very, very sick.

McKenna's door was ajar, and he pushed it open and walked into the kitchen where Mary was standing by the hob grate stirring a pot.

"There's a bit of dinner here for you," she said gently, and told him to put his hat and his Bible on the dresser and to sit at the table.

Robert sat on the edge of a hard chair. He wasn't hungry. A terrible though struck him; his ma was going to die. She must be going to die when the doctor had been sent for, and it was all his fault. If he had gone, as he was bid, to Sabbath school and to church, and had prayed to God to make his ma well, she would have been better now.

"What's wrong, Robbie?" Mary came over and put her hand on his shoulder.

Robert burst into tears. "I never prayed to God for a blessing for my ma," he sobbed. "I never went to church at all." He poured out his tale of woe and Mary stroked his head.

"Don't cry," she said. "Listen to me, your ma isn't going to die. She'll get better if we say your prayer to God now to make her well. I'll say it with you."

They both knelt on the kitchen floor, but Robert had no words of prayer on his lips, only a heavy load on his heart. He sniffed while Mary prayed.

"We'll say the Our Father, and then we'll ask God and His Holy Mother to help and protect your poor ma, and then I'll tell you a wee secret."

When the prayers were over she gave him potatoes and a piece of beef from the pot on the hob, and he asked for the secret.

"You're going to have a wee baby in your house, that's what it is."

He stared at her in astonishment, and she told him there would be a wee brother or sister soon.

"That's what the Doctor has come for, Robbie, he's bringing the baby. Now, you can go off to your Sabbath school this evening, and you can pray hard for both your ma and the new wee ba."

Robert had his supper in McKenna's also, and then Mary showed him some of the treasures he had been admiring that morning, things her father had brought from foreign lands. Robert gazed at them wide-eyed, the memory of the ships at the quay still strong and full now again of his resolution of going off with Alfie to be a sailor.

"I'm going to be a sailor, Mary," he told her in a burst of confidence. "I'll sail away in a big ship to America or India, and I'll bring you lovely things back, more shawls and boxes than you need, and then," he added shyly, "when I'm big, maybe I'll marry you." He looked at her, his eyes full of excitement.

Mary shook her head slowly and smiled at him.

"Robbie, dear, you're too young yet to think of marrying, but nobody that goes to sea will ever marry me. We've had enough of the sea in this house. The sea takes away the people you love. Sure my da was just a man that came and went when I was a wee girl, and brought us money and presents, and we would all be happy. Then he'd go away again, and Ma would cry. And now our James is going to sea, too!"

"Maybe I'll not go to sea then," Robert said, with resolve.

"Is Arthur Storey still away in Antrim at his granda's?" Mary asked suddenly.

"I think so," Robert answered crossly. He didn't want Mary to like Arthur Storey. She was to be his girl.

"Arthur is very kind," Mary said softly, and turned away to clear the things off the kitchen table.

At dusk, when the shadows were deepening in Killen Street and Divis Mountain was still aflame at the edges with the setting sun, Robert went round the corner and met his father at the door. His father told him solemnly that he had got a baby sister, and that his ma was getting well again. He was allowed into the front bedroom for a couple of minutes, under Mrs McKenna's strict eye, to speak to his ma and to see the new ba. In the darkened room he could barely see them.

"Are you better, Ma?" he asked.

"Look at your wee sister." Mrs Thompson lifted a hand to the shawled bundle on the bed beside her. "Her name will be Jane."

Robert looked as closely as possible at the wee red wizened face with closed eyes. He didn't know what to say, for he really would have preferred a brother.

Suddenly a thought struck him. "Is the wee ba a Presbyterian?" he asked.

His mother smiled and Mrs McKenna laughed and said it was time for him to go to bed. Downstairs, his father was in a strange, kindly mood, and patted him on the head and told him he was a good boy. Robert thought it best not to upset anyone by mentioning the missing of church in the morning. It was the strangest Sabbath he had ever spent, and before going to sleep in his little room he thought back on the excitement of the day and wished that all Sabbaths could be so different.

During the next few weeks the Thompson household was completely disrupted by the baby. She was called Jane, and was a strong, lusty child, thriving from her first days, but added to the once placid, smooth-running household there was the disorder of her feeding times, her sleeping and crying. Mrs Thompson was none too well; she was still weak and not able for much work in the house. Mrs McKenna helped by bringing round dinner for Robert and his father, and doing bits of washing. Mrs Storey came in, but really intruded more than anything, for she certainly did nothing but talk. Alice was more help, for she loved the baby and as soon as school was over she came to rock the cradle. For her years she could hold the baby quite well, too, and kept the shawl carefully wrapped as she gently patted Jane to get the wind up.

"Maybe that'll stop her asking me for a baby," Mrs Storey said complacently. "Deafened she had me."

"Well, now, you never know," Mrs McKenna winked at Mrs Thompson.

"What? Is it me?" exclaimed Mrs Storey. "Sure woman dear, I thought our Alfie was my last. I never thought of another when wee Alice came."

"Ah now," taunted Mrs McKenna, "the older the fiddle, the sweeter the tune!"

"Indeed no woman had harder luck than me," Mrs Storey said petulantly. "Didn't I lose a lovely boy and two wee girls between Arthur and Alfie."

"Sure woman dear, didn't we all lose weans! You weren't the only one!"

Beneath the bantering tone there was an edge that betrayed the hostility between the two women. Mrs Thompson was too tired to listen to them, or join them in their talk, and she was glad when they went out, and left her to rest. That night she told her husband that she thought a change of air might be in order.

"Maybe if I got up to Moneyrea for a bit, it would do me good. My brother George will likely be in at the market on Friday. I'll just ask him if they can take us all for a while.'

Robert listened carefully, excited at the prospect. He must be sure to be about on Friday when the country cart came. Uncle George sometimes let him hold the reins for a minute before the nose bag was put on the horse, but if they were all to go to Moneyrea, what excitement would there not be? Maybe he might get driving the horse along the road.

Uncle George always had something to eat in College Place on his visits on market day, and as he sat at his bowl of tea and cuts of loaf his sister broached the subject of a visit.

"It would do me good, George, I know, to be back up in the old place. The child took a lot out of me, and I haven't got my strength back. Sure you could bring us up in the cart the next day you're coming in." She spoke easily, confident that the visit was as welcome to her brother as it was needed by her, but to her surprise, George stirred uneasily in his chair. He scowled at the empty plate and pushed the bowl round the table with his finger.

"I doubt it wouldn't do, Martha," he said finally. "It wouldn't suit..." His voice tailed off, then with a burst of speech he went on: "Two of our weans is ailing, the fever, I think, aye, a touch of fever, and your new wee ba might get it." He pushed back his chair, relieved that a suitable refusal had been found. Mrs Thompson stared at him.

"This is something new," she declared. "You never spoke of the childer ailing before, George. Sure, I was thinking your Margaret would be a right age now for helping me to look after the wee child. We'd be no trouble."

"Oh, Margaret is going into service in the Ards, with the minister's wife there. She's getting a start at the beginning of the month. No, Martha, it wouldn't do, you'd better not come ... on account of the fever."

He was on edge to get away, and promised to call and see how his sister was when next he came to market. He promised fresh eggs and recommended her to get up and going at her work to make her feel better. She was amazed and looking for an explanation but could not find one. The fever excuse was an expedient, and not a very convincing one, for the very thought of fever would have had George worried for his own and his children's safety, and up to her proposed visit he was completely unruffled.

That night, in bed, Martha sobbed weakly.

"My own brother," she told her husband, "and the house I was born and reared in! Oh, I know what it is, it's George's wife, and it's the sorry day he married her. She never liked me, her and her bitter tongue, but surely to God George isn't that afraid of her that he'd keep his own sister out of the place. Maybe it's that bad she's ashamed to have me. That's it; likely there's dung to the doorstep and the yard ankle deep in drag muck, and the children dirty and scratching!"

John Thompson had to smile as Martha's invective flowed on. Finally he calmed her down.

"Don't worry, Martha, and be charitable in your thoughts. Your brother has some reason for not wanting you to visit him, and we must accept that. But why not go and stay with your Aunt Agnes? Wouldn't she be glad to see you?"

"I declare to God I never thought of it! Her place is only a wee bit of a cottage, but I'm sure she could squeeze us in. Will you walk up the Hills one night and ask her, John?"

He promised he would, and two nights later, after a hurried evening meal, he set off. Robert would like to have gone, but was told to stay and keep his mother and sister company. It was late and dark when John Thompson returned. Robert was fast asleep in bed and did not hear him come in.

"Well, Martha," he said gently, not to wake the baby rocking in her arms, "Aunt Agnes was glad to see me. She's eager to see you and you have a warm welcome waiting for you. It'll keep her company, you know, for she sees little of the Moneyrea people. George comes over now and then and never leaves empty handed, but his wife calls only rarely and then it seems only to make a poor mouth of it. You and Robert are to go with the baby, and I'll walk out from work on the good nights."

"Aunt Agnes." Mrs Thompson's face softened. "She's one of the best, and her living her lone now, her man and her two big sons all dead. I'll be glad to see her again."

Robert was terribly excited about the holiday in the hills. He had never been from home for even a night before and he pestered his mother with questions, how long would it take to get to the Hills, what was Aunt Agnes like and had she any horses. His mother was every bit excited, but at the same time concerned as to how she was to get out to Aunt Agnes's cottage, which was a mile or so down the hill from her old home in Moneyrea. Her plan that George would take her she discarded; if he refused her shelter in his house, she wouldn't be beholden to him for a ride in his farm cart. Walk she could not, being too weak as yet, and as for hiring a conveyance, it would cost a mint of money.

The problem was solved almost as soon as it was created by Mr Aspinall. John Thompson had asked for an hour off work one evening for the express purpose of bringing his family out to the Hills; he had favoured using George's farm cart, no matter how unbeholden his wife wished to be, but when Mr Aspinall heard of the purpose of the time off, he asked all details, and confused John Thompson by insisting on sending his carriage and horses to bring the party out to the Hills. It was typical of the man, John Thompson thought ruefully, and the act emphasised to him his former opinion that young Mr Aspinall was not quite right in the head. However, a refusal would not be taken, and on the day arranged, at five o'clock in the afternoon, Mr Aspinall's carriage drove up to the Thompsons' house. Immediately a crowd gathered, and a cluster of children swarmed round the horses and the carriage, to the coachman's disgust. Mrs Thompson was excited as much by going in a carriage as going away. She would have enjoyed the experience only for the sensation they were causing in the street. Alice Storey was to come with them, as she was so useful in helping with the baby. Poor Alfie stood disconsolate, the picture of misery and dejection. He wanted to travel in a gentleman's carriage, and here was young Alice getting, and he wasn't.

"I wish you were coming, Alfie," Robert said.

"It doesn't matter," Alfie replied. "I'd be no good at minding a ba anyhow. Here, Robert, you can have the lend of this, if you like," and he passed a small spyglass from under his coat.

"Where did you get it?"

"James McKenna gave it to me. You only have the lend of it, mind now. But you can look through it and maybe see me on a ship."

"Ah, Alfie, don't go without me!"

"I can't help it. I can't wait if you go running off and not take me. Ask your da if I can go out some night with him. I never was in them Hills up there."

Robert promised he would, and the carriage being ready, he was pulled into it by his father. Mrs Thompson was seated with bundles and parcels around her, and baby Jane in her arms. Alice was beside her, demure but excited. The coachman wrapped a rug round Mrs Thompson, adjusted his hat, flicked his whip, and they were off, Robert sitting beside his father trying not to jump up and down in the commotion. The carriage bumped gently over the cobbled streets of the town and onwards the two and a half miles to the foot of the Castlereagh Hills, Mr Thompson pointing out places of interest on the way. He knew Belfast well and could tell the name of each church they passed and what the big buildings were used for. It was, in truth, the first time any one of the party had ever been in such a carriage before, and the novelty of bowling along was as much as they could cope with.

From the foot of the Hills the road was steep and the horses had to slow down to a walk, then at the next turn, the hill was so steep that the coachman made all except Mrs Thompson and the child get out and walk. For the remainder of the journey they had spells in the carriage, and out walking, until they came to the head of the lane leading to Aunt Agnes's small holding and cottage, which was a small two-storey building with a thatched roof, fronting a cobbled yard enclosed by trees and bushes, giving a dark and gloomy appearance.

Inside the big kitchen Aunt Agnes greeted the travellers, once the varied selection of parcels and bundles had been disposed. There was a great reunion between her and Martha Thompson, after years of separation. Robert was carefully scrutinised and declared to resemble his grandfather. It was now dark and the lamps were lit which did not reveal much of the interior of the room. Alice sat huddled beside Robert on the settle near the fire, and scarcely opened her mouth. By and by, when they all had tea and soda bread and boiled eggs, Alice fell asleep, clutching Robert's hand. Mrs Thompson carried her into the small room off the kitchen and put her to bed. Later, Robert was shown where he was to sleep, in the barn-like room upstairs, with a tree waving against the window. He was too tired and sleepy to feel frightened of the strange surroundings, and slept soundly until morning.

He wakened early, knowing that something was strange, and realised that he missed the sounds of the street at home; no milk cans clattered, no carts over the cobbled streets, or factory whistles blowing. The silence of the country made him lonely, and he went, half-dressed, down into the kitchen where his father was coaxing a flame from the fire.

"You're wakened, boy. We'll go to the well for water," and his father took a bucket and opened the creaking front door, and led the way across the cobbled yard and through a little gate opening into a field.

After a few yards' uphill climb, the panorama of the whole town of Belfast below in the morning haze was revealed. Both Robert and his father paused for a minute to take in the view. It was a clear September morning with just a hint of early frost. The far-off houses, mills and warehouses were merged in the mist of the morning and the winding smoke from the chimneys. Belfast Lough stood out sparkling, and beyond the limits of the town, Cave Hill and Divis Mountain looked smaller than seen from the lower plain of the streets.

Robert had his spy glass with him, tucked in the sleeve of his jersey. He took it out and tried to focus it on the view.

"What's that you have?" asked his father.

"Alfie Storey lent it to me."

"Let's see," and Mr Thompson took it from him and put his eye to it. "A very excellent thing this. Why, I can see things very clearly. I wonder now, could I see Aspinall's place, it should be over here on this side of the river, in Ballymacarret. And there's the harbour, and ships in it, too. Why, I declare, you could almost see Lord Donegall's park at Ormeau; those trees must be part of it."

Robert was dying for a look himself, and when at length his father handed it back to him, he screwed his eye to have a good look for Killen Street and Alfie.

"Come on, come on boy," his father snapped testily, "hurry and get some water."

On the way back from the well, Robert was instructed that he was to help his Aunt Agnes by getting water, by gathering firewood, and by doing any other jobs required; he was to be a good boy and not get into any mischief while he was at the cottage.

"And I trust you to look after the Storey child, too," concluded his father. "She's a good little girl and helps with our baby, but she must get into the air as well. And, by the by, you will read your book sometime during the day, so that your absence from school will not signify. I'll set sums for you to do, too."

Robert's heart sank. It seemed he was to be kept busy and the carefree holiday he had hoped for was going to be overshadowed by all these instructions. However, as the days went by, he found that life in the Hills was free, as Alice and he roamed through the fields and lanes, gathering blackberries, and bringing in huge bundles of sticks and dead wood for the fire. They ran barefoot and soon the sun and the wind brought colour to their cheeks.

Mrs Thompson improved in her health, and her strength came back gradually. Aunt Agnes and she greatly enjoyed each other's company.

"Ach, it's grand, having a full house again," the old lady sighed. "Sure I'm that long on my own, since my Eddie died of the cholera, that I have near forgot what company is."

Her niece nodded sympathetically. "You're too long on your own. I wish I'd known sooner, but I thought our George and his ones would have been round to see you more."

"Oh, them! I'm sorry to say it, Martha, of my own nephew, but I'm pained to see he took a dirty clart for a wife. Any time any of them comes, it's for something. I declare to God, if they do give me a bit of a hand about the place now that I'm stiff with the pains, be sure they get paid for it, in some way. It's always looking this and wanting that, but of course, I know fine well what they do want! It's the same thing that made them try and keep you from coming near the Hills!"

Martha didn't understand what the old woman meant, but her heart was full of sympathy for the lonely old woman. On an impulse she said, "Would you not come and stay a wee while with us this winter? Sure you'd be lost up here when winter comes on and nobody to do a hand's turn for you."

The old lady thought for a while, then said firmly, "It is lonely, I'll not deny it. And I can't feel the same to George, knowing what he's after. Do you know, many's the time, before my pains made me too stiff, I used to walk up the well field, and stand and look down at the town below. All them houses down there, rows and rows of them, and I wondered what it would be like, living besides people, and never wanting the sound of a neighbour's voice."

"Well, there's room for you in College Place, and a welcome too, and you'd get the worst of the winter over with a bit of comfort. We have the gas, you know," Martha felt a touch of pride, "and the running water. It makes a great difference."

The old lady sighed. "Sure I haven't put a foot in the town of Belfast since the day our William John went back to Americky in the sailing ship, and that's a brave whiles back. Let's see, he was killed in Virginia, in 1850. My poor man never got over it. It killed him, and then me a widow, wasn't my only other son took from me in the cholera. It was a black year for me."

Martha patted her. "It's all in God's hands. I'll speak to John, and we'll arrange for you to come back with us. You can leave the place for a bit. Won't Samuel James McDowell look to the animals for you?"

"Oh, I'll not fret about that. George'll have one or two of his boys about the place, getting all they can." She chuckled. "But they'll not get what they hope they'll get."

John Thompson had walked out that evening from work, to spend the night, and Martha confided to him her talk to the old lady and her invitation to come and stay with them. Mr Thompson was quite agreeable; the old lady had a tremendous respect for him, and he could see she was very fond of Robert.

He walked out most good evenings, and enjoyed the good air after the long hours in the wareroom. It was a brilliant autumn, though frost came most nights. The Thompsons stayed in the Hills while the good weather lasted, and Robert and Alice and the baby were getting the good of the outdoor life. Alice would sit on a stool outside the door, nursing the baby, while Robert roamed far and wide. He missed Alfie's company very much; there was no encouragement for Alfie to come out to the cottage, however. Occasionally Alice was homesick, and the first time Robert found her sitting crying softly to herself, she was in the well field, on a grassy bank, looking down at the town.

"What's wrong, Alice?" he asked.

"Nothing," sniffed Alice, "I just want to see my da, so I do."

Robert sat down beside her and put his arm round her.

"Sure we'll be going back home soon, Alice, and you'll see him then."

"I want to see him now, and Ma, too, and Alfie and our Arthur."

Robert had a brilliant idea, and took out the spy glass that Alfie lent him. He carried it with him all the time, and had spent hours looking through it at the birds and the trees and landscape. Now he thought it would comfort Alice to look through it in the direction of home.

"Look, Alice, put your eye to this, and you'll see Killen Street, as plain as anything."

Alice wiped her eyes with her pinny and screwed up one eye. "I can't see nothing," she sniffed."

"Here, let me see," and he grabbed it from her. "You have to look away far, over at the other side of the town."

He couldn't see much himself, except a mist and a jumble of chimneys and rooftops, but he pretended he could see right into Killen Street.

"There's Alfie!" he shouted, excited.

"Where? I can't see him!" She took the glass from him.

"Well, he must have gone into the house! I'll look again. There's your ma scrubbing her front step, and it's Mary McKenna going along the street with a parcel."

Alice was comforted and whenever she was homesick, she asked Robert to look through the glass for her da, and he never failed to have a good story for her.

Robert had hoped to have the company of his cousin, Danny, from the other farm. Any time Danny had come with his father to College Place on market days, he had been most friendly and had allowed Robert to ride in the cart and hold the reins. Danny was three or four years older than Robert, and now was tall as a man, with a deep voice and the makings of a beard on him. Danny or his father now came down nearly every day to Aunt Agnes's cottage, to do any turns she might need about the place, and from the first day of the Thompsons' visit, both had shown resentment at them.

Robert went one evening to see Danny at his own home, seeking company and hoping Danny would show him how to do things about the farm. Danny had been bringing in the cows and Robert walked alongside him up the loaning. It had been a lovely day and was now a clear evening with the sun lingering and warm. In the silence of the countryside a distant bell could be heard. Robert stopped, and listened. He was almost sure it was the bell of St Malachy's Chapel. Maybe it was ringing the Angelus. Anyhow, it had a magical sound, and filled Robert with a strange delight.

"Listen, Danny, do you hear it? It's St Malachy's Chapel bell."

"I know," Danny snapped. "What do you want to be listening to that for, it's only the growls of Popery."

Robert was crestfallen, and somehow the happiness of the previous moment was gone. Danny was most unfriendly. Another day, Robert went boldly into the byre where Danny was milking. Several of his brothers and sisters were playing around, but they hid when Robert came.

"What do you want?" Danny asked, surly.

"I wanted just to see what you're doing."

"Away on out of this! Don't be coming up here, putting your neb in, looking for news. Away on, wee suck-up! Sucking-up to your Auntie for what you can get."

Robert felt bewildered, and went slowly out of the byre, and walked down the 'yard' of the house. The other children came out of hiding and putting their heads round the byre door shouted after him, "Oul' suckey-up from the town. Couldn't even milk a cow."

His mother noticed him quiet that evening and he told her what had happened, not to be a talebearer, but seeking some explanation. Aunt Agnes was listening.

"I declare I don't know what's come over George and his family," Mrs Thompson said. "There's something very queer about the way he's going on, him and his yarn to me about the weans having the fever! And I can see he resents me here. It's hard to understand."

"Not a bit," Aunt Agnes chuckled quietly, "if you knew all the ins-and-outs of it, you wouldn't think it a bit hard to understand."

"Well, I wish somebody would tell me."

"Ah, you'll find out some day. But never bother yourself, Martha, dear. I know what's behind it all, and I'm not missing any of what goes on."

Martha had to be content with this observation, but she was hurt that her brother treated her this way, and hadn't even suggested she might want to go up and look at the farm that was her old home before she was married.

The next week the weather broke with wild storms and heavy rain, and Mrs Thompson was anxious to get back home to College Place. She had asked Aunt Agnes for her decision but the old lady wouldn't say whether or not she would go with them, until the wild weather came, and then she said decisively one morning that she would.

"Sure, I'd miss you all that much, I might as well treat myself to the trip and the company when I can. The dear Lord knows there's nobody else anxious to do much for me but yourself, Martha, dear."

How to make the return journey was a problem to both Mrs Thompson and her husband, and they discussed it many times, both being agreed that under no circumstances would they go in George's farm cart.

"I'd walk first!" Mrs Thompson declared, "and carry my Aunt Agnes on my back!"

"It will hardly be necessary to go to such an extreme." Mr Thompson smiled. "I have an idea that Mr Aspinall will again offer his carriage; he keeps asking me when we return, and if he does offer again, I'd find it hard to refuse."

Mr Aspinall did offer, and one morning in October the carriage arrived at the head of the lane for the downward journey to Belfast. Aunt Agnes was doubly excited. The prospect of going to the town of Belfast for a visit was thrill enough, but to go in a gentleman's carriage nearly overpowered her. Her bundles and parcels, along with the Thompsons' luggage, filled a seat of the carriage, and they looked like emigrants when the children were squeezed in. The coachman was greatly annoyed. He was not used to such loads in his carriage, and he showed it.

CHAPTER FIVE

Aunt Agnes settled down very well to town life. She took a great interest in everything that went on in College Place and in Killen Street, and above all seemed to enjoy the constant coming and going of the neighbours up and down the streets. Most afternoons she enjoyed a walk and usually Robert or Alice accompanied her, for she was very nervous of crossing over the roads, and would stand waiting for even the slowest horse and cart to pass before she would venture.

"I'd be afraid of my life with all them horses dashing up," she told her niece. "That's one thing about the town that I find very frightening and that's all the traffic."

She was greatly impressed by the district that the Thompsons lived in, although their house was a small one, in a small street, at the back of the big houses of College Square.

"Robert was pointing out to me the houses where the professors from the college live, and we had a very agreeable chat with a fine girl that's a parlour-maid in the wine merchant's house. Mary Murtagh her name is, and she knew the childer."

One afternoon she was returning slowly from a walk slightly far afield, with Alice to lean on, and their slow and tired progress was caught up on by Mrs Storey, dressed in her good bonnet and dress. She fell into slow step with the old lady.

"I was just round seeing the great bargains in blankets in the Emporium," she said, "and I was wondering if Mrs Thompson was needing any. Fancy this, two blankets for eight shillings! It's part of a shipwrecked cargo they say, but there's not a mark on them."

"Eight shillings!" echoed the old lady. "Do you call that cheap? That's a power of money."

"Cheap enough these days, though mind you, I'm not needing any myself, for my da is in that line of business and he'd give me anything I need at the best price."

"Well, it seems a lot of money to me," persisted Aunt Agnes.

"Sure what length does money go these days anyhow," sighed Mrs Storey. "Do you know, you couldn't stand foot to the expense in our house, with butter prices at tenpence a pound, and a loaf sevenpence. I say it's just as well my man earns good money. He's a baker you know," she added in a polite tone, "and they earn very good wages."

Mrs Thompson was smoothing with her flat iron when the old lady sank thankfully into a chair.

"You know, Martha," she remarked thoughtfully, "that Storey woman was telling me the price of things. It must take a lot to run a house in the town. Things is very dear."

"Oh, I don't pay too much heed to Mrs Storey," Mrs Thompson replied quickly. "Not, mind you that it doesn't take all a man earns to keep a family. I'm sure and certain that my John doesn't earn as much as her husband, yet I could make money go further. She's very wasteful."

"Tell me this, what religion is she at all? She took pains to tell me that wee Mrs McKenna is a Roman Catholic, and she doesn't seem very fond of her, foreby they live next door to each other."

Mrs Thompson laughed. "Right enough, there's no love lost between them. The Storeys is Methodist one Sunday, and the next they go to our church. If you ask me they're everything in turn—except Roman Catholics, of course."

"Well, she's no ornament to any church, that one," the old lady declared. "If you ask me it's her and the likes of her would stir up trouble between people and cause riots. Sure I find the people round here is all very nice, and wee Mrs McKenna is as good a neighbour as a body would want."

"Don't pay too much heed to Mrs Storey. No doubt she's got wind of her big son Arthur being sweet on Mary McKenna. To her mind, nobody from these parts would be good enough for a son of hers."

The old lady seemed thoughtful all evening, as if she had something on her mind. Next morning she came down the stairs with her old, worn purse in her hand.

"Likely George will be in today, if he's at the market. If he comes I want to give him the rent, for the rent day's near hand."

"Sure you've no notion of going back yet?" her niece asked hastily. "You wouldn't go back to face the winter on your own."

"I've no notion," the old lady murmured, "but I want to pay my rent and keep the place in my name yet a wee while. What I want to tell you is that I have been thinking things over and it's only right I should give you something now and then," and she handed over a gold guinea piece.

Mrs Thompson was taken aback.

"Aunt Agnes, dear, you've no call to give me money. Sure didn't we all stay up in your house and never a word about money. It's that Storey one has put it in your mind, her and her talk about hard times. You keep that guinea for yourself, Aunt, and buy yourself a nice new shawl."

Aunt Agnes pressed the coin back into her hand.

"It pleases me now to give you the wee present, Martha, and just take it."

Mrs Thompson told her husband of the incident later when the baby was fast asleep in her cradle, and Robert and the old woman up in bed.

"Wasn't it good of her, John? Dear knows, for all the talk about her having money, I don't think she has much. How could she, and her has only the wee holding there and nobody to work it much."

"Your brother George seems to think she has something," Mr Thompson remarked drily. "It occurred to me that was his reason for refusing you hospitality. And look how they all resented you visiting Aunt Agnes, and the things Danny said to Robert. George has hopes,

I would say."

"Well, he's far off his mark, if you ask me. If she has a few more guineas in her purse I'd say that would be the height of it. It was good of her, though, to give me the guinea. I'll give it to you, John."

"No, keep it and tomorrow bring Robert round to the tailors in High Street and get him a new suit."

"A new suit! His Sunday one is as good as new!"

"He'll require a new one," her husband said firmly. "I'm hoping to find an opening for him as apprentice, and he'll need to go well dressed."

He had not mentioned the possibility to his wife, although he had been excited himself by the prospect of Robert being taken as an apprentice in the big linen firm of Stuart & Mount. Old Mr Stuart had been a close friend of the late Mr Aspinall, and knowing this, John Thompson had sought out Albert Meekin, a departmental manager in the firm, and asked him if there was any likelihood of his son Robert getting in as an apprentice. He explained that Robert had been promised an apprenticeship in Aspinall's, but that seemed a very remote possibility now, in view of the state of things. Albert Meekin promised to speak to Mr Stuart on Robert's behalf; it was a good time to ask, as apprentices were coming out of their time and new boys being taken in. Stuart & Mount was one of the biggest linen firms in Belfast, and if Robert was lucky enough to get taken, he would have a good training and wonderful prospects.

About a week after John Thompson had enquired, he met Albert Meekin outside the Linen Hall. He had known Albert for a long time, ever since his apprenticeship days. He was a lonely country boy from Lisburn then, and had met Albert in the church choir, and a friendship had sprung up between them. Somehow, of recent years he had not seen much of his friend; Albert was a married man, also, and lived at the other side of the town from College Place, and went to another church, so that John Thompson and he had drifted apart.

"Well, John, I've news for you," Albert said heartily. "I spoke to Mr Stuart about your son, and he says he will see him, if I think him a suitable candidate."

"He's a good boy, and quick at his books," John said. "Will you call round at the house and speak to him, and try him out?"

"I'll do that, though I'm sure if he's like you were at his age, he'll pass the Governor's scrutiny. I'll call round tomorrow evening, if that's all right."

Robert was dressed in his good Sunday suit immediately after school, and had to sit in the parlour doing sums and reading his book. He had been told the purpose of Mr Meekin's visit, and warned to make his best efforts at displaying his knowledge. He would have much preferred to be out this lovely afternoon, but his father had given him a long lecture and impressed upon him how important it was that he should get an apprenticeship in the linen trade.

Robert still had the attraction to ships that was born on his Sunday visit with Alfie and Alice to the quays. He hoped fervently that it could be arranged for him to go away to sea in a big sailing ship with Alfie and James McKenna, but he had sense enough not to mention these dreams to his father. In his heart he knew that he was destined to work in a linen firm, and supposed from what his father said, and his mother's delighted reaction to the prospect, that it was a great honour for a boy to be taken as apprentice in such a big firm. Not every boy would be taken that wanted to be in the linen trade; it was as good a position as the railway, but for all that, Robert thought longingly of the ships.

His mother had taken him down to High Street for a new suit. There was an exciting shop to go to, with the sewing machines on view and the rows of dress coats, vests and trousers hanging, waiting to be tried on. His new suit was for Sundays, for the present anyhow, but was to be worn on this occasion of Mr Meekin's visit.

Mr Meekin was a tall man, and towered over Robert. There was a great fuss made of the visit. His mother's face was flushed with excitement and she spent the afternoon tidying and cleaning, and urging Robert to be sure and answer well. He read his book to Aunt Agnes and she assured him he was very good at his books.

"Just look at him, sitting there, Martha," the old lady sighed. "Isn't he the spitting image of your own father? Oh, there's no doubt about it, he favours our side of the family. Doesn't he read his book well and him in his wee black suit. He'd put you in mind of a wee minister, wouldn't he, he's that good and solemn looking!"

Mr Meekin came, listened to his reading, and set him some very stiff problems in addition and division. With the anxious eyes of his parents on him, Robert did them correctly, and to Mr Meekin's satisfaction.

"A fine boy, John," he said with a shake of his head. "We'll see what Mr Stuart thinks of him. I'll speak for him and let you know the outcome."

Robert breathed a sigh of relief. He had passed one test. The next one was the following week, when, according to Mr Meekin's instructions, Robert was to present himself at the firm of Stuart & Mount as a possible apprentice. Mr Meekin kindly said he'd meet him in Castle Place and escort him himself. The night before the interview Robert was given a bath, in front of the kitchen fire, and on the morning was dressed in the new suit, squeaky new boots, a stiff hat, and a white shirt. He felt very grown-up and important.

He had wakened early and lay in bed in the darkness of the December morning, listening to the wakening sounds of the town, the factory hooters, the scurrying of feet on the cobbles of the street outside, the banging of doors and the tinkle of milk cans against bowls on doorsteps. If he got to be an apprentice he would start work at eight o'clock; other boys and girls of his age and a bit older would be at the mills and factories at half-past six, and the weavers and spinners of the linen mills would have the looms and shuttles started.

The linen mills and factories, the shipyard, the ropework, the tanneries, all had their host of workers in the busy town, an army of workers starting another day's toil. On this day, he, Robert Thompson, was to take his place with them. School was over for him, now that the world of industry was to be his, at the age of almost thirteen. Boys younger than Robert started earlier to work, as half-timers, and at his age were thin and tired with too little sleep, hard work and lack of nourishment. For Robert, there was the gilt-edged security of a good future in the linen industry.

Dressed in his best, he set off with his father, who was to escort him to Castle Place and Mr Meekin. His mother came to the door, holding baby Jane in a shawl, to see him off, and Aunt Agnes called "God bless you, son," from upstairs. Robert felt strange, and walked upright beside his father, restraining an impulse to take his hand, and fighting off a choking feeling in his throat.

The front door of Stuart & Mount was imposing in mahogany, surmounted at either side by huge brass plates and handles. Inside was dark and majestic, rather like a church, Robert thought, as he entered at Mr Meekin's heels. He was left in a dark little room to sit on a hard chair, until it should please Mr Stuart to see him. He tried to remember the advice his father had drummed into him incessantly over the past few days: "Rise when a superior comes into the room; remember the boss is called the Governor, and should be addressed as 'sir' respectfully; take off your hat entering anyplace; be always willing to do anything you are asked; knock a door before you enter." His head buzzed as he tried to remember.

After a long wait, he was ushered into the private room of Mr Stuart, the Governor, and told to take a seat. A quick look round the large room gave the impression of walls half-timbered in pine, pictures of bleach greens on the walls, glass cupboards, a large mahogany desk, and a bentwood office chair. Mr Stuart was a white-haired gentleman, with twinkling eyes and a pink complexion. He was smoking a cigar and blew smoke as Robert entered stiffly and nervously behind a boy not much older than himself, who had escorted him.

"Well, young man, so you are John Thompson's son?"

"Yes, sir."

"Well, sit down, young Thompson." Mr Stuart sat down himself and motioned Robert to the chair on the other side of his desk. Robert sat on the edge.

"So you want to come into the linen trade? I have a good report from Mr Meekin, he says you are a good scholar. Is that so?"

Robert didn't know what to say. He smiled weakly.

"I know your father. A fine, upright man. He's still in Aspinall's, I believe?"

Robert replied in a choked voice that it was so.

"What do you know about linen?" Mr Stuart asked him suddenly, and Robert took a deep breath and wondered what to answer, absolutely tongue-tied. He could feel his heart pounding in his ears, and managed to utter that "it was a very interesting thing".

"Interesting, is it?" Mr Stuart smiled at him, friendly, and Robert lost a little of his awe. He nodded his head and smiled.

"What do you find interesting? Come along now, boy, I'm sure your father's son knows a lot about linen. What interests you most?"

Robert thought for a moment, remembering all he had ever heard his father talk about linen and its manufacture. Many was the lecture he had got about the trade, and had been taken walks to show him the factory, mill and warehouse where linen goods were produced, and also had seen the long white strips of cloth on the bleach greens outside the town.

"Sir, I wondered ... I think it is interesting to know ... where the linen comes from," he said nervously.

"Where do you think it comes from?" Mr Stuart shot at him.

Robert swallowed hard. "From Lisburn?" he whispered, and went on in a burst of breathlessness, "I mean, sir, I know that the cloth is bleached in the greens, and is made up in the warehouse, and before that in the factory the thread is made, but it's where it comes from before that."

Mr Stuart smiled. "A good question, young man, and the first time I've ever had a prospective apprentice display such interest. You'll find out where it comes from in due course." He added briskly, "Yes, I think you'll do for us all right, Thompson. We'll take you on a month's trial, and then at the end of that time, if you prove satisfactory, we'll have you indentured. You may start right away," and he rang his bell on the desk. The young man who had escorted Robert in now appeared.

"Ah, Gourley," said Mr Stuart, "this is Thompson, take him to Mr Meekin."

Robert stood stiffly and gave Mr Stuart a little nod of his head. "Thank you very much, sir, Mr Stuart, sir."

"Not at all, Thompson. Pray present my compliments to your good father."

The interview was over, and with relief, Robert followed Gourley out of the office and into a large room where Mr Meekin stood at a sloping desk, leaning over a ledger. Gourley stood by while Mr Meekin directed Robert to leave his hat on the peg outside.

"Gourley will show you round the place. It will be all very confusing for a while, but you'll soon get to know your way around."

It seemed a vast building to Robert, as Gourley led him from the offices to the counting house, then around the floors and departments of the factory and warehouse. It was a three-storey building, and a succession of reeling, spinning, doffing, weaving, stitching and ornamenting departments were shown to Robert in a bewildering succession. Girls at looms and at sewing machines shouted "Yo-ho" at him, knowing he was new; others looked with curiosity at him, and paused momentarily in their work as Gourley and he went by.

"This is the factory and the wareroom," Gourley said carelessly—as if he owned the place, Robert thought. "There's the mill, at Ligoniel, and of course there's the scutch mills out in the country."

Robert nodded, as if he understood everything. He was absolutely dazed, and his day was one of endless impressions. When he got home with his good news, he had to try and recall to his father every word spoken at his interview, and every place and person seen during the day. His brain was whirling. His father was delighted that he had been taken on, and was in a benign mood strange to him.

In the next few days at the firm, Robert was able to sort out the confusion and could find his way around fairly well. He was assigned to the counting house, during his month's probation, and got to learn the intricacies of the letterpress, and found out how to take letters and parcels to the post, and how to write bills of sale and forwarding notes in careful, clear writing. The firm specialised in tablecloths and handkerchiefs, and was one of the really big firms of the trade, with its own spinning mill, factory and making-up warehouse, with an enormous business in Great Britain and North America. Daily, his father quizzed him as to his actions of the day, and Robert faithfully told any detail he thought important.

"A boy was sent to Mr Stuart today," he told. "He's a two-year apprentice and he refused to go to the post with parcels. He said it wasn't right a two-year old apprentice should go and not a new boy. Mr Meekin was angry and sent him to Mr Stuart. If he is insubordinate again, he may be discharged."

And another day he reported, "One of the boys from the country gets a parcel of bread from his ma every week, and do you know he shut himself up in the privy to eat all the tatie bread himself!"

Robert became friendly with Charley Gourley, who had shown him around on his first day, and a boy called John McIlhagga. Both were from Ballymena and lived in the same lodgings and went for walks together on fine evenings. His first month passed quickly for

Robert and he was given his indentures to take home and get signed by his father. It was a happy evening for Mr Thompson to put his signature to the deed that bound 'Robert Thompson to the services of Stuart & Mount for the term of five years, to be taught the trade of the linen merchant'.

Rarely now did Robert see Alfie. When he got home at night it was dark and cold and he didn't go out, but soon after Christmas, in the cold, crisp days of January, the two boys, Gourley and McIlhagga, invited him to come walking with them. These were his new friends, and very much to his father's liking. Alfie and Alice were in the life he had grown out of, the life of school and boyhood. Now he was a man. In a bare month or so in the trade, he could talk glibly of warp and weft, of pirns and cops, and could find his way from the ornamenting room, or the counting house to the looms in the weaving factory without having to ask the way. Now and then, when he remembered, he blushed to himself as he remembered his display of abysmal ignorance at his interview with Mr Stuart. Now he knew that flax, or lint—the little blue flowered plant that grew in an abundant crop in many farms in the north of Ireland—was the beginning of the whole linen industry. He had not yet seen the inside or the outside of a spinning mill, most of which were in the country districts beside the supply of retted flax from the scutch mills, but he knew of their existence and their place in the chain of manufacture of the snowy white linen tablecloths, handkerchiefs, and bed linens sent out almost daily from the Belfast warehouse of his firm.

He was happy, working at Stuart & Mount; there was so much to interest him and so many different people employed in the big building that he found the days flew faster for him than ever they did in the dingy classroom of the National Board school, with the tedium of eternal sums on slates and reading from his book to an overworked and fatigued teacher. Forgotten, almost, was the great "secret" shared with Alfie Storey, of running off to sea to join James McKenna when he would get a ship.

James McKenna did get a berth on a ship, by going to Liverpool and waiting his chance at the quays. His mother had accepted his departure from Belfast outwardly stoically, but inwardly hoped that the trip to Liverpool would disillusion him, or that having got there he would find it so difficult to obtain a place on a ship that he would come back to her. But James was very much his father's son, with saltwater in his blood, and he waited his chance patiently until a packet sailing ship bound for North America took him on.

Tearfully, Mrs McKenna showed Mrs Thompson the scrubby, scribbled note from James, to tell her his news.

"Aye, he's away from me now. The sea has took him too, and God only knows will he ever set foot in Ireland again."

Aunt Agnes nodded sympathetically, tears in her eyes.

"Woman dear," she said softly, "my heart aches for you. Didn't my own fine, strong son go off till Americky, and never come back to me! Sure I hate the sight of a sailing ship! Even the sight of one of them wee ships in a bottle makes my heart bleed."

A few days after this news broke in the district, Robert was walking briskly along Killen Street, tired, but not weary, after his day's toil. Mrs Storey was standing at the corner of College Place, under the light of the flickering lamp, peering anxiously down the steps.

"Ah, Robert! Have you seen my Alfie at all?" she asked anxiously, pulling a black shawl closer round her shoulders against the chill of the early March wind.

"No," Robert told her, "I'm just getting home from work." He felt very grown-up in his great-coat and hat, and he tipped the hat politely, in the manner he observed his father use.

"Well I wonder is Alice in your house? She might know where Alfie is." Mrs Storey walked alongside Robert down the steps. "Faith, she's never out of your house, that girl! If she'd do a turn or two in her own house it would suit her, instead of always over minding your ba."

Robert pushed open his front door and found that Mrs Storey was following him into the cosy, warm kitchen, where Alice sat on a creaky stool in front of the hob grate, nursing the sleeping baby Jane in her arms, while Aunt Agnes sat in her corner chair, dozing. Mrs Thompson was in the scullery, getting the supper ready for her husband and son coming home from work.

"I'm looking for Alfie," Mrs Storey announced.

"Well he's not here!" Mrs Thompson replied, tartly. She was annoyed by Mrs Storey walking in without as much as a by-your-leave.

"Alice, did you see him?" Mrs Storey asked, giving her daughter an impatient push on the shoulder.

"No, no," Alice answered, uncertainly.

"Well, do you know where he went till? I declare to my God, Mrs Thompson, that wee fella has my heart broke. Sure I was only round at Waring Street to see the woman that's making my new dress, and when I get back there's neither sight nor sign of him—nor of Alice either."

"Sure woman dear, if you had a guinea for every time Alfie was missing; you'd be a wealthy woman. And as for Alice, I'm sure I'm not keeping her here, if she's wanted at home!"

"Where could he be?" Mrs Storey whined tearfully, ignoring Mrs Thompson's broadside. She wrung her hands distractedly. "Alice Storey, I think you know where he is."

Alice's face got red, and she looked from her mother to Mrs Thompson.

"You do know! I'll bate you black and blue, Miss, if you don't tell me where he is!" and she caught hold of the child's arm. Alice started sobbing, and Mrs Thompson rushed forward to take her baby from the little girl's arms.

"Shouting at the child won't help, woman dear," she said firmly. "Alice, pet, if you know where your brother is, you ought to tell—

even if he made you swear a secret."

Alice looked tearfully from one to another, and then at Aunt Agnes, who had wakened up and was enjoying the commotion.

"Well, he said he was going away," she sobbed out. "He was going to go to Liverpool ... to see James McKenna."

Mrs Storey shrieked, "Liverpool! Ah God, he's dead! I know he's dead! Ah, my poor wee son," and she sank into a chair and cried and screeched in a hysterical frenzy. Mrs Thompson shook her and shouted at her to be quiet, while Robert comforted Alice; the baby had been handed to Aunt Agnes, and joined in the commotion, while the old woman shooed and shushed loudly.

In the noise and commotion, none of them heard Mr Thompson come in, and he stood in amazement for a few seconds, before enquiring in a loud but firm voice what was the reason for the outburst. Each one started to tell him, all at once, all talking together, all telling him that Alfie had run away to sea. It took a few moments for him to take charge of the situation, and to calm Mrs Storey, and to send her home on Robert's arm, with Alice trailing, sniffing, and hanging on his coat.

"Tell Mr Storey, or Arthur, the news, Robert," were the clear instructions given. "And you may add that I will be ready to give any assistance if they consider it likely that he could be brought back."

"If you ask me, a touch of the sea might do that young lad a world of good," Mrs Thompson remarked when the Storeys and Robert had gone. "It's what he's lost for, a touch of hard work. Sure he's older than our Robert, and he's no thought of finding employment."

"All the same it would be hard on a lad so young to go away to sea," Aunt Agnes said, wistfully. "His ma might never see him again."

"He'll hardly have got very far, I should say," Mr Thompson added. "In fact I'd be surprised if he has a foot on a ship yet. The tide was in a very low state as I passed the quay and I think the steamship will not go off for some hours yet."

Robert returned with the news that Arthur Storey would be coming round to see Mr Thompson, to have a talk with him about going after Alfie, and hot on his heels Arthur arrived to announce that his ma was insistent that Alfie should be brought back from Liverpool, or from wherever he was.

"She's beside herself," Arthur said apologetically, "and I doubt she'll make herself sick if we don't find Alfie. What I was wondering, Mr Thompson, sir, was if you would come the length of the quay with me to make some enquiries, and if he has gone to Liverpool I'll have to go on tomorrow's boat to bring him back."

Mr Thompson agreed readily, and got into his great-coat and hat, leaving the hot supper uneaten.

"I was remarking to Mrs Thompson that the boy may not have got far," he told Arthur as they walked / set off. "The tide was low as I passed, and the steamship likely has not yet left."

"Sure that fellow might go on anything that sails, or steams, to get to Liverpool," Arthur replied, and they walked across the Square, past the 'black man' statue, in silence, their coats pulled tight against the stiff, chilly March wind.

"I wouldn't worry too much about your brother," Mr Thompson said at last. "No doubt if he does get to Liverpool he'll want home fast enough. The call of the sea dies very quickly in the ears after a stormy night on the Channel."

"Oh, I'm not worrying about him! Tell you the truth, Mr Thompson, I think a spell on a sailing ship would do him a world of good. My ma has him spoiled rotten, pampering him like a wee girl, and giving him everything he wants. A good taste of sea life is just the thing for that fellow."

Mr Thompson found difficulty in keeping pace with Arthur's long legs. There was an eagerness about him, an excitement that was hard to understand, in the circumstances. And he had lost the pallor of the baker; now his face was healthy looking, with a touch of colour.

As if to read his thoughts, as they walked down the High Street, towards the quay, Arthur suddenly blurted out, "I'm only back from Antrim, you know."

"Oh? No, I didn't know."

"Yes, I was down a few months, staying with my granda. He's a powerful man, my Granda. He has a shop in Antrim, but forby that he's a packman, and it's a packman he was all his days, with the shop to keep my grannie busy and earn a few more shillings."

"Hard work, a packman's," ventured Mr Thompson. "From what I remember myself, in my young days in the country, they have to travel far and wide, from farm to farm, to sell their wares."

"That's right," Arthur replied eagerly. "I've been out with him, on the road these weeks past, and do you know, I feel the better of it! All the good air, and the walking miles up hill and down dale, sleeping where we found ourselves for the night, and eating all I could get, it's done me a power of good. And forby that, I've great plans. That's why I was wanting to talk to you, special like, Mr Thompson, for to ask your advice."

"Well, I'm only too pleased..." murmured Mr Thompson.

"I'll tell you what it is." Arthur spoke quickly and with great excitement. "I'm thinking of starting up in business for myself. I lost my work at Lamont's bakery, you know."

"Well, I did hear something..."

"Yes. Well, it's the best thing ever happened, for I went down to see them all at Antrim, for a bit of a holiday, like, and the granda was going off on his travels and asked me if I would go with him. They all thought I was looking pale, and that the outdoor life would do me good. Well, anyway," he went on, scarcely drawing breath, "I've had in my mind to start up for myself, and I thought I'd just ask my granda what he thought, for he's brave and long in the head, my granda, and if there's any flaw in a bit of business he's the one to see it."

"Are you starting a bakery?"

"Yes, I am, but small. That was Granda's advice. Start small, says he, for then you'll build up solid. And if any man knows what he's talking about it's him, for he started off a poor boy, helping a packman that was getting past it, carrying the pack from him, and learning the ropes you might say. And in time he started up with his own pack, and he has his rounds of the country all mapped out, three times a year, and he's known at every house he calls at for a man that drives a hard bargain and gives nothing for nothing, but straight as a rush and honest to a farthing. Then after he got on a bit he started the wee shop in Antrim, still keeping on at the journeys in the country, and with the one and the other I'd say my granda is worth a good few hundred pounds the day, maybe thousands, for all I could tell rightly."

"And you think he'll start you off on your own business?"

Arthur chuckled. "Well now, Mr Thompson, you'll excuse me laughing, but if you knew my granda you'd know he gives nothing. I told him my plan, and asked if he'd lend me the money."

"And he will, of course, to his own grandson."

"Aye, he will, of course! But it'll be at interest, of course!" Arthur laughed heartily. "I have to admire the old boy. He'd bargain an hour for a halfpenny."

They had reached the quayside now, and both men were silent as they looked sharply about them for a sign of the missing Alfie. The steamship for Liverpool was the centre of activity on the quayside. The ship was steamed up, ready for sailing, and they had to push their way through the crowd milling around the gangplank and along the quayside nearest the ship. Carts and horses and men carrying bundles added to the confusion, and there was shouting of "Make way!" from those wanting onto the ship, and the goodbyes of those leaning over the side to their friends below. A crowd of emigrants was on board, bound via Liverpool for North America, and seemingly all their friends and relations had come to bid them farewell. Some of the emigrants lining the ship's rail were in tears, and there was crying too among the crowd seeing them off. As Arthur and Mr Thompson pushed their way forward to the bottom of the gangplank, a girl started the singing, a sad, plaintive song, 'Oft in the Stilly Night', and a sudden hush fell on the crowd. It was a sad scene, Mr Thompson thought, and heart-breaking for those leaving their homeland perhaps forever. The little family groups could be picked out, the young parents with babes in arms, eager and full of hope for life in the new country; the older men and women, with their family half-reared, leaving because of bad times, and the hope of better conditions in the land they were going to. All were in their best, stiff Sunday clothes, with small bundles to augment the boxes and baskets stowed below.

John Thompson felt a sudden pricking at the back of his throat as the song was taken up by a few ashore:

"When I remember all the friends so linked together,
I've seen around me fall like leaves in wintry weather."

And he thought to himself that had he been leaving Ireland just then, it would be with a broken heart.

"What can we do here?" Arthur whispered to him. "You'd never find anybody you know in this mill of a crowd."

"Follow me," Mr Thompson said, and pushed his way to the man taking the tickets.

"We're looking for a wee boy that's run away from home," he told the man. "Did you see a wee fellow on his own?"

"Man dear, talk sense! With this crowd how could a body see anything! There's dozens of wee fellows has come on with their das and mas. Would he have a ticket, this lad you're looking for?"

"He might. Could we go on board and have a look?"

"Well..." The man rubbed his red nose and straightened his hat. "There's only but a minute or two before we pull up the gangplank, but if you hurry.... If you get carried over to Liverpool, mind, you'll have to pay, three shillings a head."

John dashed up the gangplank, Arthur following, and both elbowed their way along the deck, looking anxiously for a sight of Alfie, then they went down the stairs into the saloon, where on rows of forms sat a medley of passengers. The air was smoky from the hanging oil lamps which cast pools of dim light on the passengers. Some of them had never been on a ship before in their lives—and indeed had not been to the town of Belfast even—and sat tight on the hard forms, as if fearful of leaving their position lest they might not get to their destination of Liverpool. Others, perhaps the more venturesome travellers, had provisions with them, and sat eating chunks of cheese and large slices of bread. Mothers with children huddled around them, looked anxious and fearful.

At these groups John looked keenly, as it was in his mind that Alfie might have tacked himself on to a family party, particularly one that had something to eat.

"He's not here," murmured Arthur, glancing round. "We'll better go on. He's maybe on some other ship and halfway there by now."

They retraced their steps, and hastened as a shout of "All ashore!" was heard. But as they stepped on the gangplank to get off the ship, John saw Alfie's face in a crowd at the rail, wedged between two bulky men.

"There he is!" he shouted, and stepping over, caught the boy by the back of the collar and dragged him out from the crowd and on to the gangplank. Alfie yelled, "Let me go!" and some men in the crowd murmured and one rough-looking man tried to stop John's way.

"Leave the wee fellow be!" he said with menace, but John calmly pushed him aside.

"He's run away from home and I'm taking him to his mother," he countered, and then with a good grip of Alfie's arm ushered him down the gangplank and ashore, where Alfie stood, sullen, with a scowl on his face.

"I'll run away again, so I will," he muttered defiantly, "and you'll not stop me, so you won't."

"Ah, shut your mouth," his brother told him, pulling him roughly through the crowd. "Run away if you like, but next time tell your ma you're going!"

The two men turned away from the quay and with Alfie between them walked towards home. Every now and then Alfie would utter a protest, but Arthur simply clouted him and told him to shut his mouth.

"As I was telling you, Mr Thompson," Arthur said, "Granda is lending me the money and I'm starting up as soon as I can get the ovens built for me."

"Where do you intend having your bakery?"

"Oh for a start I'll build the ovens at the back of the house and have a wee bit of a bakehouse added on, and when I get well started, I'll take a bigger place. That's what Granda kept telling me. 'Start small,' says he, 'and then you can expand'. But what I want to ask you, Mr Thompson, is if you would be kind enough to help me."

"Certainly, I'll be at your service in any way I can, but I'm a linen man, and my knowledge of the bakery trade would not go beyond the bread I eat every day."

Arthur laughed. "Oh, I'm not worried about that end. I can do the baking all right—and mind you, I've some ideas for new lines of bread, and I can sell it, too, for there's one thing certain, and that's the number of people buying bread now. Now you take this town of Belfast, Mr Thompson, and look at all the people that's come to live in it these past five years. I've studied all this, mind you, and I read in a weekly newspaper that they think there's twice the number of people here now. And all them people is working, and they all must eat, and what do they eat but bread!"

"Of course you must remember that many people bake at home," John murmured.

"Agreed. But most of them find it easier—and cheaper—to buy their bread."

John was impressed by the young man's enthusiasm, and by his arguments. They walked in silence for a few minutes. The town was quiet at this time of night, though sounds of merriment could be heard from the taverns they passed in the street.

"What way could I assist you in your enterprise?" John asked suddenly, remembering Arthur's request.

"If you would help me in the money end, you know, working out if I'm not giving too much value in my bread—especially the new lines I hope to start—and checking the bills for flour and such like. I've no experience of that side of the business, and Granda says it's very important to know if you're making a profit. And if you could tell me how much interest I'd have to pay from time to time on the money I borrow—not that Granda wouldn't tell me that, but I don't want him to know I'm not all that smart at figures."

John promised his help in that and in any other way he could, greatly admiring Arthur's humility in asking. They crossed over Wellington Place and back home, into College Square, and then round into Killen Street. A small knot of people stood at Storeys' door, and on their arrival it proved to be Mrs Storey, Robert, Alice and Mrs McKenna. Mrs Storey rushed forward and threw her arms round Alfie.

"My darling boy! My darling child, you're back," and she kissed him and hugged him. Alfie shrugged her off, his face still sullen.

"You shouldn't have brought me back, Ma; I'll only go away again, so I will."

"Hello, Alfie," Robert said eagerly. "Were you on the steamship for Liverpool?"

"Aye, I was! And in another minute your da and our Arthur wouldn't have seen me, and I'd have been away. But I'm going, so I am! Just you wait and see."

"Come on in out of that," Arthur said to him gruffly, then he turned to Mr Thompson and thanked him profusely for his advice.

Robert walked beside his father, and together in silence they went down the steps and into College Place. John Thompson thought wryly to himself that Arthur had no reason to give him thanks for advice; he didn't recall giving any. On the contrary, he had learned much from Arthur that evening, and had much food for thought.

CHAPTER SIX

A few weeks later, in the month of April, there was tremendous excitement in the district, and in fact all over the town of Belfast. A new school was to be opened, a Model school, which many people thought was very necessary in the town of Belfast, where many children had little or no schooling and the schools already existing were inadequate for the number of children requiring education, even though there was no compulsion on them to attend.

The newspapers carried advertisements announcing the opening of this new type of school, where education was to be more extensive and children of all religions were to come together in the same classrooms. Over nine hundred applied, and seven hundred were accepted as pupils, and the school was opened with great pomp and attended by many of the dignitaries. The sanction and blessing of the united clergymen—Presbyterian, Church of Ireland, Catholic and Methodist—was given to the new school and the new era in education.

"Are you sending Alice and Alfie to the new school?" Mrs Thompson enquired of Mrs Storey.

"I'm not in soul: I'd look well, letting them sit with Papists. I don't believe in all this new-fangled nonsense. Foreby, my Alfie says he's left school. I can't get him to go at all, and Alice does rightly where she is."

"Well, I'm only sorry that our wee Jane isn't ready for school yet, but when she is, it's the Model school she'll go to. Mr Thompson thinks very highly of the new system of education and he says the children is getting great opportunities for both learning and tolerance."

"Oh, we'll see if it lasts! Like as not they'll all be fighting each other before long. You know what people's like."

"Well, I know what some people's like!" Mrs Thompson retorted.

"But if the Bishops of the churches and the Moderator himself can get on together and agree, what call has other people to stir up trouble."

She felt quite heated by this encounter with Mrs Storey and recounted the conversation to her husband at supper time. He listened, and shook his head sadly.

"It's a great chance for everyone, for the children especially, but for people, too, to forget the differences of the past and learn to live together, be they Catholic or Protestant."

He was greatly worried these days, fearing that Mr Aspinall had come to a decision and was going to close the warehouse. Nothing had been said, but there was an air of unrest and expectancy about the place, with rumours circulating the workers and making them restless and uneasy. Everyone had heard for gospel that the place was going to be kept oils then the story was reversed, with confusion the result, and no one person, except Mr Aspinall, knowing the truth of the matter.

John Thompson was summoned to Mr Aspinall's office one Saturday morning and a large piece of stiff paper was put into his hands.

"Here, read this, Thompson," Mr Aspinall told him. "You're the first to have sight of it."

The notice read:
'THIS FACTORY AND WAREHOUSE WILL CLOSE DOWN AND

CEASE BUSINESS AS AND PROM SATURDAY NEXT, 27th MAY, 1857.'

Although he had been expecting the news, John got a shock, and stared unbelievingly at the paper.

"It's bad news, sir," he said, his voice trembling. "It will be sore reading for the workers. Where will they look now for employment?"

"Yes, I know. I'm sorry, Thompson, really I am, but the truth is, business hasn't been too good and my financial advisers tell me it's best to finish off, sell the machines, and make an end of it."

"But, sir, business is bound to improve..."

"No, Thompson, I've made up my mind." Mr Aspinall threw the notice on to his roll-top desk and flung himself into a chair.

"The fact is, Thompson," he went on, "I've other business interests to see to—not in Belfast, and as well ... oh, dash it, man, I might as well tell you! Mrs Aspinall doesn't care for Belfast." He paused to light a cigar and chuckled. "Putting it too mildly that, to say she doesn't like it. Fact is, she loathes it. Would only stay a week, and it rained all the time. It's so dull here, man. You've no ideas of enjoying life, Thompson. Such a morbid sanctimonious crowd I never met, always praying or fighting each other. I simply couldn't persuade her to set up house here at all, so it's the end of everything here—the factory, the villa, the lot. Sell it all off, that's what I'll do."

John could scarcely speak, but tried to keep his feelings under control as he made his appeal.

"Would you not consider putting a manager in complete charge? Someone suitable would look after your interests very well. I am sure and certain that the business could be made to pay better."

With a wave of the cigar the idea was dismissed.

"No, Thompson, it wouldn't work! Tried it myself, didn't, I? If I can't do it, nobody could."

John could have told him how wrong he was, that any one of the senior men of the firm could have made a far better job of it than young Mr Aspinall. But what was the business to him? Other than being something of a nuisance, in a part of the world that his wife did not care for, what did it mean to him? He had other solid business interests that made him a wealthy man, and the town and the workers who had helped to lay the foundations of that wealth were now to be abandoned.

"This notice goes up today," Mr Aspinall drawled. "You senior men will have a month's salary to compensate you, and you'll have no trouble anyhow, Thompson, in getting a place elsewhere. Did you get your boy apprenticed?"

John told him that Robert was with Stuart & Mount.

"A good firm, he'll do well there. But look here, Thompson, I've just had a good idea. Why don't you start up for yourself?"

"I've thought of it often, but..."

"Well, think about it again. You'd do well. You have the right temperament for this business and this town. I tell you what I'll do for you Thompson, I'll write out the names and addresses of our best customers, and you start off on your own, and get in touch with them, and you'll do famously. How about that?" and he puffed his cigar and stood smiling benevolently at his own generosity. Then a sudden thought seemed to strike him.

"Oh, by the way, I'd pay more attention to the warehousing end of it, if I were you. My financial advisors tell me it's been a good paying part of the business here, and I seem to remember my old father used to go on and on about it, saying that one day it would be important. Not so many at that end, eh? Am I right?"

"Oh, I think I could count them on my fingers, Mr Aspinall," John said slowly, counting in his mind. "There's ourselves here, there's Stuart & Mount, and several other big ones and a few small ones."

"Well, you be another one, Thompson. There must be hundreds of merchants, these fellows buying in the linen from the weaving firms or the cottage weavers and selling it themselves. Overcrowded, that end of it, I'd say. Well, I'll get you that list. No, don't thank me, Thompson, you're a decent fellow. My father thought a lot of you, and it's my pleasure to help you."

John took his leave with a nod of acknowledgement. He hadn't been about to thank Mr Aspinall. What was there to thank him for? The firm's customers he knew better than Mr Aspinall did, and it was no favour to allow him the chance of having a list, in the remote possibility of being in business for himself. John's heart was heavy as he left the private office and went to the warehouse, knowing the gloom that would follow once the notice was posted and read.

George McCrum was one of the first to read it and he came hurriedly to John.

"So it's true? He's for closing the place?"

"I'm afraid it's only too true, George."

"It's a poor look out for us, that's what I say!" McCrum was indignant as he hurried off to spread the bad news.

Among the workers there was dismay and despair. Many of them had been working with the firm for years and would find it hard, John knew, to get another start at their time of life. For the younger ones there was hope that they might get employed elsewhere, though weeks could pass before new jobs were found, and they would be weeks of tight rations. Few, if any of them, could have saved any money on the poor wages paid in the linen trade. Some of them came to John, to ask if he could do anything for them, get them other work, imploring him to remember them if he heard of anything. He was sympathetic, realising that for many of them there was only outwork from the factories to earn a couple of shillings a week to starve on, and to add to the thousands of others in the same plight. The streets round the quays were full of such poor unfortunates, living in hovels, many of them destitute, pulling threads or 'veining' muslin for a pittance. John was angry. Employers had a responsibility, he felt, especially towards those who had served them loyally for years, but did young Mr Aspinall know how people existed when out of work, or if he did know, would he care?

John himself would be out of work too, thrown on his own resources, unless he could get another position quickly. On the way home his mind was in a whirl. Should he try for a position in a warehousing firm, or would he end up as an assistant to one of the many linen merchants who, as Mr Aspinall had correctly stated, were in their hundreds in Belfast? These merchants bought their linens either in 'loomstate'—brown, as it came from the weavers' looms—or bleached white from the bleach greens. The linen would be stored in cool storerooms until required, then was 'lapped' in the lengths required by the customers and sent out to the home trade or to the markers of the world.

Mr Aspinall's advice to John to start for himself as a warehouseman was a recurring dream, stronger than ever since talking to Arthur Storey. Little did Arthur realise that his ambitions for his bakery had fired John Thompson to have his own business. The one obstacle was capital: where Arthur had a granda willing to lend money, even at heavy interest, John had very little savings and certainly not enough to start a business. There was no one to lend him money. His brother on the farm, outside Lisburn, talked of selling up the place and going out to America things were so poor with him.

When John reached his home, there was a commotion. Martha met him at the door, her face white and frightened looking. Aunt Agnes had taken ill during the afternoon, and was still not too well.

"She's still not herself, John," Martha whispered. "I'm very worried about her, for she turned the colour of death. Put the heart across me, she did, and only Mrs McKenna happened in I'd have been distracted. And that Mrs Storey, what do you think she suggested? 'Send her to the hospital,' says she. 'Is it hospital?' says I to her. 'There's no body belonging to me was ever in one of them places, and as sure as my name's Martha Thompson, no one ever will.' Fancy, to send my poor old aunt to hospital!"

"She maybe meant well," John commented.

"Maybe! But I doubt it! Then she turns round and tells me to give Aunt Agnes hot milk and peppermint. She should set up for a doctor, she's that smart at giving advice."

The whole tale was poured into John's ears as he took off his greatcoat in the hall.

"It could have been that ling fish that made her take bad," Martha said reflectively. "I was in oul' Wilson's yesterday and he had in this new piece of dried ling, and I thought it would be tasty, and sure enough Aunt Agnes relished it but maybe the buttermilk she drunk didn't do with the dried ling. That'll be it."

The old lady was sitting in the seat in the corner of the kitchen, beside the fire. She was wrapped in several shawls and held her hands out to the glowing embers of the hob grate.

"You're not so well, Martha was telling me," John said gently, putting his hand on her shoulders.

"I'm bravely now, thank you, John, but I tell you what it was. It was that ling fish did the damage. I felt it and the buttermilk lying heavy on my stomach. I'll be right as rain in the morning."

John looked closely at her. She was a bad colour, he decided, and rather out of breath, even sitting quietly.

"Of course you'll be all right," he said in a heartier tone than he ever used, "but I think you'd be better in your bed just now. Why don't you go on up now, and get a good night's rest?"

She had a great respect for his opinion, but even so, looked at him uncertainly.

"It's lonesome, like … just lying there…"

"You'll not be lonesome, will she Martha? We'll be up and down to have a word with you." John was firm, and offered her his arm.

"Just a wee minute." Martha bustled over to the hob. "I've a brick heating here, I'll just place it in between the blankets," and she took the hot brick wrapped in an old piece of flannel and went up the stairs ahead of John and the old lady.

Aunt Agnes was shaky on her legs, and leaned very heavily on John. He urged her to take it easy, and paused after each step on the stairs. Robert came in from his work, and was called hurriedly to give assistance in getting the old lady up. It took the two of them all their time in doing so; she was sorely out of breath by the last stair, and sank thankfully on the edge of the bed where Martha waited to help her undress and get in. John thought privately that the old lady was very ill. It was more than the ling fish and buttermilk was wrong with her; the weakness of her legs and the want of breath and the sudden pain she took in her chest made him wonder if she wasn't near her end, but he kept this surmise to himself. Martha was worried enough and anyhow, perhaps a good night's rest would help the old woman.

But a while later Martha said to him anxiously, "She looks bad, doesn't she? Maybe I should sit in with her."

"Nonsense, woman! We'll take our supper and when you get the dishes done put your hat and coat on and go round and see Mrs McKenna for half an hour. Robert can read to his aunt."

Robert ventured to remark that he had hoped to go out for a walk with his friends after supper.

"Out!" his father thundered. "Again? Weren't you out to church on Sunday night? And weren't you out for a walk last week? Don't think you're running the streets every night, boy! You stay in and take your Bible and read your poor sick aunt her favourite verses!"

Martha cleared up after the supper, put Jane to bed, and as instructed, put on her hat and coat and went round to Mrs McKenna's.

"I'll not be above half an hour," she told him, thinking how kind and indulgent he was to her, but loath at the same time to be out of the house in case Aunt Agnes needed her.

The house settled in quietness. Jane slept peacefully. Robert sat by his aunt's bedside and read to her. She had her eyes closed, but by the occasional deep sighs he knew she wasn't sleeping. Downstairs, John Thompson took his weekly newspaper from his pocket to compose his mind by reading of the turmoil of the world and forget for a short while the disturbing events of the day.

There was a tap at the back door, and Arthur Storey came in, apologetic and tiptoeing.

"Would I be disturbing you, Mr Thompson? I heard the old aunt was sick."

"It's all right, Arthur, come in and sit down. She's in bed and feeling a lot better. Do you wish to talk to me?"

"I do that, Mr Thompson." Arthur sighed and took a bundle of papers from his pocket. "I don't want to be a bother to you, but I wondered if you would favour me with your advice?"

John nodded his head in agreement.

"Well," Arthur went on, "I'm worried, so I am. My granda never sent the money yet, and here I am, going on ahead, getting things started. Here's the bill for the flour I ordered, and there's the baskets, and the tins and things. And the fellow that's putting in the ovens is near finished the job and he's looking for ten pounds, and I haven't got the money yet... Granda said he'd send it to the bank, but I've went down every single morning, and they're none the wiser than I am myself. I need to give that ten pounds tomorrow."

John nodded. "Unfortunate, indeed, a hold-up at this time." He glanced at the bills Arthur held. "These seem important. Maybe I should look them over for you."

"I'd be obliged!"

John leafed over them, then studied each one carefully. "Hm, here's a mistake in this one here, an overcharge, perhaps accidental, but it's a pound too much. The others are quite correct."

"There now, you see, Mr Thompson, I could be losing money if it wasn't for you." Arthur thanked him profusely, then sat quiet, with a very worried look on his face. At length he asked, "What do you think I should do, Mr Thompson, about the money?"

"Would it be convenient to get in touch with your granda, to hurry him in sending you the money he's lending?"

"No!" Arthur was definite. "I don't think I should. He'd be like as not to take offence and not lend it at all." He sighed. "It's a great pity, for this fellow won't go on with the ovens until he gets some of the money, and I can't start without the ovens."

"Well, if it will help you," Mr Thompson said deliberately, "I can advance you ten guineas or so. It just so happens that I have some spare money by me and I'd be happy to lend it to you until such times as your grandfather sends his." He was careful not to let Arthur suspect that the amount of ten guineas was almost the sum total of his life savings. True, he would have a month's salary by the weekend, but that would be required for current expenses until he could find another position. Arthur's face cleared and he expressed his thanks and gratitude. John went upstairs to the bedroom where he kept his savings and having taken the gold coins from the hiding place, he stood for a minute on the landing to listen to Robert's voice, steadily reading through the Psalms, with Aunt Agnes's heavy breathing as a background.

Next morning, he recommended his wife to keep the old woman in bed for a few days. She said she had slept well and felt much better, but was easily convinced that rest would be good for her. Martha sat with her as much as possible during the day, and was happy that there seemed a great improvement.

Towards dusk she took an oil lamp to the room and sat it on the shelf behind the bed. It was a still evening and with the last remnants of daylight the chimneypots glimpsed through the window sat out black. She fixed the pillow and pulled the old woman's shawl round her.

"Keep yourself warm, Aunt love, there's a chill in the air yet, foreby it's near summer. Ah, sure it'll be lovely to see the summer again, and God willing, you'll be out and about to enjoy it."

Aunt Agnes patted her hand. "You're good to me, Martha, and so is your good man John, and wee Robert too. Ah, God knows I'm well looked after. You're very good to me."

"Now why wouldn't we be? Aren't we all very fond of you?"

"You're too good to me, so you are." She sank back on her

pillow and signed deeply. "I don't mind telling you, Martha, I got a wee fright yesterday. I thought maybe my time had come."

"Nonsense! Sure wasn't it just that oul' ling fish and the buttermilk! God knows I regret ever getting it."

"I don't know—I've been sick before with my stomach, but yesterday it was different. Anyhow, sure I'm feeling better today and thank God for it. I want you to do something for me, Martha," and she directed her niece to open a wicker basket she had and take out a calico bag that was tucked in the folds of a nightgown.

"Now look inside that pair of black stockings I have in the press. There's another wee bag there. And there's one in my good shawl at the bottom of the bag in the corner there."

Martha brought the three bags over to the bed, and Aunt Agnes sat up and emptied the contents onto the cover. A shower of gold coins spilled, shining, before their eyes. Martha had never seen so much money before in her life and for a second she was transfixed. Then, alarmed, she dashed to the window and pulled over the curtain, to hide the money from the possible gaze of any who might, by some means, observe it from the rooftops.

"Aunt Agnes, sure it's all the money in the world!" she gasped.

"'Deed it's not," chortled the old woman, "but it's a good fistful. It's a surprise to you, isn't it, Martha? Sure I knew fine well you'd no notion I have all this, and yet you look after me and worry over me like you did it for love. That's why I'm going to give it to you. Your brother knows I have it, but he doesn't know how much, and he'll not get his hands on it, for I'm going to give it now, when I'm well enough, and it'll be disposed of -fee way I want it."

Martha gasped again. "Will I call John up?"

"Aye, do," the old lady replied, and lay resting peacefully until he came into the room at Martha's heels.

"You'll wonder how I got all this," chuckled Aunt Agnes. "I'll tell you how I got it. You see, our William John went out to Americky, and got on well, worked hard and wanted the rest of us out to him, his da and me and his brother Eddie. He kept sending home the money for our passages on the sailing ship with a good friend he had that worked on a ship. Every time he come into the port of Belfast he brought me the gold from William John. It's all there, every piece of it, for it's never been out of the wee bags since we heard that William John was killed out in Americky. Then my poor husband died, and Eddie was taken from me too. I've needed nothing that I couldn't get from my bit of a holding of land, and it could have been bags of buttons lying there all these years instead of gad gold. Now I want to give it to you."

John quietly put the coins back into the calico bags, and pushed them under the pillow.

"You'll need to sleep on this notion," he said softly. "It's a lot of gold, and you know there's more than Martha to leave it to."

"It's mine!" the old lady said fiercely. "And I'll leave it where I please. Them ones up in the Hills have had plenty from me, but they never rested day or night, trying to get this off me too. George has always known I had it, and it made him very grasping."

"Well now," John said soothingly, "I think you should have your wishes noted by a man of law. Some people might think we took it off you, if you were to hand that gold over to us now."

"You're right, John Thompson, sure you know best. What way will I do it?"

"Leave it to me," he replied. "I'll attend to your wishes and see to it tomorrow."

He had decided that it would be more prudent to have a lawyer attend to the business. There was a Mr Crone he knew, who did business for Aspinall's. He'd call at his office in Arthur Street and arrange for him to visit the house the next evening.

He felt excited at the sudden wealth that was soon to be theirs, but would not allow himself to dwell just yet on the possibilities it opened. Martha was equally excited and later, downstairs, whispered,

"Oh, John, imagine all that money! What would we do with it?"

Only then did he tell her that he was soon to be out of a position and that Aspinall's was to close down, and in the exhilaration of the moment, he told her of his dreams of a business for himself, a dream that now seemed a reality, thanks to Aunt Agnes.

Next evening Mr Crone came, and being acquainted with the situation, went for a private conference with Aunt Agnes, to take note of her wishes, and to be sure that no undue pressure was to be put in disposing of the money. Mrs McKenna and Arthur Storey were called in hurriedly and asked to witness the document which the lawyer then drew up. John sat, trying to compose himself, waiting for the lawyer to come downstairs. His mind was in a whirl, but uppermost he wondered and marvelled at the great good luck of Aunt Agnes disposing of her money at this particular time, when it would be most use to him.

Arthur lingered a moment, after he had signed the document, to report the progress of his ovens.

"With luck I should start baking next week, Mr Thompson."

John nodded. "Good. Good. I'm very glad." He paced the floor for a while. "I don't mind telling you, Arthur, that I hope to start in business myself, very soon. There has been a stroke of good fortune to myself and my family, and I'll be able to start my own linen firm." Arthur was warm in his sincere congratulations, and agreed, when asked, to keep the news to himself, also the fact that he was a witness to Aunt Agnes' will.

"Don't fret, Mr Thompson, sure I tell nothing to nobody, I keep everything to myself. I wouldn't tell my ma a thing for she would tell the neighbourhood. My da knows where I'm getting the money for a start, but she doesn't."

The lawyer came into the kitchen, followed by Martha, and sat down at the table.

"The old lady seems quite sure and certain that she wants to dispose of her money now, and I can tell you, Mr Thompson, what her wishes are. I suggest the gold be placed immediately in the bank." He cleared his throat. "Well, to continue, she wants a sum held over for burial expenses, to augment the benefit of the burial society, the paper for which she has in her possession. Then a sum of ten pounds is to go to her nephew George, the same to her niece, Martha, and a similar sum to you, Mr Thompson."

John sat upright, a sudden shock going through him.

"The rest of the gold," went on Mr Crone, "a very good amount indeed, over one hundred pounds, is to go to your own son Robert, but as I understand he is yet a boy, it is to remain in the bank until he is twenty-one."

Like a man in a dream John listened. The bulk of the money to Robert. That was a surprise. He gave no outward sign of surprise, however, and listened attentively to the lawyer's proposals and instructions. At length the man was gone, and John sat quietly down, utterly dashed.

"Now wasn't it good of her, leaving her money to us," sighed Martha. "Though, mind you, our George will have something to say when he hears all." As an afterthought, she remarked, "Sure isn't it all the same thing, giving it to Robert? Can't you take the lend of it from him?"

"No, I'm afraid not!"

"Ah, can you not? Well, I'm sure Aunt Agnes will change it all, if she knows you need it to start a business. I'll ask her."

"No, Martha, you'll do no such thing. Aunt Agnes left her money as she felt inclined, and you must promise me solemnly that you won't say a word to her."

"You're disappointed, John. I can see you are."

"I will own to a little disappointment, but in truth it was a bit too good to be true; don't worry, Martha, it's a great thing for our Robert to have a fortune to look forward to, and it would be flying in the face of Providence to wish it arranged to suit my purposes."

He was ruined and blamed himself for building up hopes of starting business for himself. He would content himself now with looking for another situation and if not in the linen trade perhaps in cotton. After all, the cotton trade was far and away more important an industry in Belfast than linen, and with his experience he should find an opening. Still ... his mind had, in the short time of hope, made all sorts of plans. Regretfully he put them aside.

Arthur had left Thompson's house as soon as the lawyer came down the stairs. He strolled slowly round from College Place to his own house, enjoying the air and the moment of relaxation after his busy day attending to the details of starting his baking. At the corner of the street, just under the lamp of College Place, Mary McKenna stood, catching the light of the lamp against the evening twilight, to finish her stitching. She saw Arthur come up the steps, but made no sign to him, continuing to sew deftly at the piece of linen in her hands.

"Hello, Mary," he said softly, and then added, "love." She didn't answer him, but tossed her head and strained her eyes towards the lamplight.

"I haven't seen you for a good bit," Arthur said.

"Oh, you're the right stranger," she answered pertly. "Away visiting your grand relations in the country, from what I hear, and now, it seems, going to put all the bakeries in the town out of trade!"

He caught her arm. "Don't tease me, Mary! Sure you know rightly how it is with me. Will you come with me on Saturday, over to Dargan's Island in the pleasure boat? We could have a great day, walking round the island, and seeing all the birds and the flowers. It'll likely be the last outing I'll get for many a day. I'm starting up on Monday, Mary."

Impatiently Mary pulled away from him.

"Oh, don't interrupt your important business for the likes of me! I'll not be the one to keep you from your work!" There was an edge of hurt and anger in her tone that puzzled him.

"What's the matter, Mary? Sure you know rightly that everything I do is for you! You'll have your own carriage and pair someday, and a big house with a garden. Just you wait!"

"Ach, don't talk so daft. Sure you haven't baked a loaf yet!"

"What's wrong, Mary? Sure you know I am daft—but I'm daft about you. You know rightly that you're my girl."

"Don't be just so sure, Arthur Storey! What will your ma say about all your fine plans? Will she let you marry a Catholic?"

"Sure I told you before, Mary, it doesn't matter to me what religion you are. We can go our own ways."

Mary's face softened a bit. "Well ... your ma has said some very cutting things about Catholics, since the Model schools has opened. And you know, rightly, Arthur that you wouldn't put your foot in a Catholic church. You said so, remember, that day at St Malachy's?"

Arthur took her hand and pulled her to him.

"Mary, you like me, don't you?" She didn't answer, but she didn't pull away from him, and he put his arm round her. "Come on a wee walk with me, Mary. Sure it doesn't matter what my ma says, or what your ma says. We're the ones that matters. Sure you must know how I feel, Mary—I'd lay the world at your feet if I could, and just you wait till I get started at my baking business, and I'll be able to do more than talk."

Mary looked behind her, at the hall of her house, as though expecting her mother to come out suddenly and order Arthur Storey away, but the house was as silent as the street.

She smiled at him and whispered softly, "Well, just a wee walk, Arthur. My eyes is tired from the sewing. I'm sorry I was so cross."

As the week wore on, John Thompson's spirits dropped lower and lower. It was a sad thing, to see the murder of a good thriving business, to witness to near despair so many hard-working people about to be thrown out of work.

"What do you think the old man, old Mr Aspinall, would say to all this?" George McCrum asked him, and John knew that he would have been angry.

"He's probably turning in his grave," he told McCrum fiercely.

How he would love to offer employment to at least a few of the workers, he thought sadly, and how near he had been to it, too. No doubt Martha could have persuaded Aunt Agnes to change her will and give the money to them, now, instead of leaving it to Robert when he was a man. It had been a sore temptation, but regretfully, he put it aside. To his mind, it would be morally wrong, and every bit the same as taking the money unjustly from Robert. He could maybe justify such an action by saying it would be 'borrowing', but what security could he give that a business started on this money would succeed? He could easily lose it, as many a man had lost all in a business venture. In his father's eyes, Robert was a fortunate boy—indentured apprentice in an important linen warehousing firm, and now, heir to a fortune when he became twenty-one.

Saturday came and went, and it took all and more than his usual prayers in church on Sunday to lift John's heart and mind, and to reconcile the events of the past week to the will of God. The future he put in God's hands, and determined that Monday should find him looking for a situation that would be immediate, be it in linen, cotton or any other trade.

On Monday morning, however, Arthur Storey was an early caller at College Place. He looked worried, and burst into Thompson's kitchen as they were all eating their porridge.

"You'll excuse me coming so early," he declared, "but I would favour your advice, Mr Thompson."

John took him into the sitting room, where Arthur put a document from his pocket on the little table beside the family Bible.

"The money has come. Granda sent it, through the bank."

"That's good! Capital! Now your worries are over."

"But they're not, Mr Thompson," Arthur interrupted. "Oh, leave it to my granda to do the thing an awkward way! He's the sly oul' bugger! Look what he done!"

John took the letter in his hand, and read it. It was an order on the bank to pay to Arthur Storey the sum of one hundred and fifty pounds. He read no further.

"What's wrong with that?"

"Sure what do I want with a hundred and fifty pounds?" Arthur snapped, his eyes flashing with temper. "I need nothing as much money as that!"

"Well, tell him—send it back! Good heavens, I never heard anyone complaining about too much money before."

Arthur sighed and sat down, rubbing his head with his hands. "Aye, it sounds daft, I know, but the thing is, Mr Thompson, that I'm to be charged interest on the whole one hundred and fifty pounds—not just on what I use of it, the way I wanted. And if I send some of it back, I know what will happen—Granda won't lend me any at all! Oh, you don't know him, Mr Thompson, but he's as sly and cunning as an oul' weasel. He knows I'm not much hand at business, and he'll be chuckling away to himself, wondering how I'll get out of it."

John didn't know what to say. It was an unusual situation but he could see the force of Arthur's objection to paying interest every quarter on money he didn't want to borrow. It would be quite a charge on such a small business as the bakery would be for some time.

Arthur sat tapping his fingers on the document. "I'll tell you what I was thinking, Mr Thompson, if you don't think it too forward of me. You remember telling me the other night you were going into business for yourself? Well, in the linen business you might be needing more money to start than I do in the baking, so if you would consider the idea of taking part of the loan with me, say the hundred pounds of it, at the interest charged, it would be a great help to me."

John sat down on the hard deal chair by the window. He didn't speak for a minute or two. In fact he was speechless. Here was opportunity offering him a chance. Should he take it? Was this the answer to his prayers for direction? It was a good enough proposition that Arthur made him. One hundred pounds at quarterly interest, with his month's salary, plus the few guineas he had saved—including the ten that Arthur owed him—would that give him a small start as a linen merchant? What if he lost it all? His grave face gave Arthur no guide to his thoughts as he turned the offer over in his mind. He closed his eyes and made a brief intensive prayer. *Oh God, direct my actions this day to do what is right.* If he turned this down would he ever get the chance again? Perhaps when Robert was of age his legacy could be used—but that was seven years hence, and would Robert want to invest his money?

"How long is the loan for? When does your granda want his money back?" he asked Arthur.

"There's no time mentioned, so long as he gets his interest he'll not look for the money. Will you do it, Mr Thompson?" Arthur asked eagerly.

John wanted time to think over the offer, but it was evident that Arthur was anxious for a quick decision.

"Suppose—just suppose—one or other of us should fail in business, what then? Your grandfather would lose his money, and one of us would be under a heavy load of debt." This was the remaining doubt in the part of John's mind that wanted to accept the money, the part that was in conflict with the cautious, careful other half that took no chance.

Arthur's eyes widened. "Fail?" he said. "I'll not fail—at least I don't think so." Then he added hastily, "Of course I'll look to you, Mr Thompson, to help me with the accounts and such like. And you'll certainly not fail." He chuckled. "Sure aren't you all your life in the linen business? You must know it inside out by now."

"But circumstances could go against a person in business; at times of depressed trade in the country all of a person's efforts and knowledge would not be enough."

"Well, I don't intend to do anything but succeed!" Arthur declared vehemently. "I want to have a carriage and pair and a big house and plenty of money in the next five years."

John permitted himself a smile. "A worthy goal, surely! I'll be content with less myself. Well ... thank you, Arthur, I will accept your offer of the money, but on condition of strictest secrecy, and I mean by that that nobody must know, just the two of us."

"You can depend on it, Mr Thompson." Arthur jumped up. "Will you come with me to the bank and arrange it? This letter from Antrim is all I have to go by, and I don't know what to do next. Isn't it odd— my oul' granda can hardly write his name, but he can lend out a hundred and fifty pounds of his money and not miss it. God, I'd love to see the oul' devil's face when he knows I'm taking all the loan! He'll not know what to make of it!"

"That's one thing, Arthur, I'd like to mention. I think you should moderate your talk about your grandfather. It's not seemly!"

Arthur looked abashed. "Aye, right enough, I talk a bit loose at times, and it's no more than the oul' fella does himself, but I must mind it. I will."

John got his greatcoat and hat, and telling Martha simply that he had some business to attend to, went with Arthur into the town to the bank. Both men were silent as they walked along the streets, immersed in plans for their separate ventures.

Now that the decision was taken, John felt relieved and happy, and decided to put all fears and doubts behind him. It had been Arthur's youthful enthusiasm that had finally decided him to take advantage of the loan and to start up for himself. He undertook it in God's name. He would work hard, and do his best endeavours to succeed. If he didn't, then—and not until then—would he worry.

At the bank, John did the talking. He had suggested to Arthur, who had readily agreed, that it would be best if the money was withdrawn there and then, and divided as agreed, fifty to Arthur and one hundred to him, and placed to their separate credits in another bank in the town. In that way their business would be known to none but themselves. The interest would be paid quarterly to the first bank, for transfer to Antrim.

"That's a power of money," said Arthur as they left the first bank to walk down the town towards the second one. John agreed, reflecting that this was the second time inside one week that he had the handling of large sums of money, more than ever he had to deal with personally in his life before.

At the second bank, the manager greeted him with deference when the money was lodged to the two accounts. So well he might, thought John; the gold for Robert, and the other bequests that Aunt Agnes had named, were in this bank. No wonder indeed that the manager walked to the door with them, opened it, and said respectfully, "Good-morning, Mr Thompson, and Mr er, Storey.

CHAPTER SEVEN

The town was quiet as the two men walked out of the bank and turned towards their homes. John's mind was in a whirl; he hoped and prayed that he would ever remember this day, Monday, 29th May, 1857, as a turning point in his life. Having made his mind up, he now had many things to do, to start quickly in his own business and to take advantage of Aspinall's recent closing.

Arthur was eager to start his baking that very night, and he talked excitedly as they walked.

"I'll get our Alfie to help me at first, to take out the basket and round the houses, though God's my judge, I don't think he'll be much use. He's still mad daft on the sea. My ma watches him like a hawk, but he'll elude her one of these days."

"Better let him go, I'd say."

"Indeed aye." Arthur was silent for a moment, then he said impulsively, "Mr Thompson, I want to thank you for all your help. I'd never have got a start only for you. I'll not forget it."

John murmured some acknowledgement, his mind busy planning his own affairs.

"When I make my mind up to a thing," Arthur said earnestly, striding along, as tall as John Thompson, but lacking his breadth, "nothing will keep me from it. I'd like to tell you, Mr Thompson, that my heart is set on something else," and he confided then his feelings for Mary McKenna and his hope to marry her.

"You're young enough to think of marriage," said John.

"It's Mary for me, and nobody else," Arthur said softly. "I knew the first day we moved to Killen Street that she was the one for me. Though, mind you, her ma is against it, and mine will be when she knows."

"Aye. You're different religions. I don't think Mrs McKenna will favour it, and your own mother, if you don't mind me saying it, doesn't approve much of Roman Catholics."

"Don't I know it?" Arthur sighed. "However, I mean to have Mary, if she'll have me, like it who will."

"You might change your mind yet, you're young enough, only nineteen or so, isn't it?"

Arthur shook his head. "No," he said softly, "Mary's the one for me. Sure you must have felt the same, Mr Thompson. Didn't you know that your wife was the one for you, no matter who or what she was? I wouldn't care Mary was a pagan, I'd still want her to marry me."

John did not reply. He could not have agreed with Arthur in any case, as his own selection of a wife had been rather more cautious and in keeping with his character. He had seen Martha Milling—as she had been then—at the manse in the Hills, and had admired her dark looks, her stern countenance with eyes that could suddenly smile. But his decision to marry her had been made more on his observations of her good training as a housekeeper and cook at the manse, and on knowing that her father had a snug farm in the hills and was a good respectable Presbyterian. John had been looking for a wife. His selection was by no means hasty, though he would have admitted— had he been asked—that Martha had made him a good, loving and dutiful wife, and that he was happy and contented in his life with her.

When he reached his house in College Place he told Martha very briefly that he had been able to make arrangements to go into business for himself. He then retired to the little front parlour to compose his mind and lay his plans. Martha shooed little Jane, who was toddling around, to the kitchen, and told her to keep quiet, that Pa was thinking. Dearly would Martha have loved to know how John had accomplished this matter of business, but she knew him well enough not to ask questions. He would tell her what he thought she ought to know, and nothing more.

The first thing to do was to find a place suitable to his purpose, not too large, and not too high a rent. Then he would see Mr Aspinall, or whoever was attending to the winding up of the firm, and try to buy some of the equipment he would require; tables, maybe some sewing machines if he could get them cheaply enough—though they were new enough in the trade, John saw them as useful and a coming trend. And there were odd pieces of linen of varying lengths that would be useful to him. He would have to watch his money carefully until the business started. Expenses were not high in the house; fifteen shillings to a guinea would do for the weekly expenses, and he knew that Martha would exercise every economy to save and do with as little as possible. Then he would write quickly to Aspinall's good customers, particularly in the English market, and introduce himself. He would have to have some workers—his mind flew to Minnie Hamill, one of the girls in Aspinall's warehouse. Minnie was a great worker, and if she hadn't got a start elsewhere he would offer her a job. And he would need a storeman, one that could make himself useful in packing and general duties in the new firm. Paddy Burke was a likely fellow; he had been many years in Aspinall's and would sure enough find it hard to get a job now that he was getting on in years, but he would suit. He knew enough about the work of a warehouse to be able to turn his hand to anything.

Late that evening the smell of baking bread permeated Killen Street and College Place. Arthur's venture had begun. His first loaves were in the baking and the morning saw him out with his basket, round the houses in the district, selling his bread. Mrs Thompson was one of his first customers, and the other neighbours in Killen Street and College Place bought from him too. Boldly he knocked Mrs McKenna's door and asked if she wanted any bread.

"You've a right cheek on you, coming here," she said, "after what your ma thinks of us."

"Look, Mrs McKenna," he said tersely, "do you want bread off me? I wouldn't pass your door in case you think I've any part in my ma's quarrels. What you and her say to each other is nothing to me. Do you want a loaf?"

"Well I suppose I might as well take it off you as anybody else. What does your da think about you starting? And I'm sure Mr Lamont wonders at you starting on your own."

"I'm sure oul' Lamont is worrying about me, but sure didn't he start the same way himself, with the basket round the doors, and you wait and see, Mrs McKenna, it'll not be many years afore I'm as well off as he is, the oul' skin flint."

Mrs McKenna's good nature had to smile. "Well good luck to you anyway, Arthur Storey! I hope you succeed with your Protestant loaves!"

John Thompson's affairs proceeded as he had hoped. He was able to rent a small store at the rear of Bedford Street, at a nominal rent, and over at Aspinall's he found young Mr Aspinall in a benign mood and was able to get all he wanted and a bit more at extremely good terms. The letters had been written to potential customers and he waited results. Meantime, the store had to be scrubbed out, and Martha and Mrs McKenna between them tackled the job and soon had it in a clean condition. Martha was greatly excited that her John was starting business for himself, and if nothing else it brought colour and excitement into her life. Mrs McKenna offered her services as an outworker, to do sewing, Mary and herself. They had been doing sewing at home for some time now for the man in Hamilton Street, but Mrs McKenna had no love for him and would gladly change, if Mr Thompson had the work to keep them going.

The store was not far away from Stuart & Mount's large warehouse and factory, and John met his friend, Albert Meekin, one morning shortly after he had taken the place.

"Well, what's this I hear?" asked Albert.

"It's true, I've started for myself," John told him.

"Good luck to you," Albert said heartily. "I wish you well."

"There's one thing worries me," John told him, "and that is, what will Mr Stuart think? It won't harm Robert's chances in the firm, will it?" This had been on his mind, and he had been hoping to meet Albert to ask him this particular question.

"I won't worry too much about that," Albert said. "In fact," he added with a wry smile, "the Governor did mention something to me—you know how news goes round the trade, and everybody knows that Aspinall's is closed down and that you've ventured on your own. Mr Stuart was remarking that you would be doing the right thing for yourself, but that he didn't suppose you'd do his trade any harm for a bit yet. He meant that as a wee joke, you know," he put in hastily.

John smiled ruefully. Indeed it was most unlikely that he, in his small way, could do harm to the well-established trade of such a big business as that of Stuart & Mount. He was glad, though, that Mr Stuart knew of his venture and did not take it amiss. It was important that Robert should complete his apprenticeship there, and after that, when he was a journeyman, John hoped to have a nice little business for Robert to come to, and make it John Thompson & Son, Linen Merchants.

The days went by quickly for him, with all the details he had to attend to, and with most of the preliminaries dealt with, the little warehouse would soon be ready to start business. John called to see Minnie Hamill one afternoon, at her mother's house in Lagan village, over the bridge and the River Lagan in Ballymacarret town. As he had hoped, Minnie was quite ready to work for him, and it was arranged that she should start on Monday, 12th June. Minnie could have had other work if she had been anxious, but she had been taking life easy, and was very pleased that Mr Thompson had come to ask her to work for him. He explained that he would be in a small way at first and that her work would vary, to be stitcher, ornamentor, and packer if need be, until the business grew.

He took Robert with him the following evening, to see if Paddy Burke needed the job he could offer. Paddy lived in a very small house in a narrow lane off the Cullingtree Road, not very far in distance from Killen Street and College Place, but far removed in size, comfort and social standing.

It was a clear June evening, with a slightly cool breeze blowing down from the mountains, though warm enough for greatcoats to be discarded. When they had walked leisurely down Cullingtree Road and into the lane where Paddy lived, it seemed to be a different climate; the lane was dark and narrow, and there was a dampness in the air. No gleam of the evening sun reached in. The street was dirty, with heaps of refuse lying on the road, and a sour smell rising from them. Paddy's house had a brave air of attempted respectability, with the windowpanes clean, the curtains faded but not too dirty, and the front step scoured. A crowd of children playing outside their doors and on the waste grounds that edged the brickfields beyond had followed the Thompsons, and now stood, barefoot, half clad, but intensely curious, peering at them.

At a knock from John Thompson, Paddy Burke opened his front door. He was a small man with grizzly sandy hair, and a brick-red complexion. His eyes were red-rimmed, and he peered for a second or two at his visitors before flinging the door wide open with a hospitable gesture.

"Mr Thompson, sir!" he exclaimed. "And Master Robert, too! Come in, come in," and as he ushered them into the darkness of the tiny kitchen which was pitch black to them after the comparative brightness of outside, Paddy shouted at the children who by now were standing on the window-sill and gaping in. "Away home with yez! Away on out of this!" he shouted, and dispelled them.

Robert took stock of the room. There was very little in the way of furniture, and the hob grate was empty of a fire, with the huge black kettle pushed to the back. In a rickety chair by the side of the empty hob sat an old man sucking an empty pipe. There was a strong resemblance in the wisps of still-sandy hair and sidelocks and in the weak eyes and ruddy cheeks to the younger man, and he was at once introduced with deference to Mr Thompson as Paddy's father.

"Sit down," Paddy said, and put forward the only other rickety chair in the room for Mr Thompson and a small stool for Robert. Paddy apologised for his wife's absence. "She's away at the Chapel, but maybe she'll be back before you leave. She'll be real vexed to think you called and her not here to welcome you and offer you a bite to eat."

"Never fear, Paddy." John Thompson smiled, "It's yourself I'm here to see, though I would think it a pleasure to meet your good wife."

The polite interchanges over, Mr Thompson then asked, "How are things with you, Paddy?"

"Well, none too good, none too good at all. Work's hard to find, though it's not for the want of looking."

"Good! Capital!" Mr Thompson hoped he wasn't too hearty. It was clear to him from the bare look of the house, from the empty grate and from the poorly clad look of both Paddy and his father, that things were desperate with the Burkes. However hospitably Paddy might mention a bite to eat to his visitors, Mr Thompson was sure and certain that there was very little food, if any, in the house.

"I was hoping you'd be free," he ventured. "Did you not hear that I am commencing business for myself?"

"I never did, or I'd have been on your doorstep, sir!"

"I want you to work for me Paddy, if you will. I'll treat you fair and decent, and if things go well with my venture, I'll advance you along too."

Paddy said nothing, but swallowed hard, and there was a gleam of tears in his eyes as he shook Mr Thompson's hand.

In a moment or so he was able to speak.

"God bless you, Mr Thompson! I'll work hard for you'll not deny that things has been very bad since the old firm closed, with a houseful of childer to feed and not much to give them. Poor oul' Granda here is even short of his hit of tobacco for a smoke. We prayed hard, God knows we've prayed, and now you're the answer. Just wait until herself comes home to this good news!"

Mr Thompson edged over to the old man's chair and talked to him, raising his voice when he discovered the old man was slightly deaf. He had been a mill worker in his early days, it seemed, and eagerly told Mr Thompson about it.

"A flax dresser, that's what I was," he said in his thin reedy voice. "Aye, I've worked at many's the mill in my day, from the county of Tyrone to Derry. I never stopped long in the one place. The urge was always on me to be moving, and my childer was all born in different parts of the country. Paddy here was born in the Upperlands of Derry. Aye, I've travelled around, but I'm not fit to go far now. The legs is bad on me."

John Thompson sat on talking to him, asking him questions about his work in his early days. The old man obviously enjoyed the attentive audience and brightened up as he related the hardships of work when he was a boy, and how easy the young ones were getting it now, in his opinion.

The door opened and a tall lad came in and stood awkwardly against the wall. He was barefoot and his tattered shirt and trousers draped him. He too had the sandy hair of his mother and grandfather, and was introduced as Peter Burke. He shook hands in a mannerly fashion, and Robert and he eyed each other curiously as the adults continued talking.

"There's poor Peter looking for work," Paddy informed them. "If you would hear tell of anybody needing a strong boy to work hard, Peter's the one. Do you know anyone looking a boy, Mr Thompson?"

"No, but I will keep Peter in mind if I do hear."

"He had work down at the tanner's yard, but there was fighting and stone-throwing a time or two. You know what it's like, Mr Thompson, when you get some of both sides and there's religious differences, and the tanner sent them all home, even the ones that never said a word or threw a stone."

John Thompson rose to leave then, and shook hands with the old man and nodded kindly to Peter. Paddy escorted them to the door, where the barefoot children had again assembled and had to be scattered. John put his hand in his pocket, and slipped some silver coins to Paddy.

"A little advance, Paddy," he murmured. "I can see that things are bound to be tight with you."

"Mr Thompson, you're a gentleman!" Paddy uttered with great sincerity, and asked when he would start his work. John told him to be ready soon.

The children and neighbours stared again curiously at the Thompsons as they left the lane and walked down the Cullingtree Road. They walked in silence, then John said very gravely,

"There is something wrong with this world, Robert, when people are down to that level. People shouldn't want work as badly as that. Those poor creatures are not far off starvation. There is something wrong somewhere. Wealth and work should be better divided!"

"But there's worse, isn't there?" Robert asked. "What about all those houses down off the quayside?" As he spoke, he could have cut his tongue out. His father would now want to know how he came by his information, and he would have to tell about the unfortunate walk on the Sunday, two years ago, when Jane was born, when he missed church. He never had told anyone, except Mary McKenna. Now there would be a whole investigation.

But to his surprise, his father did not ask any questions, but agreed to his remark.

"Indeed yes, I know the disgrace that area is to the town, and I'm sorry to say that many of the big firms in the trade do little to help the poor veiners of muslin that live there. Always remember, Robert, that people should be paid living wages. Some of the veiners of muslin get as little as a couple of shillings a week. How could anybody exist on a couple of shillings? It's not Christian to treat human beings like that!"

As he had hoped, John Thompson had all his affairs so arranged that on 12th June, he was nearly ready to start, as nearly ready as he would ever be, he reckoned. Some few orders had already come as response to his letters. No doubt when they saw how he dealt with orders, how quickly he could deliver, and the standard of the cloth he would supply, he would get further orders. Minnie Hamill and Paddy Burke were waiting for John on the morning of the commencement of the firm—John Thompson, Linen Merchant. It had been an early start in the house in College Place, with an air of suppressed excitement and feeling of urgent expectancy. Aunt Agnes, who had been feeling rather better in the past week, came down for her breakfast, and joined in the special prayer that John made for the success of his venture. Dearly would Martha have loved to have gone with John to his little warehouse to join in the excitement of the new business, but she was wise enough to keep her wishes to herself, knowing that her place was in the house where her work was, and anyhow, what use would she be in a linen warehouse?

John felt the importance of the moment when he made his first entry in the brand new ledger to record the orders as a merchant in the linen trade. In the evening at supper, he unbent sufficiently to tell Martha and Aunt Agnes, as well as Robert, that he had done well and felt encouraged by the day's work, and that Minnie Hamill and Paddy Burke were working well and would be of great help to him. Arthur Storey came round after supper, before starting his own work, to report on his previous week's trading.

"I'm doing right well, Mr Thompson," he reported. "I'm well

satisfied with the way things is going, but I'm afeard our Alfie is not going to be much use to me. He's a born daydreamer, and what he's dreaming about I don't know. Maybe it's the sea; maybe he still has notions of running off. Send him out with a basket to sell the bread and you don't see him for hours, and then he comes back and he's never sold a loaf. The other day he was down at the quay, looking at the boats, and the bread going stale in the basket."

"You should try and get him a job down at the shipyard. I hear this new man, young Mr Harland, is making great progress."

"Declare to my God, I'd get him a job anywhere else I could, for he's no use to me," Arthur retorted irritably.

"I know a man who is acquainted with this Mr Harland, and perhaps he could speak for the boy."

A few days after this conversation, John was startled to see Arthur coming into his warehouse with a great air of hurry about him. It wanted less than an hour to closing time, and John had still a great deal of work to do, and hoped that Arthur was not coming to bother him about getting Alfie a job.

"Mr Thompson." Arthur was quite breathless. "I've come for you! There's trouble at your house. The old lady has took bad again, and Mrs Thompson would like you to come as quick as you can. She seems very alarmed. Mrs McKenna is with her and I saw my ma going in too."

John did not delay in leaving, giving Paddy the task of locking up and leaving the key in at College Place on his way home. He knew that Martha would never send for him unless there was real urgency, and he hurried with Arthur to find, when he reached his home, that Aunt Agnes had taken a very bad turn, something the same as the last illness, only worse.

"Oh, we can't blame it on ling fish nor buttermilk this time," sobbed Martha when she saw him. "John, I'm frightened? Do you think we should get the doctor?"

The old lady had been helped up to bed and lay inert, her face grey and her lips blue.

"She complained all day of a bit of a pain in her chest," Martha whispered, "then it got worse, and I think it's a real sore pain, too."

She certainly was very ill, John decided, and he would go for the doctor immediately. He told Martha to send Robert out to Moneyrea to inform George and advise him to come in right away.

"Do you think she's bad, John?"

"I do. She's very ill. I don't like the look of her at all."

Martha sat by the bedside quietly, while Mrs McKenna stayed downstairs looking after Jane, and preparing a hasty supper for the menfolk, and when Robert came home she sent him upstairs to his mother.

"Son dear," Martha whispered, as he tiptoed into the room with an anxious, frightened look on his face, "take a bite to eat and walk out to Moneyrea and tell Uncle George that Aunt Agnes is very sick."

Robert nodded, and looked at the bed, and the still form that barely breathed. He hoped Aunt Agnes was not going to die, at least not while he was there.

"Can I ask Alfie to come?"

"Aye, it'll be company for you."

Alfie was only too pleased to escape work with Arthur at the bakehouse, and as soon as Robert had quickly eaten several slices of bread and swallowed a bowl of milk, the two boys set off. Over the Lagan they went and walked briskly up the steep hill, in the brilliance of the June evening. The Castlereagh Hills were clear ahead of them, and when they paused to rest and looked back, the mountains and the Cave Hill beyond the mist of the town sat out etched in the dark red and blue hues of the evening sky.

Alfie pulled a piece of grass and, chewing it, gazed down at the harbour.

"There's the *Blenheim*," he remarked, "getting ready to go out."

He added softly, "I'm going, Robbie, you know, I'm going."

"Are you for running away again?"

"I am! And don't you go and clash on me, for I don't want nobody coming after me."

"My da only went last time because your ma asked him," Robert said huffily. "Sure your ma was shouting the street down."

"Well, she'll not get me back this time." Alfie was firm.

"When are you going?"

"You'll not go and tell on me?" Alfie eyed him nervously, and Robert shook his head solemnly. "I'm waiting on word from James McKenna. You see," he went on eagerly, "there's a fellow works on the *Blenheim* and he knows when James's boat will be in at Liverpool. James gives him money to bring over to Mrs McKenna when his voyage is over. James is getting me on his ship, and it won't be long. I go down near every day to the quay, pretending I'm going to sell the oul' loaves, you know, but it's to be on the lookout for this fellow. I've everything ready in my bundle, too."

"Your ma'll be raging," Robert said, "but I'll not tell anybody, I'll keep your secret. But you see, Alfie, I've changed my mind. I don't want to go away in a ship now. I couldn't leave now, you see, on account of being an indentured apprentice at the linen trade." He tried to sound important, just in case Alfie thought that going to sea was more serious than being in business.

"It doesn't matter," Alfie replied carelessly. "Sure I'll tell you all about it when I come home with my fortune of money."

They walked on again, and soon reached Uncle George's farm. The shadows were deepening in the lush laneway hedges, with an overpowering perfume of honeysuckle and cut grass mingling with the down-to-earth farm smell of manure. As they walked down the lane towards the house, faces peered out of the window at them, and in the yard in front of the house some of the children stood and stared. Danny was coming out of the byre, but he eyed Robert and Alfie silently; he had nothing to shout this time Robert thought complacently.

"Come in, Robert, is that yourself," Aunt Tilly said as she opened the door, eyeing both boys up and down. Robert could see that she was impressed by his coat and hat and white linen shirt, and he took care to speak with dignity, as befitted a man of business.

"What brings you, Robbie?" Uncle George asked gruffly, standing in his working clothes beside the fireplace.

Robert told of Aunt Agnes's illness and that it was seemingly so serious that the doctor was being sent for.

"Ma said you should come, as soon as you can," he added.

"Soul, she must be bad when yous are getting the doctor," George said, stroking his stubbly chin. "Tell me," he said, his eyes screwed up, "did they get a lawyer? Did they?"

"I don't know," Robert answered innocently.

"Well, you go on down, you and your friend, and tell them that Tilly and me will come as soon as we're dressed. But tell them I said to get the lawyer. Don't forget now!"

"I'll not," Robert said, and turned hesitantly. There was nothing for it but for Alfie and himself to go. He had hoped there might be the offer of something to eat, for he hadn't eaten much supper, and the walk up the Hills had sharpened his appetite, but not even a cup of milk was offered, or a cold potato, and the boys had to leave feeling very much let down.

The walk downhill was quicker than the upward climb had been, and when they reached College Place Robert saw that straw had been laid on the road, to deaden the sound of footsteps for the poor, sick old lady. Leaving Alfie to go on to Killen Street and his work at the bakehouse, he went to his own door. A large black crepe bow hung on the knocker. He pushed open the door softly; his mother came out of the kitchen, her eyes red from crying. He looked at her enquiringly.

She nodded her head. "She's gone, son, she's gone! Poor old

Auntie is dead! Did you tell Uncle George to come?"

"I did, and Aunt Tilly and himself will come when they're dressed. He says you're to get a lawyer."

"Did he say that?" she asked, pursing her lips and sighing deeply. "Now you sit down and take your supper. I'm sure you're starved. Did they give you nothing out at the farm? No, I thought not." She busied herself in getting him his supper. "What exactly did Uncle George say?" she asked, after a while.

"He said that Aunt Tilly and him would be down..."

"Yes, I know that, but about the lawyer?"

"Had you got a lawyer, that's what he asked me." Robert looked curiously at his mother.

"And what did you say?"

"I said I didn't know. What would you want a lawyer for? Oh, was that the gentleman that came one night to talk to Pa and you, and Aunt Agnes?" He dropped his voice as he mentioned the dead woman's name. He wasn't too sure of how she should be spoken of now.

"Yes." Mrs Thompson sighed deeply. "Son, dear, you might as well know that your Aunt thought very kindly of you, and she's left most of her money to you."

"To me?"

"Aye, to you, son. She was very fond of you, and you should never forget her. But I doubt your Uncle George won't be pleased. He likely thinks she's left it to them. I hope he won't get angry about it." She sighed again and some tears trickled down her cheeks.

"Don't cry, Ma." Robert bent awkwardly to put his arm round her neck. "Don't cry. I'm sure Uncle George won't mind. Sure it wasn't his money anyhow. It was Aunt Agnes's."

"I know, son. I'm just crying a wee bit because I'm sorry about Aunt Agnes dying. She was always very good to me. When my own ma died it was Aunt Agnes was kind to me."

The rest of the night and the following two days were like a dream to Robert. It was very late when he went to bed on the first night; his mother and Mrs McKenna laid out the dead woman and even at the late hour, some of the neighbours from College Place and Killen Street came in to offer sympathy and pay their respects, and they sat in the kitchen and in the parlour talking and chatting. Mrs Storey sat longer than any, and to all comers talked grandly of Arthur's bakery as if—as Mrs McKenna put it—he was baking for the whole town instead of for a few streets. It was very late when the noise of the country cart outside heralded the arrival of Uncle George and Aunt Tilly, and Danny, the three of them attired in their Sunday clothes, with well-scrubbed faces, and, on crossing the threshold, with suitably melancholy expressions.

"It's very sad," Tilly remarked, looking with darting eyes around the parlour. "She was powerful fond of our Danny was Aunt Agnes."

George and John Thompson discussed the funeral arrangements. She was to be waked two nights, and buried in Moneyrea burying ground, in the grave with her husband and son. George sent news of the death to some of Aunt Agnes's relations by marriage, in Comber, who called to tell the minister of Moneyrea Church that one of his flock had gone.

John had mixed feelings; he was sorry that the old woman was gone and determined that she should have every last respect paid to her with a decent, respectable funeral, but he could not help wishing that the mournful event had happened at some other time. He could ill afford to be away from his newly founded business; orders had to be attended to, and letters written to customers, and with only Minnie Hamill and Paddy Burke working for him, he himself was needed to attend to these matters. He would have to go round to the warehouse for a few hours at least, and let the relations and friends think and say what they liked.

He, too, was apprehensive of a scene from George over Aunt

Agnes's money, but it was part of the general worry and anxiety. For the while, anyhow, George seemed more concerned in working out the proper order of 'lifts' for the coffin, from the house for a decent walk before putting into the hearse, then at the graveyard, from the gate to the grave on the slope at the back of the church.

His wife, Tilly, sat in the parlour taking stock of the callers, saying little except at intervals, "It's very sad. Our Danny was her favourite, you know."

Mrs McKenna was a tower of strength to Martha. She helped to cook and serve up the meals, and washed the dishes, and arranged for Jane to be cared for by Mary during the days of the wake. She brought in a baking of soda bread and oat cake—for the extra company, as she put it.

"Though I'm sure you got plenty of stuff down from your brother's farm, eggs and butter," she remarked to Martha.

"Deed and I didn't get any such thing," Martha replied drily. "And into the bargain, they're all coming back here after the funeral for a bite to eat. I thought it would have been more the thing to go to George's house, seeing that it's nearer hand the graveyard than here, but no, he says that Tilly is very upset about Aunt Agnes, and that she wouldn't be fit to handle such a crowd."

"Well, she'll be the well-rested woman after it's all over, that's all I can say," Mrs McKenna remarked acidly, "for she's never raised herself from the chair the whole time that I noticed. What will you give them to eat? I could get a bit of boiling bacon if you like, and boil it down on my hob."

"You're far too good, but if you do get it, and I think it would work in well, I'll give you the money for it. You can't be going paying out your own on my account."

"I'm not doing too badly, what with the sewing that Mary and me gets, and now that Mr Thompson has a bit of stitching for us, sure we'll be well off. And did I not tell you that James has sent me his few shillings every now and then?"

Martha sighed apologetically. "Sure amn't I forgetting all about James. I'm letting my own trouble come between me and my friends. How is the wee boy doing at all?"

"Doing rightly, thank God! He has only went short sails so far, round the coasts I think, and every time he's sent me money over with his friend that's on the Liverpool boat I send him over his clean clothes and his stockings, but now it looks like he's for a long voyage, this lad tells me. I mightn't see him now for a couple of years." Tears came into her eyes and she rubbed them hastily with the corner of her apron.

"God grant him safe home," Martha said softly, putting a comforting hand on her shoulder. "Sure now, the time will go in, you'll not feel it, and you'll have him back safe and sound. Sure he's a good boy, James is."

Mrs McKenna dried her eyes, and smiled weakly.

"Aye, God's good indeed, and we have both a lot to be thankful for. I say," she said, deliberately bright, "that's a nice looking lad of your brother's. Danny, isn't it? I think he favours you a wee bit in looks. Your sister-in-law tells me he was the great favourite of his aunt's."

"Oh aye, she's kept chanting on at that since she put her foot over the door. Mrs McKenna, dear, I'll tell you something, just between the two of us, but there'll be trouble before my poor old Aunt is cold in her grave. You remember the night you were asked in as a witness?"

Mrs McKenna nodded excitedly.

"Well, all I can tell you is that poor old Aunt didn't leave what she had to leave in a way that's going to please our George and Tilly. Oh, there'll be words spoke, you mark what I say!"

"Were they cut out?"

"Not exactly, but they'll not like it!" Martha didn't feel free to tell her friend any more of her affairs, but she was glad to voice her apprehension to someone that there would be trouble over the will.

On the day of the funeral Mrs McKenna came to bring Jane out of the way, and Martha asked her to come back and stay with her after the coffin had been carried down College Place and along the Square, towards the Hills and Aunt Agnes's resting place. Martha, in her sorrow, couldn't help noticing how well Robert looked in his good coat and hat, with the black band on his arm, solemn and sad looking, and she compared him with Alfie walking behind, and Danny walking beside him.

As if she read her friend's thoughts, Mrs McKenna whispered, "Isn't Robert getting to be the fine looking boy?"

Mr Storey and Arthur were at the funeral, as well as other neighbouring men, and Albert Meekin came, representing Stuart & Mount. Robert had been given the few days off work, of course. Altogether, Martha was satisfied that her poor old aunt had got a good turnout, a good respectable following of friends and mourners, and she felt satisfaction that the best had been done to make it a very nice funeral.

When her tears were dried, Mrs McKenna and she turned to prepare the meal for the men of the family coming back, most likely very hungry, from the funeral. Tilly was with them, and suggested that she would help tidy up Aunt Agnes's room and sort out her things. It seemed soon enough to Martha, but she agreed. Tilly was in no two minds of her own wishes, and ended with practically all of Aunt Agnes's clothes, her bonnets and shawls and her petticoats. There was a large bundle ready to go into George's farm cart when it came to take Tilly home.

"Soul it's as well she let the old lady have a nightgown for a shroud," remarked Mrs McKenna. "You're too soft, Mrs Thompson, I wouldn't let her have everything. She has a taking hand, that one, if you don't mind me saying so!"

"Let her have what she wants, sure I don't need the things, and foreby they wouldn't fit me."

"I doubt they'll not fit her either, but that's little odds."

Martha didn't really care what Tilly took, but she was annoyed at the haste with which she took them, and as Mrs McKenna and herself got the meal prepared, she felt again the anticipatory worry of the coming row with George. In this, however, she had reckoned without her husband. He informed George, before being asked, on the way back from the graveyard, of Aunt Agnes's will, and George's anger was spent considerably before College Place was reached. He sat, surly and silent during the meal, but before he and Tilly left to step into the farm cart that Danny had driven down from their farm, he spoke his mind briefly to Martha.

"Yous is the right sly ones! No wonder that John Thompson can start up business for himself and him getting the gold that should have been left to our Danny! You worked it well, Martha, bringing the oul' aunt down to live with you and wheedling her money out of her!"

Martha would have answered him, but John restrained her and said calmly, "I told you before that Robert comes in for most of what Aunt Agnes had to give. You'll hear from the lawyer that it was all done straight-forward and the way she wanted."

"We can get lawyers too! Don't think this is the end of it. I'll see more about it! Come on home out of this, Tilly! All their gowls o'sorrow about the old lady and them with their pockets lined," he shouted.

"You're not going empty-handed anyhow!" Martha answered back. "And if I know you, George, you've spoken to the agent and got her holding for yourself, and didn't she give you all she had on her wee place."

"Come on out of this," George retorted, pushing past and into the hall.

Tilly walked behind him, lugging the huge bundle of clothes, and murmured as she went out, "She was powerful fond of our Danny, you know. It's a wonder she didn't think of him."

Martha wept bitter tears then, and when Mrs McKenna, who had been a silent on-looker, tried to comfort her, sobbed, "I've lost my poor aunt, and I've lost my brother, too!"

"Sure he'll soon forget it!" Mrs McKenna spoke soothingly.

"Not him! I know him! Say what you like, our George will never forget, nor forgive, either."

"Mrs McKenna knows as well as you and I do," John spoke deliberately, "that everything was straight-forward. Now dry your eyes, Martha. We'll retire early tonight. We haven't had much sleep these past few nights."

Mrs McKenna agreed, and quietly bade them goodnight. As she opened the door and stepped into the quiet street, Mrs Storey came running round from Killen Street and pushed past her into the kitchen.

"He's away! My Alfie's gone! Will you bring him back for me, Mr Thompson?"

Wearily, John looked up. There was no end to this day and its troubles.

"Woman dear," he said calmly, "let him go. He wants to go to sea, and nothing will stop him. It's the best thing that could happen to him."

"Look at Mrs McKenna's wee boy," Martha said, to comfort her. "Sure he's away now on a long voyage and she'll not see him maybe for two years."

"Ah, God oh, that's who he's with," Mrs Storey wailed, and sank into a chair to throw her apron over her head and sob. "He's away to meet James McKenna! Oh it was the sorry day I ever came to live next door to them ones!"

By and by she quietened down and went home, and the

Thompsons retired to bed. Robert felt tired and sleepy, but he was excited too. He had never been to a funeral before, and although he was sorry about Aunt Agnes dying, he had felt very important walking beside his father behind the hearse, up the hills to Moneyrea. Added to this was the feeling of wonder at being left so much money. It was to be his, some day. Alfie was going to bring back a fortune from the sea but he had already got one; he had only to grow older to get it.

Martha felt very lonely in the days that followed. She had got used to the old lady's company, but now the house was quiet, when her husband and son went off to work in the mornings, and she had only baby Jane to talk to, unless she found time for a chat with Mrs McKenna.

Robert found that he missed Alfie. The street seemed much quieter without him, and he kept wondering how Alfie had got on and whether or not he had met James McKenna in Liverpool. Alfie's mother wondered, too, for not a line did she get from him, and for days she waited, pale-faced and unusually quiet, for the post to come.

It was Mrs McKenna who was able to give her news when she herself had a letter from James. She told Mrs Thompson about it, as the two of them sat for an afternoon chat.

"Sure what else could I do? Wasn't the woman near out of her mind with worry? Though her and me has had many's the cross words I couldn't find it in me to deny her to news that I had from James. Alfie and him is on the one ship, and by all accounts they're bound for America. She can sleep easy now, the poor soul."

Any gratitude Mrs Storey might have felt was soon dispelled by the turn of events in Belfast, after the yearly 12th July procession of Orangemen. Riots broke out and there was fighting and stone-throwing and window-breaking not far away from Killen Street. A disorderly mob of two or three hundred assembled in Durham Street and had to be dispersed by the police. The sub-inspector who charged with a naked sword in his hand and the mob broke up and fled.

The riots lasted several days and the people in the district were terrified.

"Thanks be to God my poor Aunt Agnes was spared this," Mrs Thompson sighed. "She would have been horrified."

"I was real frightened myself," Mrs McIlvenna admitted, "for some of them come running down past the street and I thought that all my windows was going to be broke."

Mrs Thompson and she were standing talking at the corner when Mrs Storey came out of her door. She snorted.

"I'd think you'd have better to do than waste your time talking to Papists!" she shouted. "Tell them all to go back where they came from."

"Who started it anyhow?" Mrs McKenna shouted back. "It wasn't the Papists that was walking on the Twelfth, was it? Who always starts the trouble in this town?"

Mrs Thompson tried to calm them, unsuccessfully, and there was danger of a riot breaking out there and then in Killen Street.

Later that evening another mob gathered, and had to be dispersed by the police. The people scattered in all directions and some came running down from Durham Street into Killen Street, with the police hot on their heels to make arrests. Robert had been standing at his door, listening to the shouts and commotion when a lad came running towards him, blood streaming from a gash in his head.

"They're after me!" he gasped, and Robert recognised him as Peter Burke.

"Come on in," he shouted and, pulling Peter into the hall, closed the door.

Footsteps were heard coming from Killen Street, down the steps into College Place, then a loud voice shouted, "Nobody here!" and the footsteps went away.

Peter leaned against the wall, trying to staunch the blood. Mrs

Thompson came anxiously to find out the cause of the commotion and pleased when she saw a strange boy bleeding in her hall.

"It's Peter Burke," Robert said hastily. "His da works for my da now."

Peter's head was bathed with warm water and a bandage of white linen wrapped round his head. Mr Thompson arrived home while this was in progress: he had hurried home earlier than usual these few nights for fear of getting involved in a mob.

"What happened to you?" he asked Peter.

"I was with the ones out of our side," Peter replied defensively, "and them ones from Sandy Row was clodding stones."

"And did none of you throw stones?"

"We did, until the polis comes, and we all started running and I got hit with a stone. How will I get home? The polis is looking to arrest anybody they can get."

"It's all quiet now," Mr Thompson said in a weary voice. "I think you can venture. But Peter, this won't do. You mustn't get mixed up with a mob like that."

"Sure they're all in it." Peter's eyes were shining. "It's great, so it is, if you don't get hit, or lifted."

"Well you'll have to change your ways," Mr Thompson said sternly. "I might be able to get work for you, but you must promise not to go out fighting."

Peter readily promised and Mr Thompson said he would let him know if the promised job turned up, and opening the door cautiously, he listened. All was quiet.

"Away home with you now," he said and Peter went on his way.

Mrs Thompson sat on a chair, quite weak after this excitement.

"John, dear, what's the meaning of it all? Why does people have to fight over religion? Sure Mrs McKenna and Mrs Storey were at it only a wee while back. Mrs Storey says the Catholics started it."

"And Mrs McKenna says the Orangemen started it," Robert

chimed in. "You should have heard the two of them!"

Mr Thompson sat down.

"I wonder when the people in Belfast will have sense, fighting against each other, blaming each other. It's not Christian."

"Aye but who starts it all?" Martha asked.

"Well, you know how it is after every Twelfth. It doesn't take much to start a riot, but this time nobody seems right sure what the cause was. Some say it was a fellow dressed up as an Orangeman and waving a flag marching down the Cullingtree Road started it all. They say he only did it for a joke, but he was taken seriously and the stone throwing between the Cullingtree Road Catholics and the Protestants of Sandy Row was the result. We can only hope it doesn't last too long and that the people will learn a bit of sense, and live in peace together."

In a few days it was all over, and except for the court appearances of those who were arrested, and the subsequent fines and imprisonment, life in the town settled down.

John Thompson approached Arthur Storey to take on Peter Burke as a helper and Arthur agreed.

"Don't tell my ma he's a Catholic, though," he grinned. "She'd sooner I employed the devil himself."

In a few weeks Arthur was able to report that Peter was a good worker and an excellent bread salesman.

"He can sell loaves the best you ever saw," he exclaimed. "And I hardly ever have stale bread left. Peter has more customers looking stale loaves in his own street than we have the bread for. He'll do fine, though I'll have to keep my eye on him next Twelfth," he added with a sly smile. "People is not normal in this town. You're a decent, respectable, hard-working fellow for fifty-one weeks of the year and a rascal of a Papish or a Prod the other week!"

Mrs Storey had the last word on the whole affair. "What do you think of your great Model school now?" she taunted Mrs Thompson.

"It didn't last long did it, until the Catholics and Protestants was fighting over it? Sure they tried to burn it down, I hear!"

"Well, it's still standing," Mrs Thompson retorted acidly, "and to the best of my knowledge, the Catholic and the Protestant children are still sitting beside each other in the desks. And let me tell you, Mrs Storey, that when our wee Jane's old enough, that's the school she'll go to. So there!"

"Aye, maybe she will—if it's still there by then!"

PART TWO

CHAPTER EIGHT

Robert hurried down the stairs from the fancy linen department of Stuart & Mount's warehouse, pulling his greatcoat on as he went. Behind him his friend, Charley Gourley, jumped the stairs in two great leaps to keep up with him.

"Hold your hurry there, Thompson! Is there a fire?"

"Don't keep me back, Charley, I want to get home and get my supper over quick. Alfie Storey's home! He just landed this morning off the Liverpool boat. I haven't seen him for near a year now."

"Where was he this time?"

"America again, I think, but I don't rightly know. He's been near everywhere in the world now. Many's the time I wish I'd gone to sea with him. I could have, you know. I knew he was for running away when he did, over three years ago."

Charley laid his hand on Robert's shoulder and mockingly smiled at him.

"Sure, Robbie dear, you're too good a wee boy to do anything like that. You couldn't run away to sea without bringing your ma with you."

"Quit that!" Robert's face flushed with anger. "It's all right for you, Gourley, you hardly ever see your ma for a year at a time. You've forgotten what it's like to have anybody belonging to you, you're that long in lodgings."

"Sorry, Robbie, I'm only gagging! I know rightly you could have run off if you'd had a mind to. I'll tell you something, though."

"What? Don't keep me beck, with your dawdling; didn't I tell you

I'm in a hurry?"

"I'll not keep you! But many's the time I envied you, having your own home to go to, and your Ma and your wee sister dancing attendance on you and treating you like God Almighty."

Robert gave a sneer. "Ha! And did you envy me my da, too? Did you not think it would be great to have a da that treated a fellow of sixteen as if he was a baby, and wouldn't let him out at night when he wanted to go? Sure you don't know you're living, Gourley! You come and go as you please."

"Well, true enough, I do, but I can tell you that sometimes I get tired of lodgings. Sure it's all right for the first month or so. 'What'll you take for your tay, Mr Gourley? Would you not like a bit of boiled bacon for your tay?' Ach, after a wee while, it's a different tune, it's 'Here's your tay, Mr Gourley, and take it and lump it!' "

"Ach, it's the great pity of you," Robert said, good-natured again, and thumping him on the back. "I tell you what; I'll ask my da to say a wee prayer for you."

"Never bother, he has enough to do, praying for you! What you can do, though, is to ask me home with you for my supper. My landlady's sick, and I'm sure there's nothing in for the tay but stale bread and rancid butter."

"Come on then, and I'm sure our Jane will be glad to see you, if nobody else is. She thinks you're great."

"I hope your ma won't mind..." Charley said, smiling.

"She won't, and you needn't worry about my da; he won't be home from his blessed warehouse for an hour or more yet."

The two boys walked quickly along Bedford Street, at a breakneck pace, and raced each other from the Black Man statue in College Square, to arrive, panting, on the doorstep of Robert's home in College Place North. Mrs Thompson was only too pleased to see Charley Gourley and made him welcome. It made a little excitement in the quiet house and brightened Robert. He was normally a quite lively boy, but she noticed that the peace and quiet his father demanded in the home made him resentful and dull. John Thompson liked his house ordered and quiet when he came home from his warehouse at night, often with several hours' work of letter writing and bookwork to do. If, as sometimes happened, Robert's high spirits got the better of him, and he would chase Jane and Alice Storey up and down the stairs—catching them, he would say, to put them in Arthur's bakery oven—the moment his father's step was heard at the front door all merriment would cease, and the little girls' delighted shrieks of fright would stop. A gloom would then descend upon Robert, and although his mother noticed it, she could do nothing to alter her husband's mood. She thought him too hard on Robert, too stern and unbending in his treatment, and she tried, in her quiet way, without openly opposing her husband, to make life a little brighter for her son. She gave Robert a more open demonstration of her pride in him and her affection for him than came naturally to her. She knew that John Thompson felt the same for his son, but could not show it. She saw that Robert took the stern countenance and the disapproval for the true feeling. And when John Thompson spoke—as he did often—of the time when Robert should be finished his apprenticeship at Stuart & Mount's and come into the business with him, she saw the dread that came into Robert's face at the prospect.

And so she was glad that Charley Gourley sometimes came home with Robert for the evening meal. On this evening, in the sharp frosty December weather, she provided them with a tasty, hot supper for their keen appetites.

"Alfie's home, did you know?" she asked Charley.

"So I hear, Mrs Thompson, and I'm looking forward to hearing all about his travels."

"Aye, Alfie's the one that can spin the yarns," she smiled. "A funny thing, you never hear James McKenna speak a word of his voyages."

"Sure you'd think James had never travelled further than the Copeland Islands for all he ever tells," Robert put in. "He just says, 'Aye, it was a good trip', but Alfie ... he's the boy that can tell the tale." His face glowed and his brother saw the admiration that had grown in him for his boyhood pal.

After supper the two boys went round the corner and knocked on Storeys' door in Killen Street. Robert was elated: Storeys' house was such a contrast to his own, with some of the neighbours dropping in for a gossip in the evenings, and as often as he could, Robert would escape from his own house for even a short visit. And another thing, he might see Mary McKenna, for she sometimes called to speak to Arthur in his bakehouse at the back of the house, and had to come through the kitchen to get at it. Robert's heart pounded at the thought. Mary was his secret love, and even to speak to her for a few moments was enough for him. He compared Mary to every girl he met, and still thought her the most beautiful, kindest, and loveliest girl on the earth. He hoped and prayed that she never would marry Arthur Storey, and took comfort from the fact that they had talked of getting married ever since Arthur had started his baking business, over three years ago. Arthur still kept saying that Mary was the one for him, and that he would marry her and deck her in furs and jewels—someday. It was Robert's hope that Arthur's talk was so much blethering, and that Mary McKenna would never marry him. If only he was a little older himself, but at sixteen, on an apprentice's wages, he could scarcely consider marriage. Let him get out of his apprenticeship, though, then he could think of it, and at twenty-one wouldn't he have the fortune that Aunt Agnes left him!

Alfie was sitting in front of the fire, and shouted a greeting when he saw his friend Robert and Charley walk into the kitchen. Mr Storey was pottering round, putting on his boots, and getting ready for his work at Lamont's bakery. Mary was sitting in the corner, quietly stitching. She smiled at Robert.

"Alfie's telling us tales of his voyages, but I say he makes them up. Our James never has any such talk, and sure aren't they both on the one ship?"

"Aye, but James wouldn't like to frighten you!" Alfie declared. He had grown a beard, and lucked much older than his years as he sat, in his seaman's jersey, broad shouldered and grown tall, smoking at a huge cigar.

"Did you bring them home with you?" Robert asked.

"We took these off a ship in the Atlantic." Alfie nodded, looking wise, and winked at Robert. "A pirate ship it was, full of treasures from the Orient."

"You did no such tiling!" Mary retorted. "You bought them likely in the same shop that our James bought some for my uncle. And your other presents was all bought in the same town of Boston. Sure James told me!"

"Ah, but James doesn't want you to know the dangers we faced. He wouldn't tell you, for you'd never sleep in your beds at night if you knew the half of it."

"Well, mind you don't frighten yourself to death." Mary smiled.

"What's it like in America, Alfie?" Robert asked keenly.

"I'll tell you one thing," Alfie replied solemnly, "and you can believe it or not, but it's the gospel truth. There's going to be a war."

"Talk sense," Mr Storey said in his quiet voice. "Sure there's peace and quiet in this town for this many a year past."

"No, I don't mean here in Belfast, nor nowhere in Ireland. I mean in America. There's going to be a war out there, as sure as my name's Alfred Storey. They were all talking about it before we sailed."

"Oh, in America, is it," Mr Storey commented. He sat down on a chair and took out his pipe for a quick puff. "Aye, there is talk of it, in the papers. You'd better mind yourself, boy. Don't you go on no more voyages next or near America. You don't want to get into any fighting; it's no concern of yours."

Alfie hooted. "Damm the fear of me not being near it! Sure maybe we'll be fighting the Yankee boats in the ocean."

Mary looked serious. "Right enough," she said, "our James says there might be a war. Something about slaves. Isn't that right, Mr Storey?"

He nodded. "They want to free the slaves, it seems. At least, one part of America does, but the ones that has the slaves doesn't, and they're ready to go to war about it."

"Well, I think slaves should be freed," Mary declared. "God knows it was bad enough taking them out of their own country without selling them to work in the fields. It's a downright sin and a shame. God pity them that brought the poor craturs out to America and made fortunes out of them. They'll have the hard time explaining it when they go to their Maker. At least there was never no slave boats in Belfast."

"We nearly had," Mr Storey said softly, knocking out his pipe and putting it into his pocket. Slowly and deliberately he took his cloth cap from the dresser and held it in his hands. "There was one fine gentleman once tried to get up a fund to buy a slave boat, but I'm glad to say the merchants of Belfast would have nothing to do with it. I heard tell of it when I was a lad, and I remember it well. Though by the same token, many a merchant in Belfast made his money from the West India trade as they called it. It wasn't the tea and the cotton and the brandy that made them wealthy. They had money in the slave trade that was run from other ports over in England." He twisted his cap and paused, his usually quiet manner gone, and an unusual excitement showing in his face.

"I mind it well," he went on. "I was only a wee lad in Antrim when it was read out of a newspaper. This man that was trying to get a slave boat going put it to a meeting of business gentlemen in Belfast town here, and one of the gentlemen stood up and uttered a curse. He said to them all, 'May God wither the hand and consign the name to eternal infamy of the man who will sign the document!' And not one man there would sign it, they were that terrified of being cursed. It was all long ago, but I knew the man had the newspaper and kept it and he would read it to us all."

"That's a terrible curse." Mary shivered.

"But what's it really like in America, Alfie?" Charley Gourley asked eagerly.

"It's a powerful country," Alfie told him solemnly, and proceeded with a description of Indians and stagecoaches, of vast forests and enormous mountains.

"Are the girls nice? Are they good looking?" Charley asked.

"Well..." Alfie shrugged like a man of the world. "Some of them isn't too bad, but others is nothing but bold hussies, and all they want is a seaman's silver."

Mary laughed. "Don't heed him, boys! Sure what does he know? All he sees is the quayside of a town for a wee while, after being on the ocean for weeks."

"That's where you're wrong, Mary," Alfie told her, "but I won't argue with you. Someday you'll know I was speaking the truth."

"Well I haven't time now to listen to any more of your travels, for I only stepped in for a wee minute to speak to Arthur. But I tell you, Alfie, you're lost here. It's lectures you should be giving to the people on your travels. You'd make more money that way."

Mary gathered up her stitching and went out to the bakehouse to see Arthur. Mr Storey stood by the door and pulled his cloth cap onto his head. He looked keenly at the boys.

"There are yous for the night?" he asked.

"Maybe we'll take a wee bit of a walk," Alfie replied, looking enquiringly at the other two.

"Well, see and conduct yourself, Alfie," his father said. "You've got a bit rough in your way this last trip on the sea. You stay here until your ma and wee Alice comes home."

Alfie didn't reply, but as soon as his father went out, and the front door could be heard closing behind him, he turned to Robert and Charley.

"Well, lads, what'll we do? How about a walk around the town, and a glass or two at the tavern? We could go on to the music hall!"

Robert looked embarrassed.

"I'd better not, Alfie. You know what way Da is. He wouldn't approve of them places."

"Ah for God's sake grow up, Robbie! You're a man now, and every man should be able to take a glass or two. What about your da, Gourley? Would he mind too?"

"He'd be hard put to know about it, seeing he's in Ballymena, but I'd guess he wouldn't approve any more than Mr Thompson would."

Alfie shrugged impatiently. "Ach, sure you don't have to tell. Say you're at the Bible class or something."

Robert shook his head impatiently. "Talk sense, Alfie. You know rightly that if I put a foot in a public house anywhere in the lamps of Belfast there'd be somebody running to tell on me."

"Aye, and another thing," Charley ventured, "suppose they heard about it at work. You know what Mr Stuart is like about drink. We wouldn't get time to get our hats!"

Alfie held up his hand. "All right! All right! I forgot I was back in holy Belfast! It's not the same sin everywhere, you know, but I tell you what we'll do. I've a wee bottle of spirits I brought home with me. We can go out and down the entry and take a wee slug each out of the bottle. Will that do? And then maybe we can walk as far as the music hall, and see if there's any excitement."

Robert nodded his head hesitantly, and Charley said very uncertainly, "Well, maybe that wouldn't be any harm..."

The three boys went out, after Alfie had taken a dark brown bottle from the dresser and hid it under his jacket. They walked down Durham Street and paused at the first dark entry.

"Here, this'll do," Alfie called. They huddled round while he pulled a broken cork out of the bottle and handed it first to Robert. "Take a drink of that!"

Robert shrank back. "No, you go first," he whispered in a hoarse voice. He knew he was disobeying every one of his father's rules about his conduct as a good Presbyterian and the grandson of a precentor of the church, but he didn't want to show himself up in front of the other two as a spoilsport. His father abhorred all forms of alcohol, all smoking, all music halls and such like vulgar displays, and yet here he was, his son, about to sample spirits, maybe even accept a cigar from Alfie, and later to go and look at the crowds at the music hall, if not enter the place.

Alfie grabbed the bottle. "What about you, Charley?"

But Gourley shook his head and murmured, "You first."

Alfie took a long swig from the bottle and handed it to Robert, who timidly raised it to his lips and drank, a good swallow. Gourley took his swig too, and they passed the bottle round until it was empty.

"Now for the music hall!" Alfie declared, but Robert found that he could not move. His head was dizzy and he felt sick.

"What on earth was in that bottle?" he groaned.

"Rum—I think," Alfie said. "Are you all right, Robbie?"

Robert turned away and vomited. "Ah, God, I'm dying!" he muttered. Gourley announced that he felt queer.

"Are you not coming then?" Alfie asked, and when they made no reply he announced that he was off for an evening on the town and would maybe see them later. After he left, the other two stood for a while, backs to the wall, until the dizziness left.

"I'm for home," Gourley announced. "It's bed for me. That's terrible stuff. If that's drink, I want no more of it."

"Ah, stay a wee while," Robert pleaded. "Sure I couldn't go in home like this. They'd know what I'd done."

"Robert Thompson, don't ask me to stay," Gourley protested.

"Just let me get back to my lodgings and into my bed. I was never as sick in my life." He walked away and left Robert in the dark loneliness of the entry.

Robert pondered, reluctant to leave the firm support of the entry wall, but in a while he walked slowly back the way they had come, down Durham Street and into College Square. He couldn't go home in this condition. Maybe he could stop in for a while at Storeys' and sit until he felt better, and trust them not to tell on him. But when he walked down Killen Street in its lonely darkness, Storeys' door was closed. Next door, McKennas' had the door ajar, and he tapped lightly and walked into the hall. Mary came out of the kitchen and peered into the gloom.

"Is that you, Arthur?" she whispered softly, but, then, as Robert approached, she recognised him and caught hold of his arm and pulled him into the light of the kitchen.

"Robbie, what in God's name ails you? You're as white as a piece of linen sheet. Come on in and sit down," and she forced him into a chair.

"I'm awful sick, Mary," Robert cried, "and I'm going to be sick, so I am!" He dashed for the backyard door to stand and vomit in the grating. After a while, he felt better enough to go back into the kitchen, where Mary questioned him closely. The whole story of the night's work came out.

"But don't tell on me, Mary, sure you won't?" he pleaded, near to tears. "I don't want my da to know, and my ma would be terrible upset."

"I'll not tell. Did I ever tell? Did I tell the time that Alfie took you end wee Alice away down the quays and you missed your church? I'll not breathe a word, and if my ma or James don't come in, they'll never hear of it, but I'm going to speak plain and straight to you, Robert Thompson. You have behaved very badly this night. Oh, no," she held up her hand, "don't blame Alfie, you took that drink of rum of your own free will, though I don't blame Alfie for offering it. You shouldn't let him lead you into things. He has no sense, that fellow. You've more sense yourself, for you know when you've done wrong."

"But Mary, his being at sea makes him more of a man. Look how old he seems, with his beard."

"Beard!" Mary was scornful. "You'd see better on a side of bacon! He was near a year growing that bit of down on his chin. Don't you believe all his yarns. I'm sure and certain he never tasted rum either before tonight. The captain of the ship is very strict, and he doesn't let the boys run wild. Our James told me. Alfie is only trying to do the big fella."

Robert nodded miserably, and underneath his suffering, he marvelled at Mary's kindness and sense. She was wonderful, and she always knew the right thing to do. He remembered now how kind she had been to him that day when he had missed church, the Sunday that Jane had been born. He remembered he had told her then that he was going to marry her.

"Do you remember, Mary? Do you remember that day you comforted me, when I missed church? I said that day I was going to marry you!" He took hold of her hand and looked up at her, standing over his chair. "I still want to marry you, Mary! I think you're the nicest girl in the world."

Mary smiled, and ruffled his hair.

"I'll remember that, Robbie. That's a very nice thing you've said to me. But what you need now is a good strong cup of tea to clear your head, and then you may go home, but I want you to promise me—now I'm serious—promise me you won't touch drink ever again until you're a full-grown man!"

"But I am a man, now!"

"Promise me! And another thing, don't be heeding that Alfie and following him in his capers. You just be the nice quiet wee boy you always were and do what your ma and da bids you."

"But will you marry me, Mary?" Robert pleaded.

"That's a nice question to ask, and me promised to another fellow," Mary replied in a bantering tone, and she hurried to fill the teapot from the boiling kettle on the hob, and would not answer him.

Later, after he had drunk the hot, scalding tea, she sent him home. His mother remarked he was a bit tired looking and packed him off to his bed. He sank into the bed, a sorry boy that he had tasted Alfie's rum. Perhaps though, he pondered, it had served a useful purpose in giving him an opportunity of letting Mary know his feelings for her. He thought of Alfie's warning about a war. Was that just another of Alfie's yarns? If there was a war, though, Alfie might be lucky enough to see something of it, the excitement of cavalry charges, and generals leading troops proud in uniforms. He fell asleep remembering his boyish hope of being a soldier and how disappointed he had been that the campaign in the Crimea had been over before he was old enough to join the soldiers.

The prospect of a war in America was more worrying to many others in Belfast than it was to Robert. The rumblings caused great uneasiness to the linen and cotton trades, for their fortunes were tied up very much with America—the cotton trade by reason of the supply of raw cotton from the Southern States, and linen because much of the output went across the Atlantic.

Christmas passed quietly and the turn of the year brought worry to every man connected with both trades. Wild rumours and conjectures kept up a state of suspense. John Thompson had his share of the worry: he had deliberately built up the American side of his small business and was virtually dependent upon it, and as January slid into February, and still the rumours persisted and the rumblings of a war grew louder, he was a very worried man.

Arthur Storey came to visit him in the warehouse one evening in March. John thought the visit would be an informal one, one of the many that Arthur paid him from time to time, to ask his advice, or to tell him how the bakery was progressing.

Storey's bakery had progressed by leaps and bounds. Inside the first year Arthur had two boys working for him, and in two years it took four boys to carry the output in their baskets to sell. Just recently Arthur talked of buying a baker's horse and cart which were up for sale, and John surmised that the young baker had come to a decision on the matter and had come to talk it over with him. He was totally unprepared for Arthur's sudden request that the loan should be paid back to his granda in Antrim within a month.

"I'll tell you how it is," he explained. "I'd like the money paid back before I get married." He took a sheaf of papers and a notebook from his pocket and laid them on the desk.

"I'm doing twice as much business as last year. See, these is the figures, and I reckon the horse and cart I buy will increase the turnover more. You see, Mr Thompson," he said very earnestly, leaning close to the older man, "I made myself a plan when I started business, and I said to myself that when I reached a certain figure I could afford a baker's horse and cart, and when I reached another figure, maybe I could move to a bigger place, and then—the last item in the plan—when I was really going well, I'd get married."

"And are you able to do all these things now? Has trade been so good with you?"

"Improving every day. I've found a nice house to rent up in Arnon Street—you know it, I'm sure, a nice respectable street—and by luck there's a yard nearby with outhouses that'll make a far bigger bakehouse than I really need just yet, but it'll be the very thing for when I expand. And there's a stable for the horse and cart in the same yard, everything nice and handy."

"And you're going to get married?"

"I am." Arthur's face softened, and for a few seconds the face that had got sharp with bright shrewd eyes and set lips looked like the young man he had been three years ago. "And that's why I want to settle with my granda in Antrim. Him nor none of them down there is going to like who I'm marrying. You follow me?"

John nodded agreement. "You mean they will resent you marrying a Roman Catholic?"

"Aye, that's it." Arthur chuckled. "God, I can see the oul' fella's face when he hears. He'll damn and blast me, and if the money wasn't paid, the oul' buggar would send the bailiffs on me for it." He added hastily, though politely, "Do you think I'm doing the right thing, Mr Thompson? I always look to you for advice. Sure what do I know about affairs of business."

"Oh, I'm sure you won't go far wrong," John replied drily. Arthur hadn't shown him any figures and he didn't suppose anyhow that anything he, John Thompson, could advise would be listened to with anything but politeness. Arthur had developed more than his bakery in the three years of trading. John surmised that he was his grandfather's grandson in money matters and could tell to a halfpenny what he made on a day's baking. Here was a shrewd, hard-headed, money-conscious, young self-made man, who put a price on everything, and who put his own marriage last on the list of goals to achieve.

"Well..." Arthur broke the silence. "Will it be convenient for you, Mr Thompson, to let me have the hundred pounds? No hurry, of course. Within the next month."

John swallowed hard, but kept a calm countenance.

"I don't believe it will be convenient," he stated. "The linen business is not like a bakery, you know. We don't sell all we produce as quickly as you do. And yours is a cash business. Mine is not, and as it happens I have very many accounts to be paid from my American customers. I'll see what I can do, though. Leave it for the month."

He could see that Arthur didn't like this upsetting of his plan, and that he hadn't expected it. It crossed John's mind at that second that Arthur Storey would be a very bad enemy to make, and that his quick success in his three years of business had developed a character that was not attractive.

"Well, just as you say," Arthur said. "I'll look in this day next month."

When he left, John Thompson sat at his desk, deep in worried thought. It was going to be hard, if not impossible, for him to pay out a hundred pounds at this stage. With him there had been a gradual building up of a trade, with an increasing number of customers and a proportionate rise in turnover each year, amounting to an established trade that justified the long, hard work he put into it. He had been fortunate in securing some of Aspinalls' customers in England, and made regular shipments to them of piece goods and finished linens, but far and away the bulk of his trade was with America, as indeed was most of the linen trade of Belfast. He was lucky in his American customers and it was this side of the business that he had tried to extend and develop.

What was going to happen now if America was plunged into Civil War? That would have a bad effect on the linen trade, and would cut John's turnover to a core. How could he survive any such recession in business and pay back the hundred pounds to Arthur? He resolved firstly, before coming to a decision, to make a quick estimate of his worth, how much he was owed, how much cloth he had in stock, and how much he was in debt to his suppliers. He thought himself pretty comfortable, with trade as it was at present. Paying the hundred pounds would make a different picture. He would tackle this stocktaking the very next day, and in the meantime, would try not to worry about it. Tomorrow would be Saturday, and he would have leisure to think the matter out and come to a decision.

But for all his resolve, he went home a very worried man, and scarcely spoke a word all evening to Martha.

Next day his statement of affairs looked pleasing to him. He was owed more—much more—than he owed: he had a very good stock of cloth on hand, maybe more than he needed, but useful to have against urgent orders. If the American threat blew over, and it looked as if it might be all talk all these months, he would arrange to pay Arthur, but on his own terms. He would give him twenty-five pounds each month for four months, and by July would have the debt paid. He felt quite relieved and was able to devote himself whole-heartedly on Sunday to his prayers, without any worry gnawing him.

Robert set off for church evening service ahead of the family, for he had arranged to meet his friends Charley Gourley and John McIlhagga, an arrangement that he had skilfully made to avoid walking with his parents and Jane in a parade. He argued that his friends might not go to church if they did not have a definite arrangement beforehand to meet him. His father could find no objection to raise, and Robert enjoyed the freedom he gained by this manoeuvre to have a walk with his friends after service.

He had recovered from his sickness, and comparing notes with Charley and Alfie, they had all decided that what they had drunk was something unusually strong. Alfie had admitted to being sick, too, though he had drunk rum before, many times, and had no ill effects.

"It was bad stuff, that's what it was," he declared. "And maybe the strong stuff that's never sold in public houses. Next time you'll see, it'll not turn a hair on us."

But as he walked along to meet his friends in Berry Street, Robert was determined that there would be no next time. He would keep his promise to Mary McKenna: she didn't like a fellow drinking, and that was enough, he wouldn't drink again. Sauntering down Chapel Lane he was surprised to see Mary and Arthur Storey standing in front of St. Mary's Chapel. Arthur suddenly gripped Mary's arm and tried to pull her along with him. Mary resisted, and pulled herself free, and Robert saw that she was crying. He quickened his step, but Arthur turned on his heel and walked away before Robert could reach the spot, and when he caught up on Mary and asked her anxiously what was wrong, she took hold of his arm.

"Oh, Robbie! Walk with me, will you? Will you come into the church with me?"

"What is it Mary? Did you fall?" he asked. She shook her head and dried her eyes.

"I don't want people looking at me, come on in with me," she said and led the way into the church, with Robert following. He would have followed her into Hell itself, he told himself, with a shiver of excitement and anxiety.

Mary stood at the back of the church, then sank onto a bench, an empty one in the rapidly filling church. Evening devotions were about to begin; the candles were lit on the altar and incense could be smelt from the vestry.

"What's wrong, Mary?" Robert whispered fiercely.

"It's nothing," she murmured, wiping her eyes. "Arthur and me has had a fall out, that's all. I can tell you a secret, can't I? Well, we're to be married soon, and I wanted him to come to my church, just this once, but he wouldn't. He says he'll never put foot in a Papish chapel!"

Robert was stunned. "Don't marry him, Mary," he whispered. "Sure he's always talking about marrying you these years, ever since I was a wee boy. But don't marry him, Mary! He makes you cry!"

A woman in the bench in front turned and shushed him, and some children pushed into the seat and had to be let past.

"Mary!" Robert bent close to her.

"What? We shouldn't be talking! You go on now, Robbie, go on to your own church."

"Mary! Marry me!" He spoke desperately and intensely, and the woman in front turned round and said, "Quit your talking will ye."

"Mary, I'll marry you and I'll go to any church you want. I'll soon be out of my time as an apprentice and I have a lot of money coming when I'm twenty-one. Mary, I love you! I always did! Please don't marry Arthur Storey. He'll only make you cry!"

Mary bit her lip and looked at him kindly, with tears again in her eyes. At that moment the priest and the altar boys appeared on the altar and the people in the benches knelt down, and made the responses to the prayers of the Rosary.

"Thou O Lord shall open my lips!" said the priest.

"And my tongue shall announce Thy praise," responded the altar boys and the people.

Robert tugged Mary's sleeve. "Mary!"

"Oh, Robbie," she whispered softly. "You're a good wee boy, and it'll be lucky for the girl that gets you for a husband. But I'm going to marry Arthur. I want to, Robbie! Him and me is made for each other. It's only his stubborn temper showing now. Go you on now, Robbie!"

But Robert sat where he was, in misery, not hearing anything of the prayers that were going on, conscious only that Mary was going to marry someone else. A sudden movement in the bench, and the people rising to let a man past brought beside him the person he now hated, Arthur Storey.

"Clear out of this!" Arthur whispered fiercely, giving Robert's arm a sudden pull. "Go on, away to your own church, young Thompson. This is no concern of yours!"

There were shushes from all quarters now and a man kneeling beside Robert asked impatiently, "Are you coming out or are you staying, young fella?"

Arthur had squeezed into the seat Robert had occupied, and Robert had no option but to leave. As he did, he looked at Mary, and in the dim light of the church with its flickering candles, he saw a tender look of happiness on her face as she put her arm through Arthur's and sighed deeply.

Robert found his way out and stood in the porch for a few moments, unhearing of the continuing responses of the Rosary. *"Holy Mary, Mother of God, pray for us now and at the hour of our death, amen."*

His own church was round the corner, only a stone's throw, but he couldn't go in just yet. He walked round the streets for a while, his heart heavy, his whole being steeped in melancholy. His dreams were shattered and his hopes gone. Soon he would see Mary married to Arthur Storey. All his disappointment now was turned into anger at Arthur and a strong desire to kick him and punch him. "I never liked him," Robert muttered to himself. "Ever since he spoiled the walk with Mary and me that day to St Malachy's chapel. I'll never like him, as long as I live!"

These sentiments brought him to the front door of Berry Street Presbyterian Church and he tiptoed in and sat beside his mother in the family pew. He had missed the Invocation, the Confession Prayer and the First Lesson and the Anthem, and he couldn't keep his mind on the Second Lesson, the Lord's Prayer or the sermon, for thinking of his lost love.

He nursed his sorrow secretly in the following days. He had lost all hope of Mary now, he realised that: he would always think of her as the nicest girl in the world, and he would never, never marry anyone else. His dislike of Arthur became deep-rooted and he avoided any possibility of speaking to him, though the more he thought of it the more puzzled he was as to why Mary was keen to marry a fellow like Arthur. How could she prefer him to the other admirers she certainly had, particularly himself, Robert Thompson?

As the spring wore on it seemed as if the rumblings of war would indeed erupt in America. Newspapers were eagerly sought for these days; hopes rose and fell, but on 12th April war broke out. America was in a state of Civil War. The news reached Belfast soon enough to create despair in many hearts. Groups of businessmen congregated in Bedford Street and outside the Linen Halls, worried men every single one of them. Rumours and crumbs of gossip spread around the trade, but nothing to bring comfort to the big firms or to the small one-man businesses. The weeks went by and the news was black and still blacker.

John Thompson met Albert Meekin. "This is a bad business in America," he commented, understating the case.

Albert shook his head sadly. "Aye. It could be the finish of us all. There's no knowing what'll happen. Cotton is in as in a bad a way as the linen, maybe even worse."

Another day, John met George McCrum. He had taken a post with a cotton firm after Aspinalls' had closed down, and had then thought himself lucky and improved in his prospects. He was now in complete despair.

"Ach, we're finished!" he sighed gloomily. "It's the end of us all. My employer looks to be wiped out. I just don't know what to do now. There's maybe nothing for it but to emigrate to Australia."

In this setting of gloom John Thompson had a further worry to contend with. Arthur Storey had arrived at the warehouse, a month, to the day, looking for his hundred pounds. John had to inform him, firmly, that it was now impossible to think of discharging this debt, until it could be found how things were going in America.

"I'm quite solvent, you know," he told Arthur, "but I'm owed a lot of money by my American customers. Payment hasn't come and I mightn't see a penny until the war is over."

"I hear things is very bad in the linen and cotton," Arthur remarked coldly. "Some of the firms think they mightn't survive."

"Well, we must just hope for the best."

"I'll tell you how it is, Mr Thompson," Arthur said, very deliberately, taking his sheaf of papers out of his pocket. "I think it would be best if I got the hundred pounds now. Things mightn't improve at all."

"I'm sorry, but it can't be done! There was no time limit on that agreement between us, you know. The interest has been regularly paid, and legally I'm under no compulsion to pay at this very moment."

Arthur's face flushed angrily. "Well, I've paid it! I've paid it all, the whole bloody hundred and fifty pounds to my grandad, and now you owe me your part."

"I'll be glad to acknowledge that debt, legally, before a lawyer," John said firmly. He wasn't going to let the young man bully him, or frighten him, as he was quite sure Arthur intended to do both things. Inwardly he didn't feel as calm as he sounded. Arthur was right: his little warehouse could be wiped out as well as the rest of the trade, but he would pay the debt, somehow, if he took until he was an old man.

Arthur sat silent for a moment, then in a honeyed tone he said, "You've taken me up wrong, Mr Thompson. "I've no notion of going to law. Sure aren't we too good friends for the like of that?" He laughed at the idea, then pursed his mouth and narrowed down his eyes.

"But I seem to remember, Mr Thompson, just before you started up here, the night the old aunt was took bad, wasn't there a lawyer brought to your house, and wasn't I asked to witness a legal document?"

"That's perfectly correct."

"And the rumour got around that it was young Robert that was left the old lady's money. If that's the case, wouldn't that money be lying safe and sound in the bank, waiting for him to grow up?"

"That is, in fact, the case," John replied stiffly.

"Well, now, there's no need for us to say anything more about the hundred pounds. All I need is a wee paper saying that if I don't get my money before Robert is of age, I'll get paid out of his inheritance. Isn't that simple?"

"It's not my money. It's Robert's, and his to do as he likes with it, when he's twenty-one."

"Well it's that, or some other security I want, Mr Thompson." Arthur looked round the dingy office, and through the door to the warehouse. "I don't see much signs of a thriving business here that could give me that security."

John Thompson had to agree, reluctantly, in his own mind, that he had no security at all. Robert's money was the only way out.

"Very well," he told Arthur. "I'll speak to Robert about this matter and obtain his consent. I don't know if it's legal to do such a thing, though. A lawyer should be able to tell us."

"Now all I want is a wee paper saying that I'll get my money on or before the date of Robert's twenty-first birthday. There's no need to go into too much detail. Just that, and the rate of interest. My granda was generous, wasn't he. He didn't charge us much interest. I'll likely have to charge a bit more," and he sighed sadly.

John said nothing, but his heart sank. Arthur didn't miss an opportunity.

"I don't mind telling you that I was well able to send the money down to Antrim to Granda," Arthur said complacently. "Now that you owe it to me, it will be like having money invested. I haven't done too badly, now have I, Mr Thompson? There's not many young fellas my age could have done as well."

"You've been lucky, Arthur," John cautioned, "and I pray God you may always be as lucky. You mightn't have been just so prosperous if some calamity had struck, for instance if the harvests failed and there was a shortage of flour."

It was ungenerous of him to say such a thing, and he knew it was, but he could not resist taking a peg out of the complacency and boasting of this young man.

When Arthur left, with a promise to come back in a few days to make final the details of the renewed loan, John sat in the gloom, in the depths of despair. He was ruined. What was he going to do now? How would he ever pay the interest on the loan, never mind earn a living for his family? Thank God that at least Robert was well found in his apprenticeship, and the few shillings he earned would be useful.

In another year Robert would be out of his apprenticeship and would earn more money. But then, what if Stuart & Mount's did not survive either? What was to become of them all?

In a mood of hopelessness he made his way home, and sat, unspeaking, staring at the supper Martha placed before him on the table. She said nothing until the table was cleared and Jane was sent to bed, and alone in the room—with Robert at a Bible class—she put her hand on her husband's arm.

"What's wrong, John?" she asked gently, and when he didn't reply, she went on, "Now you must tell me, share your trouble with me, it's too much for you on your own."

"It's nothing, Martha. It's just business worry."

"But tell me, John, tell me! Oh, I know you never like talking about your affairs, and I never pry, you know that, never once in all the years. But now there's something big troubling you and I must know. Talking helps."

John turned sad eyes towards her, and in a trembling voice told her, "Martha, we're ruined." He told her all that had happened, how the war had affected business, and how Arthur was now wanting his money. Martha listened patiently, without a word of interruption

"Well, it's not too bad, John," she said when he had finished. "Sure I thought it was some calamity! Robert will agree to giving his money, if it comes to that, and for the other bit, about business being bad, sure man dear, where's your faith? We must trust in God to take care of us and everything will be all right. Isn't it just like a time in the country when the harvest fails, and the poor farmer thinks he's lost, but something turns up, and he never dies a winter from starvation. Come on, John, it'll be all right! We'll pray hard for it."

Her advice rallied him, and he agreed that prayer was their best way of solving the problem, and somehow, now that he had talked to Martha about it, the whole position didn't seem just so black. It would be hard, no doubt, for him to turn his hand to some other trade.

Linen and cotton were the only things he knew, but Belfast had other industries: there was the shipbuilding, and the ropemaking and engineering firms all doing well. Even though he was a man of over forty years of age, and over-old for new skills, it would not be for the want of trying. He patted her hand, an unusual gesture of affection for him.

"You're right, Martha! We must trust in God! We'll pray hard, and the Lord will not fail us."

Robert was inwardly fuming when he was told of the plan to sign away his money, and although he did not think of refusing, did not dare in fact, his resentment was triggered mostly by the fact that it was Arthur Storey who was responsible for this. He had never thought much about his money before. He knew, in a vague sort of way, that it would be there for him, but not for many years yet, and a fourpenny silver piece in his pocket was more to his present needs. He wouldn't have known what to do with his inheritance if it had been handed to him, but from the moment his father explained the need of it as security for possible repayment to Arthur Storey, Robert felt robbed. Arthur was the villain. He took the girl Robert wanted to marry, and now he wanted the money. In Robert's eyes there was no depth to which Arthur could not sink in villainy. Arthur was his enemy.

He didn't know what his father thought about Arthur Storey for although it had been frankly told to Robert the circumstances of using his money as security, John Thompson allowed no hint to escape him that he, too, had come to dislike Arthur Storey, and had come to distrust him as well. In his eyes, anyone so fond of money as Arthur now was would not be too particular how it was made.

It was not surprising then that there was little or no enthusiasm in the Thompson household when Arthur and Mary got married soon after the legal document of security was signed. It was as much as Mrs Thompson could bring herself to do to express hope to Mrs McKenna that Mary would be happy. Mrs McKenna was greatly upset and came round to unburden herself to her friend. Though she had known of Arthur's intention to marry Mary, and of Mary's fondness for him, she did not approve of the match.

"I don't like him," she told Mrs Thompson, "and I don't think she'll be happy with him. For 'by that, the religion is a barrier."

"Now you never know, it might turn out all right," Mrs Thompson said soothingly.

"Aye, maybe they will, and maybe they won't. He's wild about her, he says, but he likes things done his way. When he says 'jump' she'll have to jump, and though likely he's doing well in his business, I'd as soon see her with a man that's not so strong willed. My Mary's too soft! She wanted married in her own church, but he wouldn't agree. It seems that the furthest she ever got him was to sit a while at the evening devotions in St. Mary's. That was the most he would do, and I suppose for him it was something, seeing he always vowed he'd never put foot in a Catholic church."

"Wasn't it St. Anne's they were married in?"

"Aye! Just fancy, a Catholic and a Methodist getting married in the Church of Ireland!"

"But was it all right, I mean did the priest not mind?" Mrs Thompson asked diffidently.

"No he didn't mind, though he didn't like it! Catholics is allowed to get married in any church, so long as it is a church and not a register office. She should have held out, though."

From Mrs Storey, who came for condolence, Mrs Thompson heard a different tale, that her Arthur was throwing himself away on a girl that was only a stitcher and that / when he could have had plenty of ladies to marry. And what, she demanded, were they going to say in Antrim when they heard? How would she face them down there, them that didn't like Roman Catholics?

"I hear they were married in St. Anne's."

"Well at least he had the good sense not to put his foot in the

Roman Catholic chapel, for if he had, I swear to my God his da and me would have disowned him!"

Mrs Thompson surmised that such a fate would scarcely deter Arthur, though she was too polite to say so. She would have loved to inform Mrs Storey that her son had, in fact, put his foot in a Catholic church, but thought it well to sow the seeds of peace, for Mary's sake.

She bustled about the kitchen with a duster in her hand, as a civil hint for Mrs Storey to take herself off. She wished Mary well but found that it took all her Christian charity to do the same for Arthur.

"Well, Mrs Storey," she said, "I have a very high regard for both Mary, and for her mother too. It's a great pity of that poor woman, losing her man to the sea, and now her only son away too, and the dear knows where he is, maybe in the midst of this war in America."

"And isn't my darling boy on the high seas too?" Mrs Storey demanded, sinking into the corner chair and wiping her eyes with her sleeve. "Sure not a word have I heard since he went off a month ago. And now my only other boy's away and got himself married and moved to a new house away from me."

"Now don't be upsetting yourself, missus." Martha was firm. "What we should all do is to pray for the both boys, neighbours from the same street in the same town, and you may be quite sure, Mrs Storey, that the God in Heaven above is not going to wonder whether it's a Catholic, Presbyterian or Methodist that's doing the praying: He listens to us all!"

When Mrs Storey had gone, Martha preened herself as she thought of the encounter, and hoped that her pointed remarks would be taken to heart. She was praying very hard herself these days, but mostly for the affairs of the Thompson family, and she had faith that things would turn out for the best for them all, although she was probably the only person in Belfast that had any hope at all of the linen industry surviving.

The weeks went by, black weeks without any rays of hope, and as the war in America raged and the campaigns in the South of the country cut off the supply of raw cotton, the industry was brought to a standstill for the want of material. But then slowly the fact emerged, and was strengthened in the weeks of improved trade, that linen was going to be stronger as a result of the failure of cotton. The demand from the English and Scottish markets grew steadily from a trickle, and soon the mills, factories and warehouses were humming with activity.

John Thompson could scarcely believe it, and cautiously at first allowed himself slight hope for the first time in many months, but as orders flowed in, his little warehouse could not cope and he had to take on several girls and a second storeman. George McCrum was taken on to help with the office work and to leave John free for supervising the preparing and shipping of the orders.

Martha saw little of him these days. It was work, early and late for him and for Robert too, but she didn't mind. She was happy that their prayers had been answered and was unshakable in her conviction that it was her prayers that turned the tide and brought prosperity to the Thompson warehouse anyhow. Of the other firms she could not say: like as not someone else had been praying for them.

The old year slipped into a new one, and in the mighty struggles between the people of America the reactions in Ireland were keenly felt. Nearly every family in Ireland had relations in America, and there was great anxiety to know how "our ones" were getting on, especially those living in the war-torn Southern States.

Blood flowed in the battles, but into Belfast and the linen trade flowed gold, as the boom continued and every mill, factory and warehouse worked at full capacity. Fields of flax were sown as speculation, in the hope of the war going on, and the cotton famine lasting. Fortunes were made by shrewd speculators, quick to take advantage of the situation.

For the mill hands and the factory workers and the warehouse workers there were jobs for all, and good prospects of things staying that way, but there were no fortunes made by the workers. Their boon and their boom was in having work. Wages were meagre and left little for more than the necessities. They had to be thankful that things were so well with them. Weren't they in employment unlike the cotton workers, reduced to destitution by the famine of raw cotton. This was in contrast with the cotton weavers in Lancashire where there was terrible distress, and riots in protest against starvation.

In Ballymacarret, to come nearer home, cotton weavers were starving too. Newtownards was the same, and Lisburn was one of the hardest hit, with frightful distress among the hand-loom weavers of plain muslin and the embroidery workers. The poor souls existed on cabbage and stirabout, until a fund was set up to relieve their plight. Families emigrated to Australia, others sought work in the now successful linen trade or in some of the new engineering works that abounded, but for those who were too old to start a new life, funds were collected and administered by the charitably inclined.

John Thompson read of these events to Martha from his newspaper on one of his infrequent early nights home from his warehouse. She was full of sympathy with the poor people in their desperate plight.

"God help them, what's to become of them?"

"It's bad for them, and for the Lancashire weavers too. If anything, it's worse for them in Lancashire. They were always used to more, and they feel the destitution all the keener. Our people never had such a high standard of living or as much to eat as the English people. Over here they can exist on cabbage and stirabout, but I think in England they had got used to butcher's meat and good bread. We were never as well fed here as the people in England."

"It's the wee childer I think of," Martha sighed, her eyes full of tears.

"And the old folk. They're worst off. Many of them are too

proud to take help from the committee giving out the money from the fund. They say they never took charity before and they won't take it now."

"It's hard to understand, isn't it, John?"

"What is?" he asked gently.

"That a war in a country so far away should bring want and misery to so many people here. Aye, it's hard to understand!"

CHAPTER NINE

It would soon be the end of Robert's five-year apprenticeship, and as the time drew near he got worried and apprehensive lest his father should suddenly demand that he leave Stuart & Mounts now that he was a journeyman, and come into his business. On the other hand, of course, there was the chance that Mr Stuart might not wish to keep him on, and that he would be handed his dismissal along with his indentures. He didn't want to leave Stuart & Mounts: his friends were there, and all his interests. The thought of exchanging the busy bustling mill and warehouse with its hundreds of workers for the comparative quiet of his father's dozen or so workers in the small warehouse filled him with gloom. There was this business of his money that had somehow been signed over as security to Arthur Storey. Robert felt that he would be bound in some way—he hardly knew how—to go in with his father on this account. He waited each day now for the summons to the Private Office to receive his indentures and to learn his fate.

John Thompson had no intention of bringing Robert into the business at this stage, unless of course his services were no longer required at Stuart & Mounts, a most unlikely happening in view of the busy state of trade and the need for as many experienced journeymen as possible. He was still a little nervous about his business, since his clash with Arthur Storey, and wanted re-assuring that business was going to stay as good as it was. Wait until this war in America was over: what would happen then? If trade was depressed again, would it not be far better for Robert to be in a good position than in the struggling firm with his father?

Typically, John made no explanations to Robert, but on the day that the apprenticeship was due to end, he told him briefly that if asked by Mr Stuart to stay on as a journeyman, he should do so, that it would be good experience for him. Robert waited, daily, for the summons to Mr Stuart's office, but two weeks after the apprenticeship ended he still had not been called. He discussed his chances with Charley Gourley and Johnny McIlhagga.

"What do you think?" he asked them.

"Aye, certainly, sure they'd be mad to let a fellow go and us so busy," Gourley comforted.

"And I'll tell you one thing," McIlhagga put in, "when they made our friend Charley here a journeyman and kept him on, they're sure to want another fool to keep him company. Don't worry, Thompson, they'll feel sorry for you, too!"

"Funny man! You weren't so sure yourself, last year," taunted Gourley. "Do you mind, Robbie, wasn't he near jumping in the Lagan for fear he wouldn't get kept?"

Robert was slightly cheered by his friends, and inside a few days his summons came. Mr Stuart wished to see Robert Thompson in the Private Office. It was the same panelled office where Robert had sat, on the edge of a chair, five years previously, and now, sitting more firmly on his seat on the other side of the Governor's broad desk, he blushed to think of the raw youth he had seen then and the silly answers he had made to Mr Stuart about the linen trade.

"Sit down, Robert," the old man said kindly, and rubbed a hand over his eyes in a gesture of weariness. He shuffled through a pile of papers in front of him and drew out the deed of indenture.

"Here we are, your indenture, all duly signed! You're a journeyman now. We nearly overlooked this with all the rush and fuss of the business we're getting. Well now, the five years went quickly enough I'm sure, and no doubt you know now where linen comes from." He chuckled indulgently. "First time a young fellow asked me that one!" He beamed at Robert kindly.

Robert thanked him formally and smiled back. He had always, in his five years, felt himself a favourite with Mr Stuart, and had got many a smile and encouraging word from him, where the other apprentices had complained of stern looks and forbidding glances. Why he should be a favourite, Robert didn't know, but Mr Stuart undoubtedly had a soft spot for him. Perhaps Robert had impressed himself at that first interview as a boy who wanted to know something of the business he was being apprenticed to.

"Well, now!" said Mr Stuart. "What are we going to do with our new journeyman, eh?"

"I'd like to stay on," Robert replied. "That is, if you'll let me."

The old man looked at him, in wonder. "Do you know, I was quite sure your father would want you to go in with him. He is getting his share?" he asked politely, as a giant to a moth, which the firm of Stuart & Mount was to the small establishment of John Thompson.

"Oh, yes, he's getting a share all right," Robert assured him, "but he said that if you wanted me to stay on, I could, that it would be good experience for me."

His heart thumped. Was he not going to be kept? Would he have to go to his father's small, dull warehouse, be in his father's forbidding company all day, under a disapproving, critical eye?

Mr Stuart pursed his lips, and nodded his head slowly. "Do you know," he mused, "I would have thought your father would have taken you. He's a wise man, though, with much more foresight than I would have credited him! Few men would have made such a decision."

Robert swallowed hard, and waited.

Mr Stuart turned slightly in his chair, to glance behind him at the portrait on the wall of his father, the founder of the firm, a much-whiskered old gentleman, flanked by drawings of the mill and the factory, as they had been many years previously.

"You know, my late father used to say to me when I was a lad of about your age, that someday the warehousing end of the business would be very important. I never agreed with him, but now, sometimes, I wonder ... when the war in America is over ... what turn the trade will take."

"No sign of it going over yet," Robert ventured.

"Indeed no, and we can hardly hope it will end, it's been such a good thing for Belfast." He paused and shook his head, as though thinking deeply. Robert wished he would hurry up and give a decision.

At last, Mr Stuart came out of his deep study and smiled genially at Robert.

"We'll be glad to have you with us, young Thompson. You'll be a useful man for us, and you'll find that Mr Meekin will have plenty of work for you. In time you may be called upon to make journeys and represent the firm in England, and it will all be good training for you. And who knows," he added reflectively, "when the war is over in America, it might be necessary for some bright, young fellow to get out there and pick up the threads for us again."

Robert was delighted, and thanking Mr Stuart properly, he eagerly rushed to tell his friends the good news, and when he got home he waited impatiently for his father to come, to put the signed indenture in his hand, and to recount what Mr Stuart had said.

John Thompson said little as he read the indenture, although Martha was sentimental with tears in her eyes as she surveyed her tall, handsome big man of a son. She could hardly believe that Robert was nineteen and had served his apprenticeship. It seemed such a short time since he had gone off, in his new suit, to start work. She did not suspect her husband's thoughts and would have been surprised how he interpreted Mr Stuart's remarks.

"Clever and subtle," was how John Thompson read it, and how he could read the effect on Robert. The boy was flattered and would be led on by hopes of travelling to England, and even maybe to America, someday, in the future. By this invisible thread could Mr Stuart keep Robert in his firm, while the boy's own father was frightened and unsure of what the future might hold for his small firm. He could only hope and pray that someday he would get out from under the load of debt to Arthur Storey, and that the linen trade would continue.

Mrs Thompson had more tears to blink back when Jane started school, a chubby five-year-old, in her starched white pinafore, with her black boots well cleaned, and her hair tied back in a ribbon. Her education at the Model School had started.

Alice Storey took on the task of bringing Jane to and from school for the first week, and Jane would set off, her hand clutched trustingly in Alice's, and reluctant to part from her friend at the door of the Model School.

Alice had decided to leave school and was supposed to be helping her Ma with the housework, but most of her time was spent between Thompsons' with Jane, and up at the bakery in Amon Street, where she watched the bakers coming and going with their baskets. She kept Mary back from her work with her idle chatter. It wasn't necessary for Alice to think of any occupation, and she had a carefree existence doing a bit of scrubbing and polishing when she felt in the mood and in visiting her friends and neighbours in her shy, unobtrusive way, but managing to hear most of the neighbourhood gossip.

She was still her father's pet, and could coax him successfully to her own way, whether it was for a new bonnet, or a dress, or to sit up late when her ma had told her to be off with her to her bed. Alice loved going for a walk, out beyond the streets and avenues to the fields, and she was able to wheedle her da to bring her when all her ma's declarations that what the man needed was good fresh air after all that stuff getting into his lungs in the bakehouse would fail.

"Come a walk with me, Pa," she would plead, her big blue eyes sad, and her long fair hair sweeping over her face.

"Sure I have to be at my work," he would protest, but Alice knew that he had plenty of time, after his daily sleep, and before he went to the bakery. She would bring his boots and kneel down and try them on his feet, smiling up at him in her appealing way. He could not resist.

"All right, pet," he would say, good-natured. "I'll have no peace, I suppose. Are you bringing wee Jane Thompson today again?"

Jane usually made up the trio, and spring and summer evenings saw the pale-faced baker and the two girls strolling leisurely on the country roads beyond the Ormeau Bridge, or up at Malone. Once they walked as far as Edenderry Village on the Crumlin Road, along the lanes whitened by the lime from the quarries up in the mountains, spilled out of the carts drawing their loads towards the bleach greens. The girls would bring back little posies of wild flowers, buttercups, meadow-sweet, or the sweet-jane from the boggy fields, tight little bunches held in hot hands and fading before home was reached. They had a walk one evening to the docks to see the ships, and Alice told Jane about the day that she and Alfie—and Robert—had missed going to church to look at the ships.

"We never thought of the time," Alice told the child dramatically, "and the first thing we knew the people was all coming out of the churches, and we'd never been in at all! I can tell you we flew home like the wind, and Robert thought his da would be angry, but what do you think happened?"

"What?" Jane asked, her eyes wide.

"That was the day you were born. The doctor came that very day and brought you."

"And was Robert not beat? Was Alfie and you?"

"We weren't anyhow," Alice said, "for Alfie met a wee boy that was at the Sunday school that morning and he knew the Bible stories that were told and the hymns that were sung, and Alfie told it all to my ma, just as if we were there, and she never knew."

"What did my da say?" Jane demanded.

"Sure I don't know. Maybe he never knew, with all the excitement of you coming. But you wouldn't remember, you were only a wee ba. And I'm sure you didn't mind going on the holiday to your Aunt's house. Oh, it was lovely! And we all went in a gentleman's carriage, and me and Robert played all the time. Robert was kind to me," she added softly.

"Did Alfie not go?"

"No, your ma didn't want him to. Sure he was wanting even then to sail away in a ship. He was always mad about ships, and my ma says now she wishes she knew he was safe and sound in one. She sits and cries about him, for we never heard news of him and he might be in the war in America."

Mr Storey had been talking to a boatman while this talk was going on, and he now rejoined the girls.

"How would you like a wee trip over to the Twin Islands one day, pet?" he asked.

Alice clapped her hands. "Oh, PA, take us now!"

"No, but maybe we'll go the first free night I can get, and we'll bring your ma. You ask your ma, Jane, if you can come on a sea trip with us."

"Will I get home again?" Jane asked, in astonishment.

"Aye, I'm sure we will, if we're all good sailors," he laughed.

When she got home, Jane reported to her mother, "Mr Storey is taking Alice and me on a ship. We're going to the Twin Islands."

"Are you indeed!" Mrs Thompson retorted. "We'll see what your da has to say. You're getting the brave bit of gallivanting about for the size of you."

It was Dargan's Island, as it used to be called in Mrs Thompson's early days, that Mr Storey proposed taking the girls to, and a few weeks later Jane set off, in a state of great excitement, in her best dress and pinny, and her new black button boots. Alice's eyes were shining and she promised to keep hold of Jane's hand, and to watch over her in the boat. Mrs Storey decided not to go on the outing; she felt low in spirits, she said, and anyhow she had been several times and saw all that was to be seen.

Mrs Thompson watched the two girls anxiously as they raced down College Place to meet Mr Storey. Jane was a very determined child when she wanted her own way, and it was her mother's fear that she might want to lean out of the rowing boat, or go too close to the edge of the quay and fall into the water. It was an anxious afternoon for her until the girls came back, and Alice stepped in to tell of the wonderful adventure.

"Oh, it was great, Mrs Thompson," she exclaimed breathlessly, her eyes sparkling. "First of all we went down to the quay, and got into the rowing boat. It costs a whole penny for each of us to get rowed over to the island."

"Was it rough?" asked Robert, sitting sprawled in his father's chair in the corner of the kitchen, listening indulgently in a big-brother fashion to the prattle of the returned travellers.

"It was," declared Jane, "and Alice's new hat near blew off into the water."

"It's a lovely hat," Robert remarked, eyeing the straw bonnet with pink and blue flowers and ribbons as trimmings. "It would have been a great pity to get a hat like that all wet."

"Mr Storey said it was the quarest looking hat he ever did see," Jane said, and a twinkle came into her eyes as she added in a lower tone of voice, "He said he supposed if it was the fashion the girls would wear it."

"Jane!" her mother exclaimed, giving her arm a sharp slap. "Don't you be vulgar."

"Well, he did say it! Didn't he, Alice?"

Alice blushed with embarrassment, and whispered "Yes" in a soft, shy voice.

Robert said hastily, "What did you do when you got to the island?"

"Ah, it was lovely," Alice told him. "I wish you had been with us, Robbie. There's a big high house, all made of glass, and there's quare looking birds in it, and fishes in water, and big tall trees that reaches up to the glass roof."

"And Mr Storey bought us sweets. Me honeycomb, and Alice got yellow-man," Jane added firmly.

"Trust you to remember what you got to eat!" her mother declared, then added, "It's time you were in your bed, and you'd better go on home, Alice love. It was very kind of your da to take our Jane on the outing, and I hope she minded her manners and said thanks."

"I did!"

"Well, it's nice for you. Goodnight, Alice, pet."

"Goodnight, Alice," Robert said, and when she had gone out of the front door he remarked, "Isn't Alice getting very good-looking? And I never heard her talking as much before."

His mother gave him a sharp look, but said nothing. Jane opined, "Alice talks to me, but when she's in her own house she never talks, because her ma does all the talking."

She got another slap. "You're a forward wee hussy!" Mrs Thompson snapped. "And you've far too much to say for the size of you!"

Jane whimpered and went over to lay her head on Robert's lap. "I'm not forward," she answered. "Alice likes me, so she does, and she likes Robbie, too, for she told me."

"Pay no heed to her Robert! Come on out of that, and stop your growling and answering back, or I'll put you in the Coal-hole! "Mrs Thompson led the child, sobbing tiredly, up the stairs. Her boots were unbuttoned and her dress dragged off, and in a few moments she was ready for bed and tucked in, sucking her thumb and sobbing to herself.

Robert was still sitting in the corner, with a faraway look on his face, when his mother came downstairs, and sank into her chair wearily, picking up her knitting to keep her fingers busy as she talked.

"That child's tired out. It's been a long day for the wean, and very exciting, going out in a boat to the Twin Islands."

"Well, she's been further afield than ever I was," Robert groused. "I never got the length of going in a rowing boat on the River Lagan, never mind seeing what Dargan's Island looks like."

"No more did I, and I'm a lot older," said Mrs Thompson. "You've neither both of you, Jane and you, got further nor me."

"What, me!" Robert retorted indignantly. "Sure where did I ever get to but to my work?"

"For one thing, you were on a train, and you've seen more of the town here, and the hills and mountains round it than ever I have. Here's me, getting on for an old woman," and she pointed a knitting needle at him, "and I can tell you that I never was in any kind of a conveyance in my life, other than a country cart, until the time Mr Aspinall sent his carriage and horses to take us up to my Aunt Agnes's in the Kills."

"Were you never even in a sedan chair?" Robert asked incredulously.

"What! A sedan chair," and Mrs Thompson laughed. "I'm not getting any younger, I know, but I'm not that old! Sure there hasn't been a sedan chair in the streets of Belfast for over sixty years now, maybe longer for all I know."

There was silence for a few moments, and Robert sat swinging his foot idly; then he poked the fire in the hoc grate to a small flame, and sat, hunched up, gazing at the spurting tongues of flame and sparks that his poking had produced.

"You'll poke that fire out," his mother commented, "and I need the kettle to boil."

"Do you know what I'd like to do?" he asked her suddenly. "I'd love to travel about, maybe in the train, or on a stagecoach, and see what the rest of Ireland is like." He didn't wait for his mother to reply, but went on enthusiastically: "And I'd love to go in a ship and see foreign lands, like Alfie, and James McKenna. It's well for them."

"Is it indeed! And how do you know whether it's well for them or not? Sure the pair of them might be lying dead at the bottom of the ocean, or maybe they might be fighting in the American war and getting themselves killed."

"Well ... it would be great to be in the war, anyhow."

Mrs Thompson sighed deeply and impatiently. "War is a terrible thing, son dear. Oh, I know you think it's all excitement, and bands and soldiers in fine suits, but do you not read the paper, or hear your da reading out the bits about the thousands of men that's getting killed out in America, and the houses that's destroyed, and the poor women and children suffering? And haven't you only to look round you in the streets here in Belfast, at the poor creatures maimed in the Crimea War? That's what was done to them in a war, and now they're on the poor list, or begging ha'pence for their bite to eat."

"That's only some of them. A whole lot has nothing happen to them."

She put down her knitting and gazed anxiously into his face. "It's always the same. More people gets hurt and killed than the soldiers that are fighting. Sure it was the same here, in the old days. I mind hearing the talk at home, up in the Hills, round the fire of a winter night, and you get the old folks started talking. They'd tell you what it was like, after the Battle of Ballynahinch that the United Irishmen was fighting. They lost the battle with the soldiers, and it was God help the whole countryside then, with houses burned and looted, and women with wee childer, and poor oul' decrepit creatures flying for their lives in what they stood up in. And that's what happened the innocent ones that wasn't even in the fighting. The ones that was in it and was caught by the soldiers was hung, or thrown in jail. Aye, many a poor fellow was sent off to the ends of the earth, transported."

"Ach, Ma," Robert muttered irascibly. "Sure that was all in the old days! I'm tired hearing all about that. What I want is for something exciting to happen now. Nothing exciting ever happens in this house."

"The trouble with you, Robert Thompson, is that you're too well walked! That's what's wrong with you! If you had more to worry you than sitting doing nothing you'd thank God you had a good home, and plenty of good food to eat, and your steady work to go to."

Robert scowled, but didn't reply.

"I'll tell you what I'd like," his mother said, in a softer tone. "I've no notion of travelling far, or gallivanting off in trains or stage-coaches. It would be the fiddle of my heart to live in the country again, away from all the smoke and noise of the town. Wouldn't it be lovely!".

"That's what I missed most, when first I came to the town, when I married your da," she went on. "I used to think the bricks and mortar was going to fall on the top of me. And foreby, wouldn't the good country air benefit us all. Do you know, son dear, I've a dread on me this past while when I hear people talking about the smallpox. There isn't the same risk of getting it in the country."

"Charlie Gourley had it when he was a wee lad, and he lived in the country," Robert remarked dully. "He told me his ma sat beside him, near all the time, and wiped off the wee poxes from his face with a feather dipped in oil. You'd never think to look at him that he ever had the smallpox. There's not a mark on him."

"No, maybe not ... but I still think the country air is a deal healthier to people. All this smoke and dust couldn't be good for people."

Mrs Thompson sat knitting for a while longer. Robert took a book and sat quietly reading. The house was still, and the clock's tick was loud. Presently her husband would be home from his work, really tired, but maybe not hungry for his supper. It wasn't easy these days, Martha Thompson thought to herself; her husband working himself nearly to death, her son moody and discontented, and herself ... well she hardly knew what ailed herself. She did yearn for the open countryside and seemed to more and more recently. She thought a lot these days about her own people up in the Hills, and she wished again, as she had done many times in the past years, that the unpleasantness with her brother George over Aunt Agnes's money had never happened.

She would dearly love to heal the breach between George and herself, and be on the old footing again, with him calling in on market day for a bite to eat, and to tell her all the news of the countryside. Recently, unknown to anyone, she had walked round the markets now and then on a morning, in the hope of seeing George, or maybe even Danny, and by a casual greeting, make friends again. She had met one of the old neighbours and he, greeting her from the top of a pile of cabbages on his farm cart, had given her the news that Danny was married and lived in Aunt Agnes's old place. She had nodded, as if this was no news to her. "Likely he'll be round someday," she had shouted back, "but when you see him, tell him I'm expecting him." The neighbour nodded, but she saw from his expression that he knew how things were and that there was no friendship with George or Danny.

Next morning, Robert was rushing out to work, late for the eight o'clock start at the mill. As he opened the front door he almost knocked down Alice Storey, standing breathless on the step.

"Oh, Robbie!" she gasped. "We've news, good news, of our Alfie," and she proceeded to tell him that Alfie's friend of the Liverpool boat was at that moment in Storey's house. Alfie had met him in Liverpool, and charged him to call in at Killen Street with the news that he was safe and would soon be home.

"My ma's that pleased," Alice sighed. "She's giving this fellow a tea breakfast, and I'm to go to oul' Wilson for bacon, but I just thought I'd let you know."

"I'm glad of the news," Robert said, "but what about James McKenna? Is there no word of him?"

"Oh, he's all right, too."

"Well, I'm sure his ma will be the happy woman to hear it. Have you told her yet?"

Alice tossed her head. "I have not! Sure she'll hear it sometime or other. My ma says she wouldn't please her!"

Robert caught her by the shoulders.

"Oh, Alice, how could you! Is Mrs McKenna not worrying her heart out for news? You should tell her."

To his surprise Alice's face fell, and her lip trembled. Tears came into her big blue eyes and rolled down her cheeks. "Ah, Robbie, are you cross with me? Are you offended?"

"I will be, if you don't tell Mrs McKenna that James is safe and well. Do it now, before you go to Wilson's for the bacon.'"

"I will, I will! I'll go now. But don't be cross with me, Robbie."

"I'm not cross," he said gently, "but I would be, if you did a mean thing like that. I'm late, Alice. I'll have to go to my work," and to his own surprise he patted her cheeks, and urged her to dry her tears. He was puzzled by this incident. Alice's quick reaction to his disapproval, with her tears and crestfallen face, stirred in him a wish to pet and comfort her. And yet, he told himself, she was only a child. He dismissed his misgivings and thought longingly of seeing Alfie again—and James McKenna, too—and hearing their exciting adventures.

It would be something to look forward to.

The news of Alfie and James went round the neighbours like wildfire, and both houses had callers to discuss the news of the two sailors and to ask questions of their adventures that only they could answer when they got home to Belfast.

Mrs Thompson hurried round the corner and found Mrs McKenna sitting at her white-scrubbed table, with a pile of white linen to be stitched in front of her.

"Is it yourself?" she said, smiling when she saw her friend. "Come on in. You'll excuse me keeping at my stitching, but it takes me all my time at it to get the rent money. It'd pull the eyes out of you, but it has to be done."

"Good news!" Mrs Thompson beamed. "Your James is safe and well, I hear."

Mrs McKenna held the white cloth to her eyes for a moment, then wiped a tear with the back of her hand.

"Aye, thank God and his blessed mother," she murmured. "My prayers is answered." She dabbed her eyes again and shook her head happily. "I took a wee race up to tell Mary."

"She was glad, I'm sure."

"Oh, indeed! But did you know that wee Alice Storey was the one to bring me the news? She raced round first thing to tell me. You know, I've misjudged that wee girl! I didn't think she had it in her to be so thoughtful. It's more than her ma would do. She's never forgave me, you know, because our Mary married her big son."

"He was a lucky man to get her!" Mrs Thompson exclaimed. "I'm sure it's himself knows it, too."

Mrs McKenna's brows puckered. "Och, times you wouldn't know whether our Mary is a bit happy or not," she said. "Oh, I suppose he's good enough to her, in his way, and she's not the girl to complain much." She leaned over and whispered to Mrs Thompson,

"I think he keeps her short."

"Of money?"

"Aye." Mrs McKenna nodded. "She has to write down every single thing she buys, in a wee book, and he adds it up at the end of the week, and he can always tell if they spend more one week than another. And you know he's plenty, for his bakery is getting bigger all the time. Maybe he thinks Mary would be slipping the odd shilling or two to help me that has just my sewing to keep me going. I don't know. And the oul' ma is never done running up to see him, and giving out advice and instructions to Mary as if the poor girl didn't know how to run her house. Mrs Storey of all people! Her that's the biggest clart you'd find in the streets and lamps of Belfast."

Mrs Thompson nodded sympathetically, then asked, with diffidence, "No sign of you being a grannie yet?"

"Divil the sign! Sure you might be a grannie before me!"

"You're joking. Me a grannie? And my Robert only a boy with no notion of looking at a girl."

"Divil the boy! You might think so, but he's the fine-looking young man, and there's many a head turned in his direction. I could name somebody we both know that thinks the world of him."

Mrs Thompson smiled and shook her head. She knew her Robert: whatever he was thinking of, it wasn't of getting married, of that she was sure.

The war in America dragged on. Prosperity in Belfast increased, and in John Thompson's little business, expansion followed expansion, with steady and increasing trade. His one goal had been to set aside the money to repay his loan to Arthur Storey, and each month he had added to the amount, as well as paid the interest.

Arthur called each quarter day to collect his interest, even though John had offered again and again to pay it through the bank.

"I like to call and see you, Mr Thompson," Arthur would always say. "You know, I favour your advice on any wee matters of business that might be vexing me."

Whatever these matters might be, John didn't know, for they were never mentioned, but he noticed that Arthur took a lively interest in all that was going on in the place.

By the month of July he had the money saved, the whole hundred pounds of it, and he looked forward with pleasure to handing it over to Arthur when he came on his next visit, unsuspecting that this one would be his last, and that John Thompson was sick of the sight of him putting his foot over the door.

Quietly and calmly John paid the interest due, then handed banknotes for £100 to Arthur.

"Here we are," he said. "It seems as good a time as any to give you this. I'd like a receipt marked, if you please, and you can send me your original agreement."

Arthur was taken aback.

"Now, what's this? Sure you know rightly, Mr Thompson, that I'm in no hurry at all. I'm not looking for payment. You shouldn't inconvenience yourself this way, Mr Thompson."

Firmly, John insisted, and Arthur had to take the money from him and write out a receipt.

"I'm sure you could have been doing with this a wee while longer," he said. "Do you not want to expand your business? I can see that you've a right thriving wee concern here, and I'd be in no way troubled to lend you even more money if you liked."

"I'd prefer to terminate the arrangement," John replied.

"Well..." Arthur looked displeased. "I must say, I'll miss the bit of interest on my wee investment. It's a grand thing having money out working for you, Mr Thompson. I'll have to look round and see if I can find another safe place to lend it out to."

John forbore to comment that it wasn't so pleasant to have to pay interest on such money. He wanted no argument, and no further dealings with Arthur Storey.

Arthur got up to leave. "And you'll not mind if I call round to see you from time to time?" he asked. "You know how I always looked forward to your advice on business. You have a good head for it, Mr Thompson. I rely on you for advice."

"Any time," John assured him, "but I think, to be honest, Arthur, that it's many a long day since you needed guidance from anyone. Don't let us delude ourselves with false humility. You could instruct your own grandfather, smart man that he is, and teach him a few lessons on the art of money-making."

"Now, you flatter me, Mr Thompson!" Arthur replied, but he flushed a little. "I'm just a poor baker trying to do a wee bit of business. But I must show you, though"—and he took out his sheaf of papers from his inner pocket—"had you any idea at all that the population of the town of Belfast had increased so much these past year or so? The people is flocking in, and it's not doing my trade a bit of harm. I've another two carts on the road, and three more boys working inside. I tell you, I'll have to think of expanding the bakery again and getting more ovens, if this keeps up."

He was preparing to read out the latest estimate of population in the town of Belfast, but John had his own work to do, and he had listened long enough to Arthur.

"I've some shipments to attend to," he declared, "so I must bid you good-day."

"Don't you fear, Mr Thompson, I'll not be a stranger. I'll be round again to see you, and if you do hear of any safe, sound investment, you'll maybe oblige me by letting me know."

John signed with relief when Arthur had gone. It was a great load off his mind to have the debt paid. Now, he could concentrate on consolidating his business and lying by a reserve in case of a slump when the American war would end. And another thing he had in mind was to move house. The time was coming, he felt, to move up a bit socially, and live in a better neighbourhood. College Place—for all its quiet position at the back of the select district of College Square with its doctors, and lawyers, and professional and business residents—was really only a back street. John had ambition. He hoped someday to live in a more select street, or avenue, in a good neighbourhood, as befitted a fairly prosperous linen merchant.

He made no mention of his hopes to his wife. Time enough to tell her about it when such a move was possible. He did tell her, though, that he was free of debt to Arthur Storey, and that Robert's money would be the boy's own when he became old enough to claim it. To Robert also the news was given, but it served only to renew his dislike of Arthur Storey, as though the baker had in some way attempted to rob him of his inheritance. Robert had still not forgiven him for marrying Mary McKenna. When he thought about it, he could still easily imagine himself in love with her, but the occasions of remembering became fewer.

John Thompson thought over Arthur's remarks about the increase in Belfast's population, and how lucky Arthur was to have so many potential customers pouring into the town almost daily. There was no doubt about it, the town was growing, and building was going on apace. Inside fifty years the number of people had increased by fifty thousand, and they all had to be housed, and—to Arthur's benefit—many of them bought bread already baked. Many of the older residents groused and grumbled about the building going on in the town. New warehouses and churches sprang up, and streets of houses appeared on the outskirts of the town and on waste ground inside the boundary.

"They'll never get enough people to live in all them houses," was a popular comment, but the houses got tenants, and the warehouses did good business. Day by day, Belfast was becoming more and more a big, prosperous town, and the magnet for country people to come and settle in it and get work.

The American Civil War and the prosperity of the linen trade that followed were partly responsible, but it was really the embarrassing financial position of the Donegall family that made the actual building in the town possible.

The titled Donegall family owned a lot of the land in Belfast. The castle in Ormeau Park was the seat of the Marquis of Donegall. The Black Man statue in College Square, which Alice had been frightened to pass in the dark as a child, had been erected to the memory of a popular member of the Donegall family by dutiful townsfolk.

They lost a lot of money, by various means, and had to sell some of their Belfast lands, but to do so, a special act of parliament had to be passed, to dis-entail the estate and allow the family to sell building ground. Up to now they had granted only short leases, and what man would chance building on a short lease? But now, the entail was broken; parcels of land in and around the town were sold, and a whole rash of red brick building broke out.

John Thompson thought it ironic that it took the disaster of a civil war and the financial embarrassment of a great family to put Belfast on its feet and give it a chance to grow. He didn't join in the rather contemptuous attitude of many people towards "these country ones, with the dung on their heels, coming into the town and doing well". He had sense enough to remember that it wasn't so long ago that he himself had arrived from the town of Lisburn to seek a livelihood in the big town, admittedly not with dung on his heels, but for all that a fairly raw country youth, eager to get his chance in the lamps of Belfast.

One evening in August, John was approached by Paddy Burke as he was supervising the packing of an order.

"Will this be in time for the boat tonight?" the storeman asked.

John replied that it should be, but that there was not so much urgency and the following night would still be in time for delivery in England, whence it was bound.

"We'll likely hold it and send another few cases down with it for tomorrow's steamboat," he told Paddy.

Paddy pushed his cap back and scratched his head thoughtfully.

"If you don't mind me saying it, sir, but I'd get it all away the night, aye, and as many others as you can," and as he caught Mr Thompson's enquiring and puzzled look, he added hesitantly, "I'd favour a word with you, in private sir, if you will excuse the liberty."

Wondering, John brought him into the little office and closed the door.

"What's wrong, Paddy? Is there trouble at home?"

Paddy shook his head.

"No, Mr Thompson sir, it's not that, but there's going to be trouble in the town—bad trouble. Did you not hear about the carry-on last night? There was a very unruly mob out, carrying a dummy of Daniel O'Connell, and they burnt it, so they did, and danced round the fire."

John listened patiently. It seemed that in Dublin, a few days previously, a ceremony was held to inaugurate a memorial to Daniel O'Connell.

"And you know how us Catholics feels about Daniel O'Connell!" Paddy exclaimed. "He was the king of Ireland to us, and he was the man that set us free and gave us the emancipation of our faith. And then them hallions up here, just out of pure bigotry, go and make a mock of it all. Could they not let the man rest in his grave and let a memorial be put up till him? But I seen it myself, Mr Thompson, I seen them, with their fifes and drums, parading the town last night in their thousands, jeering and mocking, and tossing up the dummy they had made up to look like Daniel O'Connell! Then they burnt it, and they danced round the fire like savages yelling and screaming! There's going to be trouble, Mr Thompson! That's why I have took the liberty of speaking out, for you've always been the one decent man to me, sir, and I want you to know what's going on and you'll be able to save some of your property."

"Things like this have happened before, Paddy," John told him. "You're maybe taking it all too seriously. It'll likely all blow over."

"Not this time, Mr Thompson! Don't I know what's going on in my own house, with young Peter as big a firebrand as any of them. They're not to be held down this time! There's talk of wrecking the town, and you should get all the goods you can away in the boat, sir!"

John thought the storeman needlessly alarmed. He had heard something of the previous evening's parade, and had judged it unfair to allow such deliberate provocation. After all, Daniel O'Connell had been the idol of the Roman Catholics: he had won them emancipation from the religious restrictions imposed upon them. It was ill-done of the Belfast mill workers to taunt their own townsfolk because a memorial to O'Connell was going to be erected in Dublin.

Paddy might be right, though: there could be trouble. Perhaps it would be wise to work late and get away to the cross-channel ship as many completed orders as possible. There had been riots in the town only last month, John remembered suddenly, following the Twelfth of July procession of Orangemen. There had been the usual skirmishes of stone-throwing between the Orangemen and the Catholics of the Pound district, and some of the rioters had appeared in court and had been fined, while others were jailed for riotous assembly and stone-throwing.

John was inclined, the more he thought of it all, to scoff at Paddy Burke's alarm, although it was very much in the interests of the business that the storeman had spoken up, and not from any motive of personal safety.

Within twenty-four hours, Paddy was proved right. A gang of about five hundred navvies assembled near St. Malachy's Catholic Church, and marched through the town, wrecking as they went. They got as far as Brown Square, at the foot of the Shankill Road, sweeping through the streets breaking windows and scattering frightened townspeople before them. At Brown Square a battle raged with policemen from the barracks, and the rioters were chased back.

A reign of terror began for Belfast. The Islandmen—the shipyard workers from the Queen's Island—took a hand, and clashed with the navvies in a stone-throwing battle at St. Malachy's Church. Incidents multiplied, as riotous mobs gathered in the town, and before long the Riot Act was read by the police, and charges with batons made to disperse the crowds.

At Durham Street, just round the corner from Killen Street and College Place, a huge mob collected, and marched down the street, leaving not one single pane of glass unshattered in the whole length of the street.

Martha Thompson was terrified. She wasn't alone in her fear, for every mother in the town lived in dread and terror of what was happening to their menfolk going to and from their work. Nights were worst, with sounds of glass breaking, shots being fired and yells from the mobs being chased by the police. It was all too near for comfort, but where, the women asked themselves, in the whole town, was there any safety? Cromac Street and the Ormeau districts were roused, Lagan Village had incidents, and around Hercules Street, North Street and Rosemary Street (the very centre of the town) excited crowds milled around.

"It'll pass in a day or two," John told his wife soothingly, and he bade her stay indoors and keep Jane from school. He was over-optimistic though; the riots grew worse, and attempts were made to burn down the Model School.

No child in the town ventured to school; soon, the girls going to the mills and factories could not get to their work. As they approached barricades at street corners they were stopped by rioters and asked, "What religion are you?"

If they happened to be of the 'right' religion, the same as the crowd at the barricade, they were allowed to pass. In most cases they were turned back, and many of them were beaten up.

The same tactics were used against the law-abiding, respectable churchgoers on Sunday evenings. The streets were not safe to walk in, and soon business in the town ceased altogether.

John Thompson had come home, ashen faced from his work. There had been an alarming incident in Bedford Street before his own eyes, when a respectable businessman had been struck on the cheek by a bullet. This decided John to close down his place and send his workers home. Paddy Burke had aged in the few days since the riots began.

"Young Peter's in the thick of it," he told John, "and I'm waiting in terror for him to be killed. A boy from our street is lying up in the General Hospital with his leg shattered. And did you hear about the young woman that was pregnant? She was beaten up and she's lost her child, and near at death's door herself."

Stuart & Mounts closed early one afternoon and the workers were told not to come back until things quietened down. Robert and his friend, Charley Gourley, were stopped at a street corner by a mob of men, and they had to run for their lives when it seemed they were going to be attacked. They both reached College Place breathless, but more excited than frightened, and the pair of them were only too eager to run messages to the shops for any of the neighbours too timid to risk running into any disturbance. Secretly, Robert rather enjoyed it all; there was an undercurrent of tension, with the mills closed and business disrupted, that was so much out of the ordinary to him, and was the nearest thing he could imagine to a state of war. He was sorry in a way that his firm had closed down; there would have been the exhilaration of getting there in the one piece, and of seeing some incidents on the way, and hearing how others had fared.

Mrs McKenna, living on her own, was badly frightened that her house would be marked out and wrecked, so John Thompson brought her to stay with them, where with the shutters firmly bolted and in a street more off the beaten track there wasn't the same chance of being a target for rioters. Even so, as the August nights closed in, after dark, the sounds of the police shooting into the crowd of rioters on the Boyne Bridge could be heard.

The military and the special constabulary were called out, but they were unable to stop the riots that grew worse every day. There seemed no safe haven, even for women and children. A quiet little school on the Crumlin Road was set upon by a mob, and as the screaming children scattered, their books and the benches and maps were thrown out into the street and set on fire.

Sandy Row... Cullingtree Road... Protestant... Catholic. Who was to blame? Who threw the bricks that hit innocent people? Who fired the shots that killed, who wrecked and looted the shops and threw out the furniture from private houses? The Thompsons felt like a lot of Belfast people as they pondered these things, and wondered what got into their townsfolk to turn them against each other and made them act like uncivilised savages, hating each other, and bent on inflicting harm on 'them', the other side.

The infantry dragoons were brought from Dublin, twenty-seven train carriages of them. Rumour then grew that explosives were being brought from Dublin by the rioters to use against 'the other side', and the railway became the target for crowds completely out of hand. Innocent travellers arriving by train from smaller towns in the North of Ireland were set upon and beaten.

A plea for tolerance and patience was issued by the Catholic Bishop, Dr Dorrian, and was seeming to have some effect until the funeral of a Protestant man, shot in the riots, was provocatively walked past the Catholic club headquarters and a mob rushed out and set upon the mourners.

It was only when rain fell at night that the townsfolk could expect a night's sleep, albeit an uneasy one, following the days of complete standstill of the whole town, with shops closed, warehouses, mills and factories shuttered and silent.

Mrs Storey was full of indignation at the mobs in general because several of Arthur's bread carts had been attacked and all the bread looted. She was really too frightened to express any definite opinion and she was glad to go round with Alice to Thompsons' house on a couple of the very bad nights. With her husband keeping on at his work at Lamont's' bakery at night, she looked for the neighbours' company, even if it meant the company of Mrs McKenna as well.

Daily, the courts were crowded with rioters caught by the police, and stiff fines and jail sentences were handed out. The General Hospital had almost a hundred casualties to deal with and the death toll mounted to twelve.

Potatoes and butter rose in price in the shops, as the country farmers were frightened to come into the town with their produce. A stone of potatoes went from costing sixpence to as high as ninepence.

It took a week for the riots to die down, and gradually the town got back to normal. The shops in the main streets opened, the mills and warehouses started again. There was plenty work for the glaziers mending all the broken windows, and some unfortunate people had to make repairs to the damage done to their houses.

In the local papers the long columns of riot news were published, each newspaper fiercely partisan. For a few days John Thompson found it interesting, but saddening, to compare the reports in each newspaper. He read in the Protestant paper how "the manly and sturdy stalwarts of Sandy Row dashed to defend their homes from the dastardly attacks of the murderous ruffians from the Cullingtree Road", while the Catholic press reported that "the peaceful crowd from the Pound area of the Cullingtree Road was set upon by the murderous ruffians from Sandy Row". It was the same incident, reported from opposite sides. Would they never change, these hot-headed Belfast people? It troubled John that so much bitterness and hatred existed in the name of religion, and although he counted himself a true inhabitant of Belfast, he hoped he was free of the canker that divided so many. The riots were over. The dead were buried, and the injured lay in the hospital, but would it all end there?

Would next Twelfth of July or next Fifteenth of August set it all off again? Would the Catholics be shouting "Hurrah for the Pope" and the Protestants respond with "To Hell with the Pope"? John felt that his prayers and good example of tolerance was all he could offer as a solution, in the hope that other men of goodwill might feel the same, and make the August 1864 riots in Belfast something to be looked back on with shame, by both Catholics and Protestants.

There was hope that the Civil War was coming to an end in America when early in 1865 Sherman's march to the sea seemed to foretell an early victory for the Northern States, but it was some months later, in the spring, that the South fell, reeling under the blow of defeat.

Feelings in Belfast were very mixed. *The war is over in America!* and *The Civil War is ended, the Southern states are beaten!* cried the newspapers, but secretly Belfast wondered ... was the boom over too?

The wiser heads argued that it would be some time before cotton could be planted and a crop produced from the scorched Southern States. Others declared that linen had gained a foothold in the market and could not be displaced. The businessmen set about keeping their trade, built up in the war years, in Great Britain. They determined to make a bid for the American market that had been lost to them for four years, years in which there was little linen imported into America. Representatives were prepared to cross the Atlantic to open up contracts and start the flow of linen across the sea again. Representatives were sent to England, to keep the markets gained in those years.

CHAPTER TEN

When he was sure that business had settled, and been well maintained, John Thompson decided he would be able to move house. He called at several of the well-known rent offices to enquire for house lettings, and he took time off to look at the vacant possibilities. Martha went with him. She was greatly excited at choosing a new abode, but dazed at looking at so many houses, in so many districts.

"I'd no notion Belfast was got that big," she told Robert, after one evening of walking around. "Whatever way you look there's building going on."

"The town's growing," he told her learnedly. "Did you know there's about fifty thousand more people in Belfast now than there was twenty years ago?"

"I did not," she sighed, sinking into a chair, "but I'll tell you one thing, son dear. I feel like a stranger walking round, with all these new streets and roads getting built, and droves of people and not one of them to bid you the time of day, they're all that busy."

The choice came down at last to two houses, one in Ormeau Place, and the other in Eglinton Street. It took a lot of consideration of details before the decision between them was made. The house at Ormeau was a fine terrace residence, with good-sized windows, and three storeys high. There was a neat little garden at the front, and the outlook was onto open ground stretching to the brink of the River Lagan, with the trees of the Ormeau Park—the residence of the Marquis of Donegal—on the other side. On clear days there would be a fine view of the Castlereagh Hills, Martha mused to herself, and her heart warmed to the house so that she hoped that John would choose it. It would bring her nearer her home hills, to be able to look out of her windows and see them in misty remoteness or sharp and clear with the gentle slopes of green fields and brown ploughed land, rising up beyond the town, at the other side of the river.

"A fine-looking house," she ventured to remark, "and in good healthy surroundings."

"That's what has me worried," John murmured, frowning, as they stood outside the little garden and gazed up and down the road. "You see the gasworks there, down the road a piece? Well, I hear it is to be extended, and will likely take in all the open land on the other side of the road from there. That would spoil the view, and anyhow, there is an unhealthy and unpleasant smell from the making of gas. It couldn't be healthy."

Martha had to nod in reluctant agreement. Strange, how the town had grown: Here was the gasworks growing out of all knowledge, and she could remember someone telling her that when it was first built at Ormeau, about forty years ago, it was in the country, far away from the town.

"And another thing," John pondered, "it's a rather flat part of the Ormeau district here, and maybe damp would rise up from the river on misty days. This is the part of the town, you know, where there's the Cromac Wells."

"And lovely water it is, I do hear," Martha commented.

"Then there's the stream down the road a bit, that wee river that comes out in Bankmore, there could be damp from it too!"

Ormeau would not do, and Martha was disappointed. However, her first sight of the house in Eglinton Street cheered her up. It was a fine terrace house, and in a district that was supposed to be the healthiest in Belfast, and the most desirable—at least that was what the rent agents said. It had good-sized rooms, and a lovely outlook of the mountains—Colin, Divis, and the Black Mountain—that ringed the country to the north and west of the town.

It was a most respectable street, and would be a rise-up in the world, socially, for the Thompsons. The rent was reasonable for John's income, so, Eglinton Street one over from Ormeau it was.

Inside a few days all the agreements were signed, and notice given of quitting College within the month.

There was a great sadness on Martha in leaving the house where so many years had been lived, and when the shutters were closed over for the last time, she could not keep back her tears. There was heartbreak, too, at leaving Mrs McKenna, and tears were shed by both of them on the day of the flitting.

"What'll I do without you at all?" Mrs McKenna sobbed as the last pieces of furniture were put on top of the load on the cart.

"Now sure we'll not be strangers to each other," Martha told her. "You'll have to come and visit me, for I'll be lost for the want of a good friend and neighbour."

Mrs Storey came along, in time to butt into the conversation.

"Sure woman dear, the likes of us will not be grand enough for you, living up in Eglinton Street," she said tartly.

"My friends will always be welcome, should I live in the castle itself in the Ormeau Park," Martha told her with great dignity.

"Not that I'm content to stay here myself," Mrs Storey went on. "We've had the notion of moving this many a long day, but likely we'll get something a bit further out in the country. Streets is very confining," she said politely. Martha ignored her, though Mrs McKenna and she exchanged significant looks.

Alice had a sad face and tears tripping down her cheeks, and swore to visit Jane every day.

"Wee Jane, will you miss me?" she asked the child.

"I don't know," Jane replied stoically, "I won't know till I live there. I'm going to a new school anyhow. It's a private one. I'm left the Model."

Mrs McKenna noticed that it was Robert—standing impatiently in midst all the tears and leave taking—that Alice looked at.

Furniture was the Thompsons' main preoccupation in the new house in Eglinton Street. The pieces they had brought with them from

College Place didn't look much in the new surroundings and there was an emptiness about the rooms that no amount of arranging of chairs could hide. The mahogany dresser that looked massive in the College Place kitchen seemed smaller somehow, even with its array of candlesticks and brassware.

John went down to the auction rooms and bought some new things, and Martha enjoyed a clutter when a horse and cart left off a hair cloth sofa and two new chairs for the parlour, new oil cloth and an umbrella stand for the hall and a table for the kitchen. Her husband hadn't told her of his most important purchase, and when another cart brought a fine pianoforte for the parlour, Martha's pride knew no bounds. Fancy, a pianoforte! Such elegance had never been in her wildest dreams. Then she was allowed to buy new damask curtains and window poles for all the front windows, and had an enjoyable week sewing them and putting them up. John had bespoken a cabinet maker for bedroom furniture, and a new chest of drawers and a wardrobe arrived from him, redolent of the new-wood smell of coffins, she thought. She was busy for days, putting the furniture in corners, moving it out, re-arranging, scrubbing and polishing until the house was to her liking.

She had scarcely put her foot over the door since their arrival in Eglinton Street, except for Sunday churchgoing, to their own congregation in Berry Street. There was a Presbyterian church in Eglinton Street, which in the Thompsons' eyes added considerably to the street's respectability, and the minister's residence nearby more so, but they were faithful to their own church, even though a long walk faced them from their new abode. Several evenings John tried to tempt Martha for a stroll up the road, past the County Courthouse, to enjoy the air and the freshness of the open fields beyond, but she never got past the courthouse, and at the prospect of a hill to climb she pleaded weariness and they returned home.

"Leave some work for tomorrow, Ma," Robert would tell her

when she would demand his help in yet another job. "Sure we're going to be here for years and you'll have plenty of time to get all the things done."

"It'll be years before I get a good wash out on my lines in the yard if you don't fix up that pole for me," she retorted and hurried him off into the yard.

Secretly, Martha was enchanted with Eglinton Street, and its respectable neighbours. If it had a fault, and she would hardly admit it to herself, but if there was one thing she wanted to make it perfect it was her old friend and neighbour, Mrs McKenna. If the red-haired wee woman could by some chance or other have been moved to live nearby, Martha felt she would have nothing more to ask for. It was a wider street than she was accustomed to, with a more open aspect and bright with sunshine these early spring days. The neighbours kept very much to themselves, behind their own front doors and parlour curtains, and as yet she was on no firmer a neighbourly foundation than "Good morning" or "Lovely day" with the ladies on either side of her. That didn't worry her, however, as it emphasised all the more the social uplift from College Place and Killen Street.

Of course this brought a slight disadvantage; here in Eglinton Street it would not do at all to run into a neighbour and borrow a cup of milk or a pickle or two or sugar, and it definitely wasn't the done thing to throw a shawl round the shoulders and run to the nearest shop for a message. To the ladies of Eglinton Street a shawl was the outdoor garb of a mill worker or a factory girl, wisely worn by any such to keep out the damp cold after the steamy heat in the factory, but here the women wore hats or bonnets and coats—even when going for a message. All this Martha noted: ever since her earliest days working in the Manse up in the Castlereagh Hills she had tried to notice the correct thing to do, and the right way to say a thing. In College Place and Killen Street she had kept just that little bit aloof from the over-friendliness of the neighbours, and up here in Eglinton

Street she would not make any advance towards being neighbourly until she was sure of her ground, and knew whom she was talking to.

For the men of the family, there was a longer walk to work than they were used to. John said it did him good and gave him a breath of fresh air, and Robert enjoyed the company of Charley Gourley who was at present lodging in Brougham Street, not very far from Eglinton Street. Robert met him each morning at the poorhouse wall in Clifton Street, to walk to Stuart & Mounts, and occasionally Robert would call of an evening for Charley at his lodgings to go for a walk. Each time he called he was ushered into the parlour, and was there confronted by the three daughters of the house, who happened by chance to be spread out on the sofa, or strumming at the pianoforte. It was difficult for the young men to tear themselves away from the charms and chatter of the Misses Kerr, and often as not there would be little walking done by the time the talented young ladies went through their repertoire of songs. Robert enjoyed the free and easy atmosphere of the house, and the light-hearted banter, and he twitted Charley about the beginnings of a romance between him and Minnie, the eldest Miss Kerr.

"No fear of me getting caught!" Charley would reply scornfully. "Wouldn't I be the right fool? Sure I've four women running after me now, attending me hand and foot. 'What would you like for your supper, Mr Gourley? Take that easy chair, Mr Gourley!' Ay no, Robbie boy, you'll not find Charles Gourley Esq. rocking a cradle for many's the long year yet! You'll be married before me!"

"What, me!" Robert snorted. "I've no notion of getting married. I want to see round the world a bit. I've a notion I might get sent with Mr Meekin on his spring journey to England. He dropped me a brave civil hint the other day."

"Well for you! Wish I was in your department. Fat chance I have of getting anywhere, stuck in the weaving sheds."

Robert patted him on the shoulder with mock seriousness. "Ah now, you never know! You work hard and mind your manners, and you might get sent the length of Muckamore, or even as far as Coalisland, on the firm's business."

Charley reached over and tilted Robert's curved-brimmed hat over his eyes. "Just for that, Mr Thompson, I'll not ask you in to my palatial lodgings, and you'll not be able to sit on the sofa and cuddle Miss Belinda Kerr anymore."

Robert gave him a push to send him flying into the ditch. "You've a bad mind, Charley boy! I'm scared for my life of those young ladies. They all know a deal!"

"Aye, but you'd cuddle her if you got away with it! Don't deny it. I can read it in your eyes!"

Robert chased him up the road, and towards the village of Edenderry, and both collapsed laughing against a hedge, puffed with the exertion. Robert took his hat off and let the air play round his black hair as he paused for breath.

"I'll tell you what I would like, though, Charley."

"What? A bowl of buttermilk?"

"Fool! No, it's just a notion I have that I'd love to go to America someday. You never know, they might send somebody from the firm some of these fine days. If anyone's going, I'd like it to be me."

Charley looked at him seriously. "I thought you were going into your da's business?"

"It's his idea, not mine. I don't want to be settled yet awhile. Time enough when my da is near retiring. Then I can take over."

"Maybe I'll go in with you as a partner. Gourley and Thompson—how would that sound? We'd be a right couple of linen lords, and we'd make fortunes and build ourselves mansions out on the edge of the town, and send to London for the best of food and clothes. And of course our wives will be titled ladies and the children must go to school in England."

"You're away in the head, Gourley," Robert chuckled. "Are you never serious? How many wives are you going to have, anyhow?"

Gourley pushed him and they fell laughing in the ditch, in a friendly tussle.

A week after this outing, Robert arrived home one evening in a state of intense excitement. Out of breath he threw his hat and coat in a chair in the kitchen, and caught his mother by the shoulder.

"Ma, I'm going to England with Mr Meekin. Where's Pa?"

Mrs Thompson was alarmed. "God bless us, son dear. What's taking you across the water?"

Mr Thompson arrived in the house in time to hear his son's news.

"I'm going on Monday night, with Mr Meekin to England, Pa! It's the spring trip."

"You may leave off that shirt you're wearing, and the stockings, too. How am I going to get your things washed and dried in time?" Mrs Thompson lamented.

"Never mind that," her husband told her, testily. "You've five days. Let's hear what Robert has to say."

"Well, Mr Meekin is due to go to England, to the Midlands, for a spring journey, and I hoped I might get with him. Today we were getting the samples prepared, into the big skip, and Johnny McIlhagga told me I was wanted in the private office, and when I got there, Mr Stuart says, 'Well, Robert!' and you know he hardly ever calls me Robert, always Thompson. Anyhow he says, 'You're doing well, and Mr Meekin is pleased with your work and you've had good experience in the home market and now we'll see how you do over in England.' So Mr Meekin and me is going on Monday night and we're getting the Liverpool boat, and we'll be away about two weeks."

"Oh son, dear, I'll not have an easy minute and you on the high seas!" Martha sat down and bit her lip to keep back sudden tears.

"Nonsense, woman," her husband snapped. "He's not a child."

"I'm near twenty-three, Ma," Robert said gently, patting her shoulder.

"Anyhow," John went on, "it's nothing these days crossing to England or Scotland, a matter of hours and all the comfort of the new steam ships nowadays. Why, you'd think he was going off to the ends of the earth in a sailing ship to look at you."

Jane had been sitting quietly at the table, munching a huge wedge of bread. Well she announced calmly, with her mouth full, "I'm going to be a sailor when I grow up. I'm going away in a big ship with Alfie Storey. He promised to take me."

"Listen to her!" her mother snapped. "Bold as brass, sitting there, making up lies."

Mr Thompson beckoned Jane to come and stand before his chair, and he looked sternly at her and pointed a warning finger. "Look at me, Jane. Now you know you're not telling the truth, don't you? You know it's very wrong to tell lies."

Jane stared at him stolidly for a second or two, then her face creased into a broad smile and she reached up and put her arms round her father's neck and hugged him tight.

"Ah sure it's not lies, Pa, it's only wee stories," and she kissed him and stroked his whiskers.

"All right now, that's enough flattery," he said and put her arms from about his neck. "You must remember what I say, no more of these wee stories." He looked stern but Robert knew that he was not displeased, and he marvelled at the incident, as he did each time it happened when Jane wheedled her pa. He thought of himself at her age, nine years old, and how he had trembled at his father's shadow. Jane was not in awe of either parent, or of her mother's hard hand.

Mrs Thompson now took her daughter in hand. "Did you practise playing your pianoforte the day, miss? No, I thought not, and your da here good enough to buy such a valuable instrument never mind paying out the fortune for lessons. Away you go now, and practise like you're bid."

Robert's own opinion was that it would be easier to teach a cart horse to play the piano than his little sister, and as he listened to the solid thumping on the instrument he wondered how long his father would endure the agony of the noise before coming to the same conclusion.

The next few days were busy for Robert, preparing for the trip to England. There were many details to attend to and he was late each evening getting home. On Saturday the last samples were packed in the warehouse, and letters sent to advise of Mr Meekin's and his coming to the various towns and cities in England where the firm had trade, and it was quite late when he sat down, at last, to his supper, which had been kept over for him. It was an Irish stew, and as he ate ravenously out of his bowl, Jane came over and got a spoon to help him to eat it.

"I've a message for you Robbie," she whispered, spooning stew into her mouth. "Alice Storey wants to see you. She says you're to be sure and call before you go away."

"I won't have time."

"She was crying something awful and her da was saying to her 'Now Alice pet you must be a sensible girl' but she kept on crying."

"Is this another of your wee stories?" Robert asked, smiling, but lifting his bowl out of her reach.

"Give us a taste more stew! No, it's not a wee story at all. She was crying, and she told me not to miss telling you that you were to be sure and call and see her. Leave us a taste of your stew at the end of the bowl!"

"You're a greedy wee gorb!" Robert teased her, and gave her the bowl to scrape. "A body would think you were starved."

He didn't know whether or not she was having a joke with him. It was hard to decide, looking at her innocent face and big eyes. Why would Alice send for him of all people? He scarcely ever saw her these days since leaving College Place and he certainly had not given her many thoughts. It was another of Jane's 'wee jokes', he decided, and reached over and tweaked her nose.

"No more of your tricks," he said solemnly. "It's not Pa you're dealing with. Take care or I won't bring you a doll from England, if you keep telling me wee stories."

"It's not a wee story! It's not! It's not!" she shouted, her face red with temper. "And I don't want an oul' doll, I want a real live monkey."

Robert pulled her hair, and left her scraping the stew bowl, laughing to himself at her antics.

On the morning of the journey, Robert could hardly contain his excitement. The tickets for the steamer and the railway journeys in England were purchased, and the wicker skips of samples were sent down to the gangside of the boat. From the boys in the firm Robert had to take a lot of good-natured banter. Charley Gourley clapped him heartily on the back.

"Take a good hearty supper, Robert boy! Then you'll have something to be really sick with! Isn't that right, Johnny?"

McIlhagga nodded solemnly. "Aye, though they do say that rice is a good thing to eat. It brings everything up clean as a new pin!"

"And when the boat starts heaving just after you pass Donaghadee and the Copeland Islands, that's when you'll start heaving, too!" Charley added.

"You're the right pair of boys to give advice," Robert taunted. "Sure you never were over any water rougher than the River Lagan. Don't tell me you were sick in a rowing boat! Just you wait—divil the sick I'll be!"

Robert was glad to get home, with barely enough time to get washed and changed into his good clothes and have his supper before boat time. He could have been sick with excitement and anticipation without putting his foot on the Liverpool boat, and found it hard to eat the good, nourishing meal his mother thought necessary for a traveller embarking on a journey to another country across the water. The whole house was in a state of unrest until the moment when, washed, shaved, in clean linen and good suit, with greatcoat on his arm and his hat in hand, he stood to say goodbye to his mother and Jane. His father was to accompany him to the boat.

"Alice was up with Jane, and she was sorry not to see you before you went," his mother told him. "She would have stayed, but I thought it getting too late for her to be out on her own. I just told her, though, to say a wee prayer that you'll be safe and sound."

"Ach, Ma," Robert said, "it's not the ends of the earth I'm going to."

Jane sidled over to him and put a piece of paper in his hand. She whispered up to him, "There's a wee letter for you, from Alice. She told me to give it to you."

Robert smiled. "All right! I suppose you wrote it yourself! Is this to remind me about your monkey? You're the great wee dreamer!"

"It's a real letter, so it is! And you must read it!" Jane said solemnly.

"I will. I promise," he told her, and pushed the letter into his pocket.

"Well, don't forget!" Jane warned him, and added in a whisper, "Alice said it was very particular."

Mrs Thompson pushed her aside.

"Ach, stop your nonsense, Jane! You're the forward wee hussy. Let me look at you, son," and she surveyed him fondly. She could hardly see him for tears, as she reached for an imaginary speck of dust on his coat. Her big, black-haired son, she thought proudly as she looked at him, his hair carefully brushed back flat, his eyes bright. How handsome he looked in his good suit, with braided lapels, his white shirt gleaming and the stiff collar and the dark tie making him older looking than she wanted him to be. She was saying goodbye to her wee boy that suddenly had become a man. He was going out of her house and across the water, and she wouldn't know an easy minute until he put foot in the house again.

It made a painful leave-taking, and when they had gone, the two men striding down Eglinton Street, with the portmanteau swinging in Robert's hand, her tears flowed freely. It was Jane who comforted her, hugging her and telling her not to cry.

"Look, Ma," the child said, "I'm not crying. And I'm very sorry that Robbie is away and didn't take me with him. But sure next time, maybe he'll let us go to the boat with him."

There was the usual crowd at the quayside when Robert and his father arrived, and the normal clutter of boxes, bundles, barrels, cattle and some horses were being loaded on the steamer with the utmost confusion and plenty of noise. Mr Meekin was waiting, and after a few words together, the travellers went aboard. They were travelling cabin, and the steward who directed them knew Mr Meekin quite well, as a regular traveller. The older man elected to stay below and settle himself, but Robert stood eagerly by the ship's rail, watching the throng of people boarding the steamer and occasionally waving at his father standing on the quayside cobbles. He felt elated; he was actually on a boat, and he was going to England in it. His father stayed until the gangplank was raised and the shouts and the partings from the passengers were dimmed as the steamer edged off and moved slowly from the quay and into the Belfast Lough.

The buildings faded, dim and tiny, behind the ship, and merged into a shoreline that he could not recognise as his native Belfast. Robert walked round the deck, trembling with excitement and emotion. Seagulls wheeled and flew after the ship, which was now moving smoothly but quickly on the tide. Soon the town was a blur, and a violent red sunset over Divis Mountain caught his eye. The Cave Hill stood out, black and strange in the twilight, and pinpoint lights appeared along the coastline. Carrickfergus Castle was a landmark, but the shorelines then became unrecognisable in the fast falling darkness. In a little while the thin air penetrated, and the waves of the tidal swell slapping against the ship's side sent Robert below deck to find Mr Meekin, and to lie in a bunk and try to sleep.

It was a long night for Robert; he slept ill in the strange surroundings, and did not feel at ease when the boat rolled.

"We're passing the Isle of Man," Mr Meekin remarked in a sleepy voice in the early hours, when the sea suddenly became choppy. The oil lamps, suspended, swung like pendulums and made Robert dizzy to look at. He could have been sick, he felt, but was determined to lie still and quieten the heaving of his stomach which came with every roll of the ship. Sleep came eventually, but it was fitful, and through it all, he felt the motion of the waves and knew he was on a ship. In the early morning he was wide awake, while Mr Meekin slept heavily and snored.

Robert slipped out of the cabin quietly and made his way up on to the deck of the ship. A seaman told him they were going up the Mersey, and he stood at the rail, glimpsing the flat coast through the morning mist, and wondering what lay before him. He was excited; he was exhilarated and happy. Before him lay the wonderment of a different world that England would be to him, visiting the country for the first time. There would be long train journeys, new people to meet, strange houses to stay in, meals eaten in dining rooms and maybe even taverns.

He had his hand in his jacket pocket for a handkerchief and drew out the letter Jane had given him. He expected a couple of pages of his little sister's copy book, with yet another request for the real live monkey, but to his surprise, it really was a letter, and it really was from Alice.

In a childish, sprawling hand she had written,
Dear Robbie,
Ma and Pa wants me to marry Mr Skinner he has offered for me but oh Robbie I don't want to marry him his mouth is wet and he has yellow teeth please

Robbie help me I am crying all the time.

Robert thought it was a joke thought up between Jane and Alice. A child like Alice to be married! But was Alice a child? She was about nineteen now; hard to realise it, he thought. Maybe it was true, perhaps she *had* sent a message through Jane... What could he do? When he got home he could at least call and see what was going on. She sounded so unhappy, and he didn't like to think of her crying. But he could do nothing now, so he would just have to put it out of his mind until he got home.

He was able to inspect the Liverpool skyline and the approaching quays with awe and wonder, and gaze open-mouthed at the vast array of ships in the port. Alfie could no doubt tell him about them, if he were only here. *He* would know where the big packets were sailing for, and what all the small ships and the huge new steamships were doing in the port of Liverpool. By comparison, Belfast quay seemed small now.

Time passed quickly for Robert as he stood and watched, and when Mr Meekin appeared from his berth and complained of the length of time it took the ship to reach the quay and tie up, Robert thought him impatient.

"I'm watching for my usual barrow-man," Mr Meekin said. "I hope to get him to take the skips for us. He knows the rounds. He's an honest man. I believe he's an Irishman, too, for he has the hint of a brogue behind the Liverpool accent. Probably came over from Ireland after the Famine, to get a ship for America, and never got further than Liverpool. It happened to thousands of them."

As they walked ashore together, Robert felt a thrill. He was setting foot for the first time in another land. His adventures and travels as a linen trade representative had begun...

Back in Belfast, the first couple of days after Robert's departure seemed like weeks to Mrs Thompson. She cried a little, worried a lot about his safety, then like the sensible woman she was, decided she was doing no good by such behaviour. She started and gave her house a thorough cleaning and polishing that it didn't need in the least.

If only she had someone to talk to, she thought longingly, after her husband had gone to his work, and Jane had been despatched to the private school that was to make a young lady out of her. She decided, on an impulse, to go and visit Mrs McKenna. She really did need some butter, and say what they would about old Wilson, he did keep good butter. Fortified by her justification she set off happily, and on the way down the street had the pleasure of returning a gracious bow from two ladies. They were the wife and daughter of the tea packer, three doors up, next door to the muslin manufacturer and the foreign language teacher on the other side. It was a nice street, Eglinton Street, but still... Killen Street was more attractive at the moment, with Mrs McKenna to chat to.

Mrs McKenna's door was ajar, and Mrs Thompson tapped and walked in. Her friend was sitting with a pile of white linen in front of her.

"Well, you're a sight for sore eyes!" she cried out, rising quickly to her feet. "I'm awful glad to see you!"

"And me you! But your eyes are sore!" Martha added anxiously, noticing the red rims and the crusted lashes.

"Ach, sure that's nothing new. Isn't this oul' white linen sewing pulling the eyes out of me. I'll be blind if I keep it up."

"They do say that cold tea is a good cure."

"So I hear, and that's what I'm using," Mrs McKenna replied, pushing Martha into her best chair. "And just to show you how glad I am to see you, I'm going to make us a wee drop of tea, and any leftover will do to bathe my eyes."

She pulled the kettle forward on the hob, and soon it was boiling and the tea wet. Comfortably, they both sat sipping, and Martha told her friend how much she missed her.

"I think I'd have lost my reason if I hadn't somebody to talk to this very day," she sighed.

"And this place isn't the same without you, Mrs Thompson. It's lost I am, for the want of a good chat. I suppose you heard the news? That Alice Storey has an offer?"

"Alice? And her so young! Who is it?"

"Some oul' fella by the name of Skinner. They say he's rotten with money, and now he's looking round for a young wife. But, if you please, Miss Alice is crying her eyes out, and says she doesn't want to marry him."

"Right enough, our wee Jane was talking about Alice crying, but you never know if that child is making up things. I beat her till I hurt my hand, but I needn't bother for all the good it does. But tell me this, is the Storeys making Alice take this oul' fella?"

Mrs McKenna raised her eyebrows. "I doubt it," she declared. "That's a very strong-headed wee girl, and if she makes up her mind to a thing she gets it. I think she has something else in mind, but whatever or whoever she wants, it's not Mr Skinner. Her ma and da is telling her to be sensible, but there's a crying match going on near every night. I can hear it through the wall, and of course you know the ma, big in the mouth, she can keep nothing to herself. The whole street knows all about it."

"Well, it'll be for the ma and da to decide what's best for their own wee girl," Martha sighed complacently. "At least I've nothing like that to worry about for a while until Jane grows up, though what that bold wee hussy will be looking for next I don't know. She asked Robert to bring her a real live monkey as a present from England."

Mrs McKenna laughed. "Sure didn't she order my James to bring her a parrot, and she plagued Alfie Storey to bring her with him last time he was going to sea! She's a caution, your Jane."

"Who is this Mr Skinner?" Martha asked.

"If you ask where he came from, nobody can tell you," Mrs McKenna replied. "They says he's rotten with gold, and that he came in from behind the bogs somewhere. Likely followed a cart to Belfast in his bare feet and the backside out of his britches, like many a one that's done well. He's plenty of money now; foreby they'd tell you he hadn't a farthing piece to his name ten years ago."

"Alice is a nice wee girl. I'd like to see her happy."

"So would I, but I'd want no daughter of mine married to an old man like that, rich and all as he's supposed to be. It would be a good match, I grant you that, but Alice is over-young for her age and she'd be far better off with some young fellow she could laugh with."

Mrs Thompson nodded agreement. "She was always the da's wee pet, you know, and likely she's a bit spoiled. You know as well as I do that if she ever wanted anything she just cried and the da gave it to her."

"Aye right enough, she is a bit of a whinge. But sure, woman dear, it'll all end someway!"

Mrs McKenna sighed deeply and looked serious, and for a moment Martha thought her sick looking, with her pale face and bad eyes.

"Are you keeping all right?" she asked anxiously. "Foreby your eyes, I mean? I just thought you looked worried."

For a few seconds Mrs McKenna didn't reply, then she shook her head, sadly and reflectively.

"I've a weight on me, Mrs Thompson dear, a weight of worry, and I don't know what I'm going to do at all." Then, quietly she told her friend her troubles. Her son, James, had decided to leave the sea, and settle in America. He wanted his mother to come out, as soon as he was fixed in the good job he was promised, and he'd make a home for her. Mary was aghast at the idea, and implored her mother not to leave Ireland.

"So what am I to do, Mrs Thompson dear? What advice would

you give me?"

Martha gasped. "Oh, Mrs McKenna, I wouldn't know what to tell you. Do you want to go to America?"

"If I went I'd have a good home and my son to support me, but if I stay, well, I suppose I'd have to keep on at the sewing, to make my living, though my eyes is giving out. God knows, and you'll excuse me for saying it, but the pay is very poor working for linen firms. I know that Mr Thompson has to do what the others do, though left to himself he'd be very generous. But they never think of the work and the strain on the eyes for all the wee money they pay out."

Martha nodded. "Then, if you did go out to James, and he took the notion to get married, it mightn't be all that pleasant with a wife in the same house."

"I've thought of that; Mary implores me not to go, but she's not able to help me, and won't be able to, for *he* keeps her that tight he'd hardly let her give me a stale bap."

"I can only say a wee prayer for you!"

"If you would do that itself, and I'm wearing my own knees out in the chapel, and the nuns is praying for me. Mary went to their school, you know, and they're very kind to me."

Martha rose to go, reluctantly, for she enjoyed being with her friend again, but time had flown and she had to think of a meal for her husband coming home from his work.

"I'll see you soon," she said. "Why don't you come up and visit me?"

"I will, please God, some of these fine days. Maybe all my troubles will pass, and something happen that I can do what I've always wanted to do."

"What's that?"

"Open a wee shop for myself—but that's something you can't do on dreams!"

Later in the evening, after the meal was eaten, the dishes and pots washed, and Jane sent to bed, Martha recounted her talk with Mrs McKenna.

John listened to her, then remarked reprovingly, "It's an odd thing to me that you women can find so much time for idle gossiping. Wouldn't you both have been better employed attending to your house duties?"

Martha felt flattened. She applied herself, in silence, to her knitting.

Robert and Mr Meekin progressed on their journey, doing good business and acquiring some new customers in each city and town they visited. Each visit to a warehouse was fairly standard: Mr Meekin did most of the talking, after introducing Robert as "our young Mr Thompson". Robert took the samples as required from the skips, and noted down the details of the orders—made-up goods, some fancy boxed, piece goods in finished state, or loomstate linen, as ordered. Robert's private opinion was that Mr Meekin talked too much on each visit, and he amused himself by imagining how he would conduct each call, supposing he had the chance.

There wasn't much time to see around the towns and cities they visited by the time they had returned to the hotel or lodging house and had sent a fair copy of the day's orders to the firm in Belfast. The days were full and busy and the nights all too short for Robert to get his sleep.

Two weeks went by and the journey was still uncompleted; at least another week's travelling would be needed to cover the ground, but when they reached Birmingham and had got to their hotel and had an evening meal, Mr Meekin declared he had caught a chill on the train journey, and felt most unwell. Next morning he felt worse and could not rise from his bed; his legs and arms ached and his head throbbed; he was in a fever and could eat nothing. He directed Robert to do the best he could by himself with the calls in the city, and, reluctantly, Robert left him, hoping that the housemaid would be as good as her word to look in on the invalid from time to time.

Robert found his way to the first warehouse on his list by taking a cab, having directed the barrow-man with the skips to go ahead. He was very nervous as he displayed the samples and found to his amazement that he was talking feverishly, and saying almost exactly what he had heard Mr Meekin say on practically every call they had made.

He was exhausted by the evening when he returned to the hotel to recount to his superior his day's calls and the orders he had got. Mr Meekin had a "well done" for him. He was far from well, and after a restless night, was no better in the morning.

"We'll head for home," he declared when Robert went to see him very early, and waved aside all Robert's fears of travelling with such a chill on him. "I'll be better at home," he said. "An hotel is a poor place to be sick and I'll depend on you to make all the arrangements and find out about the trains and see that the skips are put on."

He was weak and exhausted when they left the hotel in a cab and got to the train. Robert arranged all the details and the journey was uneventful except for his worry about Mr Meekin's health.

They went to the steamer at Liverpool and the steward got Mr Meekin to a bunk immediately and served him hot drinks. It was a rough night's crossing of the Irish Sea, and Robert didn't sleep a wink, partly from the tossing of the ship and partly from the feverish mutterings of Mr Meekin.

In the morning, as soon as the ship was tied up at the quay, Robert, with the assistance of the steward, got Mr Meekin to a cab and drove to his home, thankful to pass the responsibility of looking after her husband to the anxious and surprised Mrs Meekin. Robert then went up home, to Eglinton Street, and gave his mother the shock of her life by walking in on her as she was scrubbing out her washing.

He had time only for a quick meal, a wash, and a shave, before reporting to the firm, where he spent a busy morning going over the details of the journey with Mr Stuart. He felt very much the man-of-the-world, quite the experienced traveller, and if he hadn't been so sleepy after his restless night, he would have enjoyed his triumph all the more.

Mr Stuart was not slow to send one of the senior members of the firm up to Mr Meekin's house for a report on the journey and Robert came in for praise for the manner in which he had handled the important calls on his own in Birmingham. He really felt—though he did not express the thought—that he could have capably carried on with the rest of the journey by himself, only for the responsibility of getting Mr Meekin back to Belfast.

John Thompson was proud of his son when he heard the story of the business trip, but as usual, he made no outward show of his feelings. How glad he was now that Robert had stayed on at Stuart & Mount's, and had gained such valuable experience as a journeyman, and now as a representative. The time was ripe, John felt, for an expansion in his own firm. Trade was still booming in linen, with absolutely no signs of any slackening. John was looking out for suitable, larger premises, and then ... *then* he'd ask Robert in with him. The boy's legacy would be useful, too, in the planned expansion. They would be able to go after the English market better by calling personally on established and prospective customers. He sometimes thought it strange that Robert had never shown any interest in his legacy; even when he became twenty-one, and knew that it was his, he had never suggested taking as much as one penny out of the bank.

At the evening meal Robert yawned frequently and remarked that he would be going to bed early to make up for a sleepless night on the boat.

Jane scowled at him. "Alfie Storey says that real sailors don't get to sleep for a whole lot of nights."

"And am I not a real sailor?" he teased her.

"You're an oul' cod, so you are! You never brought me nothing, and I wanted a real live monkey!" Jane was angry.

"I told you, I hadn't time for a present, and there wasn't a monkey in any of the places I was in," Robert said.

"Well, there's monkeys in all foreign lands, and you went away in the boat and never brought me my monkey!"

Mrs Thompson said sharply, "If you mention that monkey again, Jane, you'll get put to bed. Didn't Robert tell you he couldn't get one."

"By the way," Robert said suddenly, "talking of Alfie Storey—what about Alice? What's all this about her getting married?"

"How did you know?" his mother asked, surprised. "Sure I heard nothing about it until after you went to England."

"Well ... ah ... you see, she wrote me a wee note before I went," Robert admitted, feeling a bit abashed. "She didn't seem to relish the idea of marrying this man that had offered for her."

"She doesn't like Mr Skinner," Jane announced loudly and deliberately. "She says his feet smells, and she isn't going to marry him. She likes our Robbie though. She told me."

Mrs Thompson reached over and gave Jane a smart slap on the face. "That's enough out of you, miss! Did you ever hear the like of such talk in your life! It's a good thing for you, Jane Thompson, that your da is still at his work and didn't hear you talk like that—and him paying out good money to try and make a lady out of you at that private school."

Jane sat, red-faced and defiant, her mouth tight closed.

Mrs Thompson then proceeded to tell Robert about Alice's offer.

"And of course, she must be a good girl and do what her ma and da bids her."

"But if she doesn't like this old man..." Robert faltered.

"A girl doesn't always know what's best for her. Alice will marry who she's bid like many another."

"All the same, I hate to think of her crying. She mustn't be happy," Robert said anxiously.

"Well, it's no concern of ours," Mrs Thompson replied sharply. "Alice has a ma and a da to look after her. It was a bit forward of her, writing to you, son. Sure what could you do?"

To himself, Robert thought, *what indeed?* But he decided all the same that he would call and see Alice, and perhaps put in a word with her that her parents' choice was the right one.

"You never went to see Alice," Jane spoke up again, "and she asked you to. I told you!"

"You're for your bed," her mother said firmly. "I think we've heard enough out of you for the one night."

Robert left it until Sunday evening, after church, to call at Storeys', and he walked briskly round to Killen Street. The trees were budding in College Square, and there was a hint of summer in the soft spring air. He walked past College Place, past their old house, for sentiment's sake. It looked different now, somehow, and it seemed queer for him to be passing as a stranger the house where he had lived so many years.

There was a light in Storeys' parlour, and Mrs Storey responded to his firm tap on the door.

"Oh, it's you, Robert!" she exclaimed in a surprised voice. "Are you back from England? Did you like it? It's a pity Alfie isn't here or you could talk to him about your travels, but he's away in America again, or is it Australia? I forget; these places all sound the same to me."

She pushed him into the parlour where Mr Storey was sitting

stiffly on a hard chair in his good suit and best boots. Alice was in the corner, on the edge of a chair, pale and miserable looking. Her face lit up when she saw Robert coming into the room.

"Here's Robert Thompson to visit us," Mrs Storey announced. "We have company, here, Robert. Mr Skinner is here." She spoke in a very polite voice, somewhat louder than her usual tone.

Robert looked intently at the strange man sitting in the chair by the window. He was a middle-aged individual, with small black eyes and large yellow teeth. He was dressed in a heavily braided black suit of good cloth, and his white shirt was of good linen. But despite his clothes, he looked common and coarse, Robert decided, and he had not been many seconds in his vicinity before he had to agree that Jane's comments from Alice were right—the man's feet did smell.

"Evening," Mr Skinner remarked to Robert civilly. "Fine spell of weather, for the time of year."

Robert murmured a reply, and sat in his chair in silence, but was inwardly seething. Mr Skinner and Mr Storey indulged in a laboured conversation on the state of the baking trade, and Alice sat mute, looking appealingly at Robert. Mrs Storey had gone out of the room on Robert's arrival, but now returned with a bottle of port wine in her hands, and some drinking glasses.

"We're having some refreshment," she said, demurely. "Will you take a drop, Robert?"

"Thanks, no," Robert declined hurriedly. "I called in just for a wee minute," and he rose to his feet, and made for the door, murmuring "Evening all" as he went. Alice slipped after him into the hall and pulled the parlour door closed after her.

"Robbie" she whispered, "I hoped you'd come!" She opened the front door and whispered to him, "Can I talk to you for a minute?"

They went round the corner into College Place, deserted now in the twilight. Alice leaned against the shutters of the house that had been the Thompsons'.

"Oh, Robbie," she sighed. "My ma and da wants me to marry that oul' fella, and I don't want to!"

All Robert's good intentions of telling Alice to be sensible had left him at first sight of Mr Skinner. How could he tell her now that she must take her parents' advice, and not to worry, that they knew what was best for her? It was a shame, he thought furiously, and he didn't know when he had been so angry before. How could the Storeys push Alice into marriage with such a man as Skinner? Poor little Alice, the gentle, soft little creature, with her appealing big eyes and her trusting nature. Skinner wasn't for her. He would not stand aside and see it happen, and even if it meant speaking to Mr Storey and risk being told it was none of his affair, he would make his protest. After all, he was a friend of the family and had known Alice since she was a little girl. Surely his protest on Alice's behalf would carry some weight. And surely they could pick some more suitable suitor for their daughter.

Alice plucked his sleeve timidly. "What will I do, Robbie?"

"I'll tell you what, Alice," Robert said decisively, "I'll speak to your father! Now just you leave this to me!"

Alice looked at him incredulously. "You'll speak to my da for me?"

"Yes, I will. It's maybe a bit late, but he'll have to listen to me."

"Oh, Robbie, you're not just saying it! You will speak for me?"

"Yes I will, never fear."

"When will you see my da?"

Robert paused to think for a second. "Let's see, the sooner the better! I'll call round tomorrow night."

Alice looked at him, her eyes full of tears. "Oh, Robbie!" she gasped. "I'd always hoped you would, and I've prayed to God you would! I thought you would never get back from England in time! I'll be a good wife to you Robbie! I never wanted to marry anybody but you, never! Oh, Robbie!" She put her hand to her mouth to stifle the sobs.

Robert exclaimed, "Alice!" in a weak voice.

"I'll cry no more," she said. "I'm happy now."

From round the corner came Mrs Storey's voice shouting, "Alice! Are you there, Alice? Come on in out of that!"

"It's my ma!" Alice exclaimed. "I'll have to go! But tomorrow we can talk. Will it be early tomorrow night?"

"What? Oh, as soon as I finish work and get my supper," Robert said breathlessly.

"I'll try and keep it to myself until you speak to my da."

Mrs Storey's voice came shouting again, "Alice, will you come in out of that?"

"I'll have to go! Goodbye, Robbie love!" She pressed his arm and was off, light as a fairy, her golden hair swinging over her shoulders, her face radiant.

Robert stood against the wall, shaking. He felt as weak as the night he had taken drink in the entry with Alfie and Gourley, and he doubted if his legs would carry him down the street.

What had happened? What had he said? How had Alice taken him up wrongly? He tried to remember his exact words, but his mind was swimming with confusion. One thing was clear, and that was that Alice considered herself bespoken to him in marriage and likely would lose little time in acquainting her ma and da of the fact.

In a daze, Robert walked off, hardly knowing which direction he was taking, and whether it took him long to get up to Eglinton Street.

When he got home he still felt dazed, and presented such an appearance that his mother immediately concluded he was sickening for something and advised him to get off to bed.

He took his candle and mounted the stairs wearily, but there was neither sleep nor rest for him. His mind was occupied in trying to find a way of telling Alice, without hurting her, that she had misunderstood his intentions. In God's name, how could he do it! And yet, he had no thought of marriage, and certainly it had never occurred to him if he had thought of it to marry Alice Storey, wee Alice that was still a child to him! His plans were for more journeys to England for his firm, with the big hope of being the selected representative sent to America. So he would have to find some way of telling Alice, some way that would be gentle to her feelings that while he was very much against the proposed union with this Mr Skinner, he had not thought of offering himself as the alternative.

With this resolve, in the early hours, Robert tried to get some sleep, and although he dozed now and then, the night passed with no comfort, and in the morning he pushed aside the breakfast his mother sat in front of him, and set off for his work. He had half thought, at one time during the night, of asking his father's advice. But surely at his age he could act the man and not run like a wee boy to his da. And anyhow, didn't the whole situation make him look rather foolish?

On the way to work, he was sure of one thing: that there was no way of telling Alice the mistake he had made. He just couldn't do it to her. She was such a trusting wee thing, and it would be cruel to tell her she had taken him up wrongly. Wearily, Robert went about his duties, wondering what on earth he was going to do.

During the morning he chanced on Charley Gourley in the cobbled yard where carts were loading webs of cloth for delivery to merchants in the town. The urge to discuss his plight was strong, and he asked Charley if he could spare a minute or two.

"What's up, boy? You look like death warmed up!"

"Slip into the storeroom at the end of the passage," Robert said quietly, and went himself into the room with the webs of brown linen lining the shelves. He upturned a box and sat on it, his hands covering his face.

"Well, well, what's the trouble?" Charley breezed in. "Tell your Uncle Charley what's the matter."

"First thing is cut out the funny man act," Robert said fiercely. "I'm asking you for some advice, because I look on you as my best friend, but if you're going to do the funny man, you can clear out."

Charley's face became serious. "All right, I'm listening," he said and he perched on a pile of webs, his feet dangling.

"I don't know if you heard," Robert started off, "but some oul' fella by the name of Skinner has offered for wee Alice Storey."

Charley nodded and Robert told him the whole story.

"And now I don't know what to do," he concluded. "I just couldn't tell the wee girl the mistake she made. I thought I could, but I just couldn't."

"It was an unfortunate remark, that 'I'll speak to your da'," Charley said quietly. "But if you ask me, Robbie, you can't tell her. You would have to say you had no intention of offering for her."

"It would be a terrible cruel thing."

"And maybe worse than you think," Charley said. He looked thoughtfully at Robert for a second. "You must never have noticed, I'm thinking, that wee Alice has always been powerful fond of you. Now I could see it the few times I was in your house that she was there. Her face would kind of light up when she saw you, and she would sit and gaze at you. You're a lucky enough fella, if you ask me, to have somebody thinking that much of you and being so fond of you."

"Well, maybe I am, but I'd no notion of getting married for a long while, Charley. Ach, when I was a wee fella I thought myself in love with a girl, but sure I was only dreaming. I've given no thought to marrying."

"You've two roads open to you, Robbie boy. Either you tell the wee girl she took you up wrong, or you let the hare sit and get married to her."

Robert shifted in his seat uneasily. "I had a whole lot of plans made, and getting married wasn't one of them. You know how I've set my heart on getting to America someday."

"Well, what's to hinder you having a wife to go with you?"

"Maybe you're right, Charley."

Charley slid off his perch and roamed the small storeroom.

"There's another point you've overlooked, Robbie. You'd be getting a girl that turned down a very wealthy man for you. Many's a girl would grab a man with money, no matter what he looked like. Take Miss Minnie Kerr, now, the one you thought I was sweet on. Well, she's a nice enough girl on the face of it, but I've more sense I hope than to be taken in by her. I know rightly that she's holding me in her mind's eye as a possible reserve, in case nothing better turns up, you see. But if some oul' lad like Skinner would even look twice at her, she'd grab him that quick and have him in front of the minister before he could tie his boots. I'm Mr Gourley, in the linen trade, you know," and he mimicked a girl's voice, "but if some brave boy with a fifty pounds a year more than me was to turn up, out I'd go. So you see, it's because of yourself that Alice likes you."

Robert thanked him for his counsel and they walked back to the cobbled yard.

"You've helped me to make up my mind, Charley," he said

quietly. "I can see now the way I should go."

His talk with Charley had served to crystallize his thoughts towards the only action he knew, in his heart of hearts, to be possible. He would go round tonight and see Mr Storey and make his application for Alice's hand. He would have to think of Alice now as the girl he was going to marry, and not as the wee girl round the corner, the playmate of his little sister, Jane.

Mrs Thompson was sorely troubled about Robert. He looked ill enough last night, but when he went out to work without eating a bite, pale and haggard looking, she was sure he was sickening for something serious. But before she could decide just which disease he was taking, there was a knock on the front door, and all her conjectures as to who could be calling at this time of the morning before the things were cleared off the table were proved wrong when she opened the door to Mrs McKenna.

"Come in and welcome!" she exclaimed. "I'm that glad to see you! Sure you're early afoot this morning!"

Mrs McKenna came in, and looked round her and commented on the house with brief words of praise.

"Mrs Thompson, dear, this is not the way for me to come and visit you in your new house for the first time. It looks lovely, so it does, but you'll have to pardon me, for I haven't come to see the house at all. To tell you the truth I'm near dead with curiosity, and I just says to myself, I'll take a wee race up."

"Sit down, woman dear! What's amiss at all?"

"Tell me this, and tell me no more! Is your Robert going to marry Alice Storey?" Mrs McKenna fired the question at her.

Mrs Thompson sat hard and suddenly on the nearest chair. "God love us, Mrs McKenna dear, where did you get the notion? It's the first I heard of it."

"Well, Mary come in hot-foot this morning, full of the news. It seems Robert was down in Killen Street last night after church, and him and Alice must have fixed it up between them."

"It's news to me! Not a word have his father nor me heard of this. But he come in late last night, sort of sick looking, not talking, and went to his bed. And this morning he went off without as much as limping the breakfast I put before him. It's very strange!"

"I'm sorry to give you such a shock," Mrs McKenna said, contritely, seeing the shocked took on her friend's face. "But I knew you wouldn't think it amiss of me to come up with the news. Mary says there'll be wigs on the green, though. The oul' ma is dead against it, and Arthur is fit to be tied."

"Mind you, Mrs McKenna, I can tell you this much," Martha spoke quietly, "between ourselves, Alice wrote to him before he went over to England. I thought it forward enough of her. So whatever's happened, it was her gave it the push."

"Now you know rightly, missus dear, she's had her eye on him this many a long day. God knows I gave you a hint of it often enough, for I seen the way she used to look at him."

Martha sighed. "Och dear, what will the next of it be! I suppose he could do worse, though."

"Aye, she's not a bad wee girl. She's not as timid as she looks, mind, and I never knew her to want a thing she didn't get. Sure the da spoiled her."

"Is she a bit of a whinge?"

"Aye, I'd think so."

They sat talking for a while and had a cup of tea to help them, and when Mrs McKenna left, her friend was sore troubled and perplexed by the news. What should she do, she wondered: should she go down and tell John, or wait until he came home? Likely he'd tell her she shouldn't be gossiping either way, so maybe she'd better wait until he got home. It would be a long day for her, with nobody to discuss the news with until the men came home—except Jane, and it wouldn't surprise her one wee bit if Jane didn't know the whole story.

At supper time, Robert was serious, and ate little. He went upstairs and changed into his Sunday black suit, after having a careful shave. He dreaded the coming interview with Mr Storey, and couldn't make up his mind whether to tell his parents his news before, or after, the meeting. However, he found the opportunity when he found his mother and father sitting quietly in the kitchen, with Jane in the parlour practising at the pianoforte.

"I've something to tell you," he said. "I'm going down to speak to Mr Storey and to ask for Alice. If he lets her, Alice and me is getting married."

His father looked up quickly from his newspaper.

"This is a bit sudden, isn't it? You never mentioned the possibility."

Robert mumbled something about things turning out all for the best and rushed off, leaving two very perplexed people. Martha then thought it expedient to mention Mrs McKenna's visit and her news of this morning.

"Well, you might have let me know of these happenings," John told her gruffly. "You can prattle about things not so important at other times."

Martha nodded miserably; she knew that whatever way she did it would be wrong, but she was too much distressed at the moment to take his rebuke seriously.

"John I'm worried. Do you think Alice is the right girl for our Robert?"

"Well, he could do worse, and she could do a lot better by all accounts. But I think we're too previous in our worry. I doubt very much if Mr Storey will allow Robert's offer. This man Skinner has a lot to offer. They'll likely settle for him."

Martha hoped he was right, though she couldn't imagine any girl turning down the chance of marrying her Robert. Still, she had never, in her wildest dreams for him, thought of Alice as a possible bride.

Robert walked purposefully towards Killen Street. This had to be gone through with, and he hoped he would manage to make his offer in a dignified and manly way, without a tremor in his voice to betray his nervousness and apprehension. When he tapped Storeys' door it was Mrs Storey who opened it, and she glared at him, and bid him curtly to come in. In the kitchen Mr Storey sat smoking his pipe, his unlaced boots before him, just as he sat every night, preparing to go to his work in the bakery. He nodded to Robert in his usual manner and remarked on the state of the weather.

Alice emerged from the scullery, her face aglow when she saw Robert. He smiled weakly at her.

"Well, what's this we hear?" Mrs Storey started off. "Alice had some nonsense about you offering for her. Sure you know rightly, Robert Thompson, that Mr Skinner has offered for Alice and it's near all fixed up."

"I don't like him! I'm not going to marry him!" Alice muttered, a sob in her voice.

"That's why I'm here, Mrs Storey, and Mr Storey," Robert began, and he made the little speech he had rehearsed, of how he wished to make offer for Alice's hand, that he had a good safe position in the linen trade with excellent prospects, and had money in the bank foreby. He would be good to Alice and she would never regret her choice.

"That's a good wee speak, Robert," Mr Storey said kindly, "but sure we know all about you and you've no need to go making a speech to us. Myself, I only want the wee girl's happiness, but herself here is all for Mr Skinner."

Mrs Storey sat down and folded her arms and faced Robert, her face flushed with annoyance.

"What call had you to come and upset things?" she asked Robert. "Sure you knew rightly that Mr Skinner had offered. I've nothing against you, Robert, you're a nice wee fella, but it's Mr Skinner that Alice is going to marry and you might as well save your breath and your fine talk."

"I won't! I don't like him!" Alice whimpered.

"Hold you your tongue, miss," Mrs Storey snapped. "Sure what does a wee girl like you know who or what she likes or doesn't like. I'm tired telling you that you'll do what you're bid."

Robert didn't know what to say. He had made his offer and that was as far as his resolve would carry him at the moment. He took a deep breath and decided to make his protest at marrying Alice to Mr Skinner, but before he could do so, the door opened and Arthur came into the kitchen, with Mary walking behind him. Arthur strode the few steps over to Robert, and stood surveying him.

"Well," he demanded, "what's this I hear about you making an offer for our Alice? Man, but you were always the one to shove your neb in where it wasn't wanted!"

Robert replied quietly that he had made a sincere offer for Alice's hand and hoped he would be allowed to marry her.

"Do you indeed?" Arthur snapped. "But did nobody tell you that Alice is bespoke to a Mr Skinner? Why don't you go home and mind your own business, young Thompson. I suppose you think you've a right to interfere now that you're so well up in the world and live up the road?"

"I told him! He knows Mr Skinner has offered," Mrs Storey chimed in.

Alice had commenced sobbing and sat on the sofa with Mary trying to comfort her.

Robert felt all his dislike of Arthur Storey coming to the surface. Many times in his life Arthur had come between him and what he wanted, or had tried to, but now ... Robert's mind was made up. He was going to prevent Alice from marrying Mr Skinner, if not by marrying her himself then by some other means.

"Whose choice was this?" he demanded hotly from Arthur. "Whose idea was it to marry such a nice wee girl as Alice to an oul' hallion like Skinner? Sure you know rightly the girl doesn't want him."

"Does she not now? And who does she want then?"

"I flatter myself she would take me," Robert retorted. "I'll be well able to support her, and I have money in the bank, a legacy left me that I've never touched."

"Oh we know all about that legacy! It done wonders, didn't it, when your da was near down and out. Sure I could have had those few pounds any time I'd a mind to!"

"You were well paid for your loan, if I remember rightly," Robert replied. "And another thing, you weren't above getting a loan yourself when you started, and you were very glad to ask my father's advice and counsel at the same time."

"I could buy you and your father, and never miss the few ha'pence," Arthur sneered. "Sure beside Mr Skinner you haven't more nor a farthing piece." He turned to his father. "Are you going to let this good match fall through? Mr Skinner won't wait forever for our coy young miss to make up her mind. There's other girls in the town of Belfast would be glad of him. And here's me going to all the trouble of introducing him to the family circle, and him and me on the best of terms doing business together, and you're letting a brat of a linen clerk come in and spoil it all." He spoke with great heat, but Mr Storey sat placidly puffing his pipe.

"I've been thinking," he said slowly, "maybe he has more money, this Skinner man, but I don't want to see our wee Alice not happy. She's crying her eyes out. I think she'd do better married to Robert here."

"This is foolishness and madness!" Arthur snapped.

"You weren't always so opposed to people following their own heart," Robert said firmly. "I seem to remember you having strong views."

"Well, I was easily led in them days. If I had things to do over again I'd do them different!" Arthur said savagely. Robert glanced at Mary and saw her face turn crimson before she buried her head in her hands.

"Come on home out of that, you," Arthur barked at her, and at the door turned to address the company. "You can do what you've a mind to, but mind this, don't come whining to me for the loan of money, young Thompson, and tell your da the same applies to him! This is all the thanks I get for all the favours I've done! Come on, woman, come on out of this," and he pushed Mary out into the hall in front of him and banged the kitchen door.

Mrs Storey stayed silent, glowering at Robert.

"Well," she said at last to her husband, "is that to be your decision?"

"Help me on with my boots, Alice pet," he said. "Sarah, I can't see the wee girl not happy. Robert, you needn't make any more speeches. Just let you and wee Alice make your arrangements."

Alice threw her arms round her father's neck and hugged him.

Mrs Storey said, "I hope you don't expect me to throw me arms round you, Robert Thompson. I suppose our Alice could do worse, but I don't mind telling you I'd hoped she would have done better. She would have been rich if she'd taken Skinner. He'd have given her a carriage and pair and furs and jewels."

Robert's head was spinning when he got home, but he was more able to tell his news than when he had left, and this time the villainy of Arthur Storey had to be told. Somehow, Robert felt that he had bested Arthur, for the first time, and the shared indignation of his mother and father at Arthur's scathing remarks took their minds off the sudden decision of Robert and Alice to get married.

Mrs McKenna was able to recount a few days later to her friend, how Robert had stood up to Arthur, and the wonder of the coming wedding was rather lost in the general indignation of Arthur's behaviour.

Robert decided that wherever he lived, it would not be with his mother-in-law, but there was no reason to delay the event to search for a dwelling. It seemed likely that Robert would be sent by the firm on other trips to England and it was judged best by the Thompsons—and Alice agreed—that in the meantime the young couple should have the back bedroom in Eglinton Street. They would get a house of their own, of course, just as soon as they had time to look round. Meantime, at home with his mother and father would suit Robert well, as the climate was more cordial than in Killen Street, where Mrs Storey was finding it hard to forgive Alice for turning down a good match, and Robert for not being Mr Skinner.

Quietly, on a June morning, in Berry Street church, they were married. Charley Gourley stood for Robert as best man, and Alice had a school friend, Lizzie Harper, to stand for her.

CHAPTER ELEVEN

John and Martha Thompson found it very hard to treat Alice as a married woman, and their son's wife. They were inclined to regard her, from the very first day of the marriage, as the young girl who used to live round the corner from them, the quiet child who was a wee friend for Jane and took her to school and out for walks. Alice did little to help them away from this attitude, and in Eglinton Street, as Mrs Robert Thompson, was as quiet and timid as she was as Alice Storey. With Jane she had more to say, and the child of nine and the bride of nineteen would talk and laugh when alone, only to fall silent when the older people came into the room.

With Robert, of course, Alice was animated and lively, though only when they were on their own, in the back room, or out walking. In the first weeks after the wedding they paid visits to Killen Street to the Storeys, where Mrs Storey received Robert stiffly, and to Mrs McKenna, who was always very pleased to see them. One evening Charley Gourley asked them for a visit to Brougham Street where they were kindly received by the Misses Kerr who inspected Alice with keen eyes, and asked each other later what on earth Robert Thompson had seen in that shrinking, timid wee thing.

Mrs Thompson Senior decided conscientiously that it was her duty to instruct her daughter-in-law in the proper running of a house, and she went about the job with more zeal than tact. Like most house-proud women she was convinced that her way, and only her way, of doing things was the right one, and telling Alice that she would soon no doubt be having her own place, it was only right that she should learn how to look after it.

"But my ma has always showed me how to do things," Alice ventured. "I always helped her in the house."

"Well, I'll show you how I do things and I think you'll find my way's the best. Now, we'll start with the front step. You must always keep a clean front step, for that's how your neighbours judge you." Then she went on to demonstrate a good clean-out of the parlour. The linoleum was washed and polished, the windows cleaned, ornaments dusted, and even the leaves of the plants were carefully wiped with a damp cloth.

Alice told Robert tearfully about it that night. "And the parlour wasn't needing a turnout at all, there wasn't even a speck of dust on it. Oh, Robbie, when are we going to get a place of our own?"

"Soon, love, but you see, I'm likely to be sent over to England very soon again, and you wouldn't like to be by yourself for weeks on end, now would you?"

"No, I wouldn't," she sniffed, "but I could always stay at my ma's house."

"Well that wouldn't answer, for your ma isn't too fond of me for marrying you, and if I'm not welcome, my wife isn't to stay there. Now don't you take things so serious, wee love, sure my ma means all for the best."

"She treats me like a wee girl so she does, and not like a married lady at all," Alice said petulantly, but Robert laughed at her and stroked her fair hair.

They walked out together most evenings after supper, either visiting, or enjoying sauntering along in the cool of the June evenings, along the roads and lanes of the town. Wherever they walked, be it Ormeau, Falls or Shankill district there was great building activity going on, and Alice would eagerly look at all the new houses and asked of Robert that he make a choice of one of them as their own home. He was vague and made half promises of "someday soon", but when at length one evening Alice demanded to know when "someday soon" would be, he sighed deeply and decided that he'd have to tell her the truth.

"You see, Alice pet," he said, looking down at her serious blue eyes, "there's a reason," and he explained carefully to her the possibility of some one man in the firm being sent to America. "I thought it was just for a visit," he told her, "but now it seems that Mr Stuart wants someone in North America all the time, to open an office for Stuart & Mount, and I think I have a very good chance. I'm sure I have, for Mr Stuart asked me what I thought of the idea and I said it was very sound." Robert's voice trembled with excitement at the thought. He was glad to tell Alice of the hopes that had built up inside him, of the dreams he had cherished for years of getting to America. "Wouldn't it be a great thing?" he asked her eagerly.

"But Robbie," she faltered, her lip trembling, "where would I be?"

"You'd be with me, you daft thing! We'd be in America together, and we could have our own house out there. Wouldn't that be great, eh?"

"I suppose so," Alice said hesitantly, but Robert did not notice her lack of enthusiasm. He had enough for two, and pledging her to absolute secrecy, he told her all he knew—and imagined—about life in America.

"But isn't there Red Indians there, murdering people and setting fire to their houses?" Alice asked.

"Not at all! That's all out in the far West. We'd be in one of the big cities, New York likely, or maybe Boston, or Philadelphia. But don't breathe a word to anyone, Alice love, for you know what my da wants. He wants me to go into his business with him, and I don't want to be tied down yet awhile. I want to see a bit more of the world first, and you'll be the happiest girl ever to put foot in America."

When she was with him, Alice supposed him to be right, but when alone and her husband away at his work, she wasn't so sure that she'd like to live anywhere but in one of the new houses being built on all the roads and districts of Belfast.

The summer passed, and Robert made one journey over to

England on his own. Mr Meekin had declared himself as getting too old for travelling round the British Isles and he recommended Mr Stuart to send Robert on his own. It was a long and lonely two weeks for Alice while he was away. Mrs Thompson kept up her housekeeping instructions, and Alice couldn't even complain to her own ma about it all, out of loyalty to Robert, and because her ma would say, "Well, miss, you would marry Robert Thompson. Why didn't you take Skinner like you were bid!" Alice wouldn't admit, even to herself, that there was the slightest fly in the ointment.

Robert brought back a present for her, a beautiful ring with coloured stones, and he explained it to her, after his breakfast on the morning he came in off the boat.

"It's what they call a Dearest Ring," he told her, slipping it on her finger, on top of the broad eighteen carat gold wedding ring. "Look, each stone spells out a letter of the word 'dearest'. First 'D' for diamond, and that's a diamond, then 'E' for emerald, 'A' for amethyst, 'R' for the ruby stone, 'E' for another emerald, 'S' for the blue one, the sapphire, and 'T' at the end for the yellow-looking one, it's called a topaz. Do you like it, love? The man in the jewellery shop wrote it all down for me, and I learned it off when I was on the train, so that I could slip it on your finger and tell you what it all means."

"Oh, Robbie!" Alice had tears in her eyes, and later, she showed it eagerly to her mother-in-law, and tried to remember as many of the names of the stones as she could.

"Isn't it beautiful, Mrs Thompson? You see, it spells out the word 'Dearest'!"

Mrs Thompson looked critically at it. "I suppose it's a nice enough wee bit of a ring, but wouldn't Robert have been far better to save the sovereigns that it must have cost and put them to better use, against the time when you have your own house."

But Alice was not to be dashed, and shyly showed it to Mr Thompson too. He inspected it and remarked, "A nice little bauble, to be sure."

Jane was enthusiastic, and tried to learn off the names of the stones in their proper order.

Later in the day, Martha commented to John, "Do you think our Robert has any sense! Did you see the ring he bought her? I must say I thought it a great foolishness myself. And did you see the carry-on of the pair of them when he come in from the boat? She threw her arms round him and kissed him! She did, for I saw it with my own eyes! I don't know what the young people's coming till at all, at all! Such carry-on, in front of their elders too!"

John nodded agreement, solemnly. "Times change, and manners too. Young ones now haven't the sense we had. I think they all have it too easy. They hadn't the same striving that we had in our young days."

The summer months passed quickly for the newlyweds, and among the excursions they undertook was a long-planned one up to the Castlereagh Hills to visit Aunt Agnes's old cottage. Alice had always cherished a dream of the days she spent there as a wee girl, and wanted to return to it. It was a long walk from Eglinton Street, but they took it in easy stages. It was a warm August Saturday, and Robert had the whole afternoon free. Indeed this one and many more were due to him for the long hours he worked on the two trips to England.

Robert and Alice walked smartly to the top of the road beyond the bridge, and paused at the foot of the hill, sitting against a grassy bank, under a clump of wild rose trees and hawthorn bushes, sheltering from the warm sun. The country was at its best, the crops springing up in the fields, and the wild flowers in the hedgerows in profusion.

"I think maybe Danny lives in Aunt Agnes's cottage now," Robert explained to Alice. "I mind now that Ma met someone a while ago that told her."

Such indeed was the case, as they found when they walked into the yard in front of the house and saw Danny guiding a child's uncertain footsteps across the rough ground.

They were cordially received, and old animosities seemed forgotten. Danny's wife was a big buxom girl, very friendly and hospitable, and it was clear from her manner that she knew all about the Thompsons and the Storeys, up to the time of the quarrel over Aunt Agnes's money, but was quite prepared by quick, searching questions to bring herself up to date on all their news as quickly as possible.

Marriage had improved Danny. He was no longer the surly, suspicious boy that shouted after Robert. Now he obviously wanted to heal the breach, and after tea and soda bread and a boiled egg apiece, he brought Robert over to the farm to meet his father, Robert's Uncle George, and Aunt Tilly. Here, too, the welcome was open though not so cordial and good wishes were sent to Robert's parents and an invitation given for them to come out some day on a visit.

"You'll maybe call and see our new place next time you're at the market," Robert said politely.

"I'm very seldom in the town of Belfast these days," Uncle George grunted. "It's Danny here does most of the travelling into the market. He'll likely call, and his missus, too, for she's a girl that's fond of visiting round."

Alice was tired by the walk up the hills and over to the farm, and Danny offered to get out the farm cart and give them a ride down to the foot of the hill, an offer that was gladly accepted.

"You know, Danny," Robert remarked leisurely, sitting on the board of the cart with Alice by his side, "it was none of my doing that Aunt Agnes left me her money, nor none of my ma's or my da's either. The way it was left they got no good out of it, for it was held in the bank until I was grown up, and to tell you the truth it's there yet."

"Aye, I can see the truth of it all now," Danny nodded wisely. "It was Jinny that pointed it all out to me, after we were married. She's long in the head, Jinny is, for all she's a town girl. She's from Comber, you know."

"No, I didn't know where she was from, but I think you're very lucky in your wife. She's a very nice girl."

Danny allowed himself a slight smile of gratification. "Though mind you," he went on, "our ones weren't on for me marrying her. They thought she wouldn't be able for the country, but she manages the best. She said to me that it was no fault of you nor your ma nor da, that the oul' auntie left her gold to yous; she says that oul' weemin gets very notionate."

"Well, it's well you got the place anyhow," Robert said lamely, at last, searching his brain for something to remark.

"Aye, the agent went right till his lordship and asked for me to get the place. There was her bits and pieces too, I might as well tell you, that gave me and Jinny a start off, so maybe we didn't do so bad out of the oul' auntie, though don't let my da hear anyone say that."

They had reached the bottom of the hill by this time. Robert swung Alice down off the cart, and they waved Danny goodbye and started the long walk from the foot of the Castlereagh Hills to the Crumlin Road, on the other side of the town. Alice was tired, and after a short while had to take a rest, and by the time they had progressed through Ballymacarrett and crossed over the Lagan Bridge, she was weary and exhausted. Robert all but carried her through the town and up the Hill past the poorhouse to Eglinton Street and when they got into the house and Alice collapsed into a chair, Robert was alarmed by her paleness.

"Now you walked her too far," his mother scolded. "Sure it would tire anybody, all them miles up the Hills and down again. I don't know what you were thinking, Robert."

On Sunday morning Alice was still so tired and feeling sick that she was excused from going to church with the rest of the family. The walk down to Berry Street and back would be too far, Mrs Thompson declared. Alice didn't improve in the next few days, and Mrs Thompson wasn't surprised when Alice told her diffidently that she was going down to Killen Street to have a wee talk with her ma. Mrs Thompson had her own theory, and wasn't unduly startled to see Alice returning accompanied by her ma. The news was broken that Alice thought she was expecting: her Ma thought so too and Mrs Thompson was of the same opinion. It was Mrs Storey's plan that Alice should come home until her time came, and she added ungraciously that Robert could come too if he wanted, but Alice was firm and said she would be all right, that Mrs Thompson would no doubt look after her, and anyhow Robert wouldn't agree to go to Killen Street and she wouldn't go without him. She said all this in her timid yet determined voice and there was no arguing with her.

"Well, Mrs Thompson," Mrs Storey sat back in the corner seat of the kitchen, "it looks like we're both going to be grannies. Near time for me, you might say, if you think of the while that my Arthur is married."

Mrs Thompson made tea and cut her seed cake.

Mrs Storey went on. "I was just saying to Alice that I don't how you push up that hill past the poorhouse—it had me all out of breath. And I never seen as many dirty streets and wee barefoot childer as I did coming up here. Your street is very nice and quiet, I must say, but I don't know how you're bothered with such a long hall. It must be a torment to keep it clean."

Mrs Thompson felt her cheeks burning but kept to herself the acid comment she could have made. Quietly she replied that Mr Thompson and herself had no regret in moving up to Eglinton Street and found themselves very pleased with the situation.

"I must say, though," she allowed herself to add, "that the one thing I didn't like about College Place was the drunk men staggering the streets from the Smithfield pubs."

Into herself she added *and put that in your pipe and smoke it, for who's a better customer in the pubs than your own man!*

Alice told her news privately to Robert, and afterwards he spoke urgently to his mother.

"Will she be all right Ma? Should I get the doctor for her?"

"For dear sake have a bit of sense! Sure it's early days yet, and what would she want with the doctor? I'll look after her, and if we need anybody when she's nearer her time, we'll get the nurse from Mill Street."

Mr Thompson was informed of the coming event by his wife, and he expressed satisfaction but did not refer to the matter to anybody. Jane knew there was some mystery and quizzed her mother.

"Is Alice sick? What is she staying in her bed for? She said she would put rags in my hair and make me ringlets."

"Such a child I never did see," sighed Mrs Thompson. "What do you want ringlets for, you vain wee hussy. And foreby it would take the lightning out of the sky to curl that black hair of yours."

"Gwendoline has them. She's always tossing them at me when we're walking up to school. She's an oul' clash-bag so she is. She's always telling the teacher if you look crooked at her oul' ringlets."

"I suppose you pulled the hair off her, if I know you! I doubt they'll have the hard task making a lady out of you at your school. Away and don't bother me, and don't be tormenting Alice."

Mrs McKenna paid a visit to the Thompsons and was warmly greeted.

"Here I am," she announced, "to kill two birds with the one stone—to offer my congratulations and to pay you a wee visit."

"Did you hear then, that I'm to be a granny?"

"And didn't I always say you would be, before me?" Mrs McKenna laughed. "And wasn't the Storey woman in blowing and boasting to me, crowing over me that her Alice is in the family way and my Mary isn't, and has no sign of it either. Ah well, I'm glad at the news, but only on your account, Mrs Thompson, not for the Storeys!"

Martha Thompson had to laugh. Her old neighbour was as good as a tonic to her and she realised just how much she missed her, and told her so.

"By the way," Martha added, "I've been thinking about you and praying for you. Have you made your decision yet? Is it America and James, or will you stay on here for Mary's sake?"

Mrs McKenna looked embarrassed. She bit her lip and looked ruefully at her friend.

"I'll have to tell you! I can't keep you out of my confidence, you of all people. Sure Mrs Thompson dear, the thing was settled for me, and not very long after that day you were down with me in my house. He didn't tell you. I know he didn't."

"Who?" Martha was puzzled.

"Ah, woman dear, sure you have the best man in the lamps of Belfast, and he's dead afeard of anybody knowing it! Sure didn't your own husband come down and tell me he heard of my dilemma and offered me the lend of enough money to start up a wee shop, if that was what I wanted. I was to keep it a secret. Nobody was to know, not even Mary nor her Arthur, but sure I couldn't not tell you!"

"Well, well," was all Martha could say, remembering the rebuke that John had given her for idle gossip and wasting time talking with Mrs McKenna.

"Aye, the load's off my mind," Mrs McKenna said gaily. "I've taken his kind offer and I think I've a good chance of a wee shop in King Street, sweeties and dry goods I'll make it. Don't let on to your man I told you!"

Martha promised solemnly. She was happy for her friend, and didn't take it amiss that John hadn't thought fit to tell her of the good turn to their old friend and neighbour. When, but the once, had he ever told her anything of his business? She needn't expect it now, after so many years.

Robert had been a bit secretive, she thought, and it worried her. Was he going to be the same and keep everything to himself? It wasn't like him, but then, perhaps it was Alice who heard now all his dreams and secrets, and no doubt Alice knew why he had gone to work just the day before in his Sunday best, with his hair specially sleeked down, after a particularly careful shave. Maybe Alice didn't notice, though, for she didn't rise too early in the mornings, and it was his ma who still got Robert his porridge and hurried him out to his work. Poor wee Alice, she wasn't too well at all: not a strong girl, and likely would have a hard enough time with the baby. She needed the rest in the mornings, and Robert didn't mind at all, for her few attempts at getting him his breakfast had made him late for work: she made lumpy porridge and a couple of times had burnt it.

Robert didn't tell anyone why he dressed in his good suit. At this stage, he decided, there was nothing to tell. He had simply been asked to attend for an interview at the quarterly meeting of the company, in the firm's offices, where every three months the managers of the departments assembled, from the bleach green, the scutch mill, the spinning mill and so on, to review the business. At this particular meeting the suggestion was to be made that a permanent representative in North America would be most beneficial, and the proposed applicant inspected.

At an earlier interview, in Mr Stuart's own office, Robert had heard the general outline of the plan, and he had been asked outright would he accept the position if it was offered to him, and he had indicated that he would.

He had sat in the chair, in front of the big desk, where, as a green young lad he had been interviewed for apprenticeship, and where five years later he had received his indentures from Mr Stuart's own hands. Mr Stuart was looking very old now, he thought; he was stooped and had got a bit hard of hearing, though mentally he was still the alert, astute head of one of the biggest linen concerns in the trade.

"It's a great opportunity for you," he had told Robert. "It will mean hard work, of course, but it should be well worth while. It's up to you. I have every confidence that you will make a success of it but I have to convince some of the others that now is the time to get well in on the American market. Things are booming there now. Some of them don't see it my way but I hope they will change their minds when they have a little talk with you at the next quarterly meeting."

There was no son to succeed Mr Stuart, he had only daughters, but grandsons were springing up who would be coming into the business in several years' time; there was a nephew in charge of the spinning mill, and a son-in-law the manager of the scutch mill in Co. Derry. Robert was well aware that the scheme of having a resident representative would have gone to one of the relations of the company managers if it had been assured of success, and no doubt if it did turn out well he would be succeeded by or replaced by one of them. If it wasn't a success ... well, he would have to take that chance and wait and see.

He didn't mention anything at home. Better to wait until he had something definite to tell them, until the date was fixed. That's what he told himself, knowing full well in his heart that he shirked telling his father that he was not coming into the business with him after all.

Several days after the company quarterly meeting, at which the plan had been well received and a general plan made of sending Robert to North America in June or July of the following year, John Thompson asked his son to meet him at the meal hour. There was something he wanted to discuss. When Robert arrived at the corner of Bedford Street at the appointed hour, and stood waiting for his father to come along, he hadn't the remotest idea of what his da wanted to see him about at that particular spot. Surely anything to be discussed could take place in Mr Thompson's own little warehouse. Could he have heard of the proposed American trip, Robert wondered. It was unlikely, for it was not generally known in the firm amongst the employees. Mr Meekin knew, but he had been asked not to speak of the matter until final plans were made. How cautious they all were, how anxious that other firms should know nothing of their business. Indeed Robert had often been surprised that Stuart & Mounts' had not objected to his association with another firm, that of his father. Mr Stuart had early impressed on Robert the reading from the indentures of an apprentice—'that he shall keep his employers' secrets'—and had no doubt felt confidence in John Thompson's integrity and unlikeliness to probe the firm's business out of his son.

John Thompson arrived, out of breath but eager, to meet Robert. He took hold of his arm and led him towards Wellington Place.

"I've something to show you, Robert. A place has become available for renting, and it seems the very thing I've been waiting for. It's off Hill Street and would be most convenient in every respect— handy for shipping, nearby for the workers and not too far from Eglinton Street. I want your opinion on it before I enter into a lease."

Robert had never seen him so enthusiastic, and as they walked towards Hill Street he wondered what else his father had in mind. They reached the building, a two storied old warehouse with a small office door and a good-sized entrance gate to a store door.

"Here we are." His father took the keys from his pocket. "Now you see," he said as they entered, "here we could have a space for the office; a fireplace is handy, then a door could be made into the ground floor store."

He had obviously seen over the place several times, it seemed, for he had plans already in his head for the layout of the building. Here was to be the storeroom for the webs of linen, there was to be the space for the packing, while upstairs, in the long room with the skylights, would be put up the benches for the machines.

"There's good light here, I'm sure you've noticed. And over here can be benches for the smoothing and the ornamenting. Everything would be so handy, and with a separate store entrance the place could run very smoothly. What do you think?" He turned to Robert for comment.

Robert replied that it certainly looked a very suitable place, and seemed well suited for the warehousing end of the linen business.

John Thompson put his hand on his son's shoulder. "Well, Robert, the time has come when you'll be able to be a great help to me. Up to the present there wasn't much point in bringing you in, because we are so terribly cramped for space round in Bedford Street. There's not a spare inch and we can't expand unless we can increase our output. Now McCrum is the best fellow you'd find for the books and the invoicing end, but just between ourselves, he's not much good otherwise. Now, if you come and bring your capital into the firm we really can make the name of Thompson well known in the linen trade. I can see to the warehouse and you can do the journeys and bring in new customers. What do you say to that now, Robert? Isn't it a good plan?"

Robert had never heard his father talk so much for a long time, yet he was glad of it, for he had to decide how he was to break his own news. He paused, looked round the empty and dusty building for a moment then quietly told his father that he hoped to be going to North America on behalf of Stuart & Mount, to reside probably in New York, and to develop the trade there and in the northern cities.

"I'm sorry," he added, and when his father didn't reply, went on, "but I think you have a good thing here and you should rent this place on easy terms, and I'm sure it will do very well." He didn't look at his father as he spoke, not knowing how the news was being received, but when there was no reply, he turned sheepishly and looked at him.

John Thompson's face showed no expression. He stared at Robert, then asked quietly, "Is your mind made up? Are you sure you won't change it?"

Robert hastened to say how long he had wished for this chance, and of how good and booming things were in America since the Civil War.

"When do you think of going?"

"If all goes well, Alice and the baby and me should be on the steamer by next June."

"Have you mentioned this to your mother?"

Robert shook his head and his father added softly, "Well I think you should. It's only fair she should know."

He put his hand again on Robert's shoulder, looked at him intently, a bit sadly, Robert thought, then turned to the door, and Robert followed him.

They walked back in silence and at his work in the afternoon, Robert breathed a sigh of relief. It hadn't been too hard after all, telling his da. He had expected anger, arguments, maybe even a downright command to abandon the whole scheme, but Da had taken it very easily, and didn't seem put out. Likely he realised how good a chance it was for such a young man and how lucky he was. Well, he'd tell Ma tonight, and Alice, too, though she knew there was a chance they would be going to America, but it would be as well to tell her now, and she'd have it to look forward to after the baby was born. Would it be a boy? He hoped it would. He would call it John, after his father. No, wait, Alice might like to call it after her da. Well, William John it would be. William John Thompson and he'd be born right into the linen trade, you might say, and would be able to carry on the name and the trade. Of course it might be a girl and if it was ...

well, he'd think about a name if it happened to be one.

Near to bedtime, Robert spoke to his ma in the scullery, where she was washing pots. Jane was long since in bed, and Alice had gone up earlier: she wasn't feeling well, she said. John Thompson was at a church meeting.

"Did my da tell you?" Robert asked diffidently.

"Tell me what?" Mrs Thompson was curious.

"It's a great chance I have Ma. Oh, wait till you hear..." and Robert related his plans. His mother didn't speak, but came into the kitchen and sat on the nearest chair.

"Do you mean you'd be going to America for good?"

"Well, we'd be living there, but sure we'd likely be coming home for holidays now and then."

She shook her head sadly. "Ah no, son, nobody ever comes back from America. They all go there but you never hear tell of anybody coming back here to live. Sure what would I do without you, son dear?" She tried to bite back tears but they trickled down her face freely. "You'd be going away from us and taking our wee grandchild with you and we'd never see it again. Your da and me mightn't have many more years. What would we do at all, at all?"

Robert tried to comfort her. He put his arm round her shoulders clumsily and patted her.

"Ach don't take on like that Ma. Sure we're not going till next summer and you'd think it was the moon I was bound for. It's only America. Sure you and Pa could come and visit us." He knew he sounded lame in his comfort, but he didn't know what to say and was glad when she dried her eyes and went off to bed.

Alice's reaction to the news was to look blankly at Robert and tell him she felt sick and didn't care where she went to, but in the morning, as he was hurrying to dress himself, having slept late, she sat up in bed.

"Robbie, come here till I tell you." She took hold of his hand.

"Robbie, I don't want to go to America. I don't want to leave my da; he'd be lonely for me."

"I'm late, Alice! I'll have to hurry."

"Robbie! Do we have to go to America? Sure we could just stay here and get a wee house of our own. Or if you like we can stay here, and I'll not say a word about living with your ma. Just stay here and don't go to America."

"Oh, for God's sake be quiet, Alice!" Robert shouted at her. "Give me peace, will you. You're keeping me late for my work. I don't want to hear anything more about America!"

Alice looked as if he'd struck her, and lay down snivelling to herself. When Robert had calmed down, he tried to comfort her, but she wouldn't be comforted. She lay sobbing to herself and wouldn't speak to him, and he had to leave her to get a hurried breakfast.

His mother was calm and very quiet. Gently she asked, "Is Alice not rising this morning? Very well, I'll bring her something up. She needs her rest, poor wee girl."

Jane was bursting with excitement about the approach of Hallowe'en and kept chattering about having sport with apples on the night.

"Will we have a dumpling, Ma?" she demanded.

"Yes, love, likely we will," was the quiet reply, as Jane's unruly hair was brushed and tied back.

His ma wasn't like herself, Robert thought. There was a look of sadness on her face that made him uneasy. Probably worrying about him going to America. Oh well, she would likely get over it in a few days and be her old bustling self again. And Alice was probably sick, poor wee pet. He couldn't blame her, in her condition, but he was sorry he was cross with her. What he'd have to do, as soon as Alice's time came, was to get a good likeness of the three of them, for his ma to keep. And he'd write every week, and tell her everything about America, and she'd be able to show his letters round and say, "Isn't our Robert getting on well in America?" She'd be very proud of him.

He cheered himself with these thoughts during the day, and managed to feel quite happy about the whole thing.

He was worrying about nothing, he told himself. It was just the suddenness of the news that upset his ma and Alice. See how calmly his da had taken it? He wondered if his da would go ahead with the plans for the new warehouse. But wouldn't he need the money, the extra capital that he had expected Robert to bring in? Of course, why hadn't he thought of that! His father must have that money that Aunt Agnes had left. Robert wouldn't need it. Indeed, come to think of it, his father should have had it immediately it had come to his possession when he was twenty-one. It really belonged to him and to Ma anyhow, for it was only a whim of the old aunt's to leave it to the child that she had taken a great fancy to. After all, it was his ma and da who had been good to her. He would go round to his father's warehouse that very evening and arrange the transfer of the money to him. He'd ask out a bit early, and take his time and have a good talk with him.

Jauntily, and whistling to himself, Robert asked Mr Meekin's permission to go about five o'clock and, turning his coat collar up against the damp chill of the October evening, he walked briskly along Bedford Street to the little warehouse with the name 'John Thompson' painted on the door. He walked into the tiny office and found George McCrum sitting on his stool in front of the old sloping desk, busily writing in the leather-bound ledger. He looked over his spectacles and when he saw it was Robert, slid off the stool.

"Ah, Robert, is it yourself? How it's not often we see you round here. Come in and sit down," and he bustled to get another high stool for Robert to sit on, near the tiny grate where a few dying embers smouldered.

"Is he here himself?" Robert asked, jerking his thumb towards the store which lay beyond the office.

"Deed he's not," McCrum puffed. He had got very stout, Robert thought, and it was an effort for him to get off and on his stool. He had hastily shoved a pipe into his pocket when Robert came in, but seeing who it was, he brought it out boldly and knocked it against the grate, at the same time spitting expertly into the bowl of sawdust on the hearth. "Your da's away home," he said.

"Oh, is he sick?"

"No, I wouldn't say that now. Not so far as I can tell, do you see. At least he said nothing about being sick, and I didn't ask him. No, I wouldn't say he was sick."

"It's not like him to go home so early," Robert said, puzzled.

George McCrum laid the pipe down on the desk and swung himself up into the stool again and took up his pen. "It's not like him at all, but your da and me, Robert, gets on the best, because I do what I have to do and he never interferes and if he wants to tell me anything he'll tell me. That's the way we've got on, do you see?"

Robert sighed. "Well, I just wanted to talk to him…"

McCrum looked over his spectacles again, and put down the pen and closed the ledger.

"That's not to say I haven't wondered, do you see? I wondered why he went home early, for he never leaves until the shipping is gone, and never did a man check out the goods to the carter as careful as your da. But the night he says, 'Ach I'm away home, George,' and I says to him, 'What about the shipping, John, sure you always see to it,' and he just looks at me and he says, 'Sure you can attend to it rightly, George, it's little odds who does it', and that isn't like him, so it isn't." He paused to take breath.

"Something happened to your da, Robert, and I don't know what it was. All week and up to yesterday he was full of good humour and the best of form. But something must have happened. Yesterday he got that quiet and all in on himself, you'd think something had knocked the heart out of him. He was like a man that had a great disappointment."

"Maybe he's worrying about business," Robert faltered.

"Business, is it? Sure we're as busy as nailers! It's never been better, and if we had an inch or two more of room out in the store there we could be far, far busier, do you see? No it's not business." George McCrum's face looked concerned. "It's not business," he repeated. "Why look at this," and he rummaged through an orderly pile of papers on the desk and drew one out triumphantly. "Look at this, here's an order from a firm we've been after for years. All we ever got from them in the way of an order was a wee bit of this and a wee bit of that, and now this very morning, do you see, here comes a good big substantial order. Well says I to your da, 'What do you think of that, eh, John! At last we've got in with them,' and he just nods his head and says very quiet like 'Oh very good indeed', as if it was a couple of yards of unbleached linen."

"I mustn't keep you," Robert began, when the door opened and a red-faced carter, whip in hand, pushed his head in and yelled, "Thompsons! Shipping! Are yiz ready?"

George scrambled down from the desk.

"That's the cart now to take the shipping for the boat! I must see to it, Robert, for he mightn't wait!"

"I was just going," Robert replied hastily. "I'll see my da at the house."

He stepped out into Bedford Street, out of the dim gaslight, into the gloom of the night, with the occasional streetlight casting a yellow gleam. Slowly he walked along Bedford Street and down Wellington Place towards College Square. He was greatly disturbed by what George McCrum had told him. His da had minded, had been upset, but had never shown it. He was glad now that he hadn't offered Aunt Agnes's money to him; it would have added to the heartbreak he was causing. The uneasiness he'd been hiding from himself all day came back in full force. He couldn't conceal from himself any longer his awareness of his parents' feelings and of Alice's too. He had to face it: he was going to break his mother's heart if he went to America for good. And he had destroyed his father's hopes and ambitions that had been building up for years. He had never really understood his father, but then had he ever really tried? And Alice, what would it do to her, to be whisked away from her family and friends, to live in a strange country, to be left by herself with a young child while he travelled the cities of America? Shy, timid Alice, who was frightened of her own shadow.

He stopped, and realised that he had walked down College Square, along the College railings and was now standing by the Black Man statue. Wryly he smiled to himself: this was the first time since they left College Place North for Eglinton Street that he had made home for the wrong house. He stood and looked up at the statue. Frederick, Earl of Belfast, Belfast's Black Man, the familiar landmark, the scene of childhood play. He thought back to the night it had stood there shrouded in sheets awaiting the exciting ceremony of unveiling the following day. He had brought Alice home that night, when she was frightened, had taken her hand and comforted her. Bringing her to America wasn't the way to do it.

Robert sighed. He reflected that a man full of dreams, of ambitions and of hopes must be ruthless to carry them out, mustn't mind how many hearts he broke or the anguish he caused in getting where he wanted to go. He, Robert Thompson, wasn't made like that. He couldn't see Alice frightened.

He couldn't leave his mother heartbroken. He owed it to his father to give a try to the expansion of the firm of Thompson, to make it John Thompson & Son, and to endeavour to get to know his father, as a man, leaving the awe and sternness of boyhood behind him.

The Black Man! How long had he stood there, in his bronze stiffness? He thought back; it must be eleven years ago. It was a

Hallowe'en night, and he remembered how much he had wanted a turnip lantern like Alfie Storey's, to be able to run up and down with it. How dashed he had been when he hadn't got a turnip! Well, here he was, eleven years later, again at Hallowe'en time, and he wanted something else, something that seemed as desirable and exciting as the turnip lantern had then. It hadn't been for him to have his lantern then; it wasn't for him to have his American dream now.

He took a final look up at the Black Man, pulled his coat collar up, straightened his hat firmly on his head, and with a deliberate air, walked across the Square, towards King Street and a short cut up home to Eglinton Street.

"Time you grew up, Robert boy!" he said softly to himself.

THE END.

Map 8. Part of Belfast, 1858, from the Ordnance Survey (Public Record Office of Northern Ireland, with permission from Ordnance Survey of Northern Ireland); original scale 1:1056, reduced to 1:1958 (OS).

Irish Historic Towns Atlas 2007

The map image is taken from the "Irish Historic Towns Atlas", Public Record Office of Northern Ireland (PRONI), 2007, and dated 1858. Please note that Killen Street runs off College Square North at a 45 degree angle.

Many thanks to Andrew Dunlop and Monica Cash at the Linen Hall Library for their research and assistance in sourcing images.

Further information and maps about Belfast in early 19th century are held in the Linen Hall Library and include James O'Hagan map of 1848 held in Belfast's Linen Hall Library and an earlier map of Belfast by James Williamson from 1791.

The 1848 map depicts the Blackstaff river and it's path, disappearing under Ormeau Avenue before joining the Lagan beyond Cromac Street. It also seems to meander through the Ulster Railway Station (Great Victoria Street station). It is possible to trace the path of the Blackstaff upriver from Cromack Dock. The Farset river is not named but evident as a small stretch of water next to Barrack Street which disappears under Mill Field.

Irish Historic Towns Atlas (IHTA), no. 12, Belfast, Part I, to 1840, printed and published in 2003 by the Royal Irish Academy is a useful reference and is also available online.

RESOURCES

    As I Roved Out, Cathal O'Byrne
    Belfast Street Directories: 1845-55;1852; 1854-56; &1861-62.
    Belfast Model Schools, Centenary Books 1857-1957
    Belfast & Ulster Directory, (Historical Notes) for 1947
    Belfast News Letter, Issues Dec 1864; August 1864; & August 1857
    A History of the Town of Belfast, George Benn
    Centenary Souvenir Book: St. Paul's Convent of Mercy, 1954
    Flax and Its Products in Ireland, William Charley
    Golden Jubilee Souvenir: Holy Cross Church, Ardoyne, 1902-52
    Irish News suppl.:reprint *Belfast Morning News*, 8th Oct 1856
    History of Belfast, D. J. Owen
    Quarterly Notes: LV Publication, No. 119, December, 1937, Belfast Municipal Museum & Art Gallery. "The Cotton Famine of 1862-63".
    "Ulster Since 1800" 12 Talks Broadcast in the N.I. Home Service of the B.B.C.
    22 Talks Broadcast in the N.I. Home Service of the B.B.C.

To the above sources may be added much hearsay information, from my parents, grandparents and great-grandparents. Three great-grandfathers and great-grandmothers lived in Belfast in the period written about (1855-1866), and knowing their occupations, their places of abode and approximate incomes, has been of much value to me, as also the fact that some of my predecessors were in the linen business, in varied occupations, in the same period. I should like to express my sincere thanks to the many people who helped me in obtaining detail and information for this book, especially the staff of the Belfast Public Libraries.

    E.M.

NOTES

The ' Black Man': The statue referred to in the book is, of course, that of Frederick Richard Chichester, Earl of Belfast, which stood in College Square for 20 years, until it was moved (to make way for the statue of Dr Henry Cook), to the Old Town Hall in Victoria Street. After 13 years it was again moved, to the Public Library in Royal Avenue, from where it was finally transported to the City Hall, then newly built in 1906. Presently it is there, in the City Hall, upstairs, on the first floor.

The Wedding, Chapter 8, Page 174: It was permissible for Roman Catholics to contract marriage with those of the other Christian churches in any Christian church before a duly authorised priest or minister. The papal decree, Ne Temere, which came into force in 1908, altered this situation, but all such marriages contracted prior to this date and decree were valid and binding.

ABOUT THE AUTHOR

Elizabeth (Betty) May was born in 10th August 1916 and brought up in Belfast, the youngest of five children. She worked as a secretary before setting up her own secretarial agency above her brother James' jewellery shop in King Street. In 1955 she went into the jewellery business on High Street with James and sister Ita, on High Street near the Albert Clock. However throughout her life Betty's passion was creative writing.

Betty was a regular contributor to a wide range of periodicals, journals and magazines including, The Belfast writers' Group First Edition, The Ulster Tatler, Ireland's Own, and The Capuchin Annual. A great story teller she had her nieces and nephews enthralled with exciting stories of her own creation as well as classic children's tales and fables. Betty was a founding member and secretary of the Belfast Writers Group which had many distinguished members including Joseph Tomelty, actor and playwright, and Sam Hanna Bell, author and playwright.

It was Sam Hanna Bell who wrote the forward to 'The Name is Thompson'. 3 In 1967 'The Sunday News' serialised an abridged version of the novel in twelve episodes. Betty died in May 1997 aged eighty one.

Among the papers left after her death was the original typewritten manuscript of 'The Name is Thompson'. The idea of publishing originated with her nephew Gerard. Publishing the manuscript was carried out by her nephew Michael and grandnephew Declan, with support from her grandniece Katharine. Declan also designed the cover. We believe that Aunt Betty would approve of this publication of her novel.

Printed in Great Britain
by Amazon